WHITEWATER AWAKENING

WHITEWATER AWAKENING

RITA POTTER

SAPPHIRE BOOKS

SALINAS, CALIFORNIA

Editor - Tara Young
Book Design - LJ Reynolds
Cover Design - Fineline Cover Design

Sapphire Books Publishing, LLC
P.O. Box 8142
Salinas, CA 93912
www.sapphirebooks.com

Printed in the United States of America
First Edition – November 2022

This and other Sapphire Books titles can be found
at
www.sapphirebooks.com

Dedication

For Terra. May we continue to have amazing adventures.

Acknowledgment

I can't believe I'm writing dedications for my sixth book. Like *Whitewater Awakening*, this chapter of my life has been one hell of an adventure.

Thanks to Chris and Sapphire Books for giving me creative freedom while still offering a guiding hand.

Thanks to my editor, Tara. Even though you thwarted me from putting in misspelled words this time, it doesn't mean I won't try again.

Thanks to my family and friends. I am overwhelmed at how supportive you have all been. The number of people in my *real life* who read my books still amazes me.

A special shoutout to my work family, who continue to encourage me, even though it means I will ride off into the sunset sooner.

Thanks to my mentor Jae for your solid presence in my life. It still blows my mind that you continue to support me, even after your *formal* job is done. You are the standard I strive for.

Thanks to my growing list of author friends. There are so many of you who have impacted my life that I won't try to list you individually. I will single out two, my very first writer buddy, Lori, and my Midwestern pal Nance, you both have made this adventure so much more fun.

Thanks to my beta readers, Michele, Nan, and Cade. You make me better. Period. I couldn't do it without you. I appreciate you more than you may know.

Thanks to Terra. What can I say, you do it all. I can't even begin to list all the things you do to help me on this incredible journey. The last twenty years with you have exceeded all my wildest expectations, and I believe the next twenty will be even better.

Of course, thanks to Chumley the cat. I'm not ready to incur his wrath should I not mention him. After all, I don't want to sleep with one eye open.

And last, but certainly not least, are the readers who continue to read my stories. You have made my dream possible.

Chapter One

"Damn it," Quinn Coolidge said when the bell over the front door jangled. She must have forgotten to lock up when she went out back to the dock. Who the hell would be coming in this late? Probably an early bird weekender thinking they could score a boat rental.

Her knees creaked when she stood. *I'm getting too old for this shit.* Despite being at it for over an hour, the Jet Ski engine was no closer to running. She reached for the rag to wipe the grease off her hands. *Where the hell did it go?* It defied logic how she could lose something without moving from the spot she was working.

"Hello. Hello." A female voice drifted in from inside the store.

Fuck it. Quinn ran her hands down the back of her jeans and paused to inspect them before rubbing them down the front. As her palms reached her knees, a hint of red caught her eye. *Seriously?* She snatched the rag from under the stool and scrubbed at her hands. Making her way toward the shack that served as her storefront, she continued to clean her fingernails.

The last thing she wanted to deal with was a customer. She didn't have the time or the patience tonight.

Why were people so stupid? They'd come to her shop thinking they could rent a boat or a Jet Ski on the spot only to discover they needed reservations at least a month in advance. She used to hold back a couple of Jet Skis to appease the last-minute crowd, but she decided she didn't want them driving her equipment if they were too dumb to plan ahead.

"Hello," the voice called out even louder.

"Chill out. I'm coming, for fuck's sake." Maybe that was why her shop continually stayed at three stars on TripAdvisor. Her favorite review read, *"I wanted to throat punch the vulgar cretin that owns the joint. If I didn't have my children with me, I probably would have."* Quinn grinned. *Vulgar cretin.* She liked it.

She tossed the rag in the bucket outside the screen door as the voice called out again. With a final deep breath, she swung open the back entrance. "Would you knock it off?" Quinn shouted. "I said I'm coming."

A familiar chuckle greeted her. "You haven't changed much, have you?"

Quinn stopped dead in her tracks. Her chest tightened as she sucked in a gulp of air. *Escape! But where?* Her gaze darted around the tiny cluttered back room that offered no place for her to hide. The best hope was the door she'd just entered.

"Don't you even think about it," Mick said, stepping through the curtain that separated the storage area from the front of the shop.

How long had it been? *Two years?* Mikhala Romero looked the same, sun-kissed olive skin, short, dark, windblown hair, and a thousand-watt smile. *How the hell can someone's teeth be that damned white?*

"Don't think about what?" Quinn asked.

"I see the look in your beady eyes. You're fixin'

to bolt."

Quinn scowled. "I don't know what you're talking about. And I don't have beady eyes."

"You're still full of charm." Mick laughed. "Git your ass over here."

Before Quinn could move, Mick covered the three steps that separated them and wrapped her in a bear hug. The air escaped Quinn's lungs in a loud burst. She'd forgotten how much power Mick packed. Stella nicknamed her Popeye because of her enormous forearms. *Stella.* A lump formed in her throat as she returned the hug.

"Just in the neighborhood?" Quinn asked after being released from Mick's vise grip embrace.

"Sumpin' like that." Mick smirked and nodded.

"Isn't fifteen hundred miles a bit out of your way?"

"Fourteen."

Quinn shrugged and threw her hands out, palms up. "Ah, that makes all the difference."

"Offer me a beer, and I'll help you with that engine you're workin' on."

Quinn tried to hide her smile. She'd forgotten what a juxtaposition it was to hear a Southern twang come from the Italian American woman. People expected the Jersey Shore to come tumbling out of her mouth; instead, they got a slow Mississippi drawl.

"How do you know I'm working on an engine?"

Mick nodded at Quinn's hands. "You've got grease on your fingers, but your hands are red like you've been rubbing 'em, and some of the grime seems to be on your pants. Plus, you smell like gas-o-lene."

Quinn shook her head. Despite her slow speech, Mick never missed anything. While Quinn was still scanning her surroundings, Mick would pick up the tiniest details and make an accurate assessment. "Beer's in the fridge. Grab me one, too." Quinn stepped out the screen door and onto the dock before she smiled.

Shit. The entire area was bathed in light from the three floods she'd left on. Mick didn't need to see the repair, or more accurately, the disrepair of the property. She turned off two of the three lights and pointed the third directly at the Jet Ski lift. Still not satisfied, she adjusted it further to cast the excess light into the water.

"Jesus." Mick handed her a beer. "How are you working on that engine when it's so dark out here?" Mick made a beeline toward one of the extinguished floodlights.

"No! Don't!" *Shit. That was over the top.* "I mean, the locals hate it being lit up like a Christmas tree. It takes away from enjoying the night sky."

Mick turned. She pursed her lips, and her eyes narrowed, but instead of speaking, she simply nodded.

She knows. She must have seen the lights blazing when she'd pulled in. For now, it seemed she was going to allow Quinn her lie. "There's plenty of light where we need it." Quinn pulled up a second stool and motioned to it.

They'd been working on the engine for over half an hour when it rumbled to life, sputtered twice, caught, and roared back. Quinn cranked the throttle and listened for an unnatural whine, but none came. With a flick of her wrist, she revved the engine further but was still greeted by a smooth purr. Satisfied, she let off the throttle and hit the kill switch.

"Thanks." Quinn tossed the wrench into her

toolbox and handed Mick a rag. "I've been working on that damned thing on and off all day. Labor Day weekend isn't a good time to sideline equipment. Pisses people off."

"Happy to help." Mick ran the rag around her fingernail, painstakingly removing any signs of grease. "Aren't you curious why I'm here?"

"A little." Quinn tried to sound casual, knowing Mick moved at her own pace. It would only slow her further if Quinn pushed.

"I'll let you in on it once I get these cleaned up." Mick held up her hands.

"I've got degreaser under the sink in the bathroom."

Mick nodded and turned to go inside.

"Hey, grab a couple more beers." Quinn picked up one of the Adirondack chairs that sat against the side wall of the tiny shack. "I'll set up at the end of the dock, so we can chat."

After she placed the chairs, Quinn dropped into one of the seats. Her legs cracked and popped as she stretched them out in front of her. When had she become someone who couldn't move without her body making noise?

The night was still warm from the day, but the breeze coming off the water made it pleasant. She lay her head back, closed her eyes, and allowed herself to be transported by the sound of the lapping waves. *How much longer will I be able to do this?*

"Gorgeous night," Mick said, startling Quinn out of her reverie. Mick lowered herself into the neighboring chair and stretched out her legs. They were several inches shorter than Quinn's.

Quinn chuckled. "Are you sure you're done

growing?" It was one of Quinn's favorite lines to rub in their height difference. At thirty-six, she doubted Mick would have another growth spurt.

"I drive fourteen hundred miles to see you, and this is how I'm treated?"

"I thought you were in the neighborhood."

"Sumpin' like that."

Quinn took a long pull from her beer. The cool liquid hit the spot. She breathed in deeply, hoping the smells coming off the lake would replace the scent of gas and oil that lingered in the air. "The fish are jumping," Quinn said after a loud splash came from the left. Despite the moonlight shimmering off the water, it was still too dark to see much in the murky night.

"Still like it out here in the middle of nowhere?" Mick asked.

"For shit's sake, you act like I'm hiding out in the backwoods of Tennessee."

"Isn't that where we're at?" Quinn detected the amusement in Mick's voice. She'd always reveled in getting under Quinn's skin.

"You know damned well we're in Missouri. And I wouldn't call the Ozarks isolated."

"Tennessee, Misery...all the same to me."

"Says the girl from Bassfield, Mississippi, population one hundred fifty."

"Last census we were over two fifty."

"Population explosion." Quinn chuckled. "Do you ever plan on telling me why you're here?"

"I got a proposition." Mick brought the bottle to her lips and tilted her head back.

"A proposition from Mikhala Romero. That doesn't bode well for me." Quinn caught herself running her finger along the scar that went from the corner of her eye, down her cheek, almost to her lip. She yanked her hand away, hoping Mick didn't notice.

"Revisionist history. I've had some brilliant ideas over the years. I'd say you reaped the benefit from some of my harebrained schemes."

"Glad you admit they're harebrained. Saves me from saying it." She'd forgotten how much she enjoyed having silly conversations like this with her best friend. How many times had they sat on the dock drinking a beer and shooting the shit? *Feels like home.* Quinn stiffened; she couldn't think like that. Since Stella would never be with them again, it couldn't be home.

"Thinkin' about her?" Mick asked.

Damn it. Mick never missed a thing. Quinn thought about lying but knew she wouldn't be believed. "Yeah."

"Her parents were on the news the other day."

Quinn held up her hand. "I don't want to talk about those people." She took another large swallow from her beer.

"Whatcha wanna talk about then?"

"Jesus, after you come fourteen hundred miles, don't you think you should be telling me?"

"I reckon," Mick said, but she didn't continue.

"And...?"

"I need you to hear me out before you start hollering."

"Sign me up for what you're selling. Who could resist such a skilled sales pitch?"

Mick laughed. "I got an interesting call last week at the Pink Triangle."

Just hearing the words Pink Triangle caused

Quinn to flinch and her stomach to roil. Pink Triangle Adventures had been their dream. They'd been running the company for six years when everything fell apart. "Don't you mean the pink line?" She delivered the words she knew would rile Mick.

"How many times do I have to tell you, just because two of the three lines split on me doesn't mean it won't always be the pink triangle in my heart?"

"Split!" Quinn tried to keep the anger out of her voice. "Split is a pretty harsh term, don't you think?"

"I'm not going there." Mick held up her hand. "I want to tell you about a potential new customer."

"You drove all this way to tell me about a new customer?"

"Sumpin' like that." Mick sat back in her chair. "I got a call from a young hotshot that made her millions in Sil-o-con Valley. Sold her startup company for more money than one person should ever have, then started another one."

"She wants to buy the business?" Quinn guessed. *Sentimental fool.* It'd be just like Mick to come all this way to get her blessing, even though she'd signed over her share of the business four years ago.

"Nope. She wants to hire us."

Quinn glanced at Mick out of the corner of her eye. "Us? Got a mouse in your pocket?"

"Not today." Mick smiled, her teeth the only thing Quinn could see clearly. "Says she wants to ride the rapids with MickQ."

"Doesn't she know that MickQ is a thing of the past? Nothing left but a miscue now."

Mick ignored Quinn's attempt at humor. "She and her friends want to pay top dollar. Actually, an insane amount."

"Sounds good for business. I'm sure one of your employees will be happy to join you."

"That's the catch. It's all or nothing. She wants both of us or neither." Mick kicked at a piece of rotting wood near the end of the dock. "You could use the money to fix this place up. Or for *anything* else you might need money for."

Quinn shivered. *Anything else.* She'd never be able to earn that much in her lifetime. She glanced down at the sun-bleached boards that had seen their better days. The dock wasn't the only thing falling apart, but at least Mick couldn't see it in this lighting. No telling how much longer Quinn could hold on to the place, but Mick didn't need to know that. Although, she likely suspected. "I'm working on a couple deals that will hopefully pay off." It wasn't exactly a lie. She'd been working on a few schemes; they'd just all fallen through.

"You'll never guess which rapids they wanna do."

Quinn shook her head. *Not the Ghostrider.* "Don't say it."

"Ghostrider on the Zambezi."

Fuck. They'd run the Terminator in Chile and Bidwell in British Columbia and planned to finish their whitewater trifecta with Ghostrider in Zambia, but it never happened. Now she was out of the game. Quinn shook her head.

"There's eight of them. She offered twenty-five thousand apiece. And all our expenses paid."

"Are you fucking kidding me?"

"Nope. She started with ten thousand, but I told her there was no way I could get you out of retirement. So she asked if twenty-five grand would change your mind."

Quinn's chest tightened. "You know I can't."

"I figured that's what you'd say. But I didn't drive all the way out here for a no, so I thought I'd sweeten the pot."

"A hundred thousand dollars is pretty sweet, not sure how you can make it sweeter." Quinn tilted her head back and poured the last of the beer into her mouth.

"I'll give you the whole proceeds, two hundred thousand dollars."

Quinn nearly spit out her beer but swallowed hard before answering. "Why the hell would you do that?"

"Couple of reasons." Mick put her head back and looked at the sky.

Quinn waited for her to speak, but when she didn't, she said, "Care to elaborate?"

"Full disclosure. If I make this happen, she says she'll book all her future adventures with Pink Triangle." Mick held up her hand before Quinn could speak. "But even if she didn't, more importantly, I want to finish what we started. I want to shoot Ghostrider with my best friend."

"Why would they want a washed-up guide that's been out of the game for years?"

"You know you need to forgive yourself. And start living again instead of hiding out in the middle of nowhere."

Quinn stood. "Do you want another beer?"

Chapter Two

A re you fucking kidding me?" Gina Daughtry slammed her glass of sweet tea onto the table.

Even though they were dining outdoors on a spacious patio, to Aspen Kennedy, the loud thump filled the air. She shifted in her seat and glanced over her shoulder. *Great.* Several other patrons stared in their direction. She rested her chin on her hand, hoping to cover part of her face. "Do you always have to make a scene? It's not that big of a deal."

Gina rolled her eyes and gazed up at the greenery hanging from the wooden beams overhead. Her abundant freckles, red hair, and flamboyant clothes drew enough attention without adding her loud voice and slamming dishes. She shifted her gaze back to Aspen. "You think I'm overreacting?"

"Well." Aspen sneaked another glance at the diners who seemed to have lost interest in Gina's outburst. Not wanting to draw their attention again, she measured her response. "I think it'll be fun."

"Fun. Seriously?" Gina snorted and pretended to size Aspen up, which was a ruse since they'd been best friends for nearly ten years. "You don't exactly scream outdoorsy."

"Why not?" Aspen crossed her arms over her chest and scowled. "I'm as outdoorsy as the next girl."

"Sure you are." Gina waved her hand at the

plants hanging above. "An open-air café on Castro Street doesn't exactly count as the great outdoors. San Francisco is a long way from the wilds."

People were staring again. Luckily, Aspen was tiny, so maybe no one would notice her. To be on the safe side, she hunkered farther into her seat. "My family used to go camping when I was a kid."

"A luxury cabin in the Catskills doesn't count."

"Oh." She needed to come up with another line of defense. "This could turn out to be my thing." *Crap.* By the look on Gina's face, she'd said the wrong thing again. She braced for the onslaught.

"Ah, I see." Gina put her elbows on the table, folded her hands under her chin, and stared directly at Aspen. "Kinda like the Harley-Davidson you bought when you dated Melissa? Thank god you broke up before you got your motorcycle license. Or when you were crushing on the chef. You thought it was a good idea to remodel your kitchen and put in state-of-the-art appliances. I don't even remember her name. That's how long she stuck around."

"Sarah," Aspen said. "But you have to admit the kitchen looks nicer."

Gina shook her head. "Too bad you don't cook."

Aspen dropped her shoulders and jutted out her bottom lip.

"Oh, wait," Gina said. "Maybe it's like when you were with the painter. Didn't you convert the entire area over your garage into an art studio?"

"Now you're just being mean." Aspen scowled. "That's been gone for years."

"That's right." Gina smirked. "How often do you use the recording studio since Harlequin and the Romancers ditched you?"

"Very funny. It was Harlequin and the Sensations."

"No wonder they never made it big. I like my name better. Of course, my personal favorite was when you were with Katrina. Maybe Pink makes aerial acrobatics look easy, but you almost killed yourself. And then—"

"Stop!" Aspen held up her hands, and then put them on top of her head. "I'm just looking for my soul mate, and then everything else will fall into place. Aren't best friends supposed to be supportive?"

"I'm going to pretend you didn't say that. I'd prefer not to cause another scene."

Aspen let out the breath she had been holding. "Thank you. Am I really that hopeless?" She already knew the answer but hoped Gina would be kind. Maybe having wealthy parents and a trust fund wasn't the best thing for her. At thirty-three, she'd drifted through life searching for her elusive purpose. Gina often told her that she had more money than sense.

Gina's face softened. "Sweetie, you know I love you."

"But?" Aspen knew a lecture was forthcoming.

"But you need to figure out what you want, not follow behind whoever the flavor of the month is. How many composition notebooks do you have crammed into your closet? Maybe you better rethink starting a new journal with each new relationship. You're going to run out of room."

"Smartass." Aspen turned up her nose. "I don't just write about the women I've dated. I have all kinds of stories in my notebooks." *Damn it.* She knew she'd made another mistake as soon as Gina's eyes sparkled.

"Speaking of," Gina said. "I love your writing.

When are you going to do something with your stories?"

Aspen flipped her hand as if batting away a gnat. Afraid to jinx herself, she hadn't told Gina about submitting her first manuscript to a publisher. After nearly three months without a peep, she was glad she hadn't. *One more rejection.* She could add it to her long string of relationship failures. "That's a pipe dream."

"Says your parents."

Aspen winced. Gina was right, but talking about her parents was the last thing she wanted to do. "I'm not sure how we got off topic. We were talking about Peyton's and my trip."

"You know I'm in your corner." Gina put her hand over Aspen's. "But do you really think whitewater rafting is going to be your gig?"

"Maybe." Aspen lifted her gaze but kept her shoulders hunched. "Peyton and I need this. Things have been a bit off lately."

Gina narrowed her eyes. "You're finally ready to admit that you and baby butch aren't a match made in heaven?"

"I don't know."

"I do."

"But she's so damned cute."

"Ugh. Just when I thought we were making progress, your hormones kick in. She's a bit too cocky for me."

"Just a bit?" Aspen raised her eyebrows. Gina and Peyton had taken an immediate dislike to each other. It became clear it was in her best interest to keep them apart since their detestation grew at every meeting.

"I was being kind," Gina deadpanned. "Isn't

whitewater rafting dangerous?"

"How dangerous can it be? It's not like I'm jumping out of an airplane or anything."

"What's the name of this place again?" Gina pulled out her cellphone.

"Ghost something. Shit." Aspen dug around in her bag. "Ghosthunter? No, that's not it."

"Where is it in Africa?"

"It starts with a Z." Aspen searched her mind but drew a blank. It certainly wouldn't instill confidence if she couldn't even remember where it was. "Zimbabwe? Zaire?"

"How about Ghostrider on the Zambezi River?" Gina held out her phone.

"Yes! That's it." Aspen extracted a brochure from her bag. "Here. It's in Zambia."

Gina took the pamphlet and tossed it on the table while she continued to scroll through her phone. She glanced down at the paper, scowled, and scrolled some more. "Holy hell. Did you read some of the names of the other rapids?"

"I skimmed through it."

"The Devil's Toilet Bowl. Commercial Suicide. Oblivion. And my personal favorite, the Gnashing Jaws of Death."

Aspen laughed. "Funny. Could you be serious for a second?"

"I am." Gina pushed the pamphlet toward her. "You never read it, did you?"

What the fuck? Aspen picked up the brochure and stared at it. "Peyton's such a joker. She must have had it printed special."

"First, I don't believe Peyton has a sense of humor." Gina held out her cellphone. "And second, I

Googled it. The names are real. See?"

Aspen suddenly felt chilled, but her palms were hot and clammy. Surely, it must be a joke. "Obviously, someone had a sense of humor when they named them. Look on YouTube. See if you can find any videos."

"Way ahead of you." Gina stared wide-eyed at her phone. "Holy fuck. I can't believe you didn't research this before you agreed to go." Gina shoved the phone toward Aspen.

Oh, god. The first image made her nauseated. A raft hit a giant wave, causing the front end to shoot straight out of the water. It seemed to hover nearly vertical for half a beat before it was thrown backward, sending all the passengers into the water. "Are you sure this is the right place?"

Gina pointed to the bottom of the screen. "Read it and weep."

Fuck. She just might be sick. Air burst out of her lungs; she'd forgotten to breathe. Her stint with the yoga instructor was about to come in handy. Breathing in deeply, she let the air calm her before exhaling it forcefully.

"Are you hyperventilating?" Gina asked with a mixture of concern and amusement in her eyes.

"No, just taking cleansing breaths." Aspen continued to take in air and slowly exhale. She smiled when she noticed Gina breathing with her. They took several more breaths together before she spoke. "At least we have some hotshot guides, which should make it better. Peyton about peed herself when she got them to agree to do it. Apparently, there was an obscene amount of money involved."

"That's the only thing she's got going for her." Gina crinkled her nose. "At least she's not after your money."

"Did you just give Peyton an endorsement?"

"No! In every other way, no."

"You have to admit, it's a relief that I don't have to worry about her being after my money."

Gina's eyes softened. "Honey, do you realize that's a horrible reason for staying with someone?"

Aspen's gaze dropped to the table. "Pathetic, huh?"

"No. But it makes me sad. You don't need a relationship to make you worthy. You've got so much going for you."

"Yeah, a fat trust fund, which isn't even enough to make someone stick around."

"Damn it. I wish you'd stop searching for a woman to make you whole. Find yourself first."

"Isn't that what a relationship is for? To complete me?"

"Ugh, you know I hate that line. You complete yourself."

"Sure, easy for you to say. You've been with Steph since you were what, three?"

Gina smiled. "Try sixteen. But that's not the point. You've been through more women than a battalion of horny sailors. The worst part is, with every new *relationship*, you develop a new interest. I'm not sure what you like anymore. Do you?"

Aspen shrugged. She'd asked herself that many times over the last couple of years. The older she got, the less she seemed to know herself. Or like herself for that matter. She must have a purpose. *But what was it?*

Gina stared at her for several beats before she said, "Tell me about these guides. It might make me feel better about your safety." Gina's eyes twinkled. "I hope your life insurance is paid up."

"Very funny." Aspen glared. "You'd feel pretty shitty if something happened to me."

Gina held up her hand. "You're right. Bad joke. So what's their names?"

Aspen snatched the brochure off the table. "I wrote it down somewhere." She flipped it over a couple of times before she stopped and scowled. "Here. McCue?"

"There's only one? I thought you said *guides*."

"I did." Aspen scratched her head. "Just Google McCue. Maybe it'll lead us to the second one."

"There must be a million McCues. Can't you remember a first name?"

Aspen shook her head and shrugged. She needed to pay attention, but most times, she lost interest when Peyton and her friends talked about the things that interested them. "They have some kind of bet going about this McCue person. I was reading at the time, so I was in my own world."

Gina's thumbs played over her phone. "I'm not finding McCue anywhere, no matter how I search. Are you sure you have the right name?"

"Who knows? I guess I'll find out who they are when I get there."

"Text Peyton and ask her." Gina dropped her cellphone on the table and glared at it as if it were the phone's fault that she couldn't find what she was searching for.

"I can't do that. Then she'd know I wasn't listening." Aspen crossed her arms over her chest. "Besides, what does it matter anyway?"

"I'd kinda like to know who has your life in their hands."

Aspen rolled her eyes. "You are such a drama queen. Can we possibly talk about something else?"

"No!" Gina pounded her fist on the table.

Not again. She couldn't resist and averted her gaze to the adjoining tables. *Yep,* they were staring. This trip must be making her jumpy. When did she start caring what others thought? "Fine. What else is there to talk about?"

"When are you leaving?" Gina asked.

Seriously? Aspen fought back her annoyance. "Did you really need to do a dramatic fist slam?"

"It's my style." Gina grinned. "Besides, that was my final protest on this ridiculous idea."

"Thank God. Can we have an enjoyable afternoon? I want to shop in peace."

"Oh, goody." Gina clapped her hands together and bounced in her chair with over-the-top enthusiasm. "Do we get to shop for rafting gear?"

"No, smartass. Peyton's taking care of all that."

"Like I said, she has one plus. But back to my question, when are you leaving?"

"The first week in October."

"Holy hell. That's only a couple weeks away. Don't you have to practice or something?" Gina's voice rose again.

Aspen cringed. She threw cash on the check that the waiter had left some time ago. "Let's get out of here. We can talk while we walk."

Chapter Three

Quinn stared at the phone in her hand. Did she really want to make this call? No, but she had to. She'd been stalling ever since she'd agreed to Mick's proposal. Now it was less than a week before they flew out. She owed it to Natalie to let her know what she was about to do.

"Quinn?" the tentative voice said.

"Hi, Natalie," Quinn said. Understated seemed like the best approach. "How's it going?"

"You're kidding me, right?" Natalie's voice held controlled anger. "To what do I owe the honor?"

"Um, I'm sorry." Eloquence wasn't Quinn's strong suit. "I know it's been a while."

"Try over a year." The anger was replaced by resignation. "What do you want?"

"Why do I have to want something?" *Try charm.* "Maybe I just wanted to talk to my favorite almost sister-in-law."

"Try again." The anger was back in Natalie's voice. "Get to the point, Quinn. I have things to do, like pull my fingernails out with a rusty pair of pliers."

Ouch. This wasn't going well. "It's nice to hear your voice." It was true, but by the inhalation on the other end of the phone, she'd made another tactical error.

"Damn it, Quinn. I can't do this." Natalie sniffled. "Either get to the point or I'm hanging up."

"In other words, you don't want to hear my apologies or excuses?"

"Exactly. At least we're on the same page."

"I saw on the news that your parents are in Europe."

"So?"

"I want to see Stella." Quinn swallowed the bile that rose in her throat. It was out. She couldn't take it back.

"Wow. This call keeps getting worse and worse." Natalie sighed. "Do you have any other impossible requests?"

"I'd like to see you, too."

"Yep, and then that mouth." Natalie sighed. "What's this all about? You're planning on traveling fifteen hundred miles just to see us?"

"Fourteen."

"Goddamn it, knock off the bullshit."

"I want to see Stella." Quinn's voice quivered. "I want to see you." When the other end of the line remained silent, Quinn continued. "I'm going to be in Boston in a couple of days."

"Oh, I get it. Convenience."

Quinn could picture Natalie slumped against the back of the chair, her once youthful face etched in pain and aged by stress. "It's not like that." She recognized the pleading tone in her own voice. "Please, I don't want to do this on the phone. We have things we need to talk about."

"When will you be here?"

Hope? Quinn's heart raced. "The day after tomorrow, Friday. My flight out isn't until Sunday."

"I see. May I ask where you're flying to?"

"I'd rather tell you when I get there."

Natalie snorted. "The mysterious Quinn. Let's just forget about it. I don't need any more pain."

"No," Quinn practically shouted into the phone. "I could have lied and made up a bogus reason why I'm in town."

"Give her a gold star."

Quinn flinched. Anger she could handle, but when Natalie shifted to bitter sarcasm, nobody was safe. She could eviscerate Quinn with her words and had. "Please, Nat. I need to talk to you face to face."

There was a long pause on the other end of the phone. Quinn could hear Natalie's rhythmic breathing. She held her own breath while she waited for a response.

"Fine. I'll see you Friday. Text me with the details. Once we talk, I'll make the decision on whether I let you see Stella."

The phone went dead.

Quinn let out the breath she'd been holding. That had gone better than she'd expected.

Chapter Four

Quinn paid the driver and climbed out of the taxi. It had been over a year since she'd been back to Boston. She stood on the sidewalk and sucked in a gulp of air. The waning sun reflected off the water in Boston Harbor, one of her favorite places in the city.

She'd give anything to be on one of the sailboats, but she needed to get this done. Turning away from the solace of the water, she gazed up at the large glass structure. What would it be like to wake up and look out over the harbor every morning?

Move your feet. Standing here wasn't going to get her anywhere, except late, which would only infuriate Natalie. She stepped toward the building and tried not to gape at the lavish decor in the lobby. Apparently, Natalie's new place was an upgrade from her last, which was more than anything Quinn would ever be able to afford.

She navigated the maze of security and now stood in front of unit 3503. She thought of knocking; instead, she ran her finger the length of her scar and stared at the number.

The door flew open, and she stood face to face with Natalie. Her shoulder-length brown hair looked a bit longer than when Quinn last saw her a year ago. Despite her summer tan, she looked drawn. The playfulness that once danced in her brown eyes was gone; instead, they were guarded. Her lips pursed as she studied Quinn.

No doubt, Natalie was sizing her up. Quinn held no illusions. The past five years had done a number on everyone, especially the two of them.

She wanted to reach out to Natalie. Hug her. But Natalie's demeanor held her back. She didn't look to be in the hugging mood. "Hi, Natalie."

"Hello, Quinn." A cold veil descended. "Please, come in."

Aloof. At least she knew up front how Natalie planned on playing this. Once she entered, Natalie closed the door behind them. She wore a pair of slacks that looked freshly pressed. Not a wrinkle to be found. The shimmering material of her black blouse appeared to be silk. Her bare feet sported perfectly painted, bright red toenails. Despite being nearly six inches shorter than Quinn, her presence made her seem much taller.

Quinn's heart thumped in her chest. Why did she feel she was being led into the lion's den? She gasped when they arrived in the living room, all thoughts stopped. *What a view.* Forgetting everything else, Quinn wandered toward the bank of windows overlooking the harbor. Sailboats were everywhere. Some seemed to be coming in for the day, while others headed out to enjoy the sunset.

Natalie laughed.

Quinn started and turned from the window. The strained look on Natalie's face had softened. "Um, sorry," Quinn said. Heat rose up her neck.

"Typical Quinn." Natalie smiled. "You never could get enough of the water. Do you want to have a seat, or would you rather stand there and gape?"

"I suppose I can tear my eyes away." Quinn relaxed her shoulders. "It's nice to see you, Nat."

"I'm not sure how I feel about this." Natalie's jaw remained clenched, but her eyes softened. "Screw it. Come over here and give me a hug."

Quinn quickly covered the distance between them and wrapped her arms around the much smaller woman. At first, Natalie tensed, but Quinn tightened her hold until Natalie relaxed in her arms. While she held Natalie, her chest opened and tears threatened, so she clamped her eyes shut.

Natalie's body quivered, but she drew Quinn closer. *She's crying.* The realization hit Quinn, but she was determined to do the right thing this time. Lightly rubbing her hand over the silky material on Natalie's back, she whispered in her ear. "It's okay. Let it out."

They stood in the middle of the living room for several minutes before Natalie pulled away. Her eyes were red and bloodshot. She went to wipe her arm across her nose but stopped when she noticed the silk sleeve. "I need to go freshen up." She disappeared before Quinn could react.

Quinn walked to the window and watched the sun disappear into the horizon. The light would hold for a little while, but soon she'd be unable to see the bay. Her eyes weren't focused on the scenery anyway. Instead, she played the last several minutes with Natalie over in her head. Hopefully, with the ice broken, they could have a good conversation. A productive one.

"Would you like something to drink?" Natalie asked when she returned. No sign of her earlier tears remained.

"Do you have any iced tea?"

"Ah, staying away from alcohol?"

"I thought it was for the best." Quinn turned from the window and met Natalie's gaze.

Natalie nodded. "As much as I could use a drink, I'd tend to agree. Please have a seat. I'll be right back."

Quinn stared at the white leather couch and matching recliners. Where would Natalie want her to sit? She was still debating when Natalie returned with two glasses.

"Aren't you going to sit?" Natalie motioned toward the couch.

Good. At least she knew where Natalie wanted her. *Crap. The end or the middle?* Natalie pulled out two coasters and placed them on opposite ends of the table. *Okay.* More clues to where Natalie wanted her. With more confidence than she felt, Quinn sat.

Natalie took her place on the other end of the sofa, put her feet up, and hugged her knees to her chest. She looked so small. So vulnerable. "Care to tell me what's going on?"

Quinn took a sip of her tea before answering. "Getting right to the point, I see."

"I don't think either of us is up for small talk."

"True." Quinn nodded. "Mick came to Missouri to see me about a month ago."

"Two sides of the Pink Triangle back together again?" Natalie's voice held a distinct edge.

"Nope. At least not permanently." Quinn stirred her tea, using it as a distraction.

"Come on, Quinn. Just get to the damned point. Don't make me drag the story out of you." Natalie pulled a blanket from the back of the couch and wrapped it around herself.

It's not cold. In fact, the condo felt extra warm.

"Where would you like me to start?"

"Why are you here? Why do you want to see Stella? Why haven't you returned any of my calls?" Natalie's delivery was rapid-fire.

"Well, that narrows it down." Quinn's attempt at humor fell flat. "I guess I'll start with Mick's surprise visit."

Natalie listened intently, but her unreadable expression made Quinn uneasy. She found herself rushing through the story, pushing to get to the end, so she could hear Natalie's reaction.

"You're seriously on your way to Zambia? Ghostrider? Why would you do that?" Natalie's questions seemed accusatory, or maybe it was just Quinn's guilt.

"You disapprove?"

Natalie bit her lip. "No. I'm just surprised."

"I'm only doing it for one reason."

"Which is?"

"The money."

Natalie's brow furrowed. "That doesn't sound like the Quinn I used to know."

"The money isn't for me. It's for Stella." Quinn's chest tightened, as it always did when she spoke Stella's name.

"You still can't say her name without getting that look, can you?"

"What look?" Quinn bristled. She surely didn't have a look.

"Cut the outrage. I don't have the patience for it." Natalie flicked her wrist in Quinn's direction. "The look that's a cross between somebody kicked your puppy and you just lost your best friend."

Quinn nodded. "That about sums it up."

"What good is the money going to do for Stella? She's getting top-notch care."

"I want to hire a lawyer."

"What?" Natalie scrunched up her nose, and her eyebrows drew together.

"I can hire a lawyer to fight your parents."

Natalie threw back her head and laughed.

"What's so damned funny?" That wasn't the reaction she'd expected, and it pissed her off.

"Do you really think a couple hundred thousand dollars would be enough to fight my parents? Do you know how much they paid for this condo alone? It was my birthday present."

Quinn shrugged. She wasn't about to make a fool of herself by hazarding a guess.

"Try nearly three million dollars."

Holy fuck. "I know two hundred thousand is chump change to your family, but it would still allow me to finally hire a good lawyer. At least get my foot in the door."

"Oh, Quinn." Natalie's eyes grew sad. "That's so sweet, but I don't know if it will do any good."

"I have to try something."

Natalie slid down the couch toward Quinn and touched her shoulder. "I'm sorry. I know your heart's in the right place."

"I feel so fucking helpless." Quinn ran her hand through her short hair, causing it to stand on end. "No! More like fucking useless."

"You can't do this to yourself." Natalie wrapped her arms around Quinn.

Quinn let herself relax against the much smaller woman. Her head rested against Natalie's breast, while Natalie ran her hand over the back of Quinn's head.

She refused to cry, even though Natalie's comforting touch threatened to lay her wide open.

Neither spoke for several minutes, both seeming to draw strength from the other. Quinn exhaled deeply and moved away from Natalie. "Isn't this what got us into trouble last time?"

"Oh, so we're going there, huh?" Natalie's words held only sadness, not anger.

"Don't you think we should?"

"Fine. We're horrible people. Is that what you want me to say?" Natalie sprang from the couch and paced around the room. "We fucked each other's brains out while my sister, your fiancée, laid in the hospital on life support. Yep, we're despicable. Isn't that why you wouldn't return any of my calls?"

Each word was a dagger piercing Quinn's skin. The crudeness of Natalie's phrasing was an indication of the shame Natalie felt. The same shame that drove Quinn away from everyone she cared about. "We need to talk about it."

"Now?" Natalie glared. "After you ran away. Twice! Well, fuck you, Quinn."

Don't react. She deserved Natalie's wrath, so she needed to sit and take it. Four years earlier, she'd run away to the Ozarks when Stella and Natalie's parents had banned her from visiting Stella, leaving Natalie to handle everything on her own. After three years of licking her wounds, Quinn had returned to Boston to enlist Natalie's help to fight them. That was when they'd let too many shots of tequila cloud their judgement and, in a drunken moment of grief, fell into bed together. Quinn took the coward's way out and ran away again while Natalie religiously visited Stella every week, knowing what they'd done. "I don't expect you to forgive me. But can I at least explain?"

"Do you really think there's any excuse for what we did?"

"No! There never will be." Quinn looked to the floor. "Nor is there a defense for why I left you to handle it on your own." She looked up and met Natalie's gaze.

"Twice."

"Twice." Quinn nodded. The word like a knife to her heart. "But I have to tell you that I'm truly sorry. I love you."

Natalie cringed.

"No, not in that way. I love you like a sister."

"That seems even more gross, somehow."

"I shouldn't have left you to deal with it on your own. I was a coward." Quinn wanted to pace, but she remained seated.

Natalie circled the room but didn't speak for some time. Eventually, she squared her shoulders and faced Quinn. "I wanted to blame you. I wanted to hate you. It would have been so much easier."

Why hadn't Quinn noticed how thin she'd gotten? "It was my fault. All of it. I destroyed your sister, and then I destroyed you." The pain in her chest threatened to overwhelm her. This had been a mistake. She'd only survived by being numb, and this was too much. Her gaze darted around the room, searching for an escape.

Natalie marched to where Quinn sat and thrust her finger out. "No! Do you hear me?"

Quinn pressed herself against the back of the couch, trying to get as far away from Natalie as possible. She nodded her assent.

"Good." Natalie stepped back. "We're going to

talk about this. You will *not* run out on me again."

"Okay," Quinn said in a voice barely over a whisper.

"You've taken all this on yourself ever since the accident. I've let you, and god knows my family forced you to." Natalie resumed her pacing. Her bare feet slapped against the hardwood floor. "And after what happened last time, it would be easy to let you go on taking all the blame, but I can't anymore. I let you be the punching bag for years while I was the dutiful sister."

"Stop." Quinn moved to the edge of her seat. "You've been here the whole time. You never left her."

"Shut up, Quinn." Natalie's eyes flashed. "Just shut the fuck up and let me say my peace."

Holy shit. She'd never seen Natalie like this. Stella was always the spitfire while Natalie remained more docile and compliant. Being the younger sister left her to follow in Stella's rather large shadow.

Quinn nodded, afraid of how Natalie would react if she spoke.

"I let you take all the blame, and I never spoke the truth. Especially not to my parents. Stella was headstrong. Nobody told her what to do. Not my parents. Not me. And certainly not you. She was the smallest package of attitude I've ever known." Natalie sighed, and her gaze traveled from Quinn's head to her feet and then back again. She swept her hand as if displaying Quinn to a studio audience. "Everyone wanted to believe that this five-foot-ten wall of a woman, a butch woman no less, could control the petite five-foot-three Stella. What a perfect scapegoat we had in you."

Quinn started to protest, but Natalie silenced

her with a look. The same look Stella used to give her. Goose bumps traveled up Quinn's arms.

"You need to hear this. There was absolutely *nothing* you could have done. It was an accident. Nothing more. You'd run those rapids hundreds of times." Natalie shook her head. "Mick told me you begged her not to do it."

The scene flashed in her head. Exhaustion had set in at the end of the day, but Stella insisted on doing one more run since the water had gotten livelier. Quinn tried to talk her out of it, but once Stella got something in her head, nobody could tell her anything. Reluctantly, Quinn had joined her despite her fatigue. Maybe if she'd refused, Stella would have backed down. *Right.*

She'd been angry at Stella, so she'd taken off in her kayak first. Her only thought was to get it over with, so they could return to the campsite and enjoy the warm fire. Maybe if she'd not been irritated, she'd have realized Stella was in trouble sooner.

"I know that look." Natalie pointed at her. "You weren't responsible for her equipment. She was. We'll never know if it was a defective helmet or user error. But you did everything you could to save her."

Quinn buried her head in her hands. "I wish I hadn't."

"Hindsight is twenty-twenty. Instinct kicked in. Anyone in your situation would have resuscitated her."

"But I should have known she'd been under too long. What it had done to her brain."

"No. We're not having this conversation again. We've covered this ground so many times we've worn a path."

"Fine. But don't you think we should talk about what I did to you?"

"The mighty Quinn. Do you have a god complex or what?" Natalie threw her hands in the air and raised her voice. "Maybe you didn't get the memo, but you're not responsible for everyone. Or every bad thing that happens."

A lump caught in her throat. This was *all* her fault. Why couldn't Natalie admit it?

Before Quinn could speak, Natalie continued. "Since we're assigning blame, let's talk about me before we get into what *we* did. I've let her rot in that hospital for the last five years while Mommy and Daddy control the puppet strings."

"No, that's not fair." Quinn rose from the sofa.

Natalie pointed. "Sit your ass back down. You came here. You wanted to talk, so now you're going to listen."

Quinn lowered her bulk back onto the couch. "The floor is yours."

"I let myself be bought." Natalie went to the window and peered out at the night. "This condo was bought with hush money. I could have spoken up about what they did to you. I could have tried to fight for Stella's wishes. I sold my sister's soul for a view. That's who you slept with." Natalie turned back, and her gaze met Quinn's. "That's what should make you want to vomit. You slept with a soulless woman."

"Can I say something, or are you just gonna swear at me some more?"

"Go ahead."

"You have *no* control over what your parents do. *None!*"

"Maybe not, but I don't have to go along with

them."

"So you can get cut off from Stella like I did? You can beat yourself up all you want, but it doesn't change the fact you have no power, either. You chose the lesser of two evils."

"My parents are as evil as they come. You know this has nothing to do with Stella. It's all about their fame. They've been touring all over Europe spewing their religious crap. Talking about their miracle daughter that God will awaken one day. I don't even think they believe it, but the money is good. There's something I've never told you because I was too embarrassed."

This can't be good. "What is it?"

"They don't even visit her."

"What? They're all over the news making their weekly vigil to their daughter's bedside."

"Yep, they go to the hospital with cameras flashing when they enter. Even if it's only their PR firm doing it now. But they never go into her room."

"How do you know that?" Quinn's face felt hot.

"The staff finally told me. They go in and talk to other families, spreading their BS, and they schmooze the staff. They haven't stepped foot into Stella's room in years."

"I'd seen something on the news a while back accusing them of it, but I didn't believe it."

"That's because they screamed fake news and threatened to sue."

"Fuckers." Quinn hated them more than she'd ever hated anyone. Stella didn't want to live this way, and Quinn had failed to set her free. She'd set her up to spend a life connected to machines. The woman who had so much life packed into her tiny body lay wasting away, alone. Quinn's stomach clenched.

"I hate them, too." Natalie's sunken eyes were haunted.

Quinn took a calming breath. Natalie needed reassurance, not her anger. "If you alienate them, there won't be anyone to look out for her. You've done the right thing."

"Do you mean that?" There was a glimmer of hope in Natalie's eyes.

Quinn knew she was the only one who could make that glimmer grow. "Absolutely," Quinn said with force. "We need someone on the inside. I'm just sorry the burden falls completely to you."

Natalie appeared to deflate and slipped into the nearby recliner. She pulled her legs under her and wrapped her arms around herself. Her eyes glistened, but no tears fell. "But I had sex with you."

"And I had sex with you, too."

"I'm not even gay."

"I know."

"Then why did I do it?"

"The same reason I did."

"Which is?"

"To feel connected to Stella."

"Oh, god." The floodgates opened, and tears streamed down Natalie's face.

Quinn stood and went to Natalie. With that truth spoken, she no longer feared they'd repeat their mistake.

Chapter Five

The echo from their footsteps pierced Quinn's skull while the corridor's white tile floor cast a blinding glow. *Stop.* Her senses were on overload, or more aptly, overdrive. She doubted the sound was as loud as she imagined nor the brightness as overpowering.

Out of the corner of her eye, she watched Natalie's confident stride. Blood pounded in her ears, and she struggled to keep her breathing even. How did Natalie find the strength to do this week after week? Quinn fought the desire to grab her hand. As if sensing her discomfort, Natalie slowed and looped her arm through Quinn's.

Thank you. Quinn smiled at Natalie.

"It'll be okay," Natalie said. "I know it's hard."

"It's been over a year since the last time you snuck me in." A lump caught in Quinn's throat. "Will she look different?"

"Probably, but for me, the changes are gradual since I see her every week. For you, they'll be more dramatic."

Quinn balled her hands into fists to stop the tremor. "Does she still do... Um, does she still make those...?"

Natalie stopped walking and turned to Quinn. "Yes, she still makes noises. And she still has those involuntary twitches if that's what you're asking."

Quinn nodded.

"Are you sure you're up for this?" Natalie asked.

"How do you do it?" That wasn't how Quinn wanted it to come out, but it was too late now.

Natalie shrugged. "I don't know. I just do."

"Sometimes, I think your parents did me a favor by kicking me out. Is that wrong?"

A frown formed on Natalie's lips. She shook her head. "No. Is it wrong that sometimes I'm envious of you?"

"No." Quinn gazed into Natalie's pain-filled eyes. It made Quinn furious knowing that Stella's parents didn't visit her anymore. *Sick fucks.* Leaving one daughter in a vegetative state while relying on the other one to carry the burden was seriously fucked up. "Why do you still do it?"

Anger flashed in Natalie's eyes. "I won't desert her."

Quinn's chest tightened, and heat climbed up her neck. "Like I did?"

"No! My parents left you no choice." Natalie's voice was strong. "I know you. You'd come with me every week if you weren't banned."

"Sometimes, I wonder if that's true. People say they would, but then they don't. Maybe I'm one of them. Maybe I'm no better than your parents."

"Damn it, Quinn. Stop!" Natalie's voice was full of conviction. "You're here now at the risk of being arrested."

Quinn groaned. "Don't remind me. Don't you think the restraining order has expired?"

"I'm sure my parents file a new one every time it comes up for renewal. More publicity for their martyrdom. Don't you get notice of it?"

"Probably. But I don't always open my mail."

Natalie looked around at the people passing them. "We can't continue to stand in the middle of the hallway. We're starting to attract attention, and someone is bound to tell my parents if we aren't careful."

Quinn nodded. "Okay. Let's go."

When they entered Stella's wing, several staff smiled and greeted Natalie and eyed Quinn. *Do they know who I am?* By the looks on a few faces, some did.

They stopped outside of room 226. Quinn's heart raced, and her palms began to sweat. Natalie slid her hand into Quinn's and squeezed.

"Let's do this before you pass out." Natalie pushed open the door.

Quinn took a deep breath and willed her feet to move. *You can do this. Natalie does it every week.* She followed Natalie into the room, and her gaze fell on the tiny figure lying in the bed. She froze, unable to take her gaze off Stella.

Natalie nudged her forward. "It's okay. It looks like she's asleep."

"Isn't she always asleep?"

"Kinda, I guess. But sometimes, her eyes are open."

Quinn prayed she didn't open them when she was here. The last time she'd seen the vacant stare, it haunted her for months.

Natalie moved past her and went to Stella. She knelt and kissed her forehead. "Hey, sis. Look who I brought."

There was no reaction to the kiss or the words. *Can she hear?* The doctors she'd consulted said not in any real sense. Standing here now, part of her wanted to believe she could. *No.* It would mean that Stella lay here day after day trapped.

Natalie motioned Quinn toward the bed. "Come here."

Quinn took a couple of tentative steps forward.

The door behind her flew open. "Hey, girl. Did you bring that little stud with you today? Allison will be all over it if you did." The woman in scrubs stopped abruptly. Her face turned crimson. "Um, I'm sorry. I didn't...I didn't realize you had someone new with you."

Natalie laughed. "Good morning, Donna. I'd like to introduce you to Quinn."

Donna stared, her eyes enormous. Recovering, she held out her hand. "It's so nice to finally meet you."

Quinn took her hand, unsure what to say.

Natalie came to her rescue. "Quinn is feeling a bit overwhelmed. It's been a while."

"Of course. I should leave you to your visit." Donna smiled. "Be forewarned, Betty comes in at eleven."

"Yeah, I checked the schedule. That's why we came now."

Donna put her hand on Quinn's arm. "I'm so glad I got the chance to meet you." She turned to Natalie. "I'll break the news to Allison that you didn't bring her little Southern sweetheart." Donna whisked out of the room.

Mick? Quinn eyed Natalie.

"The secret's out," Natalie said with a casual wave of her hand. "Yes, Mick comes with me sometimes."

What the hell? "Since when?"

"Since you left."

"Four years? Seriously?"

Natalie nodded. "She doesn't come every time. Usually once a month or so."

"Why didn't either of you tell me?"

"Don't be angry."

"I'm not." Quinn realized the truth in her words. "I'm glad she's here for you."

Natalie smiled. "Mick is a different bird, but she's got a kind heart." Natalie glanced at the clock. "We need to get on with this visit. You can't be here when Betty gets in. My parents have her in their pocket." She held out her hand.

Quinn took it and let herself be led to Stella's bed.

The pallor of Stella's skin was a harsh reminder of the accident. Up until then, Quinn had never seen her without a tan. Even more striking was her resemblance to Natalie now that her hair had grown out to shoulder length. She'd always worn it short, so she didn't have to worry about it during all her outdoor adventures. *Her parents' doing.* They probably equated her short hair with being a lesbian and wouldn't stand for that.

Natalie pulled up a chair next to the bed and motioned for Quinn to sit. Once seated, she stared at Stella for several beats before she reached out and took her hand.

Natalie made the visit easier by reminiscing about the old days. Quinn found herself laughing as Natalie talked about their hike to the bottom of the Grand Canyon. It had been a perfect trip.

She gazed at Stella and tried to see the tan woman with flushed cheeks and unruly hair practically skipping down the trail. Quinn turned away, preferring to remember the vision in her head.

More than half an hour passed as they told stories and laughed. Natalie looked at her watch. "We need to go."

Quinn's heart sank. She took Stella's hand again. "I love you. I'm going to do right by you, somehow."

Natalie took Quinn's other hand. "Regardless of what happens here, you have to start living again."

Quinn wanted to protest and tell Natalie she'd been living but knew it would be a lie. "Once this is over."

"No, this may never be over." Natalie glanced at Stella with tears in her eyes. "You go with Mick, and when you come back, you start your life. Do you hear me?"

"I'm going on this trip for the money and to get past my fear of the rapids. Not to find myself."

"Damn it, Quinn." Natalie's voice rose. "Mick and I didn't just lose Stella five years ago. We lost you, too. And it's time to come back to us."

Quinn flinched and released Stella's hand. She'd never feel alive as long as Stella lay trapped in this bed, but she couldn't tell Natalie that. Instead, she gave Natalie a sad smile. "Thanks for bringing me here."

Chapter Six

A spen rubbed her eyes. After traveling for over twenty-four hours, they felt gritty. Being on a private plane helped, but it was still exhausting. She hadn't expected the Victoria Falls Airport to be so tiny. She snorted at her own naïveté. What did she expect? They were in the middle of Africa, after all.

While they waited to disembark, Peyton had gotten up to talk to the others. It gave Aspen the perfect opportunity to dash off a quick text to Gina before she had to go into *radio silence,* as Peyton called it. It would have been nice had Peyton told her before they were on the plane, but she wasn't going to argue in front of the others. She suspected Peyton had calculated that.

Her fingers flew. *Hey, Gina. Just landed in Africa. I found out on the plane that Peyton insists on no cellphones during these adventures. Says it's the only way the group will disconnect from their jobs and relax. Not that it applies to me, but I have to be a sport and play along. This will be the last you hear from me for a week or so. Wish me luck :). BTW...I was wrong about McCue. The guide's names are Mikhala Romero and Quinn Coolidge. MickQ. We are staying at some Elephant Camp a couple days before they get here. I miss you. Xoxo.*

"Hey, babe. Hand it over." Peyton plopped down

in the seat next to her.

Nobody had the right to look this damned good. Especially after traveling. Aspen would never get tired of Peyton's piercing blue eyes, made more striking by her nearly black hair.

Aspen looked longingly at her phone before powering it down and handing it to Peyton. "Do you really have to enforce this with me? It's not like I'm going to be checking in on work."

"Gina's a thousand times worse than work." Peyton slid Aspen's cellphone into the pocket of her carry-on.

Don't take the bait. There was nothing worse than having her best friend and girlfriend hating each other. "I can't believe we're in Africa. And that I'm going on a whitewater rafting trip." She flashed a flirtatious smile. "You're a bad influence on me."

Peyton laughed, obviously forgetting Gina.

Dodged that bullet. "Are you positive this is safe?"

Peyton groaned. "God, why do you talk to that Debbie Downer?"

Shit. Gina was back on Peyton's radar. "Gina didn't say anything about it being unsafe," she lied. She ran her finger up Peyton's arm and gave her a shy smile. "I'm just a little nervous is all."

"Aw, babe. You don't have anything to worry about. I'll protect you." Peyton puffed out her chest and sat up straight, trying to get the most of her five-four height.

Adorable. Apparently, she had a thing for small butch women. Gina's mocking face flashed in her mind. She could hear Gina ticking off the variety of women she dated, so she couldn't claim a type.

Peyton leaned over and planted a lingering kiss on her lips. They were interrupted by a catcall.

"Jesus. Would you two knock it off?" DaKota Lee, Peyton's best friend, said. "It's time to get off this fucking plane." She made eye contact with Aspen. "Last chance to bail. I'm sure I could get the pilot to fly you home."

Aspen put on her best smile. "I'm sorry I didn't catch that. What did you say?" *Kill them with kindness.*

The sneer didn't leave DaKota's face, but it didn't worsen, either. "Are you sure you don't want to back out? You know you put Peyton in a rough spot, having to lie for you."

Without thinking, Aspen raised her eyebrows and turned her gaze to Peyton.

"Oh, god, you didn't tell her, did you?" DaKota smirked. "Priceless."

Peyton grimaced and shot daggers at DaKota, who either didn't notice or didn't care.

Peyton took Aspen's hand. "There is that little thing I forgot to tell you about."

DaKota snickered.

God, I wish she'd shut up. Aspen faked a smile. "What is it you haven't told me, baby?" She wouldn't let DaKota get the satisfaction of seeing her rattled.

"The guides...well...they kinda think we're all experienced rafters, so I need you to go with the flow and not give anything away."

"And why would they have that impression?" *Good,* she'd kept her voice calm and measured. DaKota's gaze bore into her, but she kept her focus on Peyton.

"Because I really wanted you to come." Peyton took her hand and kissed her knuckles. "They wouldn't have let you on the trip if they knew."

Aspen took a cleansing breath to stave off her anger. A few months ago, she would have been flattered that Peyton wanted her here so badly she'd lie. Now the manipulation annoyed her, but DaKota didn't need to witness it. Laying it on thick for DaKota's sake, Aspen wrapped her arms around Peyton's neck. "Of course I'll play along. Besides, how hard can whitewater rafting be, anyway?"

"Mark those words down." DaKota smirked. "Because you just might live to regret them."

Aspen tensed, but Peyton gave her a pleading look. She checked her watch. "One forty on September 30. It has been duly noted." Turning her gaze back to Peyton, she said, "I'm looking forward to a couple days of fun and relaxation before we hit the surf."

DaKota shook her head. "Keep calling it the surf, and they'll have your number the first day."

"What are you three yammering about?" Tina Horton, DaKota's newest flavor of the month, said. "Claire and LeAnn have already disembarked."

They exited the plane onto the tarmac. Claire Barton, Peyton's college roommate, and Claire's longtime girlfriend, LeAnn Isaacson, stood holding hands. LeAnn laughed at something Claire said. Claire was the most low-key person Aspen had ever met, but she was wickedly funny with her monotone delivery. Aspen wondered if anything ever rattled her. Peyton and DaKota often joked that they needed to hold a mirror under Claire's nose just to make sure she was still alive.

LeAnn let go of Claire's hand and waved to Aspen. When Aspen waved back, LeAnn hurried to greet her. "I'm sorry we didn't get a chance to chat much on the plane. I think I slept more than I was awake." Of all of Peyton's friends, Aspen was most comfortable with LeAnn. They'd hit it off the moment they'd met.

"No worries. We've got plenty of time to catch up. I didn't get the chance to tell you that you're looking good."

LeAnn blushed and ran her hands along the side of her body. "I've been getting ready for this trip, so I've dropped a couple pounds." LeAnn was a full-figured woman, but her curves were in all the right places.

"Good for you, but I've always thought you were a knockout just the way you are."

"Stop." LeAnn playfully slapped Aspen's arm. "Well, maybe you could go on a little."

Aspen laughed. The others began the short walk to the terminal, so they followed. Aspen gazed around the modern glass structure. It wasn't as primitive as she'd expected it to be. Somehow, she figured they'd be surrounded by jungle, but it could have been a small airport in any of the tropical locations she'd flown to before.

Before she had time to take it all in, a guide whisked them away to an air-conditioned van. He handed out flutes of champagne as they climbed aboard. "Welcome to Zimbabwe," he said. "Sit back and relax. It's only about twenty minutes to the Elephant Camp."

"I thought we were in Zambia," Aspen whispered to Peyton.

The guide must have had bat ears. "Ah, Zambia is our neighbor to the east. I'm sure you will visit her on your stay here. Shall we depart?"

"What about our luggage?" Peyton asked.

"Not to worry, it is already on the way to your tentalow."

"What's a tentalow?" DaKota asked.

The guide smiled. "It's a cross between a tent and a bungalow. A tentalow."

Aspen snickered. "I love it. Although I'm not so sure how I feel about the tent part."

"Not to worry, miss. You're in for a real treat. The best of both worlds. The camp is exquisite with all the luxuries of the best resorts while you'll have the opportunity to enjoy the natural beauty of Zimbabwe and Victoria Falls. Go on a safari by day, and then enjoy dancing in your finest into the night." He counted the women and held up a paper. "I'm supposed to pick up eight today, and then two later. Has there been a change?"

Peyton nodded. "You only have the six of us. Unfortunately, two of our friends couldn't make it. Ransomware."

The guide's eyes grew large. "Ransom here? Or back in the States?"

DaKota smiled. "No, no. They haven't been kidnapped. Their company computers were hacked."

"Machete or a knife?" the man asked. Peyton began to explain, but the man let out a deep belly laugh. "I'm just messing with you. I know what hacking is. Just a little African humor."

Aspen laughed along with the others. She took a drink from her flute. Peyton seemed relaxed and in good spirits. Maybe getting away from the stress of her company would be just what they needed.

The guide put the van into drive, and they pulled away from the terminal. The paved roads seemed to be in good repair and trees sparse. This wasn't what Aspen expected.

As they drove, the trees became denser, and the paved road turned to dirt. Now she felt like they were in Africa. They talked little as they watched out the windows for signs of native animals.

Their guide chuckled. "It's my favorite part of the job to see the looks on my passengers' faces as they experience Zimbabwe. I am assuming this is your first time here."

"You assumed right." Peyton's face flushed. "I suppose we're embarrassing ourselves acting like naïve tourists."

"Nonsense," he said. "I'd be worried if someone saw this splendor for the first time and wasn't a little in awe. Hopefully, the elephants will oblige you with a visit. We'll be turning into the camp soon, so keep your eyes open."

They bumped along in silence as the road grew rougher. Dust rose around them from the dry sandy terrain.

"Look," DaKota called out and pointed. "I see one."

"Two," Tina added.

"Yes, yes." The guide chuckled. "It looks like our progress may be delayed. I believe they are standing in our path."

Aspen ducked her head and strained to see out the front window. Being seated behind the driver made it hard to make out what the others saw. As a child, she'd seen many elephants in zoos and circuses, but seeing them in the wild gave her goose bumps.

Peyton scooted over in her seat, put an arm around Aspen, and pulled her closer. "Here, can you see now?"

Aspen squealed. "Oh, my god. Elephants." Heat spread across her face. *How embarrassing.* "I didn't mean to scream like a little girl."

"That's okay, honey," LeAnn said. "Squeal away."

The guide pulled up about ten yards from the animals.

"Can we get out and pet them?" Peyton asked.

"Not these. We'll enjoy our friends from a distance. We pride ourselves in our rescue, rehabilitate, and release program, so you'll have plenty of opportunities to meet our elephants."

"Awesome," DaKota said and turned to Tina. "That will be so cool."

Aspen couldn't help but smile. Even though DaKota often irritated her, seeing DaKota with so much childlike wonder gave her hope for the trip.

The elephants meandered along the road for several minutes as they watched. Finally, the driver edged the van closer until the animals moved along.

"You must be lucky," the guide said. "This is the first time they've come out to greet our guests in a couple weeks."

"I'm going to consider it an omen," Aspen said and held up her nearly empty champagne flute. "To the trip of a lifetime."

The others tapped glasses and drank down the last of their drinks.

The rest of the drive to the camp was uneventful until they pulled up to the front entrance. They were greeted by another man in a white suit, holding another bottle of champagne.

"Welcome. You must be our guests in the west

camp."

"We are." Peyton stepped up to the man. "It's my understanding that we'll have the entire four units to ourselves."

"That is correct, ma'am. If you'd like, we'll take you to your accommodations now."

※.※.※.※

"Holy shit," Aspen said. "You weren't kidding when you said we were staying at an Elephant Camp." She was exhausted from traveling, but this place might wake her up. She flopped down on the mosquito-netted, king-sized bed. The netting draped over the canopy and was tied back on all four corners. Aspen touched the mesh. "I'm glad we have these after everything I've read about the diseases mosquitoes carry."

"Let's not talk about bugs." Peyton chuckled. "Isn't this the coolest place?"

"Remind me to give my regards to DaKota and her travel agent." Aspen rolled around on the luxurious bedding. "Can you believe we're in the middle of Africa surrounded by elephants?"

"Isn't it great?" Peyton's blue eyes sparkled. "You should've seen your face when you saw the tents. I thought you were going to demand to be taken back to the airport."

Aspen glowered. It had been a shock when they'd rolled into camp. Even though the guide had told them about the tentalows, she obviously hadn't understood the concept. When they arrived, the first thing she noticed was the cream-colored canvas roofs jutting out from the trees. The primitive first impression was a juxtaposition to the palatial inside. The resort obviously catered to wealthy Westerners. Upon further examination, there was a tiny pool and a deck where they could see the mist rising from the falls. "I wasn't that bad. But you've got to admit, from the outside, they look like circus tents. I thought we were going to be sleeping with the elephants."

Peyton hopped onto the bed next to her and ran her hand over Aspen's bare stomach, where her shirt had ridden up. "Now that you've seen it, does it pass the test?"

"Uh-huh." Aspen closed her eyes and enjoyed the feel of Peyton's warm touch. Peyton's fingers danced across her stomach and made their way to the bottom of her bra. "Peyton Dorsett, are you trying to seduce me?"

Peyton flopped onto her back and groaned. "I wish, but we have to meet the others for cocktails and canapes in fifteen minutes."

"What?" Aspen sat up in bed. "Why did I not know this?" *Typical.* Whenever they traveled in a group, the operative word was *group.* It seemed Peyton and her friends were connected at the hip. She'd hoped they'd get a little couple time, but apparently, that wouldn't be the case.

"You know DaKota likes to make it an event. She hooked us up with a special pre-dinner experience overlooking the Batoka Gorge. It's supposed to be amazing. Then she splurged on a big dinner spread for everyone."

Aspen grinned and lay back down. She put her head on Peyton's shoulder and let her warm breath tickle Peyton's neck. Breathing a little harder to ensure her breath had its desired effect, she pressed her breasts against Peyton's arm.

Peyton shifted and let out a soft moan.

Encouraged, Aspen pressed in harder and moved her lips closer to Peyton's neck. She let out several breaths before her tongue flicked out and connected with the tender spot just under Peyton's ear.

"Shit." Peyton rolled away, nearly catching Aspen on the chin with her shoulder, and leapt out of bed. "DaKota will be pissed if we're late. Or worse, come looking for us."

Of course. Over the last nine months, DaKota had interrupted many a romantic moment. It was like she had a radar and could sniff out whenever Aspen wanted sex. "No, we mustn't disappoint DaKota."

"Thanks, babe."

Either Peyton didn't catch the sarcasm or chose to ignore it. Aspen suspected the latter.

"I'll freshen up really quick, and then you can." Peyton darted for the bathroom.

Ugh, really? She thought about rummaging through Peyton's bag to find her cellphone, so she could dash a quick text off to Gina. *Nope.* She'd made a promise, and she intended to keep it.

Chapter Seven

Quinn shut her book. Glancing out of the corner of her eye, she saw Mick had awoken from her nap. They'd been in the air for nearly four hours, a small dent in their lengthy flight time. Maybe she should take a nap, so they wouldn't have to talk. Done right, they could probably take turns sleeping until they landed in Africa.

They'd talked little since they'd met at the airport. Mick never questioned where Quinn had been nor why she hadn't spent the weekend at Mick's place like originally planned.

Quinn yawned and stretched. Her lack of sleep over the last couple of days was catching up with her. More than likely, once she allowed herself to doze, she'd be out for a large portion of the rest of the flight.

The weekend at Natalie's had been cathartic. No lines were crossed, nor had either of them wanted them to be. Despite their guilt, they needed to find a way back to their previous relationship. Those two days had helped them take the first step. They'd had the opportunity to grieve together, which was something they'd never let themselves do in the past. Friday and Saturday night, they'd stayed up late. Most of their conversations centered around Stella. They told stories about all the great times they shared. They'd laughed more than they cried, but they'd done plenty of both.

Eventually, curiosity would get the best of Mick, and she'd delve into questions that Quinn would prefer to remain unspoken. It was pretty impressive Mick had lasted this long.

Might as well get it over with. "Do you want to talk about the elephant in the room?"

"Which is?" Mick replied.

"Where I was this weekend."

Mick nodded. "I reckon I already know."

That wasn't the answer she'd expected, even though it was likely true. "Oh. I guess you probably do."

"How's Natalie? I haven't seen her for a couple of weeks."

Quinn tried to hide the surprise from her face. "Yeah, I hear you're a regular when it comes to visiting Stella."

"Sumpin' like that."

"Why didn't you tell me you visited her?" Quinn hoped it didn't come out accusatory.

"You never asked." Mick paused and glanced at her before continuing. "Besides, it's not like you've been really into talking to me the last couple of years."

That hurt. She couldn't deny it. She'd not exactly kept in contact with Mick, no matter how much Mick tried. It could take her weeks to return Mick's calls or texts, but to Mick's credit, she kept on reaching out even when Quinn's responses were less than prompt. "I'm sorry. I haven't been fair to you."

"It messed with your mind. I'm just hoping time with Natalie and Stella helped." Mick's drawl came out even slower as she measured her words. "And maybe this trip will be what you need to right yourself."

Quinn leaned back against her seat and sighed.

"That's exactly what Natalie told me. She said it was time for me to get on with the business of living."

"Wise woman."

"She looked terrible." Quinn ran her hands through her short hair.

"Which one?"

Astute. "I was talking about Stella, but I could've been talking about Natalie, huh?"

"Yeah. Last time I saw Nat, she looked rough. She needs to get on with the business of living, too."

"I told her the same thing. She looked right through me, shrugged, and changed the subject."

Mick shook her head. "Her parents make it tough on her."

"Those assholes are killing their daughter who's alive while pretending to keep alive the one that's already gone."

"Doesn't make much sense. Do you think they believe Stella will wake up?"

"Nope. They don't even go inside her room anymore." The heat rose in Quinn's face. "I swear they love the attention. They're the darlings of the pro-life faction, traveling all over the country, hell the world, spreading their bullshit. Meanwhile, Stella is their pawn. Their victim. Makes me sick."

"She'd hate it." Mick gazed down at her hands. "I've never met anyone so full of life. She was a little spitfire."

Quinn swallowed the lump in her throat. "Do you think she hates me for it?"

Mick's head snapped up. "For what?"

"Saving her when I shouldn't have. Then not saving her when I should."

Mick's eyes narrowed, and she repeated Quinn's

words. "Ah, I think I know what you just said. You think Stella hates you for resuscitating her when it happened, and now again for not being able to get her taken off life support?"

Quinn nodded.

"Well, get that thought out of your head." Mick's eyes blazed. "You did what anyone would do. You tried to save her. And short of landing yourself in jail, there's nothing you can do to get her off the machines."

Quinn knew it was true but still felt she'd let Stella down. If it had only happened six months later, after their wedding, things would be different. She'd have the say on what happened, not Stella's parents. *No!* She couldn't get caught in that loop again, or it would only spiral her. "It's so hard. I don't believe in hate, but I hate what they're doing to Stella."

"What about what they're doing to Natalie?" Mick asked.

"Sometimes, I hate them just as much for that, maybe more so. I worry about her."

"Why do you think I visit Stella?" Mick's gaze shifted to Quinn. "It certainly isn't for Stella. In my estimation, she's long gone."

Damn. Why did Mick keep surprising her? Probably because Quinn had been so self-absorbed, she'd not thought of anyone else. No doubt, Mick was one of the good ones. She'd been there for Natalie while Quinn ran away and hid. "Thank you."

"For?"

"Being the person I should have been."

Mick gave a dismissive wave. "Nonsense. You and Nat are too close to the situation, so you need someone like me."

"But you love her, too."

"I do. But it's not the same, so it's easier for me."

"Well, thank you anyway."

"Did you get your little problem with Natalie worked out?"

"What?" Quinn's voice came out louder than she'd expected. She glanced around at the other passengers. They all appeared to be sleeping.

Mick smirked, and her eyes twinkled. "You didn't think I knew about you and Nat?"

How many surprises was she going to get today? "I can't believe she told you."

Mick glanced at Quinn and winked. "She didn't, but you just did."

Seriously? Mick's infuriating. When would Quinn stop underestimating Mick's ability to assess a situation? "You're an asshole." Quinn meant it affectionately.

"I know." Mick flashed her white teeth. "Things better with you now?"

"Yeah, we cleared the air. We won't make that mistake again."

"Good. I don't think either of you could live with the guilt."

"Enough of that," Quinn said. "Since I'm supposed to have a fresh start this trip, tell me a little more about it."

"I sent you the email with all the info."

"Refresh my memory."

"You never read it."

"Something like that," Quinn said, stealing Mick's signature line.

Mick glowered. "I'm not sure which is worse, not reading my email or butchering my favorite line."

"My bad. I know it sounds much better with a drawl." Quinn winked. "Fill me in on our adventure."

Mick glanced at her watch. "Our guidees should have already arrived at the Elephant Camp."

"Is guidees a word?"

"It is now." Mick grinned. "Do you want to hear about our adventure, or are you going to keep interrupting me?"

Quinn leaned back in her seat. "Enlighten me."

Chapter Eight

Aspen ran her hands down her sleek black dress and turned to the side to examine herself in the mirror. *Being tall was overrated.* Despite her five-foot-three height, she'd been known to turn heads. The dress hugged her in all the right spots. Hopefully, it would be enough to get Peyton to leave the party early tonight.

She'd have to thank Tina for insisting they be given time to come back to their rooms to change for dinner. It had been hard to leave the beauty of the Batoka Gorge, but as she checked herself out, she was glad they did. They'd only have a couple of nights to wear their nice outfits before they hit the rapids and tents.

She leaned in toward the mirror and checked out her makeup. *Not bad.* The bags under her eyes were well hidden. Although, her irises looked nearly black, which tended to happen when she'd not gotten enough sleep. Traveling had done a number on her. She ran a brush through her long blond hair and considered putting it up. *Nah.* Too much work.

With one more glance at herself, she decided she'd look good on Peyton's arm. *Shit.* Gina would be all over her for thinking like that. Why did it matter how she looked on Peyton's arm? Why didn't she ever think how Peyton would look on hers?

When she walked into the main room, she found

it empty. "Peyton." No answer, so she yelled louder. "Peyton."

"I'm out here," Peyton called from the deck.

The view took her breath away. The spray from the falls caught the fading sunlight, creating several small rainbows. "It's gorgeous here."

Peyton turned. "You're even more gorgeous." She ran her hand down the side of Aspen's dress and let her hand wander to her backside. Cupping Aspen's buttocks in her hand, she gently kneaded.

Knowing she'd be thwarted again and left hornier than before, she backed away. "You said we couldn't be late for dinner."

"You're right."

Unbelievable. She must be losing her touch if this outfit couldn't convince Peyton to be a few minutes late. Maybe if she'd come out naked, but she doubted it'd work. The ache between her legs would have to wait.

Back inside, Aspen slipped on her heels. They would make her calves look good.

Peyton cleared her throat. "Do you have to wear those? I thought I asked you not to pack them."

Aspen sighed and kicked off her heels. Gina's voice rang in her head. *You're seriously gonna let her tell you what you can wear?* Aspen once thought it was cute, but nine months in, Peyton's insecurities sometimes wore on her. Tonight was one of those times. Always having to wear flats so she wouldn't be taller than Peyton depressed her.

Before entering the dining tent, Peyton slipped her arm through Aspen's. *Sure.* They hadn't touched the whole walk, but now Peyton wanted to make sure everyone saw them enter.

Cynical much? She needed to stop listening to Gina. Her best friend meant well, but her constant complaints about Peyton must be rubbing off. *Enough.* She squeezed Peyton's arm and smiled. *Better.* So what if Peyton wanted to be taller than her, it didn't have to be a red flag.

The room had a simple elegance, despite the tented ceiling. The fans and small chandeliers that hung from the tent creases looked a little out of place, but they served a practical purpose. A large table with seating for eight sat in the middle of the room. The crisp linens and place settings were meticulously arranged.

DaKota waved from the tiny bar in the corner. She wore her signature cargo shorts with a safari shirt. The cargoes were khaki and the shirt a deep brown. Aspen was pretty sure she had the same style of shirt in every color imaginable. At least she matched the vibe here and would fit right in with the elephant trainers. Finally, DaKota's fashion sense was in style.

LeAnn and Claire had yet to arrive. Aspen smiled to herself; they were probably getting it on. *At least someone was getting laid.* Since when had she become so sex-crazed? Probably since Peyton's interest seemed to be waning. Their first month together, Peyton had been ravenous, wanting sex at least two or three times a day. Nine months later, they could go weeks without any, and then only when Aspen initiated it.

Peyton waved and started toward the bar. *Damn it.* Without heels, she couldn't strut across the floor in quite the same way. She wanted to exude a presence, so maybe DaKota would back off. Since her focus was on making sure her ass swayed in just the right way, she missed whatever DaKota said. Everyone else laughed, so she faked amusement.

DaKota shoved a drink into Peyton's hand. "It was so cool seeing the Zambezi from the gorge. Just think, we'll be on the river in a couple days."

"Too bad Patti and Denise won't be here to enjoy it with us." Peyton's brow furrowed.

"Yep," DaKota said. "I still can't believe they got hit by ransomware."

"That's why I have the no cellphone rule." Peyton took a gulp of her cocktail. "Imagine if they'd gotten the call after we'd arrived. It could have messed up our trip."

Realizing nobody ordered her a drink, Aspen turned to the bartender. "I'll take an old fashioned, heavy on the bitters." Purposefully, she turned back to Peyton. "What was it you were saying?"

"Patti and Denise. That's why I insist on no cellphones." She slammed her drink onto the bar.

Was Peyton seriously taking it personally? "They had an emergency. What's the big deal?"

Peyton's ice blue eyes flashed anger. "This is a trip we've been dreaming about for years, and they blow it off like it doesn't matter. Who does that?" Peyton crossed her arms over her chest.

"Dude," Claire said as she approached the bar. "Chillax, man."

Aspen hadn't seen Claire arrive but was glad she had. Claire tended to say things to Peyton that no one else dared. Either she didn't notice Peyton's pouts or didn't care. This was the time her laid-back attitude came in handy.

"I know, but it still pisses me off." Peyton's lips were pursed in a pout, but her anger subsided. "I've been looking forward to this for so long."

DaKota stood and put her arm around her much shorter friend. "Hey now, are we chopped liver? With or without them, this will be epic."

The corner of Peyton's mouth turned up slightly. "Sucks to be them. They're gonna miss it."

"That's the spirit." DaKota lifted her glass to the others. "To us. Fuck the Chandlers."

Everyone yelled out, "Fuck the Chandlers," except for Aspen, but she did hold her glass in the air.

"We'll still get to go, won't we?" Tina said, joining the conversation.

Peyton had been appeased, but now a worried look crossed her face.

"Why wouldn't we?" Aspen jumped in, hoping to avert any additional unpleasantness.

"That's right," DaKota said with gusto. "Why wouldn't we?" She shifted her gaze to Aspen and gave a half smile.

Peyton laughed. "Dumbasses. They're out fifty thousand dollars. I couldn't get Mick to go any lower than two hundred."

"Serves them right," DaKota added.

Aspen's stomach churned. Yet another reminder of their privilege. The Chandlers just threw away more money than some families lived on for a year, and she doubted they would even care or notice.

A waiter dressed in white entered the room. "Ladies. If you please, dinner will be served shortly."

Aspen slid into the chair next to LeAnn. "I'm so glad I was able to grab this seat."

"Definitely." LeAnn gave her a warm smile and leaned in. "No offense, but Tina isn't exactly a great conversationalist."

Aspen gave her a knowing smile. "Peyton tells

me when we get back, you're starting a new job."

"Kinda. I'll be working at the same hospital, but I got a promotion."

"Congratulations."

For the next ten minutes, the two talked, and Aspen ignored the conversation around them until DaKota's booming voice broke through.

"Hand over the money, Peyton. The bet's ten thousand." DaKota reached around Tina and handed Claire a check. "Claire's going to hold 'em."

"What are you betting on?" LeAnn frowned at Claire as she collected the check from Peyton.

"It's not important." Claire smirked.

Aspen glanced at Peyton, who also had a similar grin. "What are you guys up to?"

"Nothing." Peyton waved her off. "We were just talking about our guides."

"And it resulted in a ten thousand dollar bet?" Aspen narrowed her eyes and studied Peyton. Something told her she wouldn't like the wager, but she also knew Peyton wouldn't tell her.

"That's not important." Peyton cleared her throat loudly to get everyone's attention. "What is important is how we're going to fool them into believing Aspen knows what she's doing."

Aspen glanced at the faces around the table. "You mean I'm the only one that hasn't rafted before?"

Everyone nodded but said nothing.

Aspen's gaze settled on Tina. "No offense, but you don't look like whitewater rafting is your thing."

Tina smiled and flicked back her auburn curls. "Thank you. I was born and raised in Colorado, so I grew up on the river." She leaned her head against DaKota and kissed her cheek. "I never thought I'd do it again once I left home, but this sexy woman convinced me otherwise."

DaKota smiled. "She's an old pro. Probably better than any of us."

"Used to be." She held up her long red fingernails. "I better not break one of these, or I'm gonna be pissed."

Everyone laughed.

Aspen turned to LeAnn. "And what about you? Are you a pro, too?"

"Hardly." LeAnn smiled. "But Claire's dragged me on two or three trips."

Aspen groaned. "I'm so screwed. They're gonna spot me a mile away."

"That's why we need to come up with a plan." Peyton patted Aspen's hand. "I don't think these two will take kindly to us trying to pull a fast one on them, so we need to make this believable."

"That's why Denise and Patti not being here has the potential to screw us," DaKota said.

"Why?" Aspen shot her a puzzled glance.

"Less people for you to hide behind," DaKota responded. "With eight of us, we figured it would be easy to blend you in with the rest of the group. Now with six, it gets a bit trickier."

Ugh. Why did I agree to this? Aspen's heart raced. She didn't want the embarrassment of being found out. How humiliating to be kicked off the trip.

"Worst part is, they'd probably suspend the whole excursion if they found out," Claire said.

Great. Now it wouldn't just be her affected. Another reason for DaKota to hate her. "Maybe I should just stay back and let you guys go." Peyton's face dropped. She'd obviously said the wrong thing.

"Honey, don't look like that. I just didn't want to ruin anyone's time. I'm such a burden."

"You could say that again." DaKota pretended to whisper to Tina, but her volume was enough for everyone to hear.

Aspen removed her napkin from her lap and threw it onto the table. They'd just finished their salads, but she didn't want to sit here any longer. She started to rise, but Peyton put her hand firmly on Aspen's thigh.

"No, babe," Peyton said. "We'll figure it out. Stay."

LeAnn gently patted her other leg. "It's okay. We've got you. Since Quinn and Mick won't be here until tomorrow night, we've got time to teach you a few things."

Aspen sighed and her muscles relaxed. Why hadn't Peyton thought of this before? Now she'd have to do a crash course when she could have been studying at home for the past month. *Fuck.* She wanted her phone, so she could talk to Gina. LeAnn would have to do. It wasn't lost on her that she'd thought LeAnn, not Peyton.

"Glad we've got that solved." Peyton smiled and released Aspen's leg.

"I want to know more about these people," Aspen blurted out.

"That probably should be her first lesson," Claire said. "She needs to know about the lesbian legends."

Seriously? Legends? Since when were there whitewater rafting legends? Statements like that made her question whether she belonged. She turned to LeAnn. "Are they your heroes, too?"

"Heroes might be a bit strong." LeAnn grinned. "But their story is fascinating."

"So how did you discover them?" Aspen asked Peyton.

Peyton's face lit up. "DaKota, remember the first time we saw them on YouTube?"

"Oh, man, we were hooked." DaKota's eyes twinkled.

Interesting. Seeing DaKota starstruck made her a bit more likable. Surely, it wouldn't last. "Tell me more." Aspen tried to match their level of enthusiasm.

"We started following them in high school. They were probably seven or eight years older than us," Peyton said. "Mick and Quinn met in college, and their shenanigans started then. They'd do all kinds of crazy things in the water. Jet Skis. Boats. Rafts. And their favorite, kayaks. They were always putting up videos of their exploits. Those two were *insane.*"

"Remember that time they went over that dam?" DaKota interrupted. "That was wild."

"Oh, god. I forgot that one." Peyton laughed.

"Why didn't you show me any of their videos before we came?" Aspen asked. *Easy.* Peyton knew she would've backed out if she'd known what she was getting into.

Peyton shrugged. "I never thought about it."

Sure, you didn't. "I still don't understand why it was such a big deal to get them. Didn't you say they operated a business? The Pink...uh...Pink..."

"Triangle," Peyton said. "But it's Mick's now. Quinn hasn't been a part of it for several years."

"So we brought MickQ back together again." DaKota ran her fingernails over her shirt as if she were buffing them.

"Did they get in a fight?" Aspen asked.

LeAnn shook her head. "It was tragic. After Stella's

accident, apparently, everything went downhill."

"Stella? Who's Stella?" Aspen noted the somber faces around the table.

"Quinn's fiancée," Peyton said. "They met Quinn's senior year of college while Stella was a sophomore. Quinn fell hard for her, so it wasn't long before she joined their team."

"Hence the Pink Triangle Adventures," DaKota said. "Clever, huh?"

Sure, clever. "Why didn't you guys hire Stella, too? Did they break up?"

"Worse," Peyton said. "Tragic accident. Word is, she's in a coma somewhere. Quinn flaked out after it happened. When I talked to Mick, she wouldn't tell me how to get in touch with Quinn. I heard she's got some little shack on a lake somewhere in the Ozarks. She rents out boats and Jet Skis."

How tragic. Aspen's heart ached. "Mick kept the business?"

"As far as we know," Peyton said.

"Stella fucked everything up when she came into the picture. MickQ was never the same." DaKota made a point of looking directly at Aspen. "That's what happens when a woman gets in the way of a perfect friendship."

Stella lay in a coma, and DaKota was talking trash about her. *Nice.* How could she even respond to that?

"God, you can be an idiot," LeAnn said, saving Aspen from having to say anything. "She was the love of Quinn's life, and now she's been laying in a hospital bed for years. Show a little compassion, for Christ's sake."

"I didn't mean it that way." At least DaKota

had the decency to look remorseful. "They were just the funniest pair. And the best part about it was they didn't even know it. Remember that old Kibbles and Bits commercial where the big bulldog and the little, tiny dog were buddies? That's Quinn and Mick."

Aspen crinkled up her nose. "No. I don't think I ever saw it."

"Where did you find this woman?" DaKota said to Peyton. "Under a rock?"

Peyton shot DaKota a look before shifting her gaze to Aspen. "It was a classic. The big dog was slow and lumbering, and the little one was one of those hyper yappy dogs." Peyton chuckled. "The little one bounced around and talked really fast while the big dog plodded along. And that was Quinn and Mick. Quinn is a big dyke, she must be at least five-ten and is built like a Mack truck, while Mick is a scrappy little thing."

DaKota laughed. "The funniest thing is their personalities are the exact opposite. Mick was always the thinker, while Quinn was the more impulsive doer. Remember how we used to watch those videos and laugh our asses off?"

"That was one of our first forays into computers. I think we should credit them with some of our success. Claire helped us put the Kibbles and Bits commercials together with MickQ videos and make some crazy mashups."

"I've seen some of them." LeAnn smiled. "They're an adorable pair. Quinn talks fast, while Mick doesn't get into a hurry about anything. I could listen to her slow Southern drawl all day."

"Now the truth comes out," Claire said. "I know why you agreed to come. You're crushing on Mick."

LeAnn put her fingers a couple inches apart and smiled. "Just a little."

Claire's eyes narrowed.

"Oh, don't give me that look." LeAnn laughed. "You used to crush on Quinn."

"The operative word is used to." Claire gave LeAnn a smug smile.

"I still can't believe you're so superficial. It's just a scar."

"It's hideous." Claire crinkled her nose. "I always loved her baby face. It was so cute on her tall muscular body. Now the scar makes her look mean and scary."

"How did she get the scar?" Aspen asked.

"Probably when she tried to save Stella," Claire answered. "She disappeared for a couple years after Stella's accident, and then one day, a picture of her showed up online with this nasty scar."

"Aren't chicks supposed to dig scars?" LeAnn asked.

Claire shook her head. "Not this chick."

"Let me know when you guys are done discussing whether scars are sexy." Peyton entered the conversation.

"Claire held up her hands. "Please, change the subject."

"Okay. I've got it." Peyton clapped her hands together. "We'll create a diversion."

"A diversion to keep them from talking about Quinn's scar?" DaKota asked.

"No, to throw MickQ off Aspen's trail." Peyton pointed at Tina. "And there she is."

"Me?" Tina frowned. "How am I supposed to do that?"

Peyton smiled at Tina. "You don't look the part.

Nobody would ever think, hey, I bet that woman's a whitewater rafting expert."

Tina tilted her head in Aspen's direction. "She doesn't scream whitewater rafting expert, either."

"Don't you see?" Peyton's eyes danced. "We keep Tina glammed up. The hair. The makeup. The nails. While we do the opposite with Aspen."

"Brilliant." DaKota chuckled. "Tomorrow, when we have dinner with Quinn and Mick, we glam Aspen down."

"Exactly. I think we can pull it off." The excitement was evident in Peyton's voice. "Aspen can put her hair in a ponytail and wear no makeup. It'll give her the girl next door look."

DaKota looked Aspen up and down. "She can't dress like that, either. We need to put her into something basic. Shorts and a T-shirt."

Really? First, she couldn't wear her heels, now this. Plus, they were discussing her like she wasn't even here. "Do I get a say?"

"Do you want to ruin the trip for all of us?" DaKota shot back.

Count to ten. Surely, they weren't trying to put her down. "Is this really necessary? We're on vacation, so I'd like to look nice while we're here at the resort. Isn't it a stretch to think they'll judge me by my clothes?"

"You'll look fine," Peyton said.

Fine? What a ringing endorsement from her girlfriend. She didn't have the energy to argue. Besides, she didn't want to be responsible for spoiling everyone's trip. "Okay, but I'm doing this under protest." She crossed her arms over her chest and stuck out her bottom lip.

"Perfect," Peyton said. "They should be here for dinner tomorrow night, so we've got twenty-four hours to get this down."

Aspen sighed. Deceiving the guides, this wasn't what she'd signed up for.

Chapter Nine

"These people have some serious money," Quinn said as she dropped her bags by the side of the bed. "I can't believe they sprang for our lodging, too."

"Yep." Mick tossed her bag beside Quinn's. "We've got this place for the entire time we're here."

"Shit. Makes camping less appealing. How many days did they want to sleep under the stars?"

Mick shrugged. "DaKota's travel agent was handling all the permits and porters. I gave them a couple options, but we haven't solidified anything. I'm sure we'll find out tonight." Mick flopped onto the bed. "Damn, this is like sleeping on a cloud."

Quinn turned up her nose and rolled her eyes. "You know that's the stupidest saying ever, don't you?"

"Sheesh, it's a figure of speech. Stop being so literal. And stop being a buzzkill."

"Holy shit." Quinn bounced around the room, checking it out. "Did you know we have our own deck with a mini swimming pool?"

"Seriously?" Mick rolled off the bed. "Where?"

Quinn swung open the patio door and walked outside. Past the brush, the mist from the falls rose into the air. She waited for Mick to join her. "Isn't it amazing?"

"I swear I can smell the falls." Mick inhaled

deeply and held her breath for several beats before letting it out. "Damn, it's been a long time. Getting excited?"

Quinn smiled, not sure how to answer. Part of her was exhilarated at the prospect of shooting the rapids, but the other part of her was terrified. Her love of water never stopped, despite the tragedy, but this would be her first time guiding a rafting trip since the accident.

When Quinn didn't answer, Mick continued. "Or would you rather be anywhere but here?"

"I need to do this." Quinn stared at the mist hanging in the air. "For Stella. For myself."

"No doubt. She'd be pissed that it took this long, but she'd forgive you now that you're here."

"That's what I keep telling myself. Natalie told me the same. There's a lot riding on this trip. Do you think I'm up for the challenge?" So many emotions, both good and bad, had been churning in her since they'd landed. She didn't say it, but she was glad Mick was here with her. She doubted she could do it without her.

Mick moved up beside Quinn, who clutched the railing in front of her. She stood close enough that their bodies touched. Being much shorter, Mick's shoulder pressed against Quinn's elbow. "You're gonna do this. *We're* gonna do it!"

Quinn refused to cry. When she turned to Mick, her eyes were dry. "I've gotta conquer my fear."

"No doubt. Plus, you need to start living again."

Mick's penetrating gaze left her feeling exposed, so she turned her gaze back to the scenery. "There's no one in the world I'd rather be here with than you." A lump caught in her throat, and she swallowed hard.

Mick lightly bumped Quinn with her shoulder. "It's okay. I know you'd throw me over if you could be here with a healthy Stella."

"Yeah, but that's not in the cards." Quinn tried to smile. "You'll have to do."

"Gee, thanks. But why are you questioning if you're doing the right thing?"

"Being here with you, I know, is right." Quinn paused for several seconds. "But is it right being with this group of strangers? Should we have gotten back out just the two of us first?"

"It's probably a little late for that, don't you think?"

"Yeah. I don't suppose they'd be happy after springing for all this for me to flake out."

"Definitely, no flaking." Mick took a deep breath. "It's probably going to be pretty rough, but I'll be right here with you. Once you walk through it, your life will open up, and you'll start living again."

"I've told you. That's not why I'm here. I need the money for Stella, and it's time I conquer my fears."

"Speaking of time, we're supposed to meet our party in the dining hall in a few minutes."

It wasn't lost on Quinn that Mick had changed the subject, but she wasn't complaining. Between Mick and Natalie, they'd both been pressing, so a reprieve was fine by her. "Let's do it," Quinn said with less confidence than she felt.

❧ ❧ ❧ ❧

Aspen ordered her second old fashioned. Something told her she would need it tonight. Peyton's and DaKota's level of giddiness rose as the time for Quinn and Mick to arrive drew closer. All day, while the group explored Elephant Camp and got the opportunity to learn about the animals, they'd been hyper. They'd not shut up about MickQ's imminent appearance.

As Peyton's preoccupation grew, she'd spent little time with Aspen, but hanging out with LeAnn made the day better. If Aspen were being honest, in many ways, she preferred LeAnn's company to Peyton's. *Stop.* Peyton was supposed to be the love of her life. The one who would finally stick and complete her.

Aspen sidled up to Peyton, hoping to alleviate her guilt. Absentmindedly, Peyton put her arm around Aspen's waist but didn't acknowledge her in any other way. Instead, she continued to debate Claire and DaKota about which rock band they should hire for their next blowout party.

Tina sat on the other side of DaKota and stirred her cocktail. She watched the ice swirl in the glass as if it were the most fascinating thing in the room. She might be right.

Envy rose in Aspen. Tina had dressed the part tonight. Her bright red bodycon dress perfectly matched the color of her lips and fingernails. Aspen glared at her own blue jeans and hoodie. She'd tried to convince Peyton she could dress a little nicer, but Peyton wouldn't hear of it. She needed to look like the outdoorsy type.

Self-consciously, she ran her hand through her ponytail that snaked through the loop of her baseball cap. *Excessive.* She never wore baseball caps, and she knew she looked ridiculous. Tina flipped a hand through her auburn hair that fell to her shoulders.

If Aspen didn't know better, she'd think Tina was taunting her.

Aspen yawned. Earlier, she'd lobbied Peyton to let her skip dinner, but Peyton wasn't having it. They could tell Mick and Quinn she was under the weather. It seemed like a brilliant plan, but Peyton disagreed. Now she'd be forced to test her newfound knowledge of all things whitewater rafting.

Aspen had her back to the entrance but knew immediately when Quinn and Mick walked in the door. The room went quiet. Peyton's eyes widened, and she let out a loud exhalation. Without a word, Peyton jumped off her barstool and pushed between LeAnn and Aspen.

LeAnn shook her head. "I guess we're on our own. Nothing like being left in the dust. Shall we go meet the cutie?"

"Mick?"

"Who else?" LeAnn smiled. "That woman is easy on the eyes."

Aspen grinned. "Just don't drool all over Mick."

"Tempting, but I don't want to scare her off." LeAnn's eyes twinkled. "At least not yet."

"Let's meet your crush." Aspen turned, and her gaze immediately fell on the pair at the center of the excitement.

Damn. LeAnn hadn't exaggerated; Mick was adorable. She wore a pair of blue jeans with a tight white T-shirt tucked into her pants. Casual, yet sexy. The shirt clung to her body, showing off her muscular arms and flat stomach.

Despite her body, Mick's face was what captured Aspen's attention. Her bronze skin indicated she'd spent plenty of time outside, while her messy dark black hair gave her a carefree vibe. And then she smiled. *Shit.* Nobody had the right to look that good. Aspen shifted her gaze to LeAnn, who stood staring. "Now I get your obsession. She's adorable."

"Do you see that smile?" LeAnn didn't turn to speak directly to Aspen because her gaze remained on Mick.

"Would you stop gaping, so we can do this introduction right?"

"Sorry." LeAnn finally turned to Aspen. "I'll stop staring before I make a fool of myself."

Aspen's gaze shifted. *Quinn.* She stood nearly six inches taller and had at least fifty pounds on Mick, but she still tried to hide behind her. With hunched shoulders, she kept her gaze on the floor.

Interesting. They'd said Quinn was energetic and hyper, but Aspen wasn't picking that up from her demeanor. Trying to disappear behind Mick didn't make her appear outgoing. Maybe the tragedy changed her. Caused her to withdraw.

Evidence of Quinn's baby face remained. Her unblemished skin was smooth, except for where the scar ran from the corner of her eye to her mouth. Starting at her neck and climbing up her cheek, she sported a reddish blush, giving the impression of perpetual embarrassment or physical exertion. Her short dishwater blond hair appeared baby fine.

When Mick nudged Quinn, she looked up. Aspen locked gazes with her and found she couldn't look away. *Windows to the soul.* Her light brown eyes held wisdom and pain. Quinn blinked twice, and then shifted her gaze.

Peyton waved Aspen and LeAnn forward. "Come here and meet our guides."

Aspen stepped up next to Peyton and smiled. "You must be Mick. I'm Aspen. Aspen Kennedy." She reached out her hand, and Mick took it in hers.

Mick greeted her with a smile. "It's a pleasure to meet you, Aspen, Aspen Kennedy."

Damn. White teeth. And that drawl. "This is my friend LeAnn Isaacson."

LeAnn blushed and held out her hand. Aspen half expected her to mumble or ramble incoherently; instead, she simply nodded and smiled. LeAnn's face dropped when Mick released her hand.

Aspen stifled a giggle. No doubt, LeAnn would be embarrassed once she got her bearings.

"And this big old lug is Quinn." Mick stepped aside.

Aspen held out her hand, and it was enveloped by the warmth of Quinn's much larger one. "Quinn. It's nice to meet you."

"You as well," Quinn responded.

Before Aspen could say more, Claire and Tina joined the group, and another series of introductions began. Aspen stood back and tried not to stare, but something about Quinn kept drawing her attention. *Tortured soul or wise?*

After the greetings were finished, Peyton launched into a series of questions, dominating the conversation. Quinn and Mick politely answered, but Aspen suspected they must be fatigued. Finally, Aspen could stand it no longer. She wiggled between Peyton and DaKota and put her hand on Peyton's arm. "Don't you think we should offer our weary travelers a drink?"

Peyton smiled, but her eyes flashed anger. "Oh, yeah. Of course. Where are my manners? Would you ladies care for a drink?"

"I thought you'd never ask." Mick winked at Aspen.

Peyton's jaw clenched. She held her hand above her head and waved. "Can we get some service over here?" Her voice was louder than necessary.

"Really, Peyton?" Aspen leaned in and said it so only Peyton could hear.

"We've both got two strong legs," Mick said. "I reckon we can walk to the bar."

A waiter met them halfway across the floor and began offering apologies. Mick held up her hand. "No need for that. Lead me to the bar, so I can see what our choices are."

Peyton grabbed Aspen's arm as Quinn and Mick followed the waiter. "Thanks for embarrassing me," Peyton said between clenched teeth.

"Oh, babe, I wasn't trying to embarrass you. In your excitement, you just forgot that our guests could use something to drink. No big deal." Peyton's face had begun to relax, but Aspen recognized her mistake as soon as she delivered the last line.

"It might not have been a big deal to you, but it was to me." Peyton spun and headed toward the bar.

Great. Aspen wanted to crawl in a hole. As if getting through the evening without giving away her ignorance of whitewater rafting wasn't bad enough, now she'd have to contend with Peyton's pout. How long could she safely hide away in the bathroom before someone became suspicious? She'd find out.

She'd only made it halfway across the room when someone called her name. *Shit.* Aspen put on a smile and turned around.

"Hey, girl, where are you going?" LeAnn said,

approaching her.

Oh, good. "Just heading to the restroom."

"Care if I join you?"

So much for hiding. "Of course not."

Once they were farther from the group, LeAnn leaned over toward Aspen. "How much of a fool did I make of myself?"

Aspen grinned. "Well…at least you didn't throw Mick to the ground and smother her in kisses."

LeAnn groaned. "Oh, god, was I that bad?"

"Let's just say, it's a good thing Claire's laid back."

LeAnn laughed. "I'm not worried about Claire. She's used to me making an ass of myself and knows I lust after Mick. The bigger question is, did Mick notice?"

"Do you want the truth, or do you want me to make you feel better?"

"Ugh, I knew it." LeAnn pressed her hand against her forehead. "Just tell me how bad it was. Scale of one to ten."

"About a six."

"Oh, good. I'll take a six." LeAnn pushed the door to the bathroom open. "Probably no permanent damage then?"

Aspen followed in behind LeAnn. "Nope. I think Mick was amused more than anything. My guess is with that smile and that drawl, you're certainly not the first woman to behave that way around her."

"What about you?" LeAnn turned her gaze on Aspen and narrowed her eyes.

"What about me?"

"Don't you think she's yummy?"

"Who?"

"Seriously? Mick. Who else would I be talking about?"

Shit. Yeah, who else? Certainly not Quinn. "Sorry. I'm just a little preoccupied. I'm afraid they'll see right through me and know I haven't a clue what I'm doing." Aspen's answer only told half of the story, but she had no intention of telling the other half.

"Of course, you have to be crawling out of your skin."

"Why do you think I was coming to the restroom?"

"Ah, and I thwarted your plans to hide out."

Aspen smiled. "Yep, so we better do our business and get back out there, or everyone will wonder what happened to us."

When they emerged, they found the group bent over a table with Quinn and Mick in the center. Mick's finger rested on a large map. "Here is the heart of the Zambezi, rapids one through twenty-six." Her finger trailed along for some distance. "And this is where Ghostrider is."

Quinn pointed. "The first stretch is about seventeen miles. And it's somewhere around fifteen miles from there to Ghostrider."

"Aren't there other rapids in between?" Peyton asked.

"Yeah, there's some good ones along the way. But the concentrated ones are here between one and twenty-six." Quinn moved her finger back up the map.

"The first day should be pretty intense. We'll make it through Oblivion, which is rapid eighteen, and then set up camp at Bobo Beach," Mick said. "The second day will be a little more leisurely. We'll raft to Moemba Falls and set up camp between Upper and

Lower Moemba. The third day, the grand finale, will be all about Ghostrider. We'll hit it in the raft first and get a feel for the river before running it with the kayaks."

Kayaks? What the fuck was she talking about? Mick must have misunderstood. They were here to raft. Aspen hoped her face didn't show her shock. She needed to be careful not to give anything away, so she smiled and nodded.

"Mick mentioned you might want to try your hand at kayaking some of the earlier rapids," Quinn said. "But I recommend saving it for Ghostrider. Kayaking is intense, so it can take quite a bit out of you."

Fuck. Now Quinn seemed to be confused, too. Aspen shot a look at Peyton, who quickly looked away. Her heart rate increased, and her palms instantly became clammy. This wasn't what she'd signed up for.

"Makes sense. Save it all for Ghostrider," Peyton said.

"Yeah, I like it." DaKota nodded with a stupid grin on her face. Aspen was pretty sure if Quinn and Mick said they should go down the river on an innertube wearing a tutu, they'd agree.

"The days will go quick. Plus, we need to assess your skills. I know all of you have been in rapids before, but this is a little more intense than maybe some of you are used to." Quinn shifted her gaze to Tina when she spoke the line.

Tina smiled. "I'll be fine as long as I don't break a nail." She wiggled her fingers before putting them against her chest with a giggle.

Aspen stared at Tina. Her act was a little over the top. Sensing attention on her, Aspen glanced around the circle and noticed all her friends staring in her direction. *Shit.* She'd forgotten this was where her practiced line belonged. She took a deep breath. "Tina, you'll be fine. We'll all look out for you. Won't we?"

Everyone nodded and grunted assent.

Aspen slid past DaKota and put her arm around Tina. "Stick with me. I've got ya." Like she was a person who said, "I've got ya." *Would anyone buy this?* Out of the corner of her eye, she caught her hoodie-covered arm draped over Tina's elegant shoulder. Looking like this, maybe someone would.

Tina squeezed Aspen. "Thanks. I know you do."

Aspen wanted to vomit. Nobody would be winning an Oscar tonight. The waiters descended with the first course of their meal and saved her from further humiliation.

"God, I'm starving," Quinn said, sweeping the map off the table. She folded it over a few times, obviously not in the proper sequence based on the thickness.

Mick snatched it from her, unfolded it, and refolded with a practiced ease. She shot Quinn a satisfied smile before handing it back to her. *God, they're adorable.* Maybe Peyton's heroes weren't so bad, after all.

Everyone began taking their seats, but Aspen hung back. Her mission was to sit as far from Quinn and Mick as possible. *Crap.* Her gaze darted around the table. The seat farthest away from them would separate her from Peyton. *Would that look weird?*

"DaKota," Aspen said, raising her voice, hoping to make her story believable. "I know Mick and Quinn are your idols, so I'm willing to give up my seat next to Peyton. Just this once."

DaKota looked up at her and scowled. "What? Go sit next to your girlfriend." DaKota flicked her wrist at Aspen.

Clueless. And they were worried about her blowing it. "You had your chance," Aspen said between clenched teeth. As she turned, a hand pulled her back. "What?" She spun around and glared.

DaKota sheepishly stood. "Thanks for giving up your chair. I really appreciate it."

Aspen forced a smile. "No problem. LeAnn and I have some catching up to do." She plopped into her seat and waved a waiter over. Maybe another old fashioned would calm her nerves.

༄ ༄ ༄ ༄

Quinn craned her neck around Peyton, so she could get Mick's attention. Her eyes flashed a silent question. *What the hell just happened?* Quite an awkward game of musical chairs.

Mick shrugged and mouthed, "How the hell should I know?" before she resumed her conversation with Peyton.

Quinn let her gaze wander around the rest of the room. After being waylaid when they'd arrived, she'd not had time to take it all in. Somehow, they'd turned the canvas tent into an elegant yet casual space. The splendor suited Tina in her revealing dress, while Aspen still fit in with her sporty look.

No one could deny Tina's beauty, but Quinn found Aspen's natural look more appealing. *Tiny.* Her head barely reached Quinn's shoulder, and her clothes hung on her. The hoodie must be at least two sizes too big. Maybe she'd recently lost weight, or possibly, she preferred her clothes loose. Some women did, but it wasn't a luxury Quinn could afford. Nobody her size wanted to appear bigger.

Quinn made a mental note to herself to ensure they'd brought plenty of sunblock. Aspen's pale skin would sizzle in the African sun. Quinn doubted that Aspen's blond, nearly white hair could lighten any more despite the harsh rays.

Aspen must have sensed Quinn's gaze because she looked up and smiled. Quinn's stomach leapt to her throat. She'd brushed away the first time she'd had a reaction, but a second time couldn't be so easily dismissed.

Quinn smiled back before looking away. Despite diverting her gaze, Aspen's intelligent eyes seared into Quinn's mind. The last time she'd seen that shade of blue was the water on Crater Lake in Oregon. *Damn.* She must be tired. When was the last time she'd noticed a woman's eyes?

The waiters arrived with their food, thankfully, drawing her attention away from Aspen.

During dinner, the conversation centered around the group's day at the elephant sanctuary. Quinn enjoyed listening to their stories and was fascinated by what they'd learned about the animals. Despite their wealth, they seemed genuinely in awe of their experience. While in business with Mick, they'd met some ultra-wealthy people who'd forgotten how to enjoy the simple pleasures in life, always wanting something bigger and better, so it was refreshing this group didn't seem to have that problem.

Her favorite moment was when Aspen talked of gazing into the elephants' eyes. The way Aspen told the story was poetic and lyrical. Aspen's description made Quinn feel as if she was there and was peering into the soulful eyes herself. She'd jokingly told Aspen she should be a writer, which elicited a blush. Quinn hadn't been sure why, but the rowdy conversation made it impossible for her to probe further.

Quinn was jolted out of her thoughts as the volume around the table increased. After dinner, the conversation had turned to the rafting trip. During the chaotic introductions, Quinn hadn't made out the pairings, but it hadn't taken long for her to figure out who belonged with whom. It appeared tensions threatened to erupt between one of the couples when Tina took Peyton's side in the debate.

"Seriously?" DaKota slammed her empty glass onto the table. "You're supposed to stick with me."

Tina tilted her head and shrugged.

"Don't give me that. Why are you dissing me?"

Tina reached her hand across the table, but DaKota pulled hers back. "Come on, DaKota. Hear me out."

"I'm all ears."

"I know you're bummed we have to portage around number nine, but in the span of only seventeen miles, we have twenty-six rapids. Many are class IV or V, so having to skip one isn't the end of the world."

DaKota pursed her lips. "But how can we just skip Commercial Suicide? We should at least kayak it."

Hmm. They'd obviously been doing their home-work. Quinn loved the interesting names some of the rapids had been given. Commercial Suicide ranked right up there on her list of favorites.

"What do you think?" Mick said, her gaze

landing on Aspen.

Aspen looked to each side of herself and even behind her. "Are you asking me?"

"Obviously."

"Um, well. I think that...well, the group really should decide." Aspen's gaze darted around the table and then fell on Peyton.

Peyton sat up in her chair, so she could see around Mick. "Come on, DaKota. Let's save kayaking for Ghostrider. It'll be one for the ages. Can you imagine how sick it will look with our GoPros?"

Mick held up her hand. "I want to hear what Aspen has to say. Everyone keeps cutting her off." Mick winked at Aspen. "I have to stick up for my fellow height-challenged sister."

Quinn had noticed the same. The enthusiastic group was rowdy, and whenever poor Aspen went to speak about rafting, someone always talked over the top of her. The room went silent, and all eyes focused on Aspen.

Aspen's eyes widened, and she put her hand on her chest. "I'm feeling like a turkey on Thanksgiving Eve. Does everyone need to stare at me?"

Mick smiled. "You heard the lady. All y'all stop staring at the poor woman."

A couple nervous giggles came from the others before they turned away. Quinn's gaze stayed focused on Aspen. Her already pale face drained of whatever color was left.

"I just feel that since there are so many rapids and levels that we can skip one and it will be all right." Aspen's gaze darted around the room. "And, umm, Ghostrider should be our grand finale."

"You're so right," Peyton blurted out. "It'll slow

us down kayaking Commercial Suicide."

Mick kept her focus on Aspen. "Do you prefer an oar rig or a paddle raft? Or are you more into kayaking?"

Aspen froze with her drink nearly to her lips. She recovered quickly and pressed the glass against her mouth and took a gulp of her drink.

"We won't be needing an oar rig since we've hired porters to take our equipment for us," Peyton said. "Besides, paddle rafts let us all row, which is why we're here."

Aspen pulled her drink away from her mouth. "See, a girl can't even take a drink with this group they're so enthusiastic." She chuckled. "But Peyton is right, we won't be using an oar raft. Besides, I prefer the paddle one anyway."

Quinn studied Mick. Why was she badgering the poor girl? "Mick, sheesh, lay off." Quinn shook her head and looked into Aspen's eyes. "Ignore her. She gets a bit too intense sometimes."

Mick smirked. "Sumpin' like that."

Chapter Ten

Quinn stifled a yawn, the third one she'd held back in the past couple of minutes. After dinner, they'd stuck around to chat and get to know the group better. Now, fatigue descended like a fog, clouding her mind.

"I'm beat," Quinn said to Mick. "I'm not used to traveling halfway around the world anymore."

"Does that mean you're ready to call it a night?" Mick asked.

"Afraid so. You can stay if you'd like, but I'm ready for bed."

"Nah, I'll come with you. We just need to say goodbye to everyone."

Fifteen minutes later, they were walking back to their living quarters.

"What do you think?" Mick asked.

"About what?"

"The group."

"I think they'll do fine."

"Doesn't exactly sound like a ringing endorsement."

"Lots to take in." Quinn picked up the pace. She wanted to get back to their living quarters and away from this conversation.

Mick practically jogged to keep up. "You can run, but you can't hide."

Quinn smiled. "Far as I can tell, I'm walking. It

looks like you're the one doing the running with those stubby little legs."

"Good try, but insulting me isn't gonna stop me from asking you questions."

Quinn slowed her pace. "Fine. What do you want to know?"

"Are you ready to do this? Are you going to be okay?"

Quinn sighed. She was happy for the darkness, so Mick couldn't see her face well. "I suppose I have to be."

"I'll understand if you can't do it." Mick put her hand on Quinn's back. "More than anything, I want us to do Ghostrider together but not if it's gonna be too hard for you."

Quinn stopped walking and turned to Mick. "I need to do this. I'm afraid if I don't do it now, I may never."

"But you're scared."

Quinn's gaze fell to the ground, and she nodded. "Terrified. I've been on the water plenty since that day but not in whitewater."

"I know." Mick's eyes glistened in the moonlight. "But whitewater was always your thing."

"The rush always made me feel so alive." A lump caught in Quinn's throat. "But then it took Stella's life, so how can I allow myself to enjoy it again?"

"I understand. But..." Mick bit her lip and hesitated.

"Just say it."

"You sure?"

"I'm sure."

Mick inhaled deeply. "Stella would be pissed that you stopped living and doing the things you loved because of her. Maybe this'll sound like a cliché, but isn't it dishonoring her by crawling in a hole and hiding?"

Ouch. Quinn's chest tightened, and she opened her mouth to respond.

"Sorry," Mick said. "Let me rephrase that. If you truly want to honor Stella and all that she was, you need to start living again. She'd never want you to give up something you love on account of her."

How could Quinn explain to Mick how her body betrayed her? Her heart raced and her hands trembled just standing here talking about it. What if she froze when they got to the water? Worse yet, what if she lost her shit? Then strangers, who thought she was a hero, would witness her shame. Quinn squared her shoulders, and her jaw hardened. "I want to do this. For Stella. For you. But what if I make a fool out of myself?"

"And I want you to do it for *you*." Mick grinned. "Besides, I've seen you make a fool of yourself plenty of times, so what's another?"

"You're such an ass." Quinn lightly elbowed Mick in the shoulder. "I've missed you," she said in a quiet voice.

"I've missed you, too." Mick elbowed Quinn back. "Enough of this sappy shit. What can I do to help make it easier on you?"

"I've been thinking about that."

Mick groaned. "Oh, man. What are you going to make me do?"

"Do you think you and I can sneak away tomorrow and kayak the Minus Rapids, just the two of us?"

"Really?" Mick's face lit up. "I'm not sure we

could sneak away, but I'm pretty sure the crew would like to watch MickQ in action."

"What if I chicken out? I don't need an audience."

"I get that, but maybe an audience wouldn't be a bad thing to give you a little push." Mick pursed her lips. "There needs to be trust in a crew. I don't want to start out hiding shit from them. Does that make sense?"

"You're right. Nothing good comes from keeping secrets. So we tell them our plans at breakfast."

"Yep."

"It's just like riding a bike, right?"

Mick chuckled. "Sumpin' like that."

❧ ❧ ❧ ❧ ❧

Quinn dropped the book on her face for the third time. *Damn.* She wanted to finish the chapter, but she didn't want to end up with a black eye.

She glanced over at the other bed. Mick's eyes were closed and her breathing slow and rhythmic.

Quinn set her book on the nightstand and turned off the bedside lamp. Rolling over, she clutched a pillow to her chest.

"Hey," Mick's voice cut through the darkness.

"I thought you were asleep," Quinn said.

"Kinda."

"How can you kinda be asleep?"

"I wanna be, but something keeps nibbling at my brain."

Quinn chuckled. "Ah, that explains it."

"What?"

"I think something already nibbled away a large portion."

"Very funny." Mick's voice had a playful tone, but there was a hint of something else underlying.

"Are you okay?"

"I've been running something over in my mind."

"What?"

"I'm afraid that our group hasn't been completely honest with us."

Moments earlier, Quinn was near sleep but no longer. This trip already had her nervous, so she certainly didn't need deception added into the mix. "Why do you say that?"

"There's obviously been a misrepresentation of their experience."

Quinn breathed a sigh of relief. "Yeah, that Tina is something else. Did you see her fingernails?"

"I'm not talking about Tina."

"You think there's a second one?"

"Nope. Tina knows what she's doing. I'm worried about Aspen."

"Aspen? Are you sure you don't have the two mixed up?"

Mick let out a loud sigh. "Sometimes, I don't think you pay attention at all."

Typical. No matter how hard Quinn analyzed something, Mick always figured things out first. "What did I miss?"

"Tina's a ringer."

Quinn hadn't expected that. "Seriously? How do you figure?"

"Mark my words, Tina knows what she's doing." Mick's voice held conviction.

"That still didn't answer my question. You think Tina with her sexy little dress and long painted fingernails will do fine?"

"Nope."

Ha. Finally, Mick got it wrong.

"She'll do better than fine," Mick said. "Aspen, on the other hand, could be a problem."

Quinn stifled a yawn. "Damn it, Mick. It's late, and I'm tired. Would you stop beating around the bush and get to the point? I don't see it. Aspen responded to whatever question came her way."

"Actually, that's not true. Aspen delivered her rehearsed lines perfectly, but everyone jumped in and bailed her out other times."

"Tina was worried about breaking a fingernail. Come on," Quinn said, tiring of the conversation.

"Ah, and that's what you missed. She got her rehearsed lines right, too. She'd practiced being daffy, but instinct took over a couple times."

"That sounds paranoid. You're saying Tina played dumb while Aspen pretended to know more than she does?"

"Sumpin' like that."

"I'm not buying it."

"You don't have to. Just mark my words."

"Fine. They've been marked. Can I go to sleep now?" Quinn was surprised by her own ire. No doubt, Mick picked up on more than anyone she knew, but for some reason, she wanted her to be wrong this time.

"Sure can. Good night," Mick said with a voice that betrayed her amusement.

Quinn pulled the blankets over her head. "Good night."

⁂

Mick and Quinn had been gone for at least half

an hour, but Aspen still hadn't spoken. Not that Peyton would notice since she and DaKota had been talking nonstop about their first encounter with MickQ.

Aspen had hoped giving herself time to calm down would help. Instead, the longer she sat, the more she seethed. *Unbelievable.* Peyton hadn't mentioned anything about kayaking, something she'd only done twice on a crystal-clear lake.

She'd expected Peyton to apologize as soon as Mick and Quinn left. So far, nothing. Glaring at Peyton hadn't worked, either, since she'd been doing it for the past five minutes with still no reaction.

Fuck it. "Hey, Peyton! Do you think it might have been a good idea to tell me what the plans were before dragging me out here?" Aspen raised her voice, not caring it would irritate Peyton.

"What, babe?" Peyton said.

"Seriously? That's all you have to say." Aspen stood and nearly knocked over her chair as she did. "I'm fucking going to bed."

"Whoa, what bug crawled up your ass?" Peyton asked, finally giving Aspen her undivided attention.

The room went quiet, and everyone stared, but she didn't care. Gina was right. She'd chased one woman after another, changing interests as often as she'd changed her underwear. Why did she think whitewater rafting would be a good idea?

Now halfway around the globe, she wanted to go home. Obviously, she had the means to catch a flight tomorrow. Gina would pat her head and at least wait a few days to say, *I told you so.* It wouldn't be the first time she'd put her tail between her legs and admitted defeat. The way her life was unfolding, it probably wouldn't be her last.

Pathetic. That was how she saw herself, and more than likely, how everyone staring at her saw her, too.

LeAnn was the first to move toward her. "What's going on, Aspen? Something's bothering you."

"You think?" Aspen snapped and then felt bad. LeAnn didn't deserve her hostility. "Sorry. I just need to get out of here."

"Here the dining hall? Or here Africa?" Peyton said and moved up beside LeAnn. They stood a few feet from Aspen and didn't move any closer.

"Both." Her volatility served to keep them at bay, which suited her fine at the moment. Aspen expected to see anger from Peyton; instead, Peyton's face fell.

Peyton lifted her hand and started to extend it, but she seemingly thought better of it and let it fall to her side. "Babe, I don't want you to go. Won't you tell me what's bothering you?"

Aspen brought her lips together when she felt her mouth dropping open. Peyton really didn't have a clue. It should have made her angry, but she just felt empty. She'd not started dating Peyton for her empathy, so why did she expect it now? "I'm just tired. Maybe things will look better in the morning."

LeAnn stepped forward and held out her hand. "Something has you upset. We'd like to know what it is."

Aspen looked past LeAnn and Peyton. DaKota and Tina apparently had tired of Aspen's outburst because they were slow dancing near the bar. Claire lounged in a chair sucking on her e-cig.

Aspen's shoulders relaxed, and her hand no longer trembled. Only having LeAnn and Peyton paying attention made it easier for her to speak. "Peyton, why didn't you tell me about kayaking?"

LeAnn's head snapped around. Her brow furrowed as she stared at Peyton. "You didn't tell her about kayaking?"

Peyton had the decency to look sheepish. "Well, no, not exactly."

"Not exactly, my ass. You never told me."

"I wanted you here with me." Peyton flashed her a smile. "Besides, I thought you knew."

Aspen's anger had started to wane until Peyton spoke the last line. "How the hell would I know?"

"DaKota and I have been talking about it for a couple months."

"I never listen to the shit you guys talk about."

"Nice, babe. So just because you don't listen, it's my fault now?"

LeAnn opened her mouth but shut it. Her gaze shifted between Aspen and Peyton.

"Did you want to say something, LeAnn?" Aspen asked.

"Maybe I should stay out of this." LeAnn took a step back.

"No, you were going to say something. Please, say it." Aspen hoped her calculation was right, and LeAnn would side with her in this argument.

"I don't want to cause any problems." LeAnn held up her hands and backed up another step.

"Go ahead," Peyton said. "We could use a referee."

"Oh, no, I'm no referee. Do you both really want to know what I think?"

Aspen and Peyton nodded.

"Peyton, you should have communicated directly with her about the trip, so she could have made an informed decision."

Yes. She knew LeAnn would come through for her. Aspen tried to hide her smug smile but suspected she wasn't doing a very good job at it.

LeAnn turned to Aspen. "As for you, you need to start taking responsibility for yourself. Maybe done a little research before you agreed to come. It's not up to Peyton to decide whether you can handle it or not. That's on you."

When Aspen glanced at Peyton, she realized they sported identical defensive stances with their arms crossed over their chests.

"You two can stand there glaring at me all you want, but it needed to be said." LeAnn's gaze shifted to Claire. "You two are on your own to figure it out. Claire promised me a massage and a dip in our pool." She wriggled her eyebrows.

Peyton turned away and headed for the bar. *Figures.* Having another drink seemed to be how Peyton planned on handling it. Aspen dropped her shoulders, her limbs suddenly feeling heavy. Without a word to anyone, she picked up her bag and started toward the exit. When her hand touched the door handle, she heard Peyton calling her name. Without stopping, she pushed through the door.

She'd gotten a little ways down the path when she heard footsteps pounding behind her. For a brief moment, she considered quickening her pace but thought better of it. They'd already caused enough of a scene without it culminating in a mad dash. She slowed her pace and braced for Peyton's arrival. Would she get the sheepish charming Peyton or the sullen pouting version?

"Babe, can we talk?" Peyton said.

Good. Charming Peyton. This version was much easier to deal with. "I'm upset, Peyton. I just want to get a good night's sleep, and maybe things will look better in the morning."

While they slowly walked along the path, Peyton offered her hand.

Should I? If Aspen refused Peyton's peace offering, the argument would go on for much longer. Reluctantly, she took Peyton's hand. They went the rest of the way without speaking, but Peyton whistled as they walked.

Yep. Peyton thought the fight was over. For tonight, that was fine with Aspen. She'd have a couple of days to figure out what to do, but she knew there was no way she'd be kayaking.

Chapter Eleven

Quinn secured her helmet, hoping Mick didn't notice her hands were trembling. Next, she tugged on the straps of her life vest until it was snug. Usually, she felt only exhilaration before a run, but the underlying edginess was something new. It felt as if worms crawled under her skin and up her arms. She shook her hands, wanting the feeling to subside.

The loud crashing of the whitewater made it nearly impossible to be heard without yelling, which was probably for the best. Her voice would likely betray her nervousness.

Too late. She couldn't back out now. The porters had brought their kayaks below Victoria Falls, and she refused to ask them to carry them back up. Besides, the others would be live-streaming their run, and she couldn't face them if she backed out.

Mick finished checking over her equipment and sauntered over to Quinn. *Always so chill.* Her demeanor usually put Quinn at ease, and today was no exception.

Mick flashed a smile. "Are you ready?"

"Tell me again why I decided running the Minus Rapids would be the best way to get back in the saddle?" Quinn tried to put on an easy smile, but she suspected Mick wouldn't buy it.

"There's no shame if you decide you can't do it."

Part of Quinn wanted to breathe a sigh of relief, rip off her gear, and hightail it back up to the top of the falls. She closed her eyes, searching for a vision of Stella's face. Today, her face came immediately into focus. Lately, it had become harder and harder to conjure up an image of Stella, which panicked her. When would Stella's face fade from her memory entirely?

Quinn shook her head. It was not a thought she should have on her mind right before a run. She focused on Stella's face, trying to come up with what she would say to Quinn. No doubt, Stella would tell her to get her ass in the kayak and enjoy the ride of a lifetime. She'd tell her not to be timid because class V rapids will eat you alive if you are.

"Are you okay?" Mick put her hand on Quinn's arm.

Quinn opened her eyes, her edginess gone. "I am."

Mick studied her before she nodded. "Okay. I believe it."

"Shall we turn on the cameras?" Quinn pulled on the strap of her helmet and adjusted the GoPro on top.

"In a few. I haven't finished with the water yet."

Quinn laughed. How had she forgotten Mick's ritual? "That's right, the Zen Master must become one with the rapids."

"Sumpin' like that."

As Mick climbed along the rocky shore, Quinn took a step back and sat on a large rock.

Feeling more at ease, finally, she could enjoy the beauty of Victoria Falls. Her gaze traveled up the side of the cliff. The dark basalt rock of the gorge towered around her. To an observer above, she must look like a tiny speck.

The falls were breathtaking, nearly double the height of Niagara Falls and at least twice as wide. Quinn took a deep breath and pulled the mist into her nose.

≈≈≈≈

Aspen sat clutching the tablet tighter, hoping no one would notice her trembling hands. *Something must be wrong.* She turned off the power and rebooted. DaKota held the second tablet but didn't appear agitated.

Two of the locals had brought them to a perfect spot where they could see the longest stretch of the raging river below. The guides had set up a mini camp and served drinks at an outlandish price, but Peyton tossed around cash, seeming not to care.

The tablet rebooted but still nothing. "Do you think something happened to their cameras?" Aspen glared at the screen.

"Would you relax?" Peyton said. "It'll take them a while to get to the bottom. Then they'll need to prepare before they put in."

"Or maybe Quinn chickened out," DaKota said.

"God, I hope she doesn't wimp out this soon," Peyton said.

"Quinn has plenty of courage. Most people wouldn't be out here, considering what she's been through." Aspen shot Peyton a disapproving look, but by Peyton's lack of reaction, it didn't seem to land. "You guys are something else."

"Thanks." DaKota gave her a cheesy grin.

"That wasn't a compliment."

"I know." DaKota wriggled her eyebrows before she turned to Peyton. "Your girlfriend is worried about her new girlfriend. You better watch out."

"Seriously, you two are impossible." Aspen stood and turned away from Peyton and DaKota.

"Hey, babe. Don't wander off too far. We want to catch both videos," Peyton called.

Without turning back, Aspen said over her shoulder, "I'm going to talk to LeAnn. I'll come back when they start."

Since last night, LeAnn had remained distant. At breakfast, Aspen would swear LeAnn intentionally took the chair farthest from her. She didn't know LeAnn all that well but saw her as someone she could be friends with, so she didn't want the awkwardness to drive a permanent wedge between them.

"Hey," Aspen said. She hoped it came out casual.

LeAnn smiled up at her. "Hey."

Good sign. Aspen knelt beside LeAnn's chair. "I think I'm nervous for Quinn and Mick." She held her hand out palm down, and it trembled.

"I've got a few butterflies myself." LeAnn pointed into the gorge. "That spot with all the rocks has me terrified for them."

Aspen rose a little on the balls of her feet and peered in the direction LeAnn pointed. Her stomach dropped. *Holy shit.* "Rocks? Looks like boulders to me. What happens if they slam into them?"

"I was wondering the same thing. Look at how the water is driving against the sides."

Aspen squinted and saw the spray flying as it pounded against the rocks. "That's insane. The current will push them straight into it."

"That's what I thought, but Claire said Mick and Quinn are badasses and will handle it."

"Badasses or not, that's still one hell of a possible collision." Aspen looked away. "Did you know there's such a thing as the Minus Rapids? Where do they come up with these names?"

"I hadn't until this morning. The names crack me up."

Aspen smiled. "Somebody has a sense of humor." *Clever.* Since the rapids above the falls started with rapid number one, it only stood to reason that anything below the falls would have to be minus numbers. "They weren't on the map I have."

"Mine either. I guess not many people tackle them."

"Why?" Aspen's shoulders tensed. They looked dangerous, but then again, all of it seemed dangerous from her standpoint.

LeAnn pointed. "Just look at it."

"I know. It looks terrifying, but all whitewater does."

"I'm no expert, but I've been with Claire on several trips, and that looks narrower than I'd care to run."

Aspen couldn't think about it any longer. Her sweat-soaked hands made it difficult for her to hold the tablet. "I wanted to apologize for last night."

LeAnn waved her off. "No worries. No harm."

"You're right, though. I can't rely on everyone else to *protect* me. I'm responsible for myself." Aspen smiled. Once she had gotten into bed last night, she'd not been able to sleep because LeAnn's words haunted her. "I needed to hear it."

LeAnn returned her smile. "I'm glad I was helpful. I thought maybe I overstepped my bounds."

"No, not at all. Friends should call each other out on their shit." Heat rose up Aspen's neck and settled in her cheeks. *Presumptuous much?* It wasn't like they were actual friends, more like acquaintances. "Well, I mean...you know...umm..." *Great.* It looked like she was going to dig a deeper hole.

"Relax." LeAnn put her hand on Aspen's shoulder. "I think we're becoming friends. That's why I felt so bad at breakfast. I thought I'd messed things up."

"Oh, god, no. I thought you were avoiding me because you decided I was pathetic." When did she lose her filter? "I mean, who wants to be friends with someone who follows along behind her girlfriend like a lapdog?"

"No, that's not what I thought at all."

"My best friend, Gina, calls me out on it all the time. I'm embarrassed to tell you, but I seem to gravitate toward whatever interests my latest girlfriend has. Hence this stupid trip."

"The first sign of change is recognition, so cut yourself some slack."

"Thanks." Aspen smiled. She'd already said more than she wanted, so a change of subject was in order. "Were you as shocked as I was this morning when they announced they were going to do this?"

"At first." LeAnn nodded. "Then when I gave it some thought, it made sense. From what I'm gathering, Quinn hasn't done any water this intense since the accident."

"I think it's brave of her," Aspen said.

"Me too. I can't imagine how she feels. She lost her girlfriend, and that nasty scar is a constant reminder of it. And now she's willingly getting back on the horse, so to speak."

"I can't even imagine how scary that would be. I'd puke."

"Do you think she'll go through with it?" LeAnn glanced at her watch.

Aspen held up the tablet. Still nothing. "I'm beginning to worry that she won't, but that doesn't make her a coward."

"Preaching to the choir." LeAnn glanced at the rest of the group who stood on the other end of the line of chairs. "But those guys will have a field day with it."

"Peyton won't. I'll make sure of it."

LeAnn chuckled. "You say that with such conviction."

"I hate meanness. Why would anyone ridicule someone for something like that?"

"People do it all the time."

"People suck."

"Some people. I'm rooting for her, and if she can't do it, I won't think any less of her." LeAnn leaned closer to Aspen and lowered her voice. "I've been praying for her all morning."

"Why the secrecy?"

LeAnn's gaze shifted to the others and then back to Aspen. "They make fun of me when I talk about prayers. Apparently, it's not the in thing to do."

"Fuck 'em. I think it's sweet. Quinn could use all the prayers she can get."

❧❧❧❧

Quinn adjusted her helmet one last time and ran

her finger the length of her scar. She could do this. She had to.

"You ready to go live?" Mick asked.

"Just about." Quinn averted her gaze and stared at the rocks at her feet. Her heart pounded out of her chest.

"Come here, you big lug," Mick said. "No sense the others seeing me get all sentimental."

Quinn let Mick draw her into a hug. It felt good. Reassuring. She squeezed Mick tight and let Mick's calm wash over her.

When they let go, Quinn said, "Thanks. I needed that. Just don't tell anyone, or I'll deny it."

"Secret's safe with me." Mick winked. "Let's drag the kayaks near the water before we turn on our cameras."

Quinn smiled to herself. *Sweet.* Mick must still be worried Quinn would back out, so she didn't want to embarrass her on camera. "They're probably wondering what took us so long. Maybe we should go live now. Might be good for them to see the whole ritual before we put in."

A big smile lit Mick's face.

She knows. It shouldn't have surprised Quinn since Mick never missed anything. Plus, she knew Quinn better than anyone. Turning on the cameras meant Quinn had made her decision. This was going to happen.

Quinn playfully pushed Mick's shoulder. "Put away that goofy grin, or I won't turn on the cameras. Nobody wants to see it."

Mick wriggled her eyebrows. "The ladies love it. It's my moneymaker."

Quinn laughed. "I'm going to turn mine on first."

Aspen jumped when sound came from the tablet. Her heart immediately raced. She held it up and was greeted by Mick's smiling face.

LeAnn peered over her shoulder. "Is that them?"

"Yep." Aspen rose from where she knelt. "I promised Peyton I'd go back when they went live."

LeAnn stood. "I'll come with."

"Hey, guys, Quinn's live. I've got Mick on my screen." They'd only walked a few steps when the others rushed over.

They huddled in a semicircle and stared at the screen. Aspen adjusted the volume to hear.

Mick's words came through. They'd missed the first few lines, but she seemed to be explaining the equipment they wore. "We are about ready to put on our skirts." Mick smiled and made a bad attempt at a curtsy.

"God, she's adorable," LeAnn whispered in Aspen's ear.

"I heard that," Claire said, pretending offense, but her smile gave her away.

"Seriously, folks," Mick continued. "It's key you put this on correctly and get it on your kayak right. Quinn will demonstrate in a bit. We're heading down to our kayaks now, and then I'll turn my camera on. Sorry, but then you'll have to look at Quinn's ugly mug."

"Asshole." Quinn's voice came through the speakers.

Mick laughed and made a sweeping circle with her arm. "Follow me."

"I think she's fucking going to do it," DaKota said.

"I never had any doubt," Aspen snapped back. "She's brave."

DaKota nudged Peyton. "I warned you, dude. Quinn's capturing your girlfriend's heart."

Peyton rolled her eyes. "Sure, whatever."

"Don't think your pretty face is going to save you," DaKota taunted. "Chicks dig scars."

"Would you two shut up?" Aspen handed LeAnn her tablet and snatched the one from DaKota's hands before she could object. "I want to watch what they're doing, not listen to your commentary." She turned to LeAnn. "What's a skirt?"

"It's kinda like a membrane." LeAnn pointed at the screen at what looked like suspenders holding up a skirt that bounced around Mick's waist. "That goes over the opening of the kayak to keep the water out. It'll be easier to understand when they get in."

"Thanks." Aspen stared at the black screen, blocking out the side conversations going on around her. Quinn would appear soon, and she wanted to see her in that first moment. Would she look scared?

"Okay, everyone." Mick's voice came from the tablet LeAnn held, but Aspen kept her focus on the one she clutched. "I'm going to turn on my camera, so Quinn can show you how to properly fasten your spray skirt. Of course, we'll do a hands-on demonstration, but we wanted to give you a preview."

A smiling Quinn filled her tablet. Quinn waved. *Good.* She looked serene.

"As you can see, I'm already wearing my spray skirt. I'll spare you the curtsy." Quinn moved toward her kayak.

Aspen's gaze shifted to the screen LeAnn held. She felt a moment of disorientation as the picture bounced slightly with each step Quinn took. Aspen's focus darted back and forth. First, seeing Quinn from Mick's viewpoint, and then the view from atop Quinn's helmet. Her attention settled on LeAnn's tablet that showed Quinn's point of view.

As they moved closer, the roar of the water grew louder.

Quinn arrived at the kayak and pulled it nearer to the river. Then she turned to Mick. "Do you want to tell them a little about the skirt?" Quinn's voice blasted out.

"Holy fuck, turn the volume down," DaKota said.

Aspen punched the volume button several times. Mick's voice came out of the speakers at an acceptable level. "I'm sure you all know about the skirt. But as all good guides know, it's always important not to make any assumptions and err on the side of too much information. We will go over this with you again when you take your run, so you don't need to take notes." Mick flashed a smile.

"I'm good with hearing her repeat the instructions a million times if I get to listen to that voice," LeAnn said.

"Aren't women supposed to be into Australian or British accents, not hillbilly ones?" DaKota asked.

"Hush, I'm trying to listen." LeAnn waved off DaKota.

"You started it," DaKota shot back.

Aspen adjusted the volume. "Enough, you two. I want to watch this."

"This is critical," Mick said. "The last thing you

want is for your kayak to take on water. We don't need any Titanic reenactments out here. Our skirts are made of a combination of neoprene and nylon, which is our favorite blend." Mick laughed. "I know. That sounded stupid even to me. What normal person has a favorite kayak skirt material? I'm going to make my way over to Quinn, so you can see her fasten it on."

Aspen's gaze shifted to her tablet. The camera bounced as Mick stepped over the jagged rocks to where Quinn sat in her kayak.

"Take it away," Mick said.

Quinn gazed up into the camera. Her eyes intense but no sign of fear. "Like Mick said, this is really important. You want to start in the back." Reaching behind her, Quinn pulled the material. "You want to make sure not to be sitting on any, or it could pull loose. Then get the skirt around the rim of the cockpit." Quinn's adept hands easily slid the skirt around the back, and then moved along the sides. "When you get to your hips, you want to slide your hands to the front, so your thumbs are close to the grab loop." She stopped at the front of the cockpit. "Then stretch it forward, snap it down, and make sure the handle is out." Quinn moved her fingers around the seal one last time. "It's as simple as that. I'm secure."

Quinn disappeared from the screen as Mick turned toward her own kayak.

Quinn's camera picked it up as Mick jumped into her kayak and fastened her skirt. "We are about ready to push off." Mick waved.

Aspen stared down at her screen. Mick turned her head toward Quinn, who must not have been expecting the camera to land on her. Her eyes appeared to be closed, and she moved her thumb along her scar.

"Are you ready, Quinn?" Mick yelled.

Quinn flinched and jerked her hand from her face. "Let's do it."

❧❧❧❧

No turning back. Quinn offered up a silent prayer before she pushed off with her paddle. They had a little way to go before they hit the first rapid but not far.

Mick went out ahead, and they both glided along the water. Quinn held out her hand. *Steady. Good.* Adrenaline coursed through her body, but the butterflies in her stomach were gone.

Quinn paddled harder to pull alongside Mick. She gently bumped Mick's kayak to alert her to her presence.

Mick flashed her a smile. "We never talked about how we were gonna do this. Who's going first?"

"I am," Quinn said without hesitation. Going down the river didn't scare her, but watching someone she loved do it caused her heart to clench.

Mick gave her a knowing smile. "Be my guest." She hesitated for a second and said, "You've got this, my friend. I'm right behind you."

Afraid her voice would betray her, Quinn nodded. She made eye contact with Mick one more time and spotted the camera on her helmet. *Shit.* She'd forgotten they weren't alone. With more confidence than she felt, she said, "Let's do this."

Quinn dipped her paddle into the water and shot out ahead of Mick. They were about fifty yards from where things would get wild.

9

The blood roared in Aspen's ears as Quinn and Mick approached the churning water. She was pretty sure the two women had forgotten they were on camera when they'd had their final exchange. Aspen felt like a voyeur, watching such a sweet moment.

She'd been happy to see the confidence in Quinn's eyes. The only time she'd looked haunted was when she'd run her finger over her scar. How terrible she had a constant reminder of the accident.

"Shit's about to get real." DaKota let out a whoop and chugged her beer. "I think the son of a bitch is going to do it."

"I told you." Peyton shot her a superior look. "I never doubted the Mighty Quinn."

"Don't be so smug. This is only her first hurdle," DaKota said.

Tina had been quiet most of the morning but leaned over Aspen's shoulder now. The excitement of the run finally seemed to awaken her.

Aspen glanced over her shoulder. "Do you wish you were out there?"

Tina smiled. "Am I that transparent?"

"The rapid breathing and dilated pupils might have given you away." Aspen winked. Tina puzzled her. She had trouble believing this drop-dead gorgeous woman dressed in the tight dress last night was the same woman salivating over a whitewater run. More proof that people are complex.

Weird. Why did she choose now to focus on Tina? Probably to block out Quinn's imminent arrival at the start of the rapids.

LeAnn leaned against Aspen. "She's going to do just fine."

❧❧❧❧

Quinn thought about turning back and taking one more look at Mick before she hit the rapids but decided against it. Two or three more strokes and she'd be in. *It was time.* She dug her paddle into the river.

The first wave hit her kayak and pushed her hard to the left. She paddled against the current. The movement caused the front of her kayak to lift in the air, and the first bank of water smacked her in the face. Adrenaline surged. *Yes!* She'd missed this. Digging in, she hit the next wave. Her kayak momentarily went airborne before it slammed back down.

Instincts took over when the next wave pounded her from the side, causing her kayak to list sideways. Quinn clamped her mouth shut right before her head went under water.

❧❧❧❧

"Holy fuck," DaKota said. "That was brutal."

Aspen's gaze snapped to the tablet LeAnn held. The only sound coming from the speakers was the *glug glug* of water. The screen was green and bubbly.

Oh, fuck. Quinn's head must be underwater. Aspen held her breath. Was that normal? *Oh, god, she could drown.* Who thought this was a good idea?

Aspen glanced at the tablet she held. White filled the screen. There was no sign of Quinn from Mick's camera, which meant she couldn't rescue her, either.

Shit. Aspen's hands were no longer steady as she held the tablet.

"She's up," Peyton called out. "Look at that shit. She just skimmed under that one like a surfer."

"Sweet," DaKota added.

Aspen's gaze locked on LeAnn's tablet. No longer underwater, Quinn paddled hard away from a rocky outcrop.

LeAnn nudged Aspen. "Look, you can barely see Quinn from Mick's camera."

A tiny figure bobbed ahead, but a blast of water slammed into Mick's camera, causing Quinn to disappear.

A loud whoop came out of one of the tablets.

Peyton laughed. "Did you hear that? One of them is having a blast."

"That shit does look fun," DaKota said.

Aspen didn't want to look away from the screen but quickly glanced at Peyton. "This is what you think we're going to do?"

"Hell yeah! Biggest adrenaline rush ever." Peyton grinned.

Aspen shook her head and shifted her focus back to Quinn and Mick.

❧❧❧❧

Quinn blinked the water out of her eyes, hoping to be able to see better before hitting the rapid. She'd studied several videos of the minus runs, and if her bearings were correct, she'd be coming to the giant rock that seemed to be the toughest to steer around.

Her heart raced, but she felt more alive than she had in years. With each slap of the whitewater, her smile broadened. *Yes!* She let out another whoop. *Shit. Too late.* Her open mouth took in a gulp of the Zambezi, but she spit it out before the next splash hit her in the face. *Lesson learned. No more battle cries.*

She fought the urge to look behind her for Mick. It would be fruitless, anyway. She'd likely not be able to locate her, plus she'd run the risk of losing her focus and hitting a rapid wrong. She'd already gone under twice and preferred not to do it again. Even though, in this kind of water, it was expected, it still sent an initial sense of panic through her. Being upside down, temporarily not knowing which way was up, could play on the mind very easily.

Her focus snapped back to the present. The rock she'd been looking for loomed in the distance. It was a rock, albeit much smaller, that had taken out Stella. *Stop. Focus.* Now wasn't time for distraction.

She'd watched others make this run. It required her to work against her natural instinct. Instead of moving away from the rock on this part of the river, she needed to run toward it. She took a deep breath and set her course.

❧❧❧❧

"Look." Claire pointed at the water below. "I think I see Quinn."

Aspen moved closer to the side of the cliff, and the others followed. "What the fuck is she doing?" Aspen said louder than she intended.

"Good question. She's gonna slam into that fucker," DaKota said.

"Brilliant," Tina said. "She's got a perfect line."

"Perfect? Are you nuts?" Peyton asked. "Looks suicidal to me."

Aspen shivered. Was it possible Quinn came out here for that purpose? *No!* She couldn't think that way.

"Damn, Peyton. Are you an amateur?" Tina said.

"I'm no fucking amateur."

Tina didn't respond.

Everyone stared at the bobbing figure below. The water pushed her closer to the rock as they watched. Aspen held her breath.

Quinn disappeared. Aspen grabbed one of the pairs of binoculars they'd forgotten in their excitement. She flinched when she brought them to her eyes. The rushing water filled the lens, giving the illusion she was on the water with Quinn.

The big rock blocked her view, the angry water the only thing she saw. *Come on, Quinn.* Aspen closed her eyes for a beat, but they immediately popped back open.

LeAnn let out a scream. "There she is." LeAnn held up the tablet. "Look how close to the rock she is."

At first glance, it looked like the screen had gone black, but then Aspen noticed the whitewater splashing. Quinn was inches from the boulder, but it didn't look like she would hit it.

Aspen jumped into the air and pumped her fist. "Yes! She did it."

The group erupted in cheers. They exchanged hugs and high fives as if they'd been in the kayak. The celebration was short-lived when Claire said, "Anyone see Mick?"

Shit. How had she forgotten about Mick? The tablet showed the rushing waves, which at least meant she hadn't gone under. The volume of water slapping against the camera made it nearly impossible to see much else, but Aspen thought she detected a shadow.

"Look." Aspen put her finger on the tablet. "Is that the rock?"

LeAnn leaned in and nodded. "I think so." LeAnn closed her eyes, and Aspen suspected she was praying.

"Come on, Mick," Peyton said.

"There." Tina pointed. "She's taking almost the

same line as Quinn, but she's slightly off."

"What are you talking about? It's identical," Peyton said.

Tina snorted. "Amateur."

Peyton turned to DaKota. "I've had about enough of your girlfriend's attitude."

"Shh," Aspen said. "You two can fight later. We need to watch this."

Aspen glanced back and forth between the tablets and the river below. Her frustration grew. She couldn't make out anything either way.

"She's not going to make it without hitting," Tina shouted.

Aspen clenched her fist, and her fingernails dug into her palm. *Shit.* The looming rock filled the screen.

A loud thud filled the air. Then surging water covered the screen, and the picture bounced erratically.

LeAnn gripped Aspen's arm and squeezed. "Tell me she didn't go under."

"I can't tell." Aspen glanced around at the others, hoping someone would have an answer.

Tina walked closer to the edge with a set of binoculars and peered over.

Aspen's gaze shifted to the screen they'd temporarily forgotten. Quinn bounced along, nearing the end of the roughest section. Aspen's heart clenched. Quinn was oblivious to Mick's plight. What would happen when she got to the end, and Mick didn't appear?

LeAnn held a pair of binoculars in one hand, and the other tightened its grip on Aspen's arm. "I see her."

"Where?" DaKota didn't have a set of binoculars, so she strained to see.

"She made it," Tina cried out.

Aspen exhaled loudly. Her shoulders rose toward her ears, so she consciously released them, and the tension left her body.

The group clapped and cheered.

༄ ༄ ༄ ༄

Quinn's shoulders and forearms burned. She dipped her paddle into the river one final time and surged out of the rapids. Her head dropped back, and she looked to the sky.

Holy fuck. Intense. An unexpected laugh escaped her throat. They did it.

The thought snapped her out of her celebration. *Mick.*

She slammed her paddle into the water and turned back toward where she'd just come. She scanned the area. No sign of Mick.

Shit. She didn't know how far behind Mick was since she'd never looked back. *Dumbass. Rookie mistake.* Her fear kept her from paying attention, and now Mick wasn't coming out of the run.

Quinn's heart raced. Her face felt warm despite the cool water. She paddled hard, fighting the current. She'd almost reached the edge of the raging whitewater when she spotted the tiny kayak bobbing toward her.

"Thank God," she said out loud.

Mick bounced along. When she got nearer, Quinn spotted her signature smile. Dipping her paddle into the froth, Mick blasted forward.

"You did it," Mick yelled above the raging current.

"What the hell took you so long?" Quinn said with a smile. "Did you stop and catch a few fish along the way?"

"Sumpin' like that."

"Jesus, are you bleeding?"

Mick touched her face and ran her fingers through the blood near her right ear. "I had a bit of a disagreement with that big-ass rock."

"Looks like you lost," Quinn joked, hoping to hide her concern. She paddled closer.

"Ha. That rock won't be messing with me again anytime soon."

"Bravado from a woman with blood dripping down her face doesn't quite cut it." Quinn's kayak bumped against Mick's. Quinn reached out and pushed the hair away from Mick's wound. *Superficial, thank god.* She breathed a sigh of relief.

Chapter Twelve

A spen paced the patio, trying to decide if she should take a dip in the miniature pool. Part of her craved the calming water, but the fear of what lurked in the dark held her back. After all, they were still in the brush of Africa. Hard telling what creatures of the night roamed the area.

She'd tried to talk Peyton into a midnight swim, but she'd crashed shortly after they'd returned to their unit. Once Peyton was out, it would take a circus tent full of elephants to wake her.

With a sigh, she flopped onto the lounge chair near the patio railing. She twisted the cap off her iced tea and took a long swallow. Squinting, she tried to see out into the night. The full moon gave her some light but not enough to see far.

Tomorrow would be her last opportunity to change her mind. Would she? *Ugh!* She jammed her hand into her hair and ran her fingers the length of it. *Ouch.* An occasional tangle stopped her progress until she unsnarled it.

Gina, the prophet, saw this coming from a long way off. How dangerous would it be in the raft? Peyton told her if she stayed in the middle, she'd be able to hide her inexperience. With Quinn and Mick's skills, they'd keep her safe. Wouldn't they?

She'd worried all afternoon that one of them would discover the truth. During their tour around the area, she'd stayed as far from Quinn and Mick as possible. Would they kick her out? Maybe that wouldn't be all bad, then nobody could accuse her of being a coward for backing out. She'd put up a bit of a protest and then graciously bow out. *Win-win.*

Her true test would be after lunch tomorrow. They'd decide on a schedule, get their gear together, and go over the ground rules. That was when she'd most likely be exposed.

What was that? A noise put her on high alert, making her forget her worries. She strained to see into the darkness. The sound came again. *Whistling?*

Birds didn't come out at night, did they? She didn't think so, but then again, what did she know? Maybe birds were different here.

There it was again. It seemed closer. It sure sounded like someone whistling, but who'd be out wandering around at midnight? She'd heard no mention of security personnel, but it stood to reason there might be. If one of their guests went missing, it would be bad for business.

She took a deep breath to calm herself. When she caught a glimpse of something large moving off to her right, goose bumps rose on her arms. Maybe she could slip inside before whoever it was noticed her. She slowly stood, careful not to rise to a full standing position.

Keeping her eyes on the looming figure, she took a step backward. Immediately, she realized her mistake when her foot failed to come down on a solid surface. *Shit.* She grabbed at a chair as she fell backward.

The chair scraped across the patio floor but wasn't heavy enough to stop her fall. She let go before she pulled it into the pool with her. An involuntary scream escaped her lips right before she plunged into the water.

"Shit," she cursed when her head came to the surface. So much for not getting in the pool.

She stiffened at the sound of rapidly approaching footsteps. The waves she'd created when she fell splashed against the side of the pool.

"Is everything okay?" a female voice called out.

Aspen held her breath. Should she answer? In the pool, it was harder to see into the night, but it also meant whoever was out there would have a harder time seeing her. A security guard would probably come investigate if she didn't answer. It seemed unusual they'd have female security guards patrolling late at night.

Wow. That was sexist.

A shadow approached the edge of the patio. "Aspen?"

"Who is it?" Aspen responded.

"It's Quinn."

Aspen laughed. "Thank god. Come help me out of here."

ᘓᘓᘓᘓ

The ripples danced across the surface as Quinn moved her feet back and forth in the water. When the patio door opened, it startled her. Aspen hadn't been gone long. *Did she have time to change?*

Aspen's short robe fell just below mid-thigh. Heat rose up Quinn's cheeks. Surely, she didn't put the robe on without anything underneath. Quinn averted her gaze and began to stand.

"Don't get up on my account," Aspen said.

Quinn lowered herself and let her feet dangle back into the pool. Aspen's bright red toenails perched on the ledge beside Quinn. *Cute toes.* "Do you really think you should get that close to the water?"

"Very funny." Aspen put her hand on Quinn's shoulder and dropped to the ground next to her. Their shoulders nearly touched.

Quinn stiffened. Maybe she should scoot down. She glanced at Aspen out of the corner of her eye. Aspen's hair, still wet, appeared several shades darker. "Do you mind telling me why you decided to jump into the pool with all your clothes on?"

Aspen nudged Quinn with an elbow. "I didn't do it on purpose. I heard you whistling, and it freaked me out. I lost my balance when I tried to sneak away, and I fell in."

Quinn chuckled. She'd been baiting Aspen, but her reactions were so damned cute when Quinn questioned her. "I'm surprised you didn't wake someone with the racket you made."

Aspen leaned away from Quinn and put her hand on her hip. "Really? That's the first thing that comes to mind after my traumatic experience?"

Quinn held her hands in the air and sneaked a glance at Aspen. "Okay. My bad. Nobody expects me to have social graces when Mick's around, so I've gotten rusty." Quinn cleared her throat. "May I ask if you're okay?"

"Much better. I think the only thing hurt is my pride."

Quinn heard the smile in Aspen's voice but didn't see it. Sitting so close, Quinn felt uncomfortable facing Aspen, so she kept her gaze on the rippling water.

"That's good. Well, not the part about your pride. I mean, it's good that you're not hurt or anything." Could she come off any more awkward?

"I should ask you why you were creeping around in the middle of the night."

"Now who lacks social graces? I couldn't sleep." Quinn smiled. "And I wasn't creeping around. I happened to be walking on the path."

"What if I was skinny dipping?"

The thought of Aspen naked in the pool flashed across Quinn's mind. *Stop!* "I suppose if you screamed while you were doing it, I would have gotten an eyeful." Quinn's back stiffened. It'd been a while since she'd joked with anyone other than Mick. It felt strange, but at the same time, it felt kinda nice.

"I probably would have screamed when I saw someone lurking in the shadows." Aspen's tone was playful.

"Let me get this straight. I went from creeping to lurking? Can you explain the difference?"

"Creeping is, well, creepy. And lurking is more lurky."

Quinn laughed. "I'm certainly glad you cleared that up."

"What if Mick wakes up? Won't she be worried?"

That must be her cue. Quinn put her hand on the ground and started to push herself up.

"Where are you going?" Aspen asked.

"I thought...well...I just thought you wanted me to go." Another thing she'd gotten rusty at, taking social cues.

"I didn't say that."

"You kinda did." Quinn felt Aspen's gaze on her, so she turned her head slightly and made eye contact.

Big mistake. Aspen's eyes were the prettiest blue Quinn had ever seen. *Get a grip.* "When you asked about Mick worrying, I thought that was my cue. It's okay, I understand it's late."

"For once, I wasn't hinting around."

Quinn tilted her head and gazed at Aspen. "For once?"

Aspen sighed. "Some might say I tend not to be direct, so it wouldn't be outside the realm of possibility for me to drop hints that I wanted you to go. But I wasn't this time."

"Mick says I'm dense when it comes to picking up subtle cues. That's her department. Not much gets by her."

Aspen fidgeted and kicked her feet harder, so the water splashed.

"I'm sorry," Quinn said. "Did I say something wrong?"

"And you say you don't pick up on things. I call bullshit."

"Honest, I usually don't." Quinn's feet moved faster through the water to match Aspen's rhythm.

"Aren't we a pair?" Aspen bumped her shoulder against Quinn. "Seems like I've gotten more forthright, and you've become more insightful."

"Is that good or bad?" Quinn asked. Aspen put her at ease, which didn't come easily. At least nowadays it didn't.

"Good. Definitely good." Aspen nodded. "I'm gonna make a pledge. Right here and now. For the rest of this trip, I'm going to speak my mind."

"All right." Quinn liked the determination in Aspen's tone. It may be silly, but it made her happy she could be a small part of it.

"And you?" Aspen pointed at Quinn. "You're going to be more observant. Pay attention to things outside what's being said."

"Sheesh, I thought this was a rafting trip, not a self-improvement course."

"My first opportunity to practice being forthright." Aspen shifted beside her. "I'm not buying it. Word is that you're here to conquer some demons."

"What have you heard?" Quinn responded before thinking it through. Now it would be harder to avoid the topic.

"That you've had a rough few years. You've been hiding out, and this is your first step back into the world you once knew." Aspen's voice came out higher than before, and she fiddled with the bottom of her robe.

"That wasn't comfortable for you to say, was it?" *What the hell?* She went from hiding out in the Ozarks to having an honest conversation with an attractive woman at midnight in the middle of Africa. Life could be strange.

"Damn, we're naturals at this." Aspen chuckled. "Me being all forthright and you being observant. Must be something about the mist from the falls."

"Ah, the magic mist of Victoria Falls casts a spell over the unsuspecting tourists. I sense a movie in there somewhere."

"Drama or romantic comedy?" Aspen asked.

Romantic comedy? Quinn's pulse quickened. She wasn't going to touch that one. "Or maybe horror. Don't mist and horror go together?"

"Now you're stereotyping. I think it can be any kinda movie we want it to be."

Quinn nodded. "You're right. It's your movie

idea, so it can be whatever you want."

Aspen slapped her foot into the water, causing water to spray the front of their shirts. "Uh, sorry. I got excited. I didn't mean to get you all wet."

Quinn tried not to smirk. If this were Mick, she'd not let the opportunity for a good sexual joke pass.

"Oh, my god," Aspen said. "I didn't mean it that way."

"What way?" Quinn feigned innocence but feared the twinkle in her eyes would give her away.

"Nice try." Aspen slapped Quinn's leg. "I've seen the YouTube videos of you and Mick. If I didn't know better, I would think you were both twelve-year-old boys with the juvenile things that come out of your mouths."

"Busted." Quinn held up her hands in surrender. "So what was your brilliant idea?"

"Buddy movie."

"Huh?"

"You said I could pick the movie genre. The mist and this trip will be my buddy movie."

"I thought you and Peyton were a couple."

"We are. The mist movie isn't about Peyton." Aspen turned, and their gazes met. "I've decided you're going to be my buddy, Quinn Coolidge."

Warmth filled Quinn's chest. *Odd.* It had been years since she'd wanted to let anyone new into her life. In her time in the Ozarks, she'd made no friends. Quinn smirked. "You decided that all on your own? Do I get a say in it?"

"Nope." Aspen shook her head. "You said it was my movie, so I choose."

"You seem pretty good at this forthright stuff. I

think I'm being played. You're like one of those pool hustlers or grifters."

Aspen laughed. "Literally. I threw myself in the pool just to hustle you."

"Damn, and I fell for it. I guess I've got a ways to go on my observational skills."

"Character arc. Makes for a better movie when one of the characters is hopelessly clueless."

"Let's see. So far, you've called me creepy, lurky, hopeless, and clueless." Quinn ticked the list off on her fingers. "Not a good start to a buddy flick."

"But you're sweet. So we have something to build on."

Quinn hoped her face wasn't as red as it felt. *Think.* She needed to get the focus off herself. "Tell me more about this problem with being forthright. You seem to be doing a bang-up job of it right now."

"Do you think we can find a different word for forthright? It makes us sound like eighteenth century gentlemen or something."

"I didn't know it was an eighteenth century thing."

"Hell, I don't know if it is or not. I just made it up."

"Very forthright to admit that." Quinn couldn't resist using the word again.

"Stop!" Aspen laughed. "Come on, give me some other options."

Quinn looked to the sky in thought. "Um, honest, open, direct, frank."

"No, not frank. That sounds like gangster talk."

"Since when do gangsters say frank?"

"Frank. Frank Sinatra."

Quinn narrowed her eyes, feigning disapproval.

"Frank Sinatra wasn't a gangster just because he was Italian."

"No, seriously. I read once that a lot of mafia guys hung around with him in Vegas."

"Fine," Quinn said, shaking her head. "We'll take frank off the list."

"What about straightforward?"

"Do you really want straight in the word? How about candid?"

Aspen shook her head. "Makes me think of *Candid Camera*."

"Frank Sinatra and now *Candid Camera*. Are you sure you weren't born in the fifties?"

"What can I say?" Aspen shrugged. "My parents were fanatic about all things fifties, so I grew up with it all around me."

"Old soul. Plainspoken?"

"Now who's being insulting? Old and plain?" Aspen teased. "I prefer outspoken."

"Blunt." Quinn held back a grin.

"No nonsense. Point-blank."

"Pointblank sounds like you might shoot me. Tactless."

"You keep coming up with the negative ones." Aspen pursed her lips and scowled. "I think I like direct."

"Ugh, seriously?" Quinn planted her palm against her forehead. "That was one of the first choices. We could have avoided this whole ugly fiasco."

"But where's the fun in that?"

Quinn laughed and put her arms behind her and leaned back. It had been a long time since she'd allowed herself to let go. It felt good, almost normal, sitting and talking to a *buddy*. "It's your movie and your word. So now we have a buddy film with a direct heroine and a clueless anti-hero in the mist of Victoria Falls."

"Sidekick."

"Mick can be the sidekick."

"No! You're the sidekick, not an anti-hero."

"Do I look like a sidekick?" Quinn sat up and spread her arms. "Sidekicks are tiny. I'm twice as big as you."

"You are not twice as big."

"Just about."

"You'd have to be...." Aspen counted on her fingers. "Ten-foot-six and around two hundred and forty pounds."

"You win on that. But the sidekicks are always the smaller of the two."

Aspen shook her head. "It's my movie. We're gonna shake things up. You're the sidekick."

Quinn pretended to think about it and then shrugged. "Okay. But there's nothing about tonight that gives me the impression you're anything but fran... I mean direct."

"There's something about my large sidekick that gives me courage." Aspen nudged Quinn and smiled. "Seriously, I'm thirty-three years old and have never really spoken up for myself. Or done anything I've really wanted to do."

"Including this trip?"

Aspen's head snapped around. "How did you know?"

"I didn't." Quinn's chest tightened. They'd been having such a nice time. She didn't want Aspen to be angry with her. "I don't get observation points. Mick pointed it out to me yesterday."

"How did she figure it out?"

"She thinks Tina is a ringer, and she's playing dumb to keep us from figuring you out."

Aspen's shoulders slumped. She gently kicked her feet in the water. The ripples reflecting in the moonlight. "Are you going to send me home?"

"Is that what you want?" It surprised Quinn when sadness washed over her.

"Yesterday, I would have told you yes."

"And today?"

"I don't know." Aspen turned her gaze to Quinn.

"What's changed?"

"You."

Oh. "You're killing me with your directness." Quinn smiled, hoping to lessen the tension. When Aspen didn't respond, Quinn struggled with how to continue. "What did I do?"

"Honestly?"

"Honesty is what you're known for in this film. Hit me with it."

"I watched you battle your demons this morning." Aspen put her hand on top of Quinn's.

A lump caught in Quinn's throat. "Was it that obvious?"

"The girls filled me in on your story, but even if I didn't know, I would have seen it in your eyes." Aspen smiled. "But then, after you finished your run, and Mick rowed up to you, your face filled the screen. All I could stare at were your eyes. I saw life. Hope. Something that was missing when you set out."

Quinn made a figure eight with her foot, watching the water circle around her leg. She agreed with Aspen. She'd felt so many emotions this morning. *Exhilaration. Freedom. Joy. Guilt.* "Is it wrong that I felt good today?" *Where the hell did that come from?*

"Not at all." Aspen squeezed her hand. "You can't change what happened. But you can honor Stella by living."

Quinn tensed, unsure how she felt hearing Stella's name spoken by Aspen.

"I'm sorry," Aspen said. "Did I overstep my bounds?"

Did she? No. "It's okay, Frank."

"Good." Aspen smiled. "I didn't want to scare away my sidekick this early in the movie."

"Ah, foreshadowing?" Quinn smirked. "Planning on scaring your sidekick away later?"

"One never knows. I'm pretty good at scaring people away."

"I can't believe that."

Aspen pursed her lips. "You're right. It's just girlfriends I have that talent with. My friend Gina has stuck around for years." Aspen turned and pretended to size Quinn up. "But I think friends and sidekicks are similar, so you might be safe."

"I'm glad." What was up with her? She didn't have conversations like this with people, especially ones she'd just met. Aspen felt different. Quinn sensed her lostness. If lostness was a word. *Birds of a feather? Kindred spirits?* "You still haven't given me the full answer why you might want to stay."

Aspen put her hand against her chest. "I saw your battle, and it touched me. Even after that, I wasn't sure what I wanted to do. And then..." Aspen waved her hand between the two of them. "And then this happened."

Quinn's stomach fluttered. She wasn't sure if the moment called for playful or serious. She settled on playful. "You threw yourself into the pool, so you could find a sidekick?"

"Exactly." Aspen rewarded her with a smile. "But the question is, will my guides let me stay?"

Crap. Quinn hadn't thought of that. "You don't have any experience?"

"Not a lick."

Stall. "Why did you come then?"

"Like I told you. I never speak up for anything I want. Gina says I follow one girlfriend after another. Changing my interests as often as I change my socks."

"What do you want now?"

"I want to stay," Aspen said without hesitation. "I want to go down the Zambezi River with you."

It wasn't lost on Quinn that Aspen said her, not Peyton or the rest of her friends. "Okay. I'd like that, too. But you know I'm going to have to talk to Mick about it."

"I'd expect nothing less. I'd never ask you to keep something from Mick."

"I never would. But thanks for saying that." The tension still in the air made Quinn uncomfortable. She wanted their easy banter back. "So what kind of costume does the sidekick get to wear?"

"Well, I was thinking something frilly and lacy."

Quinn groaned.

Nearly an hour later, Quinn finally said good night and headed back to her quarters.

Chapter Thirteen

"Would you stop whining?" Quinn said, walking onto the patio.

Mick sat sprawled on the lounge chair, sipping her sweet tea. She'd rolled her tank top up, exposing her stomach, and hiked up her shorts. Quinn would never admit it, but Mick still had an impressive body. Hard muscles and a tan.

Mick glared. "I still can't believe you agreed to do the touristy thing."

Quinn sat on the lounge chair across from Mick and put her feet up. "We need to get to know our guidees."

"Do we haveta?" Mick drawled.

"It won't kill you."

"It might."

"You're impossible." Quinn made like she was going to stand, waiting for Mick to stop her.

"Fine. I'll go, but I refuse to enjoy myself."

"That's the spirit." Quinn chuckled. "I've heard the Devil's Pool is kinda fun."

Mick rolled her eyes.

The Devil's Pool would definitely be considered a tourist thing, but how many people could say they sat on the edge of a waterfall? Literally, they would be on the lip as water surged around them and plunged at least twenty stories into the Zambezi River. It sounded scarier than it was, but still Quinn found she looked forward to seeing the falls so up close. It certainly wasn't something they could do at Niagara.

"Once you're done pouting, I need to talk to you about something."

Mick studied Quinn. "Words nobody ever wants to hear. Might as well ruin my day some more."

The direct path made the most sense. Quinn took a deep breath. "You were right."

"Hot damn. It's about time you admit it."

Quinn rolled her eyes. "You don't even know what you were right about."

"Doesn't matter. Just hearing you say it is music to my ears." Mick flashed a cheesy smile. "Care telling me what I'm right about?"

"Tina's a ringer, and Aspen's never whitewater rafted before."

"Oh, and how'd you find this out?"

"I couldn't sleep last night."

"So, you creeped her on social media?"

"I went for a walk. She fell in the pool." Quinn waved her hand. "But that's not important."

"Whoa." Mick sat up in her chair. "You can't just throw that out there and move on. Spill."

Quinn quickly ran through the story, leaving quite a bit out. Mick didn't need to know everything. "So that's how we got to talking."

"And she just blurted this out?" Mick eyed her suspiciously.

"It was in the context of the conversation. But once again, not relevant to the situation at hand."

"And what situation is that?" Mick shrugged. "She either heads home or stays at the resort."

"She wants to go along." Quinn shifted in her seat, waiting for Mick's reaction. It would either be an adamant no, or worse yet, she'd begin to question Quinn's motives. Not that it would do any good since she didn't understand her own reasons.

"She does, does she?" Mick's gaze locked on Quinn's. "Mind telling me why you're willing to let someone with no experience go?"

"I like her."

Mick raised her eyebrows.

"Not like that," Quinn said. "She's a sweet person."

Mick sized Quinn up but didn't speak. She pursed her lips and nodded.

"Stop. You're making it into something it's not."

"Seems like you're the one doing all the talking." Mick smiled.

Damn it. Mick had a way of turning silence into a weapon. Quinn needed to stop talking and not play into Mick's hands. After another several seconds of awkward silence, Quinn squirmed in her chair. "Well, what do you think?"

"About what?"

"Seriously?" Quinn narrowed her eyes, and her nostrils flared.

"Seems to me there's a few topics on the table that we might want to discuss." Mick smirked. "So where do you want to start?"

"As far as I'm concerned, there's only one thing on the table."

"And that would be?"

What the hell? Mick was going to make her say it. "Whether we let Aspen go down the river with us."

Mick rubbed her chin. "What do you want to do?"

"I want to take her with us. Of course, she can't

do the kayaking, but she should be able to do the rafting. We'll just need to make a few adjustments." Quinn crossed her arms over her chest.

"Okay." Mick nodded.

"Okay? That's it?"

"Yep."

"You mean you put me through all that just to say yes?"

"Sumpin' like that." Mick flashed a smile before lying back and closing her eyes. "I'm taking a nap. Wake me up when it's time to go on our expedition."

Quinn stared, but Mick kept her eyes closed. As infuriating as Mick could be, she'd missed her. Mick never agreed to anything so readily. Something was up, but Quinn knew she'd get nothing more out of her. At least, not now.

❧❧❧❧

"Did you say something?" Aspen looked up from her journal. She moved her arm, and the page stuck to it. The day, already warm, threatened to be a hot one. It would be cooler inside, but the patio called to her.

"I asked if you were ever going to get your nose out of that book and come to breakfast with me," Peyton said.

Aspen sighed. She'd wanted to get her thoughts on paper from last night, but Peyton would make that impossible. "Let me finish this paragraph, and I'll be ready."

"I can't believe you were up before me. What time did you crawl into bed last night?" Peyton plopped into the adjacent chair.

So much for finishing her paragraph. "It must

have been around two."

"Couldn't sleep?"

Shit. She'd vowed to tell Peyton the truth if the subject came up. She wouldn't be lying if she just answered the question, but she wasn't about to get into half-truths. "I had an unexpected visitor."

Peyton stared. "Visitor?"

Be casual. No reason to get self-conscious, but somehow, she suspected Peyton would have some kind of beef. "Quinn was out walking, so I invited her in. Well, after I fell in the pool, I did."

"You fell in the pool?"

Aspen filled in the bare necessities but left big chunks of the encounter out. She'd been trying to get last night down in her journal before her memory faded. "Just being clumsy."

"I see. What did you talk about?" Peyton said it nonchalantly, but there was an underlying tension in her demeanor.

"I told her the truth about my whitewater rafting experience or lack thereof."

"Why the hell would you do that?" Peyton's face reddened, and she stood from the table. "You don't want to go at all, do you?" Aspen opened her mouth to speak, but Peyton cut her off. "When are you planning on flying back?"

"Slow down." Aspen held out her hand. "I told her I wanted to go on the trip."

Peyton ran her hand through her hair. "And her response?"

"She's going to ask Mick."

"Must have been some talk." Peyton shook her head and muttered.

Aspen needed to turn around the conversation

before Peyton's jealousy reared up. "It was nice getting to know her better." That should pass for a benign answer.

"I find it interesting it made you want to stay and her entertain the possibility of letting you." Peyton's gaze searched Aspen's face. "Just steer clear of her. She's carrying some heavy baggage."

Aren't we all? Something she couldn't say. Aspen took a deep breath. *Compliance.* "Thanks, I'll remember that. We still need to wait and see if Mick gives me a thumbs up."

"Do you want her to?"

"Of course. I came on the trip with *you*, didn't I?" Aspen flashed a flirtatious smile. "So why would I want to go home now?" Aspen hoped her answer would appease Peyton.

The tension in Peyton's jaw relaxed, and she grinned. "That's my girl." She patted Aspen's shoulder. "Stick with me, and you'll be a pro in no time." She pointed at Aspen's journal. "Finish that up, so we can get to breakfast. I'm gonna run inside and freshen up."

❧❧❧❧

Peyton took Aspen's hand as they entered the dining area. Before their trip, Aspen had noticed a pattern, but during this trip, it had become more obvious. Or maybe she'd just become more aware of it. In private, Peyton was aloof and rarely affectionate. Public displays seemed to be more her thing. *Had it always been that way?* She didn't have time to contemplate it further because LeAnn and DaKota waved at them from across the room.

"Hey," Peyton called out. "Are you guys ready for some adventure?"

"Hells yes," DaKota answered.

Great. DaKota was in full-blown hyper mode. That never boded well for Aspen, or maybe it would be okay since she and Peyton would be busy acting like teenagers.

"One more fricking day," Peyton called out. Several others turned and looked in their direction, but Peyton seemed oblivious.

When they arrived at the table, Aspen slipped her hand out of Peyton's grip and slid into the chair next to LeAnn. Peyton, busy carrying on with DaKota, didn't notice.

"Hey," LeAnn said with a smile. "You ready for today?"

Aspen glanced around the room to make sure no one else was listening. She leaned in toward LeAnn. "I'm a little nervous."

"Why? Today should be a piece of cake. The Devil's Pool sounds scarier than it is."

"I'm not worried about that." Aspen leaned closer. "Last night..." she glanced around the table again before continuing, "I confessed to Quinn."

"Confessed? What?"

"That I'd never been on whitewater before."

"Holy shit, really?" LeAnn said loudly. Her face fell when the others looked in their direction. "You're really afraid of Devil's Pool?"

Good save. "I know I'm just being silly." Aspen played along, thankful for LeAnn's quick thinking. She wasn't ready for DaKota's harassment just yet. It would come soon enough, especially if Mick vetoed her.

DaKota rolled her eyes and returned to her conversation with the others.

"Sorry," LeAnn whispered.

"Great save."

"So tell me everything. Why? How? When?"

Aspen filled LeAnn in on the previous night, filling in a few more details than she'd given Peyton. "She's just so sweet. It didn't seem right to lie to her."

LeAnn grinned. "Sounds like I'm not the only one with a crush on MickQ."

"Nah." Aspen waved her hand. "It's not like that. We're buddies."

"What did your *buddy* say about letting you go tomorrow?"

DaKota let out a loud whoop followed by laughter. Aspen whipped her head around, fearful they'd overheard. Tina had a plate on her head and danced seductively around DaKota.

LeAnn shook her head. "Sometimes, I don't ask."

"Right. Anyway, Quinn said yes, but she had to ask Mick." Aspen scanned the room again, hoping Quinn and Mick would arrive soon.

"You can stop looking," LeAnn said. "Mick sent a text earlier saying they'd meet us for the expedition at noon."

"Great." Aspen groaned and flopped back against her chair. *Three hours.* "It's gonna be a long morning."

"It'll go fast." LeAnn patted her arm. "This afternoon should be fun. Did you hear DaKota bought up the whole lunch expedition, so it'll only be us?"

How sweet. LeAnn wanted to distract her from her worries. "I have to admit I haven't paid attention to talk of our excursion. I've been so freaked out about tomorrow, it's all I've thought about."

"Understandable."

Peyton wandered over and put her hand on Aspen's shoulder. "I'm hitting the buffet. Want to come with?"

No. "Sure." Aspen smiled at LeAnn. "I'll be back. Then you can fill me in."

※ ※ ※ ※

A tiny bug flew around Aspen's face, and every time she shooed it away, it came back. *Damn it.* Maybe she should go back inside, but she hadn't been able to sit still. Quinn and Mick should be here any time, and the van to take them to their tour would come soon after.

Peyton remained in the lodge. Aspen had made the excuse of wanting to get acclimated to the heat, which was only part of the story. She really wanted to find out Mick's decision.

The pair rounded the corner. Despite her size, Quinn's movements were usually fluid, so it surprised Aspen to see her lumbering. Realization dawned, and Aspen smiled to herself. For Mick to keep up, Quinn had to unnaturally shorten her stride, giving her an awkward gait. Still, Mick practically jogged to stay even with Quinn.

Butterflies danced in Aspen's stomach. Casually, she waved and smiled. She wanted to rush down the path to meet them but refrained. She'd find out the verdict soon enough.

A broad smile lit up Quinn's face, and she waved back. Quinn's pace quickened. Mick would have had to run to match Quinn's stride; instead, she lagged several steps behind.

Hopefully, Quinn's smile signified something positive, but on the other hand, she could be trying to soften the blow. Aspen's gaze met Quinn's. The warmth of her light brown eyes caused some of Aspen's nervousness to dissipate. Then Quinn winked.

That had to be positive. People didn't wink when they delivered bad news, did they? Aspen's gaze shifted to Mick, who'd just arrived beside Quinn.

"Ready for our excursion?" Mick asked.

Aspen stifled a giggle at Mick's pronunciation of excursion. LeAnn would have found it adorable. *Note to self.* She'd have to try to get Mick to say it again, just for LeAnn. "I am. And you?"

"I'm raring to go." Mick smiled. "Where's the others?"

"Still inside." Aspen motioned at the building behind them. "I told them I'd get them when the van arrives."

"I suppose you're looking forward to tomorrow's trip even more," Mick said.

What? Did Mick just tell her she could go? Aspen shifted her gaze to Quinn, who nodded and gave her a crooked grin. *Yes!* Without thinking, she leapt into Mick's arms and gave her a hug. "Thank you. Thank you so much."

Mick laughed. "It's not me you should be thanking." She motioned with her thumb toward Quinn. "She talked me into it."

Aspen let go of Mick and grabbed Quinn. At first, Quinn's grip on her was tentative, but the harder Aspen squeezed, the more Quinn's embrace tightened.

When Aspen stepped away, she felt warmth spread throughout her body. The hug put her at peace, or more likely, the knowledge that she'd get to go tomorrow did. She didn't have any more time to consider it before Mick spoke.

"Just promise you won't be a scalawag again."

Aspen smiled. "I would if I knew what I'm promising."

Quinn shook her head. "It's another one of her Southern euphemisms. Means rascal."

"It's not Southern." Mick glowered.

"Whatever." Quinn waved her hand. "Just don't be one, Aspen, and all will be good."

"I promise not to be a scalawag or a rascal." Aspen held up her hand as if taking an oath.

"Now you're just being redundant," Mick said.

"Never mind her," Quinn said. "She's a grump."

Chapter Fourteen

Quinn stood but waited for the others to exit. The short boat trip to Livingstone Island had been interesting, especially the hippo sighting, but anticipation for the main event rose.

The guides motioned for her to follow the rest of her party. She walked behind, trying to gauge the group's reaction to what came next. More precisely, how Aspen felt. During the ride, Quinn sensed Aspen's nervousness, which only intensified now that they were close to the Devil's Pool.

Peyton and DaKota scrambled toward the front like two school kids not wanting to miss anything, while Tina followed close behind. Mick walked with Claire and LeAnn, leaving Aspen to take up the rear with Quinn.

The guide continued to talk and point out various sights, but Quinn tuned him out and casually moved up next to Aspen. "You nervous?"

Aspen smiled up at her and nodded. "A little. Stupid, I know."

Quinn shook her head. "Not stupid at all. A healthy fear of nature isn't a bad thing."

"First, we'll stop at the place that David Livingstone saw the falls for the first time," the guide said in a practiced tone. "As you recall, Mr. Livingstone was the first European to see the falls, and he named them after Queen Victoria. Now if you'll follow me."

Quinn marveled at the beauty as they walked. The tiny rainbows forming in the mist from the falls were breathtaking. Quinn leaned down toward Aspen and whispered. "Hey, Frankie, there's lots of buddy mist up here."

Aspen laughed. "Gay-friendly, too."

Quinn cocked her head. "Huh?"

"Rainbows." Aspen pointed in several directions. "Lots of them."

Quinn laughed. "That was the lamest joke I've ever heard."

"Don't get me started. I'm just warming up."

Quinn groaned and tuned back into the guide.

"Livingstone's words from his diary sums it up. He said, *No one can imagine the beauty of the view from anything witnessed in England. It had never been seen before by European eyes; but scenes so lovely must have been gazed upon by angels in flight.*"

Aspen leaned against Quinn. "I wish I had my notebook, so I could write it down. It's beautiful."

"Famous quote. I'm sure you can find it anywhere. Hell, they probably put it on a T-shirt or a mug."

Aspen smiled. "You're probably right."

They began walking again, following the guide. "Do you always carry around a notebook?" Quinn asked.

"Usually. Don't tell anyone, or I'd probably lose my cool points."

"Secret's safe with me. But I didn't realize you had many cool points to lose."

Aspen chuckled and elbowed Quinn lightly in the ribs.

The guide continued to talk, but Quinn found

Aspen to be more fascinating. She'd not pegged her as someone who'd carry around a notebook.

Peyton circled back and grabbed Aspen's hand as they neared the water. Quinn should have asked what kind of things Aspen wrote about, but it was too late now. She'd question her later.

The guide pointed. "We will have to take a short swim from here. You can strip down to your swimsuits, unless you want to go in fully dressed, which I don't recommend."

"What if a hippo or crocodile comes and takes our clothes?" LeAnn asked.

The guide chuckled. "Not to worry, we'll watch out for them. Besides, they prefer to eat people rather than clothes." He must have noticed the look of horror on LeAnn's face. "Sorry. Bad joke."

Aspen pulled her shirt over her head to reveal a tiny black bikini, which she filled out nicely. Quinn averted her gaze as Aspen slid her shorts down her shapely legs.

"See something you like?" Mick asked.

"No, no…Nothing like that." Quinn waved her off. "I like talking to her. She's smart and funny."

"But no sparks?"

"For god's sake, I'm not looking for sparks." Quinn looked down at the ground. "It's been a while since I made a new friend."

Mick's eyes softened. "I like seeing you coming out of your shell. I forgot how lifeless you've been."

"Thanks…I think."

Mick chuckled. "Let's get naked."

Quinn crossed her arms over her chest and glared.

"What?" Mick's naïve act wasn't fooling Quinn.

"Don't go calling it getting naked, or I'm going in with all my clothes on."

They swam for a short distance when the guide motioned them to follow him onto the rocky area. They were closer to the edge of the falls and could clearly see the water cascading over the side.

Once everyone had climbed onto the rock, the guide held up his hand and waved it. "Welcome to the Devil's Pool at our beautiful Victoria Falls."

The others clapped, and Quinn joined in, swept up by the adventure.

"We prefer to call our falls *mosi-oa-tunya*," the guide said. "It means the Smoke that Thunders."

"Can you say that again?" Aspen asked.

Quinn smiled, figuring Aspen would want to write that in her notebook, too.

"Certainly." The guide smiled. "*Mosi-oa-tunya*. The Smoke that Thunders."

Aspen repeated the phrase after he finished.

"Very good. You are a natural." He held his hands wide apart over his head. "Are you ready for an experience of a lifetime?"

Everyone called out, "Yes!"

"Excellent," he said. "As you can see, we are at the edge of the falls. Nearly two hundred fifty gallons of water flow over the side every second. The currents are not for the faint of heart. And if that isn't enough, Victoria Falls is nearly twice as high as Niagara."

Quinn shifted her gaze from the guide and took in the grandeur. Her chest tightened. Stella had always wanted to see Victoria Falls. *No!* She couldn't do this to herself. She forced herself to tune back into the guide.

"I need everyone to pay close attention to the

instructions I am about to give you," he said. "And yes, there will be a quiz."

The group laughed.

"Seriously," he continued. "We have a nearly perfect safety record."

"Um, nearly perfect isn't terribly reassuring," DaKota called out.

"I promise you, nobody has gone over on my watch." The guide smiled. He ran down the safety rules, ones he'd probably given thousands of times.

Quinn tried to focus on his words, but her gaze kept being drawn back to the falls.

❧ ❧ ❧ ❧

Aspen drew her hands into loose fists to stop them from shaking. She was being silly. The odds of being hurt in a car accident were much greater than being injured here. Still, swimming so close to the edge of the waterfalls made her heart race.

"I'd like to go over a few more rules." The guide glanced from person to person before he continued. "Since this is a small, private group, we will let you all into the water at the same time. *But* we will only let two people at a time approach the edge of the falls for pictures. At that time, we will give you further instructions. We have been doing this for many years, and it is perfectly safe if you follow the rules. Any questions?"

Aspen glanced around. Everyone shook their heads.

"Okay." The guide smiled. "I'm sure everyone wants the opportunity to jump into Devil's Pool. We will have you enter one at a time." Without warning, he jumped backward into the water and landed with a large splash.

His counterpart, who'd yet to speak, followed suit. He bobbed to the surface and brushed the water from his face. "It's as simple as that," he said with a heavy accent and huge smile.

The first guide nodded. "Who wants to go first?"

Aspen took a step back, hoping not to be noticed. She'd need not have worried.

DaKota waved her arm and stepped up, followed closely by Peyton. "I'll go," DaKota said. The guide motioned for her, and DaKota sprang into the air. She let out a whoop right before plunging into the water. When she surfaced, she laughed and whooped again. "Let's see what you got, Peyton."

Peyton launched herself off the edge. Her distance exceeded DaKota's, and she triumphantly thrust her arms above her head. The two splashed around while one by one the others jumped into the water.

Aspen and Quinn were the last two still standing on the bank.

"Hey, babe," Peyton called. "Jump to me."

Quinn turned and met Aspen's gaze. "Are you ready?"

Aspen's heart raced. "I'm being stupid. It's not like I'm jumping over the edge of the falls, so why am I so damned nervous?"

"Cumulative effect."

"Meaning?"

"This whole trip has you nervous, and it's come to a head now. Even though there's not much danger."

Aspen smiled. "I didn't know you were a psychologist."

Quinn grinned. "One of your sidekick's hidden talents."

"Hey, Aspen, would you stop flapping your jaws and get your ass in here?" DaKota yelled. "I want to get on with seeing the edge of the falls."

"How can you resist an invitation like that?" Quinn stepped aside and motioned for Aspen to step forward.

Just go! Aspen took two steps back. *One. Two. Three.* She ran forward and leapt. As she flew through the air, she flapped her arms and kicked her legs, going for as much distance as possible. The cool water momentarily took her breath away as she went under. She kicked up and broke the surface of the water.

Aspen shook her head, letting the spray from her hair fly off in all directions. With both hands, she ran them through the length of her hair and squeezed out the excess water.

"You did it, babe." Peyton swam to her and gave her a quick kiss.

"Plus, I'll have you know, I got the most distance." Aspen danced in the water.

"Beginner's luck." DaKota pointed up at Quinn. "Besides, you're not the last to go."

Aspen met Quinn's gaze and detected a hint of mischief. What was Quinn up to?

Before she could analyze further, Quinn left her feet. Mid-flight, she curled into a ball and landed like a cannonball only a few feet from DaKota. With her larger frame, the spray was impressive.

DaKota got a face full of water, while Aspen got a little of the excess splash.

Peyton laughed and pointed at DaKota, who sputtered and wiped the water out of her eyes. Tina quickly turned away, stifling a laugh, while Mick concentrated on the spot Quinn entered the water.

Quinn bobbed to the surface and smiled. She winked at Aspen before turning to DaKota. "I guess Aspen wins. I didn't make it far enough."

DaKota's eyes darkened, but then she smiled. "You got me." She held her fist out toward Quinn.

A look of surprise crossed Quinn's face before she bumped fists with DaKota.

⁂

Quinn held back as the others laughed and joked while they splashed around in the pool. Maybe she'd been too cynical about DaKota and Peyton. Had she let their money cloud her judgment? *Probably.* While they still reminded her of frat boys at times, maybe they weren't so bad after all. A little self-absorbed, no doubt, but weren't most people?

Mick paddled over and splashed her. "That's for earlier."

"What did I do?" Quinn said, trying for an innocent expression but knowing she failed.

"You drenched her on purpose."

Quinn put her hand to her chest and opened her mouth in mock surprise. "Me?"

Mick splashed her again. "And that's for the bad acting job."

Quinn laughed. She cupped her hands, filled them with water, and threw it at Mick.

Quinn was mid-laugh when Mick sent a spray of water in her direction. *Shit.* Quinn clamped her mouth shut before the water pelted her face. "Now you're in trouble, Romero."

"Oh, it's Romero now, is it? Just for that...." Mick hit the water in front of her and sent another spray to rain down on Quinn.

Quinn retaliated, and soon they were scuffling like teenagers. Quinn hadn't laughed this freely in years. It felt good.

They finally called a truce when both were gasping for breath from laughter and exertion.

Aspen swam toward them but stopped several yards away. "Are you two children about done?"

Quinn grinned. "Yes, Mom."

"Good. We all want to get our pictures with you guys on the rim of the falls."

"I thought they'd only let two at a time up there," Mick said.

Aspen raised her eyebrows. "DaKota can be very persuasive."

Translation: Money talks. "I see. I'm game if Mick is."

Mick nodded. "Let's do it."

Last night before falling asleep, Quinn searched the internet and found hundreds of vacation pictures from this exact location. People were funny. Memorializing their trip via a photo became almost more important than the experience itself. It gave tourists the opportunity to feel the thrill of being on the edge of the falls without any real danger.

She wouldn't burst anyone's bubble by telling them she'd seen many group shots. Hopefully, DaKota didn't pay too much for the privilege.

"First we do individual pictures," the guide said when they all gathered. He ran his finger back and forth across the group with narrowed eyes. "Do we have someone brave here?"

Peyton and DaKota were the first to raise their hands.

"Step on up, my friends, or should I say swim?"

Soon they were showboating on the edge of the falls as the guides took multiple pictures. Quinn had to admit the imagery was impressive as the water rushed past them and plummeted over the falls. The guide held on to DaKota's feet as she lay on her stomach on the rock ledge and peered over the falls.

"Holy shit," DaKota called out. "What a fucking rush." She held out her arms as if she were flying as the water surged around her.

"Epic," Peyton said. "I'm next."

They each took turns, some more adventurous than others. Quinn noticed that Aspen held back, inconspicuously moving away from the action.

The guide smiled and waved to her. "Nothing to be afraid of. Come, I'll make sure nothing bad happens to you."

Aspen gave him an apprehensive smile but didn't move forward. DaKota and Peyton began chanting Aspen's name, which caused her to withdraw further into herself.

Quinn nonchalantly swam to her. "It's up to you. Don't do anything you're not comfortable with."

Aspen smiled, but her eyes held fear. "I'd like to do it." She held out her trembling hand. "But I'm not sure I can."

"Do you want me to go with you?" Quinn surprised herself by the question.

Aspen's eyes lit up. "Would you?"

"Isn't that what a sidekick is for?"

Aspen linked her arm through Quinn's. "Definitely. Let's show everyone how brave I am."

The guide gave Aspen a big smile and reached out his hand to her. "This'll be easy. Just you wait and see."

Aspen let go of Quinn's arm and took the guide's hand. Quinn gave her a reassuring smile and stepped back.

Soon Aspen was sitting on the ledge while the others cheered her on. With her flushed cheeks and huge smile, she was even more beautiful. She stretched out, put her hands behind her, and raised her face to the sun. With the falls behind her, she could have been doing a *Sports Illustrated Swimsuit Issue* cover shoot.

Quinn glanced away, hoping her face hadn't given away her thoughts. She looked back when the guide said, "Ready to see what it looks like over the falls?"

Aspen let out a nervous giggle. "Promise you won't let me go over."

"Promise." He smiled and moved into position. He motioned where she should move to. She tentatively inched forward while he held her legs.

"Oh, my god," Aspen screamed and then began laughing.

The guides snapped pictures as she looked over the edge of the falls.

When they pulled her back, a giant smile lit her face, and she splashed through the water, laughing the entire time.

"The lady has courage." The guide clapped his hands in the direction of Aspen.

Peyton swam to Aspen and dramatically planted a deep kiss on her lips.

At first, Aspen pulled back but then put her arms around Peyton and hugged her. "I did it."

Quinn looked away.

The guide called out, "Are you ready for your group photo?" His gaze landed on DaKota.

"Hell, yes. Let's do this, kids," DaKota said.

"We want the two of you in the middle." Peyton motioned to Quinn and Mick.

"If we do that, we'll have to split up the couples," Tina said.

"So? What's the big deal?" DaKota asked.

Quinn and Mick took their positions. "This might take a while," Quinn whispered to Mick.

"Yup. Care to bet on how long?"

"Nope. Getting a bunch of headstrong lesbians to agree on something is worse than herding cats."

After several minutes of debate, they reached a tentative agreement and settled on four different configurations. Quinn and Mick had it easy. They stayed in one spot while the others moved around them.

By the final picture, Quinn stopped paying attention to the musical chair routine going on around her. She gazed out over the falls, enjoying their beauty. When she realized she was happy here, a feeling of serenity washed over her. She'd missed Mick and the experience of being on an adventure.

Quinn was brought back to the present when she felt a pair of smooth legs slide around her waist from behind. She glanced to her left and saw Peyton slide in behind Mick. Her heartbeat quickened. *Who was it?* Arms reached around Quinn's neck, and she felt warm breath on her ear.

"You're stuck with me," Aspen said into Quinn's ear. "I hope you don't mind."

A shiver ran through Quinn. *Stop.* She'd been

holed up in the Ozarks for too long. *Be cool.* It was only a photo op, for God's sake. As casually as she could muster, she put her hands on top of Aspen's arms. A sharp intake of breath came from behind Quinn. *No.* It couldn't be. Just her imagination. "You're good, Frankie."

Aspen's easy laugh made her smile.

"Am I going to be stuck with that nickname forever?"

"Afraid so."

"Everyone in place?" the guide said, cutting off any further conversation. "I need a *big* smile. Say cheese!"

After several clicks on multiple devices, the photo shoot ended. Quinn's shoulders dropped when Aspen let go of her neck and her legs unwrapped from around Quinn's waist. She took a couple of steps forward into the deeper water and turned around.

Aspen met her gaze and smiled. "I think that picture is going to be my favorite."

Quinn nodded. "Mine too." Uncomfortable under Aspen's gaze and unsure what more to say, she swam away.

Chapter Fifteen

"D o you think those four are ever going to join us?" LeAnn asked.

Aspen glanced over to the bar in the corner of the dining room where Quinn and Mick had been huddled with Peyton and DaKota for nearly forty-five minutes. "They'll have to when the food comes out."

"True." LeAnn nodded. "I'm famished."

"I know, right?" Aspen's stomach growled in agreement. "I guess we burned more calories than I thought."

Claire held up her empty glass and stood. "Best way to combat hunger. I'll go see what's going on up there."

LeAnn shrugged. "And then there were three."

Tina wasn't exactly a third since she'd been engrossed in the map she'd spread out across the table. It looked to be a detailed overview of the Zambezi rapids. She'd probably be the best to discuss tomorrow's run with Quinn and Mick, but Peyton and DaKota would never hear of it.

Even though she had never warmed to Tina, seeing her study the map gave Aspen comfort. In a pinch, she imagined Tina would come through.

"The falls were beautiful," Aspen said, turning her attention back to LeAnn.

"Gorgeous. I had fun today. Did you?"

"A blast." Aspen shook her head. "I can't believe

I just said that."

"Why?"

"I know it's stupid, but I was scared to death. Then Quinn did that ridiculous cannonball, and everyone was laughing and joking. Having a good time. And I guess I forgot to be afraid."

"I love it. Forgetting to be afraid."

"Somehow, I don't think that will work for me tomorrow." Aspen's throat constricted at the thought.

"Whoa." LeAnn put her hand on Aspen's arm. "Are you okay? I've never seen someone's face drain of color so fast."

Tina looked up from the map. "Dude, you don't look good." She pushed a glass of water toward Aspen. "Maybe you better take a drink."

Aspen picked up the glass, not because she thought it would help, but to delay having to speak. She took a sip and then another. Her heartbeat slowed, and she no longer felt like she might pass out. "Sorry," she mumbled.

Tina's gaze softened. "It's okay to be afraid as long as it doesn't immobilize you. It's the people that have no fear that I worry about."

Aspen's eyes widened. "You mean you're afraid?"

"Always. Mother Nature isn't somebody to screw with." Tina glanced toward the bar. "Quinn knows that better than any of us."

Wow. Maybe there was something behind Tina's hardass, sex kitten veneer. Why did it seem she always failed to remember that lesson? She'd observed people for years and captured them in her notebooks, but still she tended to be stuck at surface level.

"Your color's starting to return." LeAnn patted her hand. "Feeling better?"

"Yes, thanks." Aspen turned her gaze to Tina. "And thank you. Coming from you, that really helps."

"I'm happy to be of service." Tina's shy smile surprised Aspen.

Damn it. How had she missed seeing this side of Tina all these months? "Can I ask what you're doing with the map?"

"Sure." Tina beamed. "Do you two want to come around here, so you can see?"

Aspen and LeAnn flanked Tina as she pointed to a spot near the top of the map. "This is where we'll put in. It's called the Boiling Pot."

"Seriously?" Aspen groaned. "Why do they make the names all sound so scary? Couldn't it be Unicorn Bay or something like that?"

Tina laughed. "Okay. We start here at Unicorn Bay." Tina's finger trailed along the map. "These are all the rapids we'll hit. Goes from one to twenty-six."

"Umm, I don't want to come off dense, but..." LeAnn stopped. Her face colored.

"Go ahead." Tina gave an encouraging nod. "The only stupid question is the one not asked."

"Why are you spending so much time studying the map?" LeAnn's face turned a deeper shade of red. "I don't mean to be offensive. It's just...." LeAnn's finger snaked along the river. "Isn't a map for figuring out which way to go?" LeAnn leaned forward and looked closer. "I don't see any turnoffs."

Tina chuckled. "Good point. There's only one way to go on the river." Her long red fingernail moved slowly down the map. "See, right here."

Aspen squinted at the markings Tina's finger rested on. She'd grown up on GPS, so she'd never learned to read a map. This one looked more foreign than most. "I'm afraid that I have no idea what I'm looking at."

"Me either," LeAnn said.

Tina tapped the map. "This is rapid number four. They call it Morning Glory." She slid her finger over slightly. "See the information box."

Aspen and LeAnn nodded.

"It explains the best way to run it. This one's fun. Depending on the water level, it has three different options."

Aspen grinned and pointed. "What's Dragon's Back?"

"One of the possible routes on Morning Glory. It shoots between two holes, which they call the Dragon's Back."

"Oh, cool." LeAnn clapped. "I want to ride the Dragon's Back."

"It'll depend on the water when we get there. Quinn and Mick will decide."

"I'm still puzzled," LeAnn said. "What good does it do for *you* to study the map?"

"I'll guarantee you that Quinn and Mick have spent hours getting acquainted with the rapids. I want to be prepared, too."

"Don't you trust them?" Aspen asked.

"Implicitly, or I wouldn't have come." Tina looked away and seemed to be contemplating. Her gaze returned. "Maybe I shouldn't say this, but it's just us girls. DaKota and I had a huge fight about it when we weren't sure if Quinn and Mick would take the job. She wanted to hire some company I'd never heard of. I researched them, and they had less-than-stellar safety precautions. I refused to go."

"I'm sure that didn't sit well," LeAnn said.

Tina scrunched up her face and shook her head. "Nope. Good thing they agreed, or I think our relationship would have ended before it had barely begun."

Interesting. Another misconception she had of Tina. Underneath the flashy clothes and coquettish persona was an independent woman. She just let everyone believe the illusion that DaKota was in charge.

"How long have you been studying this?" LeAnn asked.

"About a month. I just wanted to take one more peek and ask Quinn and Mick a few questions."

"Then why aren't you up there?" Aspen pointed. "You know more about rafting than Peyton and DaKota combined."

"That's why I'm not."

"You want to talk to them peer-to-peer?" Aspen said.

"Something like that." Tina groaned. "Oh, god, I'm starting to sound like Mick."

"You just don't have the dreamy accent." LeAnn batted her eyes.

They all laughed.

Sometime during the conversation, the tightness in Aspen's chest disappeared. She let the good feelings wash over her. Having someone other than Peyton to talk to on the trip made everything better.

"If we can get LeAnn to stop drooling, maybe I can show you a few more things before dinner." Tina winked.

"Fine." LeAnn crossed her arms over her chest in mock anger.

Tina grinned and put her finger back on the

map. "This is a grade four rapid. See the number here?" Tina pointed.

"I remember you guys teaching me about that." Aspen perked up, feeling she had something to add to the conversation. "That's a pretty powerful rapid, but there are several grade fives on the Zambezi. Even a grade six."

"Very good." Tina smiled.

"After we make it through Morning Glory, we'll be on our way to Stairway to Heaven followed by the Devil's Toilet Bowl."

"Who named these?" LeAnn asked.

"At least they're memorable," Aspen said. "I think we might just have to rename them. How about Kitten's Water Dish?"

Tina laughed. "Quinn and Mick will lose it if you guys start talking about Unicorn Bay and Kitten's Water Dish." A mischievous glint danced in her eyes, and she smirked. "Let's do it."

⁂

Quinn leaned back in her chair. *Ugh.* She'd eaten too much. It would probably be in poor taste to unbutton her shorts. She glanced over at Mick, who snagged a leftover roll. Where did she put it?

They'd made quick work of the meal. The afternoon at the Devil's Pool seemed to have left them all with an appetite. Even Aspen, who looked like she'd be a nibbler, ate her meal with gusto.

She and Mick had decided not to talk shop during dinner. The trip today had done a lot for the camaraderie of the group, so they'd wanted to preserve that feeling. An easy and familiar conversation flowed while they rehashed the high points of the day.

"Hands down, my vote is for the cannonball," Peyton said. "I think everyone at this table has wanted to do that at one time or another to shut you up." Peyton playfully elbowed DaKota.

Her friends cheered and voiced their agreement.

DaKota laughed. "Very funny." She turned to Quinn. "How much did Peyton pay you to do it?"

Quinn smirked. "Did you ever think I might have paid Peyton to *let* me?"

"Snap," Aspen said.

"Burn," Tina added.

"This is *not* how it's supposed to go," DaKota said, a huge smile still on her face.

"I'll let you off the hook," Mick said. "Now that dinner is over, we need to go over the game plan."

The side conversations stopped, and all focus turned toward Mick.

"Apparently, you have a way of quieting a room," Quinn said.

Mick shot her a look before continuing. "We're excited about tomorrow. All the cards are on the table. Which is the only way we can have a safe and successful trip." Mick shifted her gaze toward Aspen. "We know this is Aspen's first whitewater experience. We also know we have a ringer amongst us." Mick smiled at Tina. "You could probably teach us a thing or two."

"I don't think I'd go that far." Tina waved off the compliment, but the hint of a smile gave her away.

Mick launched into her safety speech. Quinn leaned back in her chair and blocked it out. She'd heard it hundreds of times before.

Today had been a good day. Something about

this place seemed to be doing a number on her. There'd been blocks of time that she'd let herself have fun without thinking of anything else. Now the butterflies fluttered in her stomach, and her chest constricted. Tomorrow would be the big test. She'd done fine on the Minus Rapids and splashing around in a harmless pool of water, but the stakes would be higher in the morning.

Other people's lives would be in her hands. Sweat beaded on her brow, so she nonchalantly picked up a napkin and dabbed at her forehead. She took a deep breath, hoping to slow her rapidly beating heart.

Shit. When she'd felt this way before, Mick tried to convince her she was having a panic attack. She didn't want to believe it, but it sure felt like she was panicking now. She took a few calming breaths. She needed to focus on something else. *Fast!*

Mick continued to talk, but her gaze stopped on Quinn. *Damn it. She knew.* Quinn looked away and tried to focus on her job. Since they'd partnered, Mick normally did most of the talking, while Quinn sat back and observed.

Quinn had a job. She needed to scan the group for potential troublemakers and weak links. She'd been concerned about DaKota and Peyton since they'd arrived, but after today, she felt better. Their earlier conversation left her with no doubt both wanted the trip to be successful and for everyone to have a good time.

Despite DaKota's bravado, Quinn suspected it was mostly for show. DaKota appeared to have a healthy sense of self, so she'd likely not do something stupid to prove herself. Quinn leveled her gaze on Peyton; insecurity lay just under the surface. Hopefully, the insecurity wouldn't cause her problems.

Quinn tuned back in to Mick's speech. "I suggest that everyone get a good night's sleep. We'll meet at seven a.m. to go over safety instructions and commands."

Chapter Sixteen

Quinn smiled at the eager faces gathered around them. She'd agreed to this trip only for the money, thinking she'd find a way to tolerate the rich protégés, but she liked them. Mick's idea to spend a few days together before they hit the rapids had been genius.

"Well, kids, I've got some good news and bad news for you. Which would you like first?" Mick asked.

DaKota groaned. "Give us the good first."

"Smart thinking." Mick flashed a smile.

Quinn stifled a giggle when her gaze landed on LeAnn. She sported the same dreamy look Quinn witnessed many times over the last couple of days whenever Mick smiled. LeAnn must have sensed Quinn's stare because she turned her head toward Quinn but quickly blushed and looked away.

"The good news is we are partnering with a local company who will be providing porters to help on this trip. They'll be arriving shortly to take us to our destination. The van will be packed with all the equipment we'll need. We'll put in near the Boiling Pot at the base of Victoria Falls. The eight of us will be in a paddle raft, and our additional porters will follow with an oar rig that will carry our camping equipment."

Aspen raised her hand. "Um, now that the

secret's out, do you mind explaining that in layman's terms?"

Quinn stepped up. "The oar rig has compartments for supplies. It is a completely different experience taking one of those down the river. In my estimation, not as fun for everyone." Quinn smiled at Aspen. "The paddle raft allows everyone to participate."

"You mean I don't get to sit in the rocking chair and let all of you do the work?" Aspen pretended to frown.

"Afraid not." Quinn winked.

"So what's the bad news?" Peyton put her arm over Aspen's shoulder and pulled her closer.

"The bad news," Mick said. "The bad news is that we aren't letting you off the hook. Even though you paid the guides handsomely, they aren't going to do all the work."

"Meaning?" DaKota asked.

"The most experienced rafters, Tina, DaKota, Peyton, and Claire, will get the oar rig ready for the trip while we give Aspen and LeAnn further instruction on basic rafting techniques."

"But I paid them to take care of everything." DaKota crossed her arms over her chest.

Quinn bit her lip. If she pouted any more, no doubt, Mick would make things even harder on them.

Mick smiled. "And I talked to them this morning and told them not to."

"Damn it, that sucks," Peyton joined in.

"Here's the thing," Mick said. "I'm not comfortable giving the impression of privileged Americans with the locals. So we help do the work."

"That includes setting up camp tonight," Quinn added.

"Now you're killing us," DaKota said, but her smile said she wasn't too put out. "Good thing we're only camping a couple nights."

"All right. I think we're ready." Mick nodded at the van that pulled around the corner. "Looks like it's go time."

⁂

Sweat rolled down Aspen's back as they rode in the Land Cruiser. She didn't want to touch anything with her hands for fear of leaving wet handprints. Her heart raced. Could she really do this? She trusted Mick and Quinn completely, but she'd started to doubt her decision since she'd woken up this morning.

They would be at their destination soon. She needed to back out now, or it would be too late. She glanced at Quinn, who sat in the seat in front of her. Her muscular shoulders reassured her. Quinn would keep them safe.

Ironic. After what happened to Stella, Quinn would probably hate to hear Aspen put so much faith in her. But she did. From everything she heard, what happened to Stella was a fluke accident with nothing Quinn could have done.

She was brought out of her thoughts when the van pulled to a stop.

"We're here," DaKota called out and bounced in her seat.

Despite not always seeing eye to eye with DaKota, her childlike enthusiasm made Aspen smile. She'd not been half bad on the trip. Being around her idols seemed to have a positive effect on her. Hopefully, it would continue on the river. One of Aspen's fears was the rest of the group becoming frustrated by her inexperience.

They piled out of the van while their guides began unloading the equipment. Quinn and Mick jumped in to help, and soon the others followed suit. Having something to keep her mind occupied suited Aspen; she didn't want to dwell on what was to come.

Once everything was unloaded, they gathered around their mountain of gear. Mick and Quinn had already stripped down to their swim trunks and swim tanks. *Damn.* Quinn's shoulder muscles were massive, and Mick didn't appear to have an ounce of fat on her. Aspen shot a glance at LeAnn and smiled. It seemed Mick's physique hadn't gone unnoticed.

Aspen inconspicuously walked over to LeAnn. "You might want to close your mouth, or a bug might fly in."

LeAnn snapped her mouth shut and chuckled. "I need to develop a better poker face."

"Even so, the drool would probably give you away."

LeAnn swiped at her mouth. When her hand came up dry, she laughed. "Very funny."

"You better be careful, or Claire is gonna get pissed."

LeAnn waved her hand. "We've got a deal. We can look all we want as long as we don't touch. And Mick is certainly fine to look at. Quinn's not too bad on the eyes, either."

"Um, I hadn't really noticed."

"Liar." LeAnn winked.

Aspen hoped the heat she felt on her cheeks didn't show. Peyton had made her way to where they stood, and she certainly didn't want to have this conversation in front of her. Aspen was saved from responding when Mick whistled to get their attention.

"We're going to break into two groups," Mick said. "I suggest stripping down to your swim clothes considering the heat, but don't forget to put on your sunscreen. We'll be up here for about forty-five minutes before we head down."

Peyton shot a glance at Quinn before she spoke. "They just want to check out our ladies." She pulled Aspen closer to her.

Mick laughed. "Sumpin' like that."

Aspen slid out of her lightweight pants and pulled off her neoprene shirt. She'd immediately fell in love with her new bikini as soon as she laid eyes on it. The vibrant red, yellow, and blue swishes were what first caught her eye, but it was the design that sold her. The criss-cross top contained her breasts better than a traditional bikini, but it also showed off more of her ample assets than the sports bra variety. The boy shorts rounded out the look.

Peyton whistled and wriggled her eyebrows. "Wow, babe. You should have told me you got a new suit. I might have sent the rest of these guys out on the river, and we could have stayed back at Elephant Camp."

What the fuck? Aspen had modeled it last night in their room, and Peyton barely tore her focus away from her magazine long enough to grunt. Now she decided to make a show of noticing. Aspen faked her best smile and batted her hand at Peyton. "Stop. You'll embarrass me."

It must have been the correct reaction because Peyton beamed and patted her on the ass. Aspen steeled herself, so she wouldn't flinch. She felt like all attention was on her and wanted the focus diverted. She glanced toward Tina and LeAnn, who had begun to remove their outer clothes. *Perfect.* It was just the diversion she needed. "Oh, my god, I love both of your suits," Aspen said, hoping her voice didn't come out too over the top.

LeAnn sported a more conservative look with a tropical patterned skirt bottom and a matching wide strap top. In typical Tina fashion, her black suit highlighted all her assets. It probably cost her a small fortune for the least amount of material. Her look would surely take all attention off Aspen.

"Damn, Tina," DaKota said. "The first whitewater we hit, you just might be topless."

Thank you. DaKota saved the day as everyone's gaze turned to Tina.

"I've never fallen out of my suit. I'm a pro. I've got this." Tina winked.

"All right." Mick glanced around the circle. "Aspen and LeAnn, you two are going to work with Quinn on rafting commands while the rest of us help the guides prepare the rafts."

LeAnn waved her hand. "But I've rafted before."

Quinn nodded. "Yep, we know, but you've got the least amount of experience next to Aspen, and it'll be better for her to practice with someone else in the raft."

"No fair," DaKota said. "She's getting off easy."

"Don't be so sure," Aspen said. "From all the reading material Quinn and Mick gave me, one of the biggest dangers with a new rower is hitting someone in the head with our paddles."

LeAnn groaned. "Lovely."

Quinn helped the guides drag the paddle raft away from the rest of the equipment. Her heartbeat quickened, and it wasn't from the exertion. Now was not the time to let panic take over. She'd been relatively calm all morning, but that could quickly change. *Focus.*

She looked over her shoulder. "Aspen, can you and LeAnn each grab a paddle?"

Aspen bent over and examined the myriad paddles strewn around the area. "There's a bunch of different ones."

LeAnn stepped up and picked up two paddles. "These are the ones we need." She handed one to Aspen.

"Grab me one, too," Quinn called.

Once the guides had left them alone with the raft, Quinn held up a paddle. "Since we don't want LeAnn to be clocked in the head, this is the best place to start."

"Thank you." LeAnn smiled.

"The best way to ensure safety is to grip it correctly." Quinn hoped the paddle wouldn't slide out of her grasp because of her sweat-drenched hands. She held it up and pointed. "See the T-shaped end? At all times, you want it in your palm." Quinn slapped it into the center of her hand and wrapped her fingers around it. "Keep a tight hold. You guys try it."

LeAnn and Aspen followed Quinn's lead and gripped their paddle. "Damn," Aspen said. "The T makes it feel like I've got a good hold on it."

"Exactly." Quinn pretended to paddle a few strokes and then let her hand slide off the T. She continued the rowing motion, and the end of the paddle swung through the air. "Did you see how dangerous that was? I could have hit anyone in the face or head. That's why you keep the proper grip at all times."

"Is it true that is one of the biggest dangers?" LeAnn asked.

"In my experience, yes. Or at least the most frequent. I've seen a few teeth knocked out in my day."

"Oh, god." Aspen crinkled her nose and looked at her paddle as if it were bent on assault. "I don't want to hurt anyone."

Quinn tried to hide her smile. The look on Aspen's face was priceless. "Just remember your T, and you'll be fine. I've found that it is usually the experienced rowers that get lazy and end up hitting someone."

Quinn kept her gaze on Aspen's hands as they practiced, trying to avoid looking at her bikini-clad body. "Okay. Let's practice commands. For that, we're going to sit in the raft. For this trip, Mick insists that I be the captain, so I'll be in the stern." When she noticed Aspen's furrowed brow, she added, "the back of the boat." You guys will sit in front of me, Aspen on my right and LeAnn on the left."

Aspen smiled. "So you'll be able to catch me if I start to go overboard."

"Yep, but let's hope you don't go overboard." Quinn winked. "Why don't you two get into your positions, so we can practice commands? I'm going to stand behind the raft, so I can watch both of you better."

Aspen and LeAnn grabbed their paddles and climbed in. Aspen sat on the seat that went from one side of the raft to the other, but LeAnn remained standing. "I don't think we're supposed to sit there, are we?" LeAnn asked.

"Nope, when you're in a paddle raft, you sit on the edge of the raft."

Aspen jumped up, her face flushed. "Sorry. Good thing you know I'm a rookie."

"No worries. By the time you're done with your lesson, you'll look like a pro." Quinn flashed her a smile. "You want to sit on the edge behind the last seat. There are footholds where you can slide your inside foot, and then slip your outside foot under that seat in front of you."

Aspen sat on the side of the raft and shoved her leg under the seat, until half her calf was lodged underneath.

"Okay, lesson number one." Quinn walked around to where Aspen's leg was and gently moved it back. "You never want to put any body part too far under something or tie yourself in."

"But I don't want to fall out," Aspen said, her lips pursed in a pout.

"I'd rather you fall out than get stuck and be trapped under the raft if it capsizes."

Aspen's lips drew into an O. "Shit. I never thought of that." She pulled her foot out, so only her big toe was under the seat.

"That's the opposite extreme." Quinn shook her head. "Tuck it in a little farther." Once satisfied that Aspen was in the correct position, she moved around to check on LeAnn, who'd positioned herself perfectly. "Are you ladies ready for your next lesson?"

She was greeted by two yeses.

Quinn moved back to her position at the back of

the raft. "Okay. We'll start with something easy. There are only two ways I will ask you to paddle. Forward or back. Or I will ask you to stop."

"I think I might be able to do that." Aspen giggled.

Quinn spent the next several minutes calling out commands, while the two women practiced.

"I think you've got that. Now for something a bit more challenging." Quinn held up her paddle. "The paddle is also used for turning. This is a simple command, too, but sometimes people get it backward. So listen up. To turn right." She pointed to Aspen. "The person on the right side needs to paddle backward, while the person on the left paddles forward."

"I'm assuming if we want to go left, the person on the left paddles backward," Aspen said.

"Yep, you've got it. Are you ready to practice?"

Aspen nodded and lowered her paddle as if it were going into the water. She had a determined set to her shoulders and appeared ready to pounce on the first command.

Quinn stifled a chuckle. Aspen's intensity was adorable. "Turn right," Quinn called out.

Both women seamlessly performed the command. In Quinn's experience, the first few times, trainees seemed to get it right because they were laser focused. It was after they let down their guard and got overconfident when the problems occurred. Once she mixed in forward and back commands, they began to make mistakes.

Aspen swore under her breath, and her brow furrowed.

"It's okay," Quinn said. "Eventually, it will become natural. That's why we practice."

They performed the commands for another ten minutes. No one would be hurt on her watch. That thought increased her pulse, and she felt sweat drip down the side of her face. "All right. Are you ready to move on?"

"Yes," LeAnn said, dropping her paddle in feigned exhaustion.

"Oh, come on, it wasn't that bad, was it?"

LeAnn smiled. "No. I've just never had such a thorough guide before." LeAnn stopped, drew in her breath, and sat up straighter. "Um, sorry. I didn't mean anything by that."

Quinn nodded. By her reaction, LeAnn's mind had gone to Stella. *Shit.* She'd not wanted to address Stella, but she feared that if she didn't, the others would be tentative around her and edit everything they said, which wouldn't be good for anyone. "I think I should probably talk about the elephant in the room. Or should I say raft?" Quinn hoped her attempt at levity would make it easier.

Aspen turned around fully and met Quinn's gaze. Her blue eyes penetrated Quinn's soul.

Damn it. Quinn needed to focus. "Yes, I am ultra-cautious because of what happened to Stella. I wake up every morning wishing I could relive that day over and make different choices. Unfortunately, I can't." Quinn lowered her gaze and stared at the paddle she held. She would not let her voice crack. "I never want to have to second-guess myself again. And ask if I did enough or if I prepared you all enough. So you're the victims of that. You'll probably get ten times the instruction you'd get from most guides."

"That's okay," Aspen said. Her voice sounded closer than Quinn expected it to. "We'll go through as much training as you need us to, so you feel comfortable."

Quinn shifted her gaze from her paddle and found that Aspen stood next to her. When their gazes met, Aspen wrapped her arm around Quinn's waist and hugged her.

Emotions bubbled up in Quinn's chest. *Weird.* Whenever she thought of Stella, it was always painful coupled with suffocating panic, but Aspen's touch added a different dimension. Peace. Comfort. "Thanks for understanding." She should say more, but no words came to her. She wanted to get back on solid footing.

As if sensing her need, Aspen spoke. "Are you ready to fill our heads full of knowledge?" She squeezed Quinn once more before letting go and jumping back into the raft.

"Now comes the tricky part," Quinn responded. "When we start to hit rough waters, following these commands will be the difference between taking a swim and staying in the raft."

"Oh, great." Aspen moaned and dramatically put her arm against her forehead.

Quinn suspected her antics were to pull Quinn completely back into the moment. Which was exactly what Quinn wanted. "There are three commands that I will use. The first is lean in. For this command, I don't want you leaning out to paddle anymore. Instead, I want you leaning in to reduce the likelihood that you fall out."

They practiced a few times before Quinn moved on. "I'm sure you've seen videos where one side of the raft is way up." Quinn held out her hand and tilted it, so one side was much higher than the other. "When the raft is in this position, it could easily tip the rest of the way." Quinn flipped her hand over. "When this happens, everyone takes a dip in the water. Which of course we don't want. So if I sense we are heading toward this, I will call out high side, which means everyone in the raft moves to the high side in hopes we can level it out. Once leveled out, you should return to your side. Any questions?"

Aspen's eyes grew bigger. "How often does that happen?"

"Hopefully, not very often. I don't like using the command unless I absolutely have to. So if I do, you know to move fast."

"Great," LeAnn said.

"You guys will do fine. Are you ready for the last command?"

Both women nodded.

"Get down," Quinn shouted out.

Aspen's head whipped around as she searched the area while LeAnn slid from the side onto the floor. "Oh, shit. I just got swept overboard, didn't I?" Aspen put her hand over her face.

"Afraid so." Quinn smiled. "Although I wasn't being fair. You'd never heard the command before, but obviously, LeAnn has."

LeAnn chuckled. "It's the one I'm best at. Someone tells me to get down, I'm diving for safety."

"That's what I like to hear. Are you two ready to try out all the commands you've learned?"

Aspen raised her hand. "Can I ask a question?"

"Certainly."

"What happens if you don't get down fast enough, and...umm, you fall out?"

"Excellent question." Quinn smiled. "Let's talk

about it." Quinn moved to the side of the raft and put her hand on the rope that circled the raft. "This is called a grab rope. If you fall out or we capsize, the first thing to do is try and get a hold of it."

"And if we can't?"

LeAnn cringed. "I hate this part. The thought just freaks me out."

Aspen stared at her wide-eyed. "That's not very reassuring."

"Oh, sorry," LeAnn said. "I should leave the commentary to Quinn."

"LeAnn is right." Even though Quinn wanted to allay Aspen's fears, she needed to get across the importance of making the right moves. "I won't lie to you. The instructions I'm about to give will sound counterintuitive. If you are too far away from the raft, you should flip onto your back and point your feet downstream."

Aspen's face drained of color. "Are you kidding me? Just let the current wash me away?"

"I know it sounds scary, but it's the safest thing to do," Quinn said. "LeAnn, have you ever seen it happen?"

"Plenty." LeAnn nodded. "It works. The current takes you faster than you'd think. You kinda bob up and down like a bobber until you come out of the whitewater."

"Remember, we'll also have the local guides behind us helping out. Just whatever you do, don't try to swim back upstream. And always flip onto your back. I've seen some torn-up feet when they dangle. You're moving fast, and they can get bashed against the rocks." Quinn made eye contact with Aspen. "I'm not saying this to scare you. I just want it ingrained in your mind should something happen. The better trained you are, the less likely you are to panic."

Aspen nodded. The color had begun to return to her face. "Am I a little freaked out? Yes. But I understand."

"Ready to practice?" Quinn continued to meet her gaze.

"Let's do it," Aspen said with conviction. "I'm ready."

Quinn lost track of how long she'd been shouting out commands until Mick sauntered over tapping on her watch. "You've been at it for nearly an hour. I think they probably have it by now."

"Has it been that long?" Quinn glanced down at Mick's watch. "I'll be damned. It has been."

"Has the captain been treating you ladies well?" Mick asked and flashed her smile at the two trainees.

Quinn's eyes danced, but she hid her smile at the look on LeAnn's face. *Yep.* No doubt by her expression she'd like to throw Mick into the raft and have her way. It wasn't anything Quinn hadn't seen many times over the years, but she'd almost forgotten Mick's effect on women.

"She's the best." Aspen leapt out of the raft. "The rookie is ready to do this."

"No fear?" Mick asked, her gaze pinpointed on Aspen's face.

"Just the normal level. I feel one hundred percent safe with Quinn."

Quinn's stomach lurched. *Stop.* She could do this. *Had* to do this. Before speaking, she took a deep breath. "They're ready."

Mick turned to her and said, "And you?" Her voice came out barely over a whisper.

Quinn closed her eyes for a beat but opened them quickly. "I'm ready."

≈≈≈≈

Aspen followed behind Quinn, admiring her broad muscular shoulders again. It was evident, despite Quinn's outward strength, a battle raged inside her. Aspen couldn't imagine how hard it must be for Quinn to be on this trip. *Money?* Was that the reason she agreed to be their guide? Hopefully, Aspen would get the chance to ask her. She'd enjoyed their talk the other night and wanted the opportunity to do it again.

The air was charged when they joined the others. As the anticipation grew, so too did the volume. Mick had to shout multiple times to get everyone's attention.

Finally, they quieted, and all focus fell on Mick. She smiled and slowly bobbed her head. "Okay. It sounds like everyone is raring to get in the water. A few things before we hit the path to the Boiling Pot."

Unicorn Bay. Aspen almost shouted out the nickname they'd given the Boiling Pot but thought better of it. She glanced over at LeAnn, who must have been thinking the same because she appeared to be holding back a giggle.

"Quinn will give a brief rundown of the commands she will use as our raft captain." Mick shifted her gaze to LeAnn and Aspen. "Sorry, but you'll have to listen to it one more time."

Aspen smiled. "I'm good with a final refresher."

Mick stepped up after Quinn finished. "Are there any questions for Quinn?" She gazed around the crowd. "Okay. Looks like we are ready to gear up then. Everyone will need to put on your helmet and PFD."

Aspen leaned toward LeAnn and whispered in her ear, "What's a PFD?"

"Personal flotation device. Or life vest."

Aspen nodded and gave a thumbs up.

"You'll also want to carry your paddle with you," Quinn said. "One, because the guides don't need to be carrying your shit. And two, it serves as a walking stick."

"Let's go." DaKota bounced on the balls of her feet. "I'm so ready for this."

"One last thing," Mick said. "Tina and I will be in the front of the raft."

DaKota crossed her arms over her chest and glared at Tina. "Why can't we trade off? We all want a turn."

Mick held up her hand. "We'll assess that as the day goes on. Tina has the most experience, and it's important to have strength up front. While Quinn will be giving the commands, the people in the front set the pace, so pay close attention and try to match the speed of your strokes with ours."

Peyton and DaKota whispered with each other, but Mick ignored it and continued with her instructions.

Once they were geared up, they began their descent. The guides went ahead, carrying the raft and all the equipment. *Damn.* Aspen had no idea how they did it.

As they made their way down the narrow path through the lush trees, the conversations halted. Partly because of the slippery terrain, but mostly because of the deafening falls. They'd need to practically shout to be heard over the pounding water. The farther they walked, the mist turned into what felt like a steady rain. Aspen inhaled, taking in the dampness.

She tuned out everything and focused on the beauty of her surroundings. There would be plenty of time to panic once they got to the Boiling Pot. She smiled to herself. *Unicorn Bay.*

Chapter Seventeen

Quinn gaped at the swirling water. The Boiling Pot was living up to its name. The water churned like a witch's cauldron. She'd heard about this spot and had seen plenty of videos, but they didn't do it justice. Another bucket list item she could check off. Her stomach lurched. Thoughts of bucket lists, after Stella, always made her uneasy.

As if sensing her nerves, Mick moved up beside her. "This is crazy, isn't it? We've seen a lot of water in our day, but this might be the coolest."

Grateful for Mick, Quinn smiled. "Amazing." She was surprised she even got one word out. The setting had her mesmerized.

"A couple of the clan are a little green around the gills, but they should be all right."

Quinn had been so wrapped up in the moment she'd almost forgotten why they were here. Feeling guilty, she glanced toward the group. "Aspen?"

"I tried to talk to her, but I didn't seem to be making any headway. I'm pretty sure she'd rather be talking to you."

Quinn's head snapped around, and she narrowed her eyes. "Me? Why?"

"Are you serious?" Mick's lip curled, and she rolled her eyes. "She hangs on your every word."

"That's what a good student does. Pays attention to their instructor."

"Sumpin' like that." Mick shook her head. "She trusts you. Which is the biggest reason I said yes to letting her come."

The breath caught in Quinn's chest. *Fuck.* Was she prepared for someone to put so much trust in her? She couldn't handle failing Aspen as she had Stella.

Mick put her hand on Quinn's back, obviously sensing her panic. "There's no accounting for taste. Apparently, I'm too much of a runt for her." Mick squeezed Quinn's biceps. "She's looking for the big guns. Although, they seem to be getting a little soft. Don't they have any gyms in the backwoods?"

Quinn laughed. Mick always knew how to lighten her mood. "I don't live in the backwoods. And yes, they have gyms. Just none like Sal-Rexah."

"Great gym. Stupid name. But I digress." Mick's head motioned in the direction of the group. "I think Aspen could use a little of your calming charm. I'll work with the others, so you can talk to her without DaKota and Peyton offering unhelpful commentary."

Mick started to turn away, but Quinn grabbed her arm. Their gazes met. Quinn blinked back the mist in her eyes. She'd pretend it was from the spray of the water. "Thank you."

"For what?"

"Being my friend. Standing by me, even when I didn't deserve it."

"Don't forget dragging your ass out here, so you can finally get back on the horse."

"Something like that," Quinn said with a smirk.

"Damn it. How many times do I have to tell you that you just don't know how to use that line or say it?"

"Ah, that's right. It's supposed to be sumpin'."

Mick's smile was large, despite the dismissive wave of her hand. "I'm done with this conversation."

≈≈≈≈≈

Bile rose in Aspen's throat, and her stomach roiled as much as the water in front of her. She'd never seen anything like this. The name made perfect sense. It truly looked like a giant boiling pot. She had no idea how they'd be able to put their raft in without it being swallowed up by the water.

She edged away from the group in case she needed to vomit. It wouldn't be a good start to their adventure, and she'd prefer no one saw it. Peyton was too busy with DaKota to notice her absence. She closed her eyes and took in several deep breaths.

She could do this. Quinn and Mick knew what they were doing. Plus, they had another set of guides following along behind should they need help. What could go wrong? *Ugh!* Weren't those the words uttered during every bad horror movie right before someone died? *Get a grip.* This isn't a horror movie, and no one is going to die.

At the thought of death, she flinched. *Quinn.* How was she doing now that they were this close to putting in? Maybe if she focused more on Quinn's plight, she could forget her own fears.

"How are you holding up?" a voice said.

Aspen's eyes popped open. *Speak of the devil.* She started to lie but stopped. She'd promised directness, so that was what Quinn would get. "I've been better."

"You look a little green. As your trusty sidekick, I recommend we sit down for a spell." Quinn pointed to a large boulder about ten yards away. "Come on."

Aspen looped her arm through Quinn's, and she immediately felt more secure as she let herself be led away from the spot she'd been riveted. Quinn's concerned brown eyes were comforting. Her heartbeat slowed as they walked.

Quinn helped her up onto the rock before she jumped onto it herself. The churning water continued to assault her eardrums. "I'm sorry I'm being such a wimp," Aspen said.

"I'd be worried about you if you weren't." Quinn's gaze bore into her. "You should always respect the power of the water."

Was Quinn just trying to make her feel better? "Really?"

"Absolutely."

"Are you nervous, too?"

Quinn's jaw tightened, and her eyes hardened. She opened her mouth but then closed it again. For several beats, she looked into Aspen's eyes. Then she gave a barely perceptible nod.

"I'd be worried about you if you weren't," Aspen said with a grin, hoping mimicking Quinn's words would break the tension.

"Touché." Quinn smiled. "So, Frankie. Are we going to do this?"

Aspen playfully lowered her shoulder and bumped Quinn. "As long as my sidekick promises she'll fish me out of the Zambezi should I fall in."

Quinn put her hand under her chin and rubbed as if she were thinking. "Hmm, well, that all depends."

"On?" Aspen shot her a sideways glance.

"Whether I get a cool sidekick name or not."

"Isn't the Mighty Quinn good enough?"

Quinn shook her head. "Cliché. Stolen from a

movie. You'll have to do better than that."

Aspen knew what Quinn was doing. Keeping her distracted, but she didn't mind. "How about Gigantor?"

"Really?" Quinn slapped her palm to her forehead. "Making fun of my size again."

"Weren't you the one whining that the sidekick can't be large?" Aspen winked. "Besides, I think your size is perfect. Makes me feel safer."

Quinn laughed. "That's what Mick said. Said you didn't feel safe with a runt like her."

"I never said that." Aspen raised her eyebrows. "Where did she get that idea?"

"Mick was being Mick. Trying to distract me from the jitters."

"Did it work?"

"I'm still here, aren't I?" Quinn gazed at Aspen with her lips pursed and eyes narrowed. "What about you, Frankie? Is the pep talk working?"

"Maybe." Aspen grinned. "I think I'm ready to tackle Unicorn Bay now."

"Unicorn Bay?" Quinn scrunched up her nose.

"Yep. LeAnn and I decided to give them all less scary names. Unicorn Bay sounds much more friendly than the Boiling Pot."

Quinn put her hands over her face and shook her head. "Where did I go wrong? I suppose there's rainbows and kittens, too."

"How'd you guess?" Aspen bit her lip, hoping to hide her grin. Little did Quinn know how accurate she was.

The few minutes with Aspen had settled Quinn's nerves. She was going to do this. Life was strange. If someone told her six months ago she would be shooting the rapids on the Zambezi with Mick, she'd have laughed in their face. These past few days had been good for her. It was the first time since Stella's accident that she felt almost like herself.

Quinn shifted her gaze to the sky and put her thumb against her scar. Funny, whenever she thought of Stella, she looked to the heavens because in her mind, Stella was already there. *I love you, babe. This one's for you.* She ran her thumb the length of her scar before shifting her gaze back to the turbulent water.

The local guides were inspecting the equipment for the final time, and Mick was checking that everyone's helmet and life vest were secure.

The excitement was palpable. Large smiles greeted her. Even the normally nonexpressive Claire had a huge grin on her face. Peyton and DaKota bounced around with enough energy to power a city.

"Looks like you guys are raring to go," Quinn said, approaching the group.

"Can't wait," DaKota answered. "This is the coolest trip ever."

"Especially doing this with MickQ," Peyton added. "We need to get a few pictures before we take off, to memorialize the occasion."

"I'm sure the guides have gotten pretty used to that by now," LeAnn said.

"Shit, speaking of pictures," Tina said with a frown. "Did anyone test out our GoPros?"

"Handled." DaKota slid up next to Tina and put her arm around her waist. "Peyton and I tested them all out this morning. We should get some epic footage."

"If there's nothing else, it sounds like it's time to get this party started," Mick said. "We'll be running rapids one through eight before we have to portage around number nine, where we'll have a little snack before moving on."

"Come on, can't we do it?" DaKota said.

Mick shook her head. "We already discussed this. It's called Commercial Suicide for a reason. It's a grade six."

"I bet if I slipped the guys some money, they'd let us do it," Peyton said.

Quinn clamped her lips together, hoping Mick would handle the situation. While Peyton and DaKota's money gave the group opportunities they wouldn't normally be afforded, this was one occasion it wouldn't be a positive.

"We're not doing it," Mick said.

Peyton started to protest, but Mick held up her hand. "We can waste a bunch more time arguing about this, or we can get into the water and start our adventure."

Brilliant. Redirection always tended to work, and today was no exception. They appeared to lose interest in the argument and hurried to the raft, leaving everyone else behind.

Quinn held out her arm to Aspen. "May I?"

Aspen smiled and took it. "Thanks."

Quinn recognized the fear behind her eyes, so she leaned in. "Just remember your training. You'll do fine. What's the key?"

"Not to panic," Aspen said and steeled her jaw.

"You've got it, Frankie. Let's do it." Quinn took Aspen's hand to steady her as she climbed into the raft.

Don't panic. Don't panic. Don't panic. Aspen repeated Quinn's words as they pushed off from the shore. She made sure her foot was firmly in the foothold and the other partially under the seat in front of her. *T-grip.* Checking her hand, she ensured the T was firmly clasped in her palm.

They bobbed through Boiling Pot, and she knew it was nothing compared to what was to come. Quinn called out commands, and Aspen concentrated on her rowing. *Forward. Back. Turn left. Turn right.* Her concentration so focused, she didn't pay attention to what lay ahead.

Quinn called out. "First rapid will be the Wall."

LeAnn glanced at Aspen. "Pink Floyd, here we come."

Aspen heard Quinn chuckle behind her but was afraid to turn. She didn't want to mess up her rowing.

"You got your angle, Quinn?" Mick called. "Looks like we have a pretty strong eddy."

"I see it."

Aspen peered at the water, trying to remember what an eddy was. She spotted the circular movement that created a whirlpool. *Duh.* Now she remembered. *Focus.* She didn't want to miss any of Quinn's commands.

"This one's called the Wall because our goal is to paddle through to the wall on your left."

Aspen braced herself. The whitewater churned in front of them. How would it feel when their raft hit it? She'd soon find out.

"Forward," Quinn called out.

Mick and Tina picked up the pace, so Aspen tightened her grip on her paddle and matched their strokes.

"You've got this, Aspen," Quinn said right as they hit the beginning of the whitewater.

Oh, shit. The raft pitched forward, and Aspen's mind went blank. Her heart raced as the water pounded against the raft.

"Turn left," Quinn yelled above the sound of the raging water.

Left. Her mind was still blank. *Backward or forward? Back.* Aspen dipped her paddle. Another wave lashed the raft, causing Aspen to bounce off her seat several inches.

"Lean in. Lean in." The volume in Quinn's voice raised.

Aspen leaned in, waiting for the command to get down. She didn't have to wait long before they were pounded, and the front of the raft lifted.

"Get down," Quinn yelled.

Aspen didn't need to be told twice; she slid to the floor of the raft. She felt like a tiny bobber adrift in the water. Her stomach roiled, but she ignored the sensation. A spray of water splashed into her face, taking her breath away. She sputtered and spat a stream of water out, nearly hitting LeAnn, who huddled near her. *Lesson learned.* She needed to keep her mouth shut.

"Paddle forward," Quinn called out.

Aspen froze, not registering what she was supposed to do. Adrenaline surged through her body and made her shaky. The others leapt back into position on the side of the raft. *Shit.* She lurched up and nearly toppled over the side.

A large hand grabbed her. *Quinn.* How embarrassing. The first rapid, and she nearly fell out. Her gaze shifted to Quinn, but a large burst of water pelted her in the face, blurring her vision, but she still felt Quinn's comforting hand holding her in place.

"You're doing fine." Quinn loosened her grip. "Just relax. You're steady, so I'm going to let you go."

"Thanks," Aspen muttered, thankful for the water that obscured her view and hopefully did the same to Quinn. Aspen dug her paddle into the river and tried to keep pace with Mick.

The Wall loomed large ahead. They were almost there. Aspen felt as if she'd been thrown into a large mixing bowl and the beaters were turned on high.

"Forward."

Aspen paddled harder.

"Turn right. Turn right."

The Wall was almost upon them, and they weren't turning quick enough. *Why?*

"Peyton, turn right. Peyton, paddle back."

Peyton followed the command, and the boat turned before it slammed into the wall.

"Paddle forward."

With a few more strokes, the raft hit calmer waters, and it bounced lightly, nothing like the beating they'd taken earlier.

Mick raised her paddle and let out a victory cry. The others joined in the cheers.

Aspen's heart raced, but pride swelled in her chest. She'd done it. Made it through her first rapid. Mick slowed the pace, so Aspen was able to look over her shoulder at Quinn.

Quinn noticed her and winked. "Good job,

Frankie."

"That was so much fun." Aspen beamed.

"Whoa, careful there." Quinn pointed at Aspen's hand, which no longer held on to the T.

Shit. Aspen grabbed the top of the paddle and firmly gripped it. "Sorry."

"No harm, no foul." Quinn shifted her gaze to the water ahead. "Relax for a spell. It won't be long before we get to our second rapid. The Bridge."

"Over troubled water," LeAnn sang.

Aspen joined in and grinned at Quinn before turning her attention forward.

"Tell me again why I put you two back here with me."

"We entertain you," Aspen said.

Quinn snorted. "True. Very true."

They approached the Victoria Falls Bridge. *Duh, not very original.* The rapid namers could have come up with something more creative.

"Holy shit," Claire yelled and pointed. "What kind of fools would do that?"

Aspen gasped as the bungee cord snapped the jumper back into the air, and the person on the other end bobbed up and down several times.

Mick laughed. "They're probably saying what idiot would raft these rapids."

"Speaking of," Quinn called out. "Show time."

∾∾∾∾

Quinn loosened her grip on the paddle and took a deep breath. *So far, so good.* They'd just come out of the fourth rapid, Morning Glory, with no issues. The group worked well together and followed her commands perfectly. Aspen and LeAnn were holding their own. Except for early on, when Aspen nearly tumbled from the raft, there had been no other incidents.

The calmer water gave them a reprieve before they hit the next rapid. Quinn took the opportunity to take in the large rock walls on each side of the narrow river. The enormity of the boulders made her feel small and insignificant in comparison.

Stella's kayak slamming into a large rock jolted Quinn out of her calm. *Stop.* She had to stay focused on the here and now, or it could become dangerous. *Keep your head in the game.* She repeated the line to herself several times before she could draw herself back to the moment.

Needing a distraction, she lightly poked Aspen with her paddle. "Hey, you ready for the Stairway to Heaven?"

"Or is it the Highway to Hell?" Aspen shot back.

Quinn groaned. "Did you two rename them all?"

"Three. Don't forget Tina."

"Seriously, she teamed up with you losers?"

"Hey now, who are you calling a loser? We handled those first few rapids like a boss," Aspen said. "Right, LeAnn?"

"Absolutely." LeAnn raised her paddle over her head. "Bring on the Highway to Hell."

Quinn pretended to cover her ears but then smiled at the pair.

"Okay, team," Quinn called out. "Forward."

Like clockwork, the rowers dipped their paddles into the river, and the raft surged forward.

This was the first true class V rapid on their journey. Quinn had researched the run extensively and knew what course she wanted to take. Too far right would take them over a large pour over, which not only resulted in a significant drop, but it would land them in a strong recirculating pool. Unfortunately, the far left would put them into a large crashing wave that had been named the Catcher's Mitt. *Time to thread the needle.*

The paddlers were doing great and had them lined up to hit where she wanted to go but were drifting slightly to the left. Quinn yelled out, "Turn right."

The raft didn't move as quickly to the right as she'd expected, so she studied her rowers. *Shit.* Aspen was still paddling forward. "Aspen, turn right."

Aspen sat up straighter, pulled her paddle out of the water, and stared at it. They were still not getting to the right fast enough. If Aspen didn't paddle soon, they'd end up in the Catcher's Mitt, which would surely lead them to capsize.

"Aspen, paddle back," Quinn called out. "Now."

The words sent her into action, and Aspen began frantically paddling backward.

Good job. Quinn leaned into her paddle and helped with the turn. Just a little more and they'd hit in the perfect spot, but would they make it?

Only a few more seconds, and they would be there. Quinn took in a deep breath and readied herself for the plunge. Even if they hit the rapid perfectly, they were in for a large drop. At least eight meters, which was higher than a two-story building.

The water churned around them as they approached the rapid. They were exactly where Quinn wanted them. "Forward."

The paddlers on the right switched directions.

"Forward," Quinn called again.

Mick picked up the pace, and the others followed her lead.

Water lashed at the raft and spilled over the sides.

The front of the raft hit the beginning of the drop. Mick and Tina disappeared from sight as the water sprayed up. The back of the raft went up.

"Get down," Quinn ordered.

The rowers scrambled off the edge of the raft.

They hunkered in the middle.

Quinn bore down, keeping her paddle in the water, directing them away from the rougher water to each side.

They began their descent.

Screams rang out.

A wall of water slammed into Quinn's face. She couldn't see anything other than the rushing waves.

Her stomach lurched. She felt weightless as they plunged downward.

With a jolt, they hit the bottom. Adrenaline coursed through her.

Yes! They'd done it, but now wasn't time to celebrate. She checked the surroundings and decided to keep them down while getting across the large wave they were soon to encounter.

It slammed against them, but the course of the raft held. Quinn continued to put her paddle into the water to keep them steady.

Now. "Paddle forward."

Like lightning, the group returned to the sides and paddled frantically to keep pace with Mick and Tina.

The rest was easy, and they shot into calmer waters.

Mick was the first to celebrate. She raised her paddle over her head. "Hell yeah."

The others joined her, all screaming their own exclamations of victory.

Quinn smiled. *Fuck*. They'd done it. It had been more than five years since she'd taken anyone over a class V rapid. It felt good. Damned good. She hoped anyone who saw water streaming down her face would think it was from the river. Quinn stood and raised her arms triumphantly. "Yes! Great job, crew."

∞⋇∞⋇∞

Aspen's shoulders relaxed. She'd not realized how tense they were until they dropped into a normal position. That had been some rush. The feeling of careening into the steep drop was both exhilarating and terrifying. She couldn't wait to get to her notebook to describe the experience.

She'd enjoyed it but didn't think she'd become a thrill seeker anytime soon. Her hands still trembled from the rush of adrenaline.

The slower pace of the river gave her time to check out the impressive surroundings. The high black rock walls somehow made her feel small. The water pounding against the sides helped her understand how water could cut through solid rock and make a canyon.

Mick and Tina kept the pace slow while Peyton and DaKota chattered excitedly, reliving the moment they plunged into Stairway to Heaven. Aspen smiled to herself. It was in these moments that Peyton's endearing qualities showed. She beamed like a child at the experience, and her excitement was contagious, but it also made Aspen realize just how different they were. Peyton was like a frat boy who constantly sought out the next adventure, while Aspen took a more cerebral approach.

She loved trying these things, too, but she preferred to cherish and savor them through her writing. The act of describing them enriched her experience, while Peyton had already moved on to the next. The churning of the water increased. It wouldn't be long before the next was upon them.

The normally chill Claire was waving her arms with more animation than Aspen was used to. Either she was upset about something, or the adrenaline finally woke her. When she turned, her huge smile told Aspen it was the latter.

As they continued down the river, the current increased. It wouldn't be long before they hit the next rapid. Aspen searched her memory but couldn't come up with the name.

As if reading her mind, Mick called out. "We're heading to the Devil's Toilet Bowl."

"Let the flushing begin," Tina added. Mick and Tina chuckled at the corny joke. They seemed to be developing a nice camaraderie, plus they'd managed the front of the raft masterfully.

"We are on to the Kitten's Water Dish," LeAnn shouted.

"You guys are killing me." Quinn groaned. "The Toilet Bowl is a short one, so we hope to be in and out."

DaKota laughed. "Demon's Swirly."

"Oh, no. Now they've got you doing it, too," Quinn said. "Mick, when did we lose control of this group?"

"You mean we had control?" Mick asked.

"True. Very true." Quinn raised her paddle. "Okay, we're about there. Time to put on our game face."

Aspen tightened her grip on her paddle, making sure to firmly set the T in her palm. Quinn calling out commands put her at ease as they approached the frothy water.

In practically a blink of the eye, they shot through the two large waves and came out the other side. Other than being drenched a couple of times, they made it through with little trouble. *This isn't half bad.* Her earlier fears were nearly gone.

When they emerged and the raft slowed, Aspen took in the breathtaking sights of the gorge. This area seemed to hold more greenery than the earlier areas.

"Enjoy the beauty and recover your strength," Quinn said.

Aspen relaxed and took in a deep breath. The fresh smell of the water invigorated her. *What a day.* The sun beat down, but the cool water caressed her skin, almost chilling her. As they floated down the river, she took in the natural beauty.

Chapter Eighteen

Quinn dug her paddle into the water to turn the raft. After the Devil's Toilet Bowl, they'd slowed their pace to let everyone catch their breath. Many did the entire twenty-four rapids in one day, but since they were doing the stretch in two, it gave them time to enjoy the scenery.

She glanced over her shoulder. The oar rig and the two guides in kayaks floated along behind. They were amazing. Day after day, they challenged the river and usually won. She wished she'd been able to watch them following behind. More than likely, they made it look easy. Maybe on one of the rapids, she'd turn her GoPro backward to see if she could capture their run. She didn't want to try it on Gulliver's Travels, though. Something told her this would be the toughest one so far. She'd thought the Stairway to Heaven would be, but it turned out relatively easy. Paranoia was probably creeping in since things had been going so well.

The crew chattered amongst themselves. Everyone seemed to be having a great time, which was what every tour company wanted. She'd missed this more than she realized, being here with Mick. Renting out boats and Jet Skis to tourists wasn't exactly the most rewarding career.

Over the last couple of years, she'd followed the Pink Triangle Adventures. It seemed Mick continually added new excursions, and if Quinn were honest, it sometimes made her sad that she was no longer a part of it. She ran her hand through her already drying hair. Now wasn't the time to lament what she'd missed; instead, she wanted to savor the moment.

The gorge rose around them, so she looked up, taking in all its natural beauty. She searched the upper banks, hoping to catch sight of an animal, but so far, she'd had no success. The sun was high in the sky, signifying it was nearly lunchtime. Her stomach growled in agreement. All the exertion was making her hungry. She was thankful they'd portaged around the ninth rapid, Commercial Suicide. Only Gulliver's Travels and the Midnight Diner to conquer before her stomach would be tended to.

Mick turned, and their gazes met. "This next one is the long one, around seven hundred meters."

"I've never gotten metrics," Claire said. "Can you give it to us in layman's terms?"

"About seven football fields," Mick answered.

"Holy fuck." LeAnn rubbed her chest. "Every time we come out of one of those, I swear my organs are loose and are sloshing around inside my body."

"For me, it's like riding a mechanical bull," Aspen said. "Something tells me that I'm going to be sore for days after this."

"Likely," Quinn said. "Your body is getting tossed around in ways it's not used to."

"I'm sure Lilliputian Lane will bounce us around plenty," LeAnn said.

Quinn smiled. "I refuse to comment on your ridiculous renaming."

❧❧❧❧

Aspen couldn't wait to tell Gina how outdoorsy she was being. *Hmph.* And Gina didn't think Aspen had it in her. It surprised her how much she'd enjoyed the experience so far. Her nervousness long forgotten, now she could simply enjoy the moment.

No doubt, Quinn was right, she'd be sore in the morning with all the jolting from the waves, but the feeling of accomplishment and overcoming her fears would make it all worthwhile.

She gazed around at the terrain, remembering she had a GoPro on her helmet. She slowly swept the area from one side to the other. Even with the pictures, she wasn't sure she could capture the scene in writing, but she would try.

"Okay, crew," Quinn said, drawing Aspen's attention back to the moment. "We will be in the midst of Gulliver's Travels before you know it. As Mick said, this is the longest one of the day. There are several different sections, but I won't tell you the names because I don't want to hear from this lot." Quinn pointed her paddle toward Aspen and LeAnn.

"Aw, come on, buzzkill," Aspen joked. "We find ourselves hysterical. Right, LeAnn?"

LeAnn nodded. "Hysterical!"

Quinn shook her head and smiled. "It's go time. Forward."

Mick and Tina dug their paddles into the river, and the raft surged forward. The speed increased when the rest joined in.

They hit the first wave of Gulliver's Travels, and the water surged against the raft, driving it closer to the rock.

Quinn called out, "Turn left."

Aspen thought for a fraction of a second and then paddled forward. The raft moved away from the danger and glided through the spray.

"Get down," Quinn called.

Aspen slid to the floor a fraction of a second before LeAnn started to move inside. They hit a large wave, and LeAnn flew into the air. Her mouth opened in an O as she began to fall backward. Without thinking, Aspen grabbed her arm and held on with all her strength. The wave listed the boat to the right, which gave Aspen the extra leverage to pull LeAnn to her.

LeAnn collapsed next to her and gasped for breath. "Holy shit. Thank you."

Aspen wanted to hug the frightened woman, but the thought was interrupted when the raft crashed into another wave. She hazarded a glance over her shoulder at Quinn. The sinewy muscles in her shoulders showed the effort she exerted keeping the raft on track. With a final hard pull to the left, they passed the large wave that threatened and hit the more stable whitewater.

"Forward," Quinn yelled.

Before Aspen moved back to the side of the raft, her gaze met Quinn's. Aspen smiled, and Quinn returned it.

"Good save," Quinn mouthed. Aspen understood the words, even though they weren't loud enough to be heard over the raging water.

"Thanks," Aspen mouthed back before she turned to the front and dipped her paddle into the water.

The next couple of rushes were less eventful than the first, although they were forced to get down several times as the water lashed at the raft. This was by far the roughest water they'd hit so far, or maybe it just seemed that way because the stretch seemed to go on forever.

Aspen wiped the water out of her eyes, for what she swore was the tenth time. From what she could tell, it didn't look much farther to the end.

"One more, babe," Peyton said over her shoulder. "You still holding up?"

Aspen nodded. "I'm good." She started to put her hand on Peyton's back but stopped when she remembered Quinn's words. *Don't take your hand off the paddle.*

"Forward," Quinn commanded.

She'd only made one pass with her paddle when Quinn called out again. "Get down."

Peyton turned to the center of the raft, and a large wave slammed against the side. Peyton hadn't had the T-grip in her palm, so the paddle drove forward and smashed against the side of DaKota's cheek.

DaKota's head snapped back. She stumbled. Then she disappeared over the side of the raft.

Shit. No! Aspen lunged toward DaKota, but she was already gone.

Peyton's mouth dropped open, then she screamed. "DaKota."

Aspen's mind went blank for a second, and then she cried out, "The grab rope."

DaKota bobbed in the water, keeping pace with the raft. Quinn skittered to the side shouting, "Take the grab rope."

DaKota's fingers wrapped around it as another wave pounded them.

Quinn glanced over her shoulder. "Peyton and Claire, drag her in. I need to steer before we hit that wave wrong." Quinn leapt to her spot at the back of the boat, while Peyton and Claire moved into action.

Aspen tried to focus on paddling while her friends yanked DaKota into the boat. Blood streamed down DaKota's face from where Peyton's paddle hit her. She fell to the floor of the raft, and her chest heaved as she sucked in air.

"You okay?" Worry lines creased Peyton's fore-head. "I'm sorry. I didn't mean to hit you."

"Get down," Quinn yelled. "Get down."

Aspen shot to the floor and looked to the front of the boat. She gasped, and her heart raced. She had to glance up to look at Mick and Tina, who must have been ten feet higher than where she sat. It took a moment for her to register what was happening. "Fuck," she screamed right before Mick flew over the top of her head, and she felt herself falling backward.

Everything seemed to move in slow motion. The raft shot straight up and then tipped backward. Aspen clenched her hands around the paddle and closed her eyes. They were going over.

The only sound Aspen heard was the gurgling of water.

Underwater. She panicked. But which way was up?

Don't swim. All her instincts told her it was wrong, she needed to save herself.

No. She didn't know which way was up. What if she swam the wrong way and went farther underwater? She held her breath and followed the instructions Quinn gave earlier.

She flipped onto her back and let her life vest push her to the surface. The water continued to rage around her, but she kept her mouth shut and hoped too much wouldn't rush up her nose. Her head popped up out of the water, and she gasped. *Air. Sweet air.* She inhaled deeper and held it in her lungs.

Now that she could breathe, she needed to get back to the raft. She glanced around and spotted it off to her left. Quinn and Mick were pulling themselves on top of the overturned raft, and the others bobbed in the water.

ᘒᘒᘒᘒ

With one final burst of strength, Quinn yanked herself onto the overturned raft. She collapsed, gasping for breath. Mick landed with a thud beside her and began coughing.

Images rushed through Quinn's mind. She shook her head, trying to clear it. She couldn't do this now, but the images continued to assault her. Stella. CPR. Surging water. Hospital bed. More angry rapids. Stella. Turning blue. Her skin so cold. Lifeless eyes.

"Quinn," she heard a voice call. "I need your help. Come back. Aspen needs you."

Quinn blinked a couple of times. *Aspen.* The images disappeared, and she was back on top of the raft. She turned and gazed into Mick's familiar eyes.

"Thank god," Mick said. "You're back."

Quinn breathed in deeply and scanned the area. LeAnn was only a few strokes from the raft. Mick and Quinn moved in unison; each grabbed an arm and lifted LeAnn atop the upside-down raft. LeAnn rolled onto her side and coughed up water.

Quinn stood, hoping to get a better view of the river. A wave hit, and Quinn nearly toppled over, but she spread her stance to regain her balance.

Tina slammed into the raft and snatched the grab rope. She pulled herself up before Quinn or Mick could help.

Mick pointed. Quinn and Tina looked in the direction she indicated. Claire and DaKota bobbed about fifteen yards in front of the craft, struggling to swim back. The harder they fought against the current, the farther away the surging water swept them.

Shit. Where was Aspen? Peyton? Quinn immediately began searching. The bouncing raft and spray from the waves made it difficult for her to see. A heaviness descended on her chest with each second that passed without spotting Aspen.

Wait. Quinn squinted into the murky water. About twenty yards out, a shock of blond hair caught her eye. *Aspen.* Quinn took a deep breath. She needed to appear calm, or Aspen would likely panic.

Quinn waved. "You've got this, Aspen. Keep your body angled toward us and paddle with your arms."

The turbulent water rushed around Aspen, and the spray lashed at her face, making it hard for Quinn to maintain a sightline on her. Butterflies fluttered in Quinn's stomach.

Images popped into Quinn's mind. Stella. *No!* "Aspen," Quinn called out. "I'm right here. You've got the perfect line. Keep your legs tucked."

Movement about ten feet from Aspen caught Quinn's eye. Peyton bobbed through a whitecap that had obscured her from view. Her flushed face held a grimace, but she appeared to be okay.

Both women were on course to intersect the raft at nearly the same time if Quinn's estimation was correct.

Peyton arrived at the raft a couple of seconds before Aspen and snared the grab line. When Aspen was only a few yards away, a large wave struck her and slammed her against the raft. She hit with a thud, and her head snapped back. She gasped for breath and frantically reached for the grab rope.

Quinn dropped to her knees and reached out her hand to Aspen. Peyton's hand shot past Aspen's and clutched Quinn's arm. *What the hell?* Apparently, it was every woman for herself.

Peyton never glanced in Aspen's direction. With gusto, Quinn yanked Peyton onto the raft, sending her skittering across the slippery surface.

There was panic and hurt in Aspen's eyes. Quinn wanted to erase both. "It's okay. I've got you." Quinn easily lifted Aspen from the whitewater that still beat against the craft.

Gently, Quinn lowered her to the slippery surface. Aspen flipped over onto all fours and coughed. Foamy water sprayed out of her mouth, and she coughed again.

Quinn put her hand on Aspen's back and knelt beside her. Another wave struck the vessel, causing it to rock in the current. Aspen gasped and grabbed Quinn.

Without thought, Quinn wrapped her arm around Aspen and held her tightly. "It's okay. You're safe. Just breathe."

Aspen took a few more ragged breaths and coughed once more before her breathing returned to normal. Once it did, Quinn released her hold and helped Aspen flop back into a sitting position. Quinn didn't say anything while Aspen took in cleansing breaths.

Quinn decided to speak once Aspen's eyes went from panic to calm. "You'll be all right. You just swallowed a little water."

"How did I manage to do that?" Aspen asked.

Shit. This wasn't good. She pointed over her shoulder with her thumb. "You just...um..."

Aspen laughed. "Joking. Sorry, by the look on your face, it was a bad joke."

Quinn's heart thumped in her chest. "You scared the shit out of me."

"Sorry," Aspen said again, giving Quinn a sheepish smile. "You do good work, though. Your sidekick status is in good standing."

"Glad to be of service, Frankie." She glanced away, not wanting Aspen to see all the emotions surging through her. More than anything, she wanted to wrap Aspen in a bear hug. She couldn't be sure if it were to comfort Aspen or to comfort herself.

"Thanks again. You're the best."

Quinn jumped to her feet. "I need to check on the others." She needed to put some distance between her and Aspen.

A look of bewilderment crossed Aspen's face, and she gave Quinn a sad smile before Quinn turned away.

The others were shaken but okay. The guides following them had sped past their watercraft, at Mick's insistence, and went after Claire and DaKota. The duo sat in the middle of the oar raft while the guides fluttered around them. *Thank god.* Everyone was okay.

Chapter Nineteen

Aspen didn't know what she'd expected from Bobo Beach, but this wasn't it. Maybe she'd seen too many movies about tourists stranded alone in the wilderness, but the large expanse of sand nestled between the rocky walls covered in greenery had a feeling of desolation. The enormous walls towering around them reminded her of the power of nature, a lesson she'd learned earlier in the swirling water.

They were the first campers to arrive and had staked out the flat area to the right of where they'd landed. It would offer them some seclusion from the other two groups that were also scheduled to camp in the area tonight but still put them near enough to the river that they could hear the water.

While the walk from the river wasn't far, the beach sloped upward from the water, so lugging the gear up the incline had proved strenuous.

"Grab the other end," Aspen said to LeAnn. They'd been helping the guides unload the oar rig, per Quinn and Mick's request. Sweat dripped off her brow and bounced off the container full of supplies.

"This shit is heavier than I thought," LeAnn said as she heaved the other end.

"No kidding. The guides throw this shit around like it's nothing."

They took several steps across the beach before LeAnn responded. "I seriously need to get back to the gym." LeAnn ran her cheek against her shoulder, trying to wipe the sweat away.

"Do you want to put it down?"

"Nah. Let's get this dropped off, then we can take a breather."

They trudged through the sand without speaking. Walking through sand was difficult enough, but with their load, with each step, Aspen's calves burned. The twenty-some yards they had left to go seemed like two miles, but her stubborn streak kicked in. This stupid container wouldn't beat her.

With only a short way to go, one of the guides trotted past them with a container bigger than the one they carried resting on his shoulders. He set it down and headed back toward the raft.

Aspen groaned. "Did you see that?"

"It was probably the light stuff," LeAnn offered.

"Yeah, that must be it." Aspen nodded toward the pile of supplies. "Let's just put it down over here."

They dropped it with a thud. Both panted, trying to catch their breath. As if on cue, they flopped onto the top of the container and bumped into each other as they fell.

LeAnn laughed. "We're such a pathetic pair."

"No doubt, but we were traumatized today, so we're in a weakened state."

"Speaking of, I didn't even think to ask you how you're doing."

"I think I'm okay." Aspen paused and smiled. "No, I know I'm okay."

LeAnn leaned her shoulder into Aspen. "That's the spirit. It's scary the first time. Hell, it's scary whenever it happens."

"I felt so helpless. Out of control. One minute

you're riding along, and then, bam, you're in the water. It was all a big blur."

"I'm just glad you weathered it so well. I think it helped having Mick and Quinn. I feel safe with them."

"Me too." Aspen smiled. "I suppose we should get that last box."

"Ugh." LeAnn got to her feet with a dramatic groan. "Fine."

"I guess it's only fair," Aspen said, glancing at the flurry of activity. "I wouldn't have a clue how to set one of those up." While Aspen and LeAnn had been carrying gear, the others had begun pitching the tents. They'd placed their three tents close together in a triangular pattern with a place for a fire in the middle while Quinn and Mick had taken their gear about twenty-five yards back.

"Can I ask you a question?" LeAnn asked as they started back toward the shore to get the last container.

"Sure." Aspen braced herself. In her experience, an uncomfortable inquiry would follow.

"Why did you decide to come on this trip?"

Yep, uncomfortable. Aspen opened her mouth to say, *it sounded like fun,* but she stopped, remembering her motto. Frank and forthright. "Because Peyton wanted me to."

"Oh." LeAnn hesitated. "You didn't want to?"

As they walked, Aspen glanced at LeAnn out of the corner of her eye. "Off the record?"

"Of course."

"Things have been a little off between Peyton and I." Aspen fought the urge to scratch her neck as heat rose. "I thought maybe it would be the thing we needed to get back on track."

"Has it worked?"

Aspen sighed.

"I'm sorry. I shouldn't pry." LeAnn put her hand on Aspen's arm and stopped walking. They stood facing each other.

"It's okay. It's nice to have a friend here to talk to. As long as it doesn't put you in an awkward position."

"Not at all. It's not like Peyton and I have deep discussions." LeAnn smiled and nodded toward the others. "Those three get into their own little world sometimes, so I'm ecstatic that you agreed to come. And for the record, I think it is damned impressive that your first experience with whitewater is on the Zambezi. It takes guts."

They started walking again. "Thank you for saying that. DaKota, and sometimes Peyton, reminds me that I'm the weak link that can't kayak Ghostrider. Makes me feel like an outsider."

"Nonsense. They both know that kayaking Ghostrider takes experience. Hell, I'm leaning toward not doing it myself."

"Really?" It would be nice to have someone else sitting on the sidelines with her, but she wouldn't tell LeAnn that. She wouldn't want to unduly influence her.

"Yep. I'll wait and see how I'm feeling by then."

They reached the container, and both stared at it without making a move to pick it up. Aspen gazed at LeAnn. "Is this going to weigh a ton?"

"Possibly, but the sooner we do it, the quicker we can put our feet up and relax."

Aspen smiled. "I like the way you think."

They each grabbed a handle and heaved. It easily lifted off the ground, and LeAnn let out a whoop. "It's our lucky day."

"The river gods are smiling on us," Aspen said.

They started back up the beach with their load. This time, Aspen enjoyed the movement of the sand under her feet since it didn't feel as if she were walking through quicksand.

"You never answered my question," LeAnn said.

"Which one?"

"Whether being here with Peyton has helped mend things."

Aspen shook her head. "Honestly, no." She knew she should say something more instead of leaving it with the vague response. "If anything, I feel even more distant. Can I tell you something that's going to sound stupid?"

"Nothing's stupid among friends."

"I feel like I'm changing." Aspen stopped walking and made eye contact with LeAnn. "We've only been here a couple of days, but something in me is shifting." Aspen shook her head. "Crazy, I know. People don't change in a couple of days."

"They do if they're ready to. If they're ripe."

Aspen held up her arm and pretended to sniff her armpit. "Definitely ripe."

LeAnn laughed. "That's one of the things I like about you. You don't take yourself too seriously. But honestly, I think when we're ready to change, the people and circumstances that we need present themselves, if we listen to them."

"You don't think I'm being silly?"

"Not at all. A trip like this can be life-changing."

"You mean I could be having a whitewater awakening?" Aspen chuckled and raised her eyebrows.

"I love it." They arrived near the campsite and

dropped their container. "Aspen Kennedy," LeAnn said loudly as she held her arms up toward the sky. "This is your whitewater awakening."

Aspen raised her arms and looked to the sky. "Yes!"

"What the hell are you two going on about?" DaKota said with a laugh as she rummaged through one of the containers.

"Girl talk." LeAnn gave her a sly smile.

DaKota shook her head. "Do you think when you're done, we can have you do something for us?"

"What's that?" LeAnn asked.

"Claire and Tina are tent-pitching machines." DaKota motioned with her head to where Claire and Tina were stretching out the canvas about thirty yards away. "They've got your tent up already, LeAnn. They wanted me to help with something on ours, but I've gotta finish helping Peyton if I can ever find the damned net."

"We can help out," Aspen said.

DaKota pointed to a small pack. "The gear got messed up. That's Mick and Quinn's, so I need someone to take it to them."

"Why don't I help Claire?" LeAnn said, looking at Aspen. "You can take that to Quinn."

꙳ ꙳ ꙳ ꙳

Quinn pounded the stake into the ground and pulled on the rope. Mick left her to set up the tent on her own, while Mick checked in with the local guides, which was how Quinn preferred it. They'd never done well putting up a tent together. While Mick was methodical and planned out everything before beginning, Quinn went right to work adjusting as she went. Ironically, both methods took about the same time to complete. They'd tested it several times over the years, and they usually finished within five minutes of each other.

Aspen wandered over. Sweat dripped down her flushed face. "We had some of your stuff." Aspen set the pack down.

"Whoa," Quinn said. "Looks like you better sit down and have some water."

Aspen sank into the folding chair near the tent. "Thanks. I didn't realize how damned heavy some of the equipment is. The guides hoist the boxes like they're loaded with feathers, but I swear they're filled with bricks."

Quinn pulled a bottle of water out of the cooler. Ice chunks rolled down the sides, so she shook it off before handing it to Aspen. "Nice and cold."

Aspen took a big gulp. "Perfect. I chose my sidekick well." She closed the bottle and ran it along behind her neck. She let her head flop back and closed her eyes.

Quinn turned away and pounded on the next stake. When she finished, she turned back to Aspen. "How was today for you?"

"It was harder than I expected but not as scary."

The answer intrigued Quinn, so she stopped and gazed at Aspen. "I'm afraid you're going to have to give me more than that."

Aspen sighed. "I can admit it now. I was terrified. I thought it would be a constant adrenaline rush. Like I was risking my life the entire time."

Quinn flinched.

"Oh, my god, I'm so sorry." Aspen's face turned

a deeper shade of red. "That was so insensitive of me."

"No, no." Quinn held up her hand. "I never want you to censor yourself with me."

"But I don't want to bring up painful memories."

"It's okay. The memories are mine. I can't hide from them or expect others to tiptoe around me. All I want is honesty, Frankie."

Aspen smiled and relaxed farther against the back of her chair. "Okay. Back to the original question. After the first couple waves, it wasn't as scary as I thought it would be. I started having fun. Actual fun."

Quinn laughed. "Care to define the difference between fun and actual fun?"

Aspen narrowed her eyes and pursed her lips. Quinn stifled a chuckle. A stern look didn't suit Aspen, but Quinn would keep that to herself.

"There's fun. Like in, sure I'm not hating it. But then there is actual fun, where you forget everything else in your life because you're absorbed in it. Everything else disappears."

"Absorbed in fun." Quinn nodded. "I like it. Maybe that should be the new slogan for Pink Triangle Adventures. We absorb you in fun."

Aspen pointed. "That'll cost you. I don't give away marketing slogans for free."

"Even after I fished you out of the river?" Quinn put her hand against her chest, feigning offense.

"Fine. You can have it. As long as you promise that you'll fish me out again the next time."

"Deal. But let's hope there isn't a next time." Quinn smiled.

A loud ruckus interrupted their conversation. Peyton and DaKota were tossing a volleyball back and forth across a net.

"Oh, god." Aspen groaned. "Where do those two get their energy? I can't believe they brought a volleyball net."

"Competitive adrenaline junkies. I've met plenty like them." *Ouch.* That came out judgmental and harsh. "I mean...I just mean that the two seem to be thrill seekers."

"Definitely." She gave the pair one last glance before turning her gaze back to Quinn. "You want the truth?"

"Always."

"Sometimes, it's tiring."

Quinn hadn't expected that response. She tried to keep her expression even. "How so?"

"It's one adventure after another." Aspen's gaze shifted to the sky. "Sometimes...I don't know...."

"You'd like a few quiet moments?" Quinn ventured a guess, not sure why she felt so free talking with Aspen.

Aspen's head snapped around, and her eyes widened. "Exactly. How did you know?"

"Adventures are fun, but they can't sustain you. At least they can't for me."

Aspen flashed a smile. "Says the woman that used to thrill seek for a living."

"Right. But seriously, at the end of the day, after the thrills are over, it all comes down to having someone you can sit and have a beer with while you watch the sunset."

Aspen gazed out at the water. "I couldn't agree more."

"Hey, you guys," Peyton yelled. "Stop the chattering and get over here and play volleyball."

The rest of the crew, including Mick, was

gathered on the makeshift court. Quinn shook her head. "I've got to finish setting up the tent."

"What the hell have you been doing over there?" Mick called.

"Sheesh." Quinn held up her bottle of water. "Can't I get a little bit of a break?"

"Slacker." Mick laughed. "Get your ass over here. I'll help you with the tent later. I need a setter."

"Damn it, can't someone else set for you?" Quinn wondered if the group would pick up on their shtick.

DaKota's gaze shifted from Quinn to Mick, and then back again, her eyes so narrow they were only slits. Quinn bit her lip, trying not to laugh.

"Wait, what?" Peyton pointed toward Quinn and then turned to Mick. "She sets for you?"

"Sumpin' like that," Mick answered.

Aspen laughed. "They're fucking with you guys." She stood from her chair and reached out her hand. "Come on, setter."

Quinn smiled and let the much smaller woman pull her up. "Do you want me to set for you, too?"

"Obviously." Aspen winked.

"Okay, we're coming," Quinn responded. "But I want it noted that Mick said she'd help me pitch the tent. I know her. She'll feign some sort of volleyball injury and try and get out of the deal."

"Yeah, whatever. Just get your ass over here." Mick launched the ball in their direction.

Quinn snatched it in one hand. Maybe she was showing off a little. It never hurt to intimidate the competition. She was having fun, something that had been a long time coming. *Maybe it was wrong.* Her heart raced, and heat ran up her neck.

Before she could think further, the volleyball

sailed from her hand. *What the...?* She glanced around
and met Aspen's satisfied grin.

"That was too easy. You're going to have to
protect the ball better if you plan on winning," Aspen
said. "Come on, let's go."

Chapter Twenty

The campfire flickered and popped. Aspen sat on the ground and rested her back against Peyton's legs. The fire mesmerized her, so she only half listened to the talk. The stiffness in her body had begun to take hold. She hoped the warmth from the fire would help loosen her muscles.

Aspen split her attention between the conversation of her friends gathered around the campfire and Mick and Quinn. They'd wandered off to put up their tent but promised to return once they were done. Aspen couldn't make out their words, but it seemed they chattered incessantly while they worked. A couple of times, she'd heard a torrent of cursing in a distinctly Southern drawl, followed by Quinn's belly laugh.

Hearing Quinn laugh brought a smile to her face. She couldn't put a finger on why Quinn touched her like she did. A sweetness surrounded Quinn, while at the same time, she seemed lost. Aspen couldn't imagine what it would feel like to have the person you loved most in the world wasting away in a hospital bed.

"You're going to watch it with us?" Peyton shook Aspen with her knee.

Shit. What was she supposed to be watching? She'd not really been listening. Should she just agree? But what if it were something she didn't want to do? Maybe she should say no.

"Typical. You weren't listening, were you?" Peyton didn't try to hide the irritation from her voice.

"Um, sorry." Aspen stretched her arms up over her head. "I'm just so full after that yummy meal. Then I got lost in the fire. It's so peaceful and relaxing out here. What was it you said?"

Peyton patted her shoulder. The answer must have appeased her. "We were talking about watching the footage from Gulliver's Travels from the GoPros. Put it up on DaKota's massive screen when we get home."

"Are you serious?" Aspen recoiled. "Why would you want to watch that?"

"I told you." DaKota pointed at Peyton and laughed. The gash in her cheek from Peyton's paddle had scabbed over, but it still looked angry. Knowing DaKota, she'd proudly display it as her war wound. "Damn it. I should have put a bet on it."

"Why, because you know you're going to lose your first bet?" Peyton shot back.

"Who says I'm going to lose? There's always tomorrow." DaKota smirked.

"Fuck you." Peyton casually flipped DaKota off.

"What is this damned bet you keep going on about?" Aspen asked.

Peyton squeezed Aspen's shoulders, bent, and kissed the top of her head. "Nothing you need to concern yourself with."

Aspen shrugged and said nothing else, knowing she wouldn't get a straight answer out of Peyton.

"Are you guys ready for the epic kayak run?" DaKota shifted her gaze to Aspen and gave her a pitying look. "Everyone but you."

Don't take the bait. Now that the secret was out,

DaKota took every opportunity to make it clear that Aspen didn't belong in the same league as the others. She decided to take the high road. "I'll be cheering you all on."

DaKota patted Tina's leg. "Peyton has her own little cheerleader. Are you going to be cheering me on?"

"No," Aspen said, no longer able to hold her tongue. "She'll be running circles around you."

"Says the woman that can't hack it." DaKota crossed her arms over her chest and glared.

"Knock it off already." Tina sat up straighter. "Leave her alone. I think she's showed tremendous courage even being out here."

DaKota started to bristle, but Tina pointed her finger at her and shook her head. "You're just pissed that Mick and Quinn wiped up the volleyball court with you."

Snap. Aspen bit her lip, so she wouldn't laugh.

Peyton snorted. "We should have been given a handicap since Quinn's ten feet tall."

Aspen tuned out as the banter continued. Her gaze settled across the way on Quinn, who finished pounding the final stake into the ground.

꙰꙰꙰꙰

"Ta-da," Quinn said and pulled the final rope taut before she raised her hands over her head.

Mick shot her a look. "You're not seriously going to celebrate taking this long to put up a tent, are you?"

"Yep. Got a problem with that?" Quinn stood and peered down at Mick.

"Back off." Mick crossed her arms over her chest

and glared up at Quinn.

"You're so cute when you're angry." Quinn playfully ruffled Mick's hair, knowing it drove her crazy.

Mick laughed. "God, I've missed your dumb ass, Coolidge."

"Son of a bitch. You must have if you let me get away with that."

"You can pat my head like a dog all you want if you come back to Boston and leave that godforsaken place."

"It's not a godforsaken place."

"It's not where you belong, though."

True. But Quinn wouldn't let Mick win that easily. "Who says?"

"Me." Mick patted her own chest, then pointed toward Quinn. "And your face. You've got some color in those cheeks and a bit of sparkle in your eyes. It's been a while since I've seen that."

Quinn tried to glare but wasn't sure how successful she was. "It's probably just a sunburn." Mick was right. It had been a long time since she felt this good. She ran her thumb along her scar. It served as a constant reminder and helped ground her. She yanked her hand away from her face.

"Good try. But I can tell you're having a good time."

Quinn's shoulders slumped. She turned away, pretending to check the tent ropes again. How could she have a good time when Stella was stuck in that hospital bed? *It wasn't right.*

"Damn it, Quinn." Mick grabbed Quinn's arm. "You can't go the rest of your life not having fun."

"I can try," Quinn said defensively, knowing how ridiculous it sounded.

Mick snorted. "Seriously? Is that the best you've got?"

Quinn fought the laugh that rose in her throat, even though she knew how stupid she sounded. She searched for a snappy comeback. When she couldn't find one, she remained silent. Maybe it would make her appear brooding.

Mick slapped her on the back. "Nice try, but I see that lip quivering. You won't be able to hold that smile much longer."

"Fuck you," Quinn said but laughed.

"You want to know the entire reason I said yes to letting Aspen come on the trip?" Mick asked.

"Sure, if you care to enlighten me." Quinn knew Mick would tell her anyway.

"First off, because you wanted her along. To be honest, it shocked the shit out of me."

Quinn narrowed her eyes and stared at Mick. "Why?"

"Taking responsibility for her didn't freak you out. I figured it would. Lots more could go wrong with someone without experience, but you were willing to take the chance."

Quinn's heart raced, and she sucked in her breath. *Shit.* She'd never thought of that. Her focus had been entirely on Aspen. Her gaze darted around the campsite, and suddenly, she wanted to escape.

"Relax." Mick put her hand on Quinn's arm. "It's okay. You look like you've seen a ghost. Come and sit down."

Quinn let Mick lead her to a chair. *Don't freak out.* A chill ran through her body. Her gaze landed on the local guides sitting around their own campfire. They could replace her. Couldn't they?

"Dude, you're white as a sheet." Mick handed her a bottle of water. "Do you need something stronger?"

"No." Quinn's hand trembled when she brought the bottle to her lips. A few drops of water escaped down her chin, but most of the cool liquid made it into her mouth. *Get a grip.* Now she was drooling like an infant.

"Talk to me. What's going on?"

Quinn took a deep breath, hoping to clear her mind. "I didn't know. I didn't realize."

"What didn't you know or realize?" Mick pulled her own chair closer.

"Oh, god." Quinn put her head in her hands. *Stella.* How could she have betrayed her like this? "I temporarily forgot."

"You're gonna have to give me more to go on." Mick put her hand on Quinn's knee. "What did you forget?"

"Stella. Everything." Quinn's chest tightened. She breathed in deeply, trying to fill her lungs with oxygen, but she just felt as if she were drowning.

"You didn't forget Stella."

"Yes, I did," Quinn nearly shouted. "What is wrong with me?"

"Slow down. There isn't anything wrong with you."

Oh, god. She must be having a breakdown. Quinn sucked in air but still didn't feel like her lungs had enough. *The tent.* She could hide there. Her breathing became shallower, so she inhaled deeply.

Mick stood and put her hand on the back of Quinn's head. "You better put your head down. I think you're hyperventilating."

Quinn lowered her head between her legs and

tried to pull more oxygen into her lungs. *Just breathe.* She closed her eyes and inhaled. After holding it for a couple of beats, she slowly blew it out. She repeated it again and again.

Neither spoke for several minutes as Quinn focused on her breathing. *Damn it, why is this happening now?* They'd been on the river all day. She'd made it through the worst of it when they'd capsized. Why did Stella haunt her now? With that thought, images of Stella flashed in her mind. Stella smiling. Stella laughing. And then Stella looking stern.

Quinn blinked several times, wanting to erase the last image. What did that look mean? Probably that Stella would be disgusted that she was here having fun. *Stop it.* Mick and Natalie had told her for years that Stella would be pissed if she knew Quinn was holed up in the Ozarks hiding from the world.

As if reading her mind, Mick asked, "What are you thinking?"

"If I have fun, I'm betraying Stella."

"Snap the fuck out of it." Mick's voice held a harsh edge.

Quinn jerked her head up. Instantly, she felt light-headed from the sudden movement. "How the hell would you feel if it were your fiancée laying in that fucking hospital bed?"

Mick's eyes blazed. "You're not the only one that loved her." Mick poked her finger at Quinn's chest. "Yes, she was your fiancée. I get it. But we all lost her, so get off the goddamned cross already."

Blood pounded in Quinn's ears, and her cheeks felt as if they were on fire. With her jaw set, she glared at Mick. Their gazes met. For the first time, she saw the pain that lay behind Mick's mischievous brown eyes.

Why hadn't she noticed before? *Too self-absorbed.* She looked to the ground. "I'm sorry," she mumbled.

"Did you just apologize?"

"Yes," Quinn answered, her voice barely above a whisper. "I've been selfish."

"You've been grieving." Mick patted Quinn's shoulder. "But it's time to start living again."

"But I don't know how."

"And that's the other reason I said yes to Aspen."

"What is?"

"Aspen brought life back into your eyes. A spark."

"No." Quinn frowned. "I'm certainly not looking for a girlfriend. And if I was, I'd never go after someone in a relationship."

"Chill out. I didn't say you were trying to get into her pants." Mick smiled. "Do you realize this is the first friend you've made since the accident?"

"Maybe." Quinn slumped against the back of her chair.

"You chased all your other friends away." Mick grabbed the front of her own shirt and pretended to straighten an imaginary tie. "Except for me."

"No, I didn't." Ire rose in her.

"Really? When was the last time you talked to Alex?"

Quinn searched her mind. Her shoulders sagged, and she let out a defeated sigh.

"We're still friends." Quinn crossed her arms over her chest. So what they didn't talk every day. Friends could go awhile without being all up in each other's shit.

"Did you know she met the woman of her dreams?"

Quinn's eyebrows shot up. She didn't think Alex would ever find anyone with the horrible taste she had in women. "No, but…"

"She's been with Jill for nearly a year. Care to tell me again how you're staying in touch with your friends?"

"Fine." Quinn threw up her hands. "So I haven't been a good friend."

"That's not the point, and you know it." Mick scowled. "Don't make me lose my shit on you again. I just want the old Quinn back. The one that was full of life. I've seen glimmers of her."

Tears welled in Quinn's eyes. "I want me back, too. During this trip, I've had moments of feeling like my old self. But I'm scared."

"What are you afraid of?"

Quinn took a deep breath and let it out slowly. "Betraying Stella."

🌊🌊🌊🌊

Aspen's eyelids felt heavy. They fluttered a couple of times as she tried to stay awake. She'd given up on Mick and Quinn returning since they'd been sitting by their tent engrossed in a conversation for some time. Disappointment rose in her. Maybe she'd slip into her tent and write in her journal.

She started to rise but stopped when she caught movement out of the corner of her eye. Quinn strode across the distance between their tent and the campfire. Her stride seemed purposeful, as if she were on a mission, and Mick wasn't with her.

"Hey, guys." Quinn smiled and waved her hand. "Sorry, we aren't going to be able to join you tonight.

We've run into a problem."

"What's up?" DaKota asked.

Quinn's head lowered, and her shoulders drooped. *Adorable.* She looked like a big kid who'd done something wrong. "I thought I'd done a bang-up job putting the tent up, but apparently, I pulled it too tight. Although, I think it was already messed up."

"So what happened?" DaKota asked.

"One whole seam has ripped out, so we have to figure out how to sew it up."

Mick bound up beside Quinn. "I told you I'd find it." Mick held up a kit. "Everything we need for repairs."

"I'll help," Aspen said without thinking. She'd become bored by the conversation around the fire, so hanging with Quinn would be fun. And Mick, she added in her thoughts. "I'm pretty good with a needle."

"Since when?" Peyton asked.

"I used to date a wannabe fashion designer, so I learned to sew to help her with her collection. She couldn't sew to save her life, so she created her own team of gullible women. Free labor."

"I'm not following," LeAnn said.

"She had four others," Aspen held up her hands and made air quotes, "seamstresses. We all worked for free. And might I add, we didn't know about each other until she hit it big. Then she dumped all of us because she could afford to hire employees."

"Ouch, babe." Peyton laughed. "That's cold."

Aspen nodded. "Yep, and the worst part was, when she broke up with me, she said my sewing was substandard. Seriously, who does that?"

"I hope you let her have it," Tina said.

Heat rose up her cheeks, and she couldn't meet Tina's gaze. How did she respond to that? Admit that she'd been a doormat and apologized for her lack of expertise? She smiled to herself when a response came to her. "Sumpin' like that," she said in a slow drawl.

The group laughed. Crisis averted. She wouldn't have to admit to more of her shortcomings. She quickly stood, and her body rebelled. Sitting so long, her legs had stiffened, and the crick in her back sent a sharp pain up her spine. *Damn, I'm getting old.* Nonchalantly, she stretched, hoping nobody would notice her awkward movements.

"I promise I won't criticize your sewing prowess." Mick pointed at Quinn. "I'm sure you'll do much better than this lug."

"Let's get this done, so you guys can come back and enjoy the fire and the conversation." She took a step, but Peyton grabbed her hand and pulled her back.

"Don't I get a goodbye kiss?"

Ire rose in Aspen, but she pushed it down. *Of course, the public display.* Anymore, half the time, Peyton forgot to kiss her good night. Not wanting to make waves, Aspen bent and pecked Peyton's lips before standing upright. "Onward," Aspen said to Mick and Quinn.

A gleam danced in Mick's eyes, and she turned to Quinn. "Hey, why don't you take a load off and hang with the group? Aspen and I can fix the tent. It doesn't take three of us."

Quinn reacted quickly. "No, no. I can work with her. Why don't you stay here?"

"Nonsense." Mick took Quinn's arm. "You did most of the work putting the tent up. It's the least I can do."

Quinn started to protest. "But—" Mick guided her toward an empty chair. "Really, I don't—" Mick motioned to the seat and nudged Quinn toward it. "Honestly—"

"Nope, I won't hear of it. Sit."

Quinn plopped into the chair. She scowled up at Mick.

Mick smiled and winked before turning her attention to Aspen. "Whew, we dodged a bullet. The last thing we need is her ripping out all of your hard work."

Disappointment rose in Aspen's chest, but she pushed it down. *Ridiculous.* Quinn didn't have to be involved in everything. She could do this without her sidekick. Resolve washed over her, and she stood up taller.

She caught LeAnn out of the corner of her eye. LeAnn pursed her lips and glared before she winked and smiled. Aspen laughed. No doubt, LeAnn would be envious of her getting to spend time alone with Mick.

Mick held out her arm. "Shall we?"

"Let's." Aspen threaded her arm through Mick's.

≈≈≈≈

Damned Mick. She didn't do anything without a purpose; no doubt, that had been calculated. What the hell would she say to Aspen? *The sneak.* She'd pay for it when Quinn got her alone.

Quinn couldn't dwell on it any further because someone had said her name. "Pardon?"

"I asked how you felt our first day went," Tina

said. She had a huge smile. Without her fancy clothes and makeup, Quinn could see the Colorado River girl.

"Great. I would have preferred not to capsize, but everyone handled it like a pro." It was true. Quinn had been impressed by the reactions. Other than Peyton's punk move not letting Aspen in the raft first, everything went well. Quinn chastised herself. She was being old school; some might even say sexist. Just because Peyton was more masculine didn't mean there should be a male-female thing going. Although with Aspen being the rookie, it should have been common courtesy.

Shit. Now she'd missed what LeAnn had just said. "I'm sorry. This is the first time I've sat back and just relaxed, and I got caught up watching the fire."

DaKota grabbed a beer out of the cooler. "Here, I think you need one of these."

"Thanks." Quinn smiled and twisted the cap off. "Okay, back to LeAnn, what did you say?"

"Despite the wipeout, it was fun. I wondered what rapid you enjoyed the most. I know I had my favorite, but I'm curious which one yours was."

Quinn rubbed her chin and stared into the fire. *Favorite?* "I loved Stairway to Heaven to start our trip. That drop got the blood pumping, but I'd have to say number eighteen. Oblivion."

"That one was wild." Peyton joined the conversation. "I thought for sure we were gonna take another swim."

"Me too." Quinn smiled. "I read somewhere that only one in four don't flip, but I don't know if that's true. After the debacle on Gulliver's Travels, I was happy to redeem myself."

"I was sure we were flipping," Tina said. "But

you called high side at the perfect moment."

"Why do I think if you were captaining, we wouldn't have tipped at all?" Quinn said to Tina.

Tina's cheeks reddened, and she looked away. She shook her head. "Ridiculous. I'm not half as good as you."

"You're just being modest. You more than held your own with Mick up front."

"Speaking of the front. When do we get another go at it?" DaKota asked.

"You and Peyton got your shot in the front."

Tina caught Quinn's eye and winked. *She knew.* Quinn had placated them by giving them a couple of the easier rapids.

"It kicked ass," Peyton said. "Any chance we get another go at it tomorrow?"

"Just like today, we'll assess as we go." Quinn didn't want to debate with them, so a change of subject was in order. "LeAnn, you asked which was my favorite, which was yours?"

"I'd say the Mick and Quinn."

"Mick and Quinn?" Quinn's forehead furrowed. "I didn't hear you use that name on the river."

"That's because we'd just come off the Terminators I and II and everyone was screaming and celebrating."

Quinn laughed. She knew which rapid came next. "Double Trouble, huh?"

"Yep." LeAnn laughed. "Aspen named it."

"Figures."

Tina pointed at Peyton and DaKota and then swung her hand toward Claire. "You three are the only ones without a rapid named after you."

Where had Quinn been, she must have missed

multiple pseudonyms. "Hit me with it. Which rapids are you ladies named in?"

"Seriously, you didn't figure it out?" LeAnn asked.

Quinn shook her head.

"Rapid twelve," Tina said.

Quinn chuckled. "Hardly." She looked from LeAnn back to Tina. "Nope."

Tina stood and twirled. "I think the Three Ugly Sisters is perfect."

"Good try, babe," DaKota said. "Nobody's falling for that."

Claire, who appeared to be sleeping the entire time, lifted her head. "I'm not buying it, either." And then her chin dropped back onto her chest.

Quinn held back a laugh. She still hadn't been able to figure out Claire or LeAnn. Who was she to question their partnership? "On a different note. Mick tells me you two have spared no expense and have a giant feast planned for tomorrow night when we camp."

Peyton's face lit up. "Yes. We're excited for everyone to see our spread."

Quinn sat back and took a swallow of beer. The cool liquid slid down her throat. *Refreshing.* DaKota joined the conversation, and Quinn relaxed further, no longer needing to take part. She could enjoy the fire and being amongst the living again. Today, even the capsize on Gulliver had been just what she needed.

Chapter Twenty-one

Aspen was no dummy. She had no doubt that Mick wanted to get her alone. *But why?* Despite her attempt at being casual, by the look on Quinn's face, she knew, too. This would be fun since it was her first time interacting with Mick one on one.

Mick had shown her the large seam that split halfway across the bottom of the tent. It wouldn't take much to fix. She suspected Mick knew that, too. *Oh, well.* She'd play along and see what this was about.

Aspen opened the repair kit and examined the contents. *Perfect.* She had more than enough to do the job. Wait until she told Gina that her time with Sylvia hadn't been in vain. She smiled to herself, imagining Gina's reaction.

"Finding everything you need?" Mick knelt beside her.

"Yep, I'll have it stitched up in no time."

"Thanks." Mick remained next to Aspen.

Should I? She'd labeled her new attitude as direct. Could she do it with a stranger? For some reason, it had come easy with Quinn, but would it be as simple with Mick? Aspen plunged in before she chickened out. "So why did you really want me to help you?" *Oh, god.* She did it.

Mick chuckled. She turned to Aspen and gave her an appraising look before nodding. "Astute. I like it."

"That didn't answer my question." *Damn.* Where did that come from? Quinn would be proud of her frankness. She held back a grin.

"You're right." Mick stood. "What say we work on the tent and talk while we do it? Before Quinn decides to crash our party."

"Deal." Aspen picked up the kit and stood.

Mick unhooked the tent, laid it out, and sat back on her heels. "So what is it you'd like to know?"

Aspen grasped the awl and pushed it through the fabric. "You obviously have something you wanted to talk to me about. Why don't you just tell me, so I don't have to guess?"

"All right." Mick grinned. "Assertive. I like it."

Aspen didn't want to tell Mick that she had no idea where her bravado came from. Was there something about Quinn that gave her confidence, or had she finally had enough? "I'm practicing. It's a newfound skill, so be kind."

"That I can do." Mick's drawl relaxed Aspen. Made her feel safe. "It's just that Quinn has had a rough few years. I'm sure you've heard the stories. Pretty hard not to since it was all over the internet."

Aspen nodded. "Yeah, Peyton and DaKota filled me in. They've followed you two for years. You could say they're some of your biggest fans."

"Just like anything else, most of what's out there is probably true, but there's always the bullshit. I've read some crazy rumors. I just wanted to make sure you had the true story."

"Of course." Aspen tried to hide her surprise. "Why me?"

"Quinn likes you. I haven't seen her take to anyone since the accident, and I don't want it to turn out badly."

Aspen glanced up from the stitch she'd just made. "Why would it turn out badly?"

Mick shrugged. "Call me paranoid, but I don't think Quinn could take another hit. And well, you guys come from different worlds. Ya know."

"Quinn's great. What do you think I'm going to do to her?" Her words came out harsher than she'd intended, but the conversation was making her uneasy.

Mick held up her hands as if in surrender. "Whoa. Let me start again. I'm sure you've heard about Stella's accident and that she's pretty much brain dead. I can't remember the official word for it now."

A lump caught in Aspen's throat as she nodded. "Yes. I've heard that story."

"Let's just say, Quinn didn't handle it well."

"Nobody would."

"Relax. Quinn's my best friend. I love that woman more than I love myself, so you don't need to be defending her with me."

"I'm sorry." Aspen's cheeks were on fire. "That was rude and presumptuous of me. Of course, you have her best interest at heart. When I see the two of you together, it's obvious how much you care about each other. I apologize."

Mick held up her hand. "No need to apologize. I've caught you off guard, and I'm afraid my normal Southern charm is failing me."

Aspen put her hand on Mick's arm. "No, not at all. I guess I'm a little more jumpy than I realized. Please, go on."

"Anyway. Since Stella and Quinn never married,

Stella's parents have complete control over her medical decisions. We all know that Stella wouldn't want to live this way, but Quinn is powerless. It's torture. Quinn feels like she failed Stella once because of the accident and then every day that she wastes away in that hospital bed."

Bile churned in Aspen's stomach. *How awful.* Her heart went out to Quinn. She'd thought about it but not at this level. "The poor thing."

"It's torn her up." Mick's playful eyes no longer held any sparkle. All Aspen could see was pain. "She went into hiding. This is the first time we've hung out in years. She's shut everyone out. She's living in a little shack in the Ozarks. I think it's her punishment to herself."

"Oh, god." Aspen let the awl drop from her fingers. She'd been working and listening, but she needed to see Mick's face. "I appreciate you telling me this, but I'm still confused."

"The entire time she's been in Misery, she's made this many friends." Mick held up her hand in the shape of a zero. "None. You're the first person since the accident that I've seen her enjoying. She pushed away all her other friends. I was just too stubborn to go away."

Aspen grinned and pretended to size Mick up. "I can see that." Mick rewarded her with a smile. "But she's friendly with everyone here, so why me?"

"I've been surprised how she's been with the group. I believe she's actually having fun. But you're different."

"Me? What have I done?"

"Don't know." Mick shrugged, and her eyes widened. "Not a clue. But when she asked me to let you go down the river without any experience, you could have knocked me over with a feather. Of course I said yes. She could have asked me to let you steer the damned raft, and I probably would have agreed."

"But why?"

"Because I saw life in my friend's eyes for the first time in years. Whatever's happening on this trip might bring her back to me. But...." Mick picked up the awl and pushed it through the canvas.

"Are you going to leave me hanging?" Aspen asked.

Mick made several more stitches before she stopped and looked up, her pain evident. "If anything goes wrong, I'm afraid it could break her. With each rapid, I was starting to see the old Quinn, and I temporarily forgot. It was the best feeling. Then that fucking Gulliver's Travels. My insides were churning. What if Quinn lost it? What if something bad happened?" Mick sat back on the ground and wrapped her arms around herself.

"It's okay, Mick." Aspen wanted to reach out to her but wasn't sure how Mick would react, so she kept her hands in her lap.

Mick took a deep breath. "When Quinn and I climbed up onto the raft, for a moment, she was gone. I thought she'd checked out. I was afraid that was it. I've tried to talk to her about PTSD, but she won't hear of it." Mick ran her hand through her wiry hair. "I told her you needed her, and it was like a switch flipped. Her eyes cleared, and she said your name. Then she was back, hauling people in while she looked for you."

"Oh." *Really?* That was the best she could do? "Wow." Not much better. "I didn't know. I'm not sure what to say." Should it make her uncomfortable? She searched her mind. It didn't. All she felt was warmth in her chest.

Mick smiled. "Sorry. This is a lot to throw on you."

"No, not at all," Aspen said and genuinely meant it. "I just don't understand why you're telling me this now. It seems like Quinn weathered it well."

"She did." Mick's head bobbed up and down. "But Ghostrider could be different. It isn't for the faint of heart. What if something happens and we lose her again? Part of me wants to call it a trip, return the money, and take the partially healed Quinn back to the States. And somehow convince her to move back to Boston."

"And the other part of you?"

"The other part knows the dumbass will never go for it." Mick shook her head, and her jaw clenched. "She thinks this will be the game changer."

"Letting herself live again?"

Mick's eyes narrowed, and her brows furrowed. "No, no. You think Quinn's doing this to heal herself. But she's not. That's why I'm doing it. Hoping this experience will bring her out of her self-imposed dungeon. For her, it's about the money."

Money. Had she misread Quinn?

"By the look on your face, that surprises you."

"Yeah."

"It's not what you think. The fool has it in her head that she's going to be able to hire a lawyer to fight Stella's parents. Me and Stella's sister have both tried to tell her that Stella's parents have more money than God. Two hundred thousand dollars will be eaten up before she knows it. But the stubborn ass won't listen."

It was as if a punch landed to Aspen's gut. How terrible. All this for Stella. "You mean that's the only reason she's doing this? Putting herself through hell?"

"The money mostly, and she wants to conquer her fears. But I just want her to start living again. And I've seen it happening this trip, especially with you."

"She doesn't have to finish. We'll pay her anyway." Aspen rose to her feet. "I'll go tell her now."

"No," Mick practically yelled and grabbed Aspen's hand. "You can't do that. She can't know we're having this conversation. Hell, I'm not sure why I'm telling you all this. Maybe I've got my own PTSD. I'm afraid Ghostrider might trigger something in her. The three of us, Quinn, Stella and I, always talked about running Ghostrider, and I'm afraid what it's going to do to her."

Finally, Aspen understood. Mick was terrified for her friend. Aspen wanted to comfort her but wasn't sure how. She'd normally wrap her in a giant hug, but the others could see them from the campfire, and it would draw attention. She needed to convey her understanding through her words. Another opportunity for being forthright.

Aspen sank back to the ground next to Mick. She put her hand on Mick's knee and smiled. "Thank you for trusting me with that story. I promise, I won't share it with anyone. Not even Quinn. You're a good friend, Mikhala Romero. A great one."

Mick met her gaze and gave her a shy smile. *Adorable.* The cockier one of the pair was even cuter when she was filled with humility. "Just promise, the rest of the group can't know this. Quinn would be humiliated."

Aspen brought her hand to her chest. "I'm honored you entrusted this with me. We'll get her through in one piece."

"Thank you." Mick flashed one of her signature smiles and handed the awl to Aspen. "Shall we finish this up before the others start to question what we're up to?"

"Absolutely." Aspen jammed the awl into the fabric, her heart full.

❧❧❧❧

The fire flickered and cast an eerie glow on the campers. It wouldn't be long before it burned out if they didn't add more logs.

Quinn stretched out her legs. She was about ready for bed anyway. After several hours of sustained conversation, the group had stopped talking. From what Quinn could see of their faces, they all looked tired.

"So," LeAnn said, breaking the silence. "Mick or Quinn, can one of you tell us why they call it Ghostrider?"

"Go ahead." Mick nodded at Quinn. "You're the Ghostrider fanatic."

Quinn rolled her eyes. "I wouldn't exactly call me a fanatic. But since Sleepy looks like she might tip over any minute, I can tell you the story."

Aspen snatched the piece of cake that sat untouched on her plate and shifted her gaze to Quinn. "I love a good story."

"I'm not sure how good it is." Quinn smiled. "I wouldn't go eating that cake like it was popcorn. It's not exactly an edge-of-your-seat type of tale."

With an exaggerated movement, Aspen tore a

piece off her cake and tossed it into her mouth as if she were at the movies.

LeAnn laughed. "Now you're gonna have to make it good, or your audience will be disappointed."

"Ugh." Quinn ran her hand through her short hair. "The pressure. Maybe I should wait to tell it in the morning when it's light out."

Mick met her gaze. The firelight bright enough for her to recognize the twinkle that danced in her eyes. "Maybe. It might give them nightmares."

Sweet. Mick had picked up on her game. "Are you sure you guys want to hear this?"

Nods greeted her.

She needed to think quick on her feet. "Well, you see," Quinn started in her most mysterious voice. "The McMillans"—where in the hell had she come up with that name—"had honeymooned right here on the Zambezi River. They'd vowed that on their eighteenth wedding anniversary, they would return to do it again."

"Really? The eighteenth?" Aspen said and put another piece of cake into her mouth.

"Yeah, that's the water anniversary," Quinn lied. How the hell would she know which was the water anniversary, or if there even was such a thing? "They'd talked about it for years. Then on their seventeenth anniversary, exactly one year before they were supposed to come here, Ted McMillan disappeared. They found his semi-truck in the Rockies. Empty. No sign of a struggle but also no sign of Ted. His company claimed that at exactly midnight his GPS signal abruptly cut out."

The eager group leaned in as Quinn told the story, except for Mick, who sat back with an amused grin on her face. Luckily, all attention was on Quinn, or they might have become suspicious.

"Lucy McMillan was beside herself and spent every dime hoping to find Ted. In her grief, she'd forgotten they'd prepaid for the trip years ago. She tried in vain to get the money back to keep searching, but the hotel refused to refund her. So her best friend convinced her to go."

"What the fuck?" Tina said. "Which one? Everyone should boycott them."

Quinn held up her hand. "That's the strange thing. When she arrived at the hotel, she planned on giving the manager an earful. But when she asked for him by name, the woman at the counter shook her head in confusion. She'd never heard of the man. Lucy pulled the email from her bag and handed it over. The clerk shrugged and shook her head. That was the hotel's email address, but nobody by the name of Edgar Hitchcock had ever worked there."

Quinn's gaze landed on Mick, who rolled her eyes. Maybe combining Edgar Allan Poe and Alfred Hitchcock was just asking to be discovered, but nobody noticed.

"That's creepy," LeAnn said. "Are you sure this is real?"

Quinn shrugged, hoping to appear casual. "It's just what I've heard. You can Google it." She knew full well none of them had brought their phones.

"What happened next?" Peyton asked, her eyes wide.

"Lucy and her friend started out at the Boiling Pot just like you guys did. If I'm not mistaken, they camped right around here their first night." Quinn paused and slowly glanced around. She made a show of looking over her shoulder.

The others followed her lead and looked over theirs, as well. Mick coughed, which Quinn suspected was to hide her chuckle.

When all attention returned to her, Quinn continued. "Lucy felt strange. Like she was being watched." Quinn leaned in for emphasis and lowered her voice. "Lucy heard her name called, but when she turned, nobody was there. In the middle of the night, she felt her covers being pulled back." Quinn let her gaze dart around for emphasis. "She told her friend she felt disoriented. Light-headed. The next day, her friend reported that her behaviors became more erratic."

Quinn stopped and took a long pull from her beer. The fire continued to flicker. The rushing water could be heard over the crackling campfire. Quinn brought the beer to her lips again.

"Jesus. Would you finish the story already?" DaKota said.

"Oh, yeah, sorry. I was just thinking about poor Lucy." Quinn rubbed her chin. "They say she was a beautiful woman, but grief aged her. Anyway, the next day, they went farther down the river. They set up camp right below Ghostrider, except then it was called the Widow Maker."

"No way," Aspen said. "You're making this up."

Quinn held out her hands palms up. "You know all the crazy names they have. Kinda the equivalent of Commercial Suicide."

Aspen nodded. "Makes sense."

Like taking candy from a baby. "So they went to bed that night, and Lucy still felt unsettled. They'd planned on an early start for the last leg of their journey, so they could raft to the end. The sun was just coming over the horizon. The mist rose over the river, and the morning was eerily quiet. Even the guides later said they'd never felt the vibes they did that day." Quinn cleared her throat. "Maybe I should stop and finish this in the morning."

"No," the group said in unison.

Quinn glanced at Mick. "Do you think I should finish this?"

Mick bit her lip and looked to the sky. "I reckon you better. They need to know the whole story, so they know what they're getting into."

Quinn slid to the front of her seat, and the others mimicked her movement. Nothing like getting them on the edge of their seat, Quinn thought. "Lucy and the rest of the party on the expedition gathered by the river. The guides were acting funny and whispered to each other. They soon discovered one of the rafts was missing. Lucy shuddered, and her entire body was covered with goose bumps, even though the temperature was in the upper seventies. Out of nowhere, a raft, their raft, bobbed down the rapids. Nobody was in it, but the guides swear that it maneuvered as if someone were steering it."

Quinn had lowered her voice as she spoke, forcing them to lean in farther. "Then Lucy screamed," Quinn said in a loud voice. Everyone jumped.

"What the fuck did you do that for?" DaKota said.

"Um, sorry," Quinn said. "Just getting into the story. Before anyone could stop her, Lucy ran to the water, screaming Ted's name and jumped in." Quinn sat back in her chair. "They never found her or her body. And that's how Ghostrider got its name."

"Don't forget to tell them about the legend," Mick said.

Quinn sighed. "You go ahead."

"The locals say, sometimes late at night or early in the morning, they see a raft coming down the river with two people in it, but then it vanishes into thin air."

"Jesus," Peyton said. "Why didn't we ever hear about this?"

Quinn shrugged. "The locals don't like to talk about it. Bad for tourism."

"And why the fuck didn't you mention it to us before now?" Aspen asked, her expression priceless. A combination of fear and anger.

Mick chuckled.

Quinn's lip trembled as she tried to hold back her laughter.

"What's so funny?" LeAnn said.

"I guess you three aren't the only ones that can make up bogus shit," Quinn said, finally allowing herself to laugh.

"Asshole." Aspen threw the rest of her cake at Quinn.

The cake ricocheted off Quinn's shoulder and grazed her face, leaving a dollop of frosting. With two fingers, she swiped it and licked her fingers. "Gotcha."

The group laughed, and all began talking at once.

Aspen glared at Quinn, but her smile gave her away. "You're still an asshole."

※ ※ ※ ※ ※

Aspen whistled while she unrolled her sleeping

bag. Peyton and DaKota spared no expense. She didn't realize they made such large air mattresses.

"You're pretty chipper," Peyton said, pulling clothes from her bag.

"I had fun today," Aspen said and meant it.

"Even with DaKota giving you shit about Ghostrider?"

Aspen rolled her eyes. "I'm used to her being an ass. I just wish you'd defend me sometimes."

"Defend you?" Peyton stopped and stared. "She's just joking. Sheesh, get a sense of humor."

"I guess we don't share the same sense of humor." Aspen tried to say it light-hearted but knew her words had a bite to them.

Peyton pulled her shirt over her head as she said, "There's lots of things we don't share."

Aspen took in a breath. She could pretend she didn't hear it, but she was tired of these games. "You're right."

"I thought you said you were having fun," Peyton said as she poked her head through the neck of her shirt. "Apparently, you were lying."

"Don't get defensive with me. You're the one that said we didn't have anything in common."

"Really?" Peyton threw her hands up. "That's not what I said."

"Then what did you say?"

"I said there's lots of things we don't share."

"Means the same to me."

"Well, it's not."

Aspen was starting to tire of the circular conversation. She'd come on this trip to revitalize their relationship, but it hadn't turned out that way. If anything, she felt more disconnected from Peyton than ever. *Did she care?* Her predominate emotion with Peyton on the trip had been irritation. "I'm not going to split hairs with you. We both know what you were implying."

Peyton stared at her for several beats before she shifted her gaze to the ground. "Do you even want to be here?"

Wow. That was a loaded question. She hadn't expected Peyton to be so direct. "I don't know."

"Yes, you do."

Aspen's feelings about this trip were so mixed that she couldn't even begin to explain them to Peyton. "I could ask you the same. Do you even want me to be here?"

"I asked you first."

Aspen's limbs suddenly felt heavy, and all she wanted was sleep. She sighed and met Peyton's gaze. "I think both of our answers speak volumes, don't they?"

Peyton's shoulders slumped. Her eyes held a mixture of pain and relief. "I suppose," she said in a voice not much louder than a whisper.

They didn't say anything more as they prepared for bed. Aspen busied herself with changing her clothes while Peyton fussed with her blankets, making sure to get all the covers tugged the way she wanted them.

They'd been in bed for several minutes before Peyton said, "I think we're just exhausted from the day. It's been a wild one." She let out a forced chuckle.

"Yeah, it has been. I can't remember the last time I've been this tired." All she wanted was to sleep.

"That's it. Things will look different in the morning. Better."

Aspen nodded. Not that she believed it, but her thoughts were getting fuzzy. "You might be right."

"I am." Peyton's voice didn't hold the conviction that her words did. "We just need to get some sleep."

Finally, they could agree on something, Aspen thought. "Definitely."

"Night, babe."

"Good night."

Chapter Twenty-two

Quinn peeked her head out of the tent flap and inhaled deeply. There was nothing like the smell of a river first thing in the morning. She sniffed again. River mixed with coffee, even better. *Heaven.*

Someone must be up, or the local guides were already working on breakfast. She glanced at the sleeping form on the other mattress. Before she could nudge Mick, a groan came from the sleeping woman. Mick raised her arms over her head and stretched, letting out another groan.

"Morning, sunshine," Quinn said in an extra perky voice. She chuckled when Mick pulled her sleeping bag over her face. After years away, some things didn't change. Mick was not a morning person. "It's gonna be a beautiful day. Rise and shine."

"Fuck you," Mick answered. She cocooned deeper into her sleeping bag and rolled onto her side.

"The coffee is already brewing." Quinn shook out her bedding and rolled her sleeping bag.

Mick peeked her head out, so only her wiry hair and dark brown eyes could be seen. "Coffee?"

"She's alive." Quinn dropped her rolled bag and grabbed an end of her air mattress. "You better get moving, or I might drink it all."

"Why are you so fucking annoying first thing in the morning?" Mick extracted her arms and stretched again.

"Part of my charm. Besides, you're the one that wanted me here. Were you listening? It's shaping up to be a beautiful day. The Zambezi awaits us."

"Joy. Just get me some coffee first, and then we can talk about it."

❧ ❧ ❧ ❧ ❧

The breakfast was amazing. Quinn couldn't believe the local guides prepared something so delicious in the middle of a beach. She'd eaten at five-star restaurants that couldn't touch the tastiness of the French toast she'd just devoured.

Before she dipped her finger in the maple syrup, she glanced around to make sure no one watched. She'd missed soaking up a small portion on her plate, and now all her French toast was gone. Subtly, she ran her finger through the sticky syrup, hoping to get as much as possible in one swipe to avoid detection.

"Do you want a little more French toast?" a voice said.

She lifted her head and met Aspen's gaze. Aspen's eyes were full of amusement. Heat rose in Quinn's cheeks. *Busted.* Maybe if she acted casual, Aspen wouldn't notice her finger remained in the sticky goo. "Um, I'm good."

Before Quinn could say more, Aspen rose from her seat and plopped half a piece of French toast on Quinn's plate only centimeters from her finger. Aspen winked. "Thought you might need something to wipe your finger on."

Quinn glanced around, and only LeAnn and Mick seemed to have been paying attention. Both chuckled but said nothing. "Thanks," she muttered when she looked up at Aspen.

"My god, we can't take you anywhere." Mick laughed.

Aspen turned and leveled a scowl at Mick. "Leave her alone. She needs to keep her strength in order to captain the raft."

"Yeah, what she said," Quinn responded in a haughty tone.

Aspen turned back to Quinn and pointed. "And you need to get some table manners."

Mick made a face at Quinn. "Yeah, what she said."

Aspen laughed and shook her head.

In an exaggerated motion, Quinn ran a piece of the toast through the syrup, making sure to saturate it. She put the bite into her mouth, closed her eyes, and let out a satisfied moan.

"You guys ready for the Morning Shave and Morning Shower?" Mick asked.

"Oh, god, I'd kill for a shower about now." Aspen touched her head. "I can feel it running through my hair now."

LeAnn ran her hands down her legs. "A little stubbly, but I don't believe I need a shave."

Claire chuckled. "I think that's the name of our first rapids."

Quinn jumped, forgetting Claire was sitting beside her quietly eating her breakfast. *Typical.* Claire faded into the woodwork most of the time. "And we have a winner," Quinn said.

"Seriously?" Aspen asked.

"Yup," Mick answered. She moved her arm in a sweeping gesture like a game show hostess. "Bobo

Beach is one of the most popular camping sites. As you can see." She pointed at the other campers who were also on the move this morning. "What better name than Morning Shave and Morning Shower?"

Aspen groaned. "These names are killing me, they're so corny."

"But memorable," Quinn said. "I'll bet you that you'll be able to rattle off several when you get back to San Francisco and Gina starts quizzing you."

Aspen nodded. "True. But they're still juvenile."

"Only if you're an old fuddy duddy."

"Seriously? Did you just call me a fuddy duddy?"

Quinn put her hand over her face. "Oh, god, it's happening. I've been hanging around Mick too long."

"The hell. I don't even say shit like that," Mick said. "I think you might be channeling the eighty-year-old woman trapped inside you."

Quinn studied her plate, and then ran another piece of toast through the syrup. "Leave me alone. I'm eating."

✺✺✺✺

The second day of rafting was going better than the first. They'd been thrashed around hard on the Upper Moemba, which was one of the largest rapids on the river, and by the look on Aspen and LeAnn's faces, they were ready to be done for the day. They held their paddles and slumped toward the center of the raft. On the other hand, Peyton and DaKota stood in celebration and held their paddles over their heads.

"Back atcha," Peyton yelled at the waves behind them as they floated in calmer waters.

"We came, we saw, and we kicked your ass,"

DaKota shouted, joining the celebration.

Quinn's shoulders stiffened, but she said nothing. *Leave them be.* Some customers liked to celebrate. It was harmless fun. She shouldn't let her superstition spoil anyone's fun. Silly, but she never wanted to tempt the river gods. The thought made her cringe. She'd never disrespected the river, but look where it got her.

"Quinn," a loud voice said.

"What?"

Aspen studied her. "Are you okay? I called your name three times."

"Um, sorry. What did you need?"

"Is this the last rapid for the day?" Aspen's eyes were glassy, and her shoulders hunched. Despite abundant sunscreen, her crimson nose had to hurt.

"It is. You look tired."

Aspen smiled. "Yeah. That last one took it out of me."

"Me too," LeAnn added. "I'm ready for a glass of wine and some good food."

"Amen," Aspen said.

"All right, gang," Quinn called out. "Let's get paddling so we can get off this river and relax for the evening."

Peyton and DaKota returned to their spots on the side of the raft. Peyton turned and smiled at Quinn. "And tomorrow, we get Ghostrider."

A chill ran through Quinn. She must have gotten too much sun. "Forward," she called out and focused on the river.

※ ※ ✍ ✍

Quinn stared into the flickering fire. The camp was quiet after everyone went to bed. They'd turned in a little earlier tonight. After two days of pounding and adrenaline surges, the body got tired easier. She wondered if the others had been able to drift off to sleep with the anticipation of Ghostrider.

Not wanting to think about tomorrow, she turned her thoughts back to their day on the Zambezi. She'd been prophetic; the weather had been gorgeous, and once again, she found that she was enjoying herself. It had amazed Quinn how well the group responded to her directions. Today, they'd moved without hesitation when she called out a command, even Aspen. Several times, their quick response prevented a possible capsize.

Despite being tired from the day, she hadn't been able to sleep. Tomorrow, Ghostrider awaited. She wrestled with her feelings, not sure if she was ready to admit them to herself. In some ways, after being on the river for two days, Ghostrider would be just another rapid, except they'd talked about it for years. Would it haunt her, and if so, how would she handle her emotions? What if she handled them as well as she had the rest of the trip? Wouldn't it sully Stella's memory?

The end of the trip loomed, and her uncertainty would return. She knew Mick wanted her to move back to Boston, but could she live in the same city with the constant reminder of Stella?

Thoughts of the future made her uneasy, so she allowed a movie of the trip to play in her head. Most of the scenes featured Aspen. She rubbed her chest, hoping to lessen the ache. In a couple of days, they'd say goodbye to the group and likely never see them again.

Quinn tossed a log into the fire harder than she intended. Tiny bits of wood and sparks flew up, looking like tiny fireflies circling the flames. She put her head into her hands and tried not to think of anything.

❧❧❧❧

Aspen glanced at the sleeping form next to her. Typical Peyton, out like a light. Peyton could sleep through a monsoon. Aspen, on the other hand, had been staring at the tent ceiling for far too long. She'd heard it said that if someone couldn't fall asleep within a half an hour after lying down, they shouldn't force themselves to sleep; instead, they should get up.

Quietly, she unzipped her sleeping bag and slid out. Hopefully, it wouldn't be too dark outside the tent. Did dangerous wild animals lurk at night? Quinn had told her that some people liked to sleep out under the stars without a tent at all. The thought made her queasy.

She'd just step out for a few minutes and hope the moonlight cast enough light to make it less scary. She glanced at Peyton once more before getting to her feet. Her hand swept along in the dark through her open suitcase until it brushed her sweatshirt. *Just in case it had gotten chilly outside.*

She shivered, not from the cold. Being outside alone felt decadent and a little scary. Aspen pulled the sweatshirt over her head; somehow, it would make her feel safer.

On her tiptoes, she made her way toward the tent flap. Peyton slept on. Looking back one final time, she slipped through the opening into the night.

She stood in front of the tent and let her eyes adjust. Even though they'd set up camp away from Moemba Falls, the plummeting water filled the night air. A small fire burned near one of the tents. Was that where the local guides set up camp? She squinted, trying to acclimate herself to her surroundings.

Her shoulders relaxed, and she smiled. *Possibly Quinn and Mick's campsite?* Did she have the courage to fumble around in the dark to check it out? A tiny woman like herself probably shouldn't be wandering around in the middle of Africa. *No.* Frank and decisive was her motto this trip, so she needed to practice it now.

Aspen drew in a lungful of fresh air before slowly letting it out. She squared her shoulders and began her short trek toward the flames. The closer she got to the fire, the surer she was that it was Mick and Quinn's.

The figure sitting near the fire appeared to be large. *Quinn?* She hoped. Not that she'd mind talking to Mick, but it was Quinn she really wanted to see. When she got within ten yards, she called out, "Mind having company?"

"Fuck," the voice said. "You scared the shit out of me."

Quinn. Aspen recognized her voice immediately. *Interesting.* She could identify Quinn's voice in the dark. No need to dwell on it. "That didn't answer my question."

"What was your question?" Quinn's familiar chuckle filled the air.

"Mind having company?" Aspen stopped a few feet from the fire and squinted across it, trying to make out Quinn's features.

"Do I have a choice?" Quinn asked.

Ouch. Quinn's response hurt more than she'd expected. She enjoyed Quinn's company and had made the erroneous assumption Quinn felt the same. All she needed to do was excuse herself and head back to bed.

Before she could speak, Quinn interrupted. "Sorry. I was teasing, but in this lighting, you probably didn't catch my smirk."

"Seriously? It's pitch black and you have this teeny tiny fire. I'm supposed to read your facial expressions?" Aspen faked outrage.

"Sheesh, Frankie. Pull up a chair and chill out. You're going to give yourself a heart attack."

Aspen walked around the fire and grabbed the chair that sat off to Quinn's right.

"Shouldn't you take that seat?" Quinn pointed to the other chair.

Aspen glanced around the area. The smoke wasn't wafting her way. "Why? Is that seat better?"

"It'd put me on your right side."

Oh, god. What a clueless dumbass she was being. Even though she hadn't acted like it, Quinn must be self-conscious about her scar. "Um, sure." Aspen leapt to her feet and went to the other chair.

Quinn laughed. "Ah, that was a joke."

Aspen studied Quinn. How could she joke about something like that? "Sorry, I guess I just don't find it funny."

Quinn scratched her head. "I thought being your sidekick was our joke."

"Sidekick? What are you talking about?"

"Right-hand man or should I say woman?"

Quinn pointed to the empty chair to her right. "Isn't that what they call a sidekick?"

"Oh, god, now I understand."

"A joke's never good when you have to explain it." In the low lighting, Quinn's features looked even softer and her eyes sad.

"No, I misunderstood. I thought you were talking about something else."

"What did you think I was talking about?"

Aspen waved her hand in dismissal. She didn't want to tell Quinn what she'd thought. "Oh, nothing."

"Come on, Frankie. Isn't your motto direct and forthright?"

Ugh. Of all times for her words to come back and bite her in the ass. How would Quinn react? But she had promised to be more honest and direct. Did that apply to this situation?

"It can't be that bad," Quinn said. "Just tell me."

Aspen diverted her gaze and stared into the fire. Would Quinn be upset or angry? Or would it just make things awkward? Only one way to find out. Aspen met Quinn's gaze and nodded. "I thought maybe you didn't want me sitting on that side because of your... um, your face."

Quinn's brow furrowed, and her eyes showed no sign of comprehension. She touched her face, and her finger brushed her scar. As if a curtain lifted, realization showed in her eyes. "Oh, this."

"I'm sorry. I didn't mean to...I misunderstood...I..." Aspen didn't know what to say to combat the discomfort.

"Relax. You didn't offend me." Quinn ran her finger the length of the scar. "It's part of me. A reminder."

Direct and frank. "How long have you had it?"

"About four years."

In all the early YouTube videos of Mick and Quinn, the scar wasn't evident, so the rumors must be true. Quinn hadn't escaped Stella's accident unharmed. "So you got banged up when Stella…when she had her…her accident?"

Quinn sighed. "Shortly after. Car accident."

"Oh." Aspen wasn't sure if she should pry. As she considered her response, Quinn spoke.

"Tomorrow's our last day on the river."

Obviously, Quinn wanted to change the subject, so Aspen asked, "Happy or sad?"

Quinn rubbed her chin and stared into the fire for several beats before answering. "Both, I guess."

"You know I'm not going to let you get away with that answer, don't you?"

"I didn't think so." Quinn grinned. "It's been good for me to get back out here on the water. Spend some time with Mick." Her gaze locked on Aspen. "And you guys have been great to work with."

"Even though Peyton and DaKota can be a bit much?"

Quinn shook her head and smirked. "They don't bother me at all. Trust me, Mick and I have had our run-ins with plenty of frat boys and machismo men. Those two are nothing compared to that. They at least listen."

"Everyone doesn't?" *Duh.* "Pretty naïve of me to think everyone listens, huh?"

"A little." Quinn held up her hand with her thumb and finger slightly apart. "That's what I like about you."

"What, that I'm naïve and dense?"

"That you're innocent. That you think the best

of people."

"Yeah, it gets me in trouble, though." Aspen ran her hands through her hair. *Lots of trouble.*

"How so?" Quinn's intense gaze bore into her.

"I always believe everyone thinks like me. Has the same motives." Aspen shrugged. "I guess it's just my privilege showing."

Quinn tilted her head, and a puzzled expression crossed her face. "Privilege? What does that have to do with privilege?"

"That's what I thought, too." Aspen sighed. "Until I dated a social activist who set me straight on some things. That is before she left me."

"Ouch. Before she left you or on her way out the door?"

Heat rose up Aspen's neck. The end of that relationship had been an exceptionally memorable one. *How sad.* She'd had so many breakups that she only remembered the ugliest, and this one certainly qualified. "On the way out the door. She never told me any of these things when we were together, but she unloaded with both barrels when she left."

"Just like that. She slammed you and walked out?"

Aspen tried to grin but feared it came out more of a grimace. "It wasn't quite that simple. She was fine when I was pouring lots of money into her cause of the month." Aspen waved her hand. "That came out wrong. Lots of her causes were excellent, and I still contribute to them now. But she seemed to want more and more money without any accounting, so I turned off the tap, so to speak."

"No more money?"

"Exactly. She stuck around for a while to see if

I was serious. But when I cut out the middleman, she bolted." Aspen rubbed her chest, remembering how awful the tirade had been. She'd been verbally eviscerated. In hindsight, it was one last gasp effort to reopen the money tap. It hadn't worked, but it had left her wounded for some time. "Bolting wasn't good enough for her, though. She had to make me suffer on the way out."

"Hence the privilege comment?"

"Yep." Thinking about it still made Aspen's chest tighten. "She was vicious. It messed me up for a while. I guess it still does." Aspen wiped her sweating palm on her shirt sleeve and held it up. "I still have this reaction when I talk about it."

"I'm sorry. We can chat about something else." Quinn stood and threw a couple more logs on the fire.

Good. It must mean she wasn't planning on running Aspen off anytime soon. "It's okay. It's been several years. I'd almost forgotten about her." Aspen chuckled. "The ironic thing is, a couple years back, I saw she was arrested for embezzling from a nonprofit."

"Priceless."

"It was. Made me feel a little bit vindicated, but I still struggle knowing she had a point."

"Meaning?"

"After her tirade, I did a lot of research. I read something that said only the privileged can be optimists."

Quinn shook her head. "I don't believe that. You can drive yourself crazy reading some of that stuff."

"And I did." Aspen frowned. "I walked around for weeks being a complete downer. But I called it being a realist. Gina finally had to intervene. She plied me with so much self-help stuff that I had no choice but to come out of my funk. She helped me understand I can't feel guilty about the hand I was dealt."

"Solid advice."

"But how can I be an optimist when I know about all the horrible things going on in the world? Isn't that selfish of me?"

"And there you go in your vicious circle."

"Yes!" Aspen groaned and grabbed her head with both hands. "Ugh, how can anyone know what to do?"

"They can't."

"Well, thanks for that uplifting message." Aspen smiled.

Quinn chuckled. "That didn't come out quite right. Let me try again. You do the best you can with the best of intentions. That's all anyone can do."

"But that's the problem. What is my best? We spent a boatload of money to come here. Maybe I should have stayed home and donated all the money to a good cause. I live in a huge house. How wasteful. I could sell it and live in a tiny apartment and give more money to charity—"

"Stop." Quinn thrust out her hand. "Stop. You're spinning yourself in a circle. You've passed my test of how to tell if someone is good or not."

Aspen tilted her head. "I have, huh? And why is that?"

"Jerks don't think about these things." Quinn crossed her arms over her chest, and a satisfied smile parted her lips.

"That's it? It's that simple?"

"In my world, it is. You're trying to figure it out and do something about it, but that doesn't mean that you have to live like a monk, either." Quinn smiled.

"Do you want a newsflash?"

Aspen gazed at Quinn out of the corner of her eye. "Sure, why not?"

"You'll struggle with this your entire life and never find an answer."

"Aren't you full of hope and inspiration?" Aspen smiled. "I don't think you'd have a career at Hallmark." Aspen held up her hands as if she were unfurling a banner. "I can see the front of the card. *Don't worry*. And on the inside, it would say, *You'll never figure it out anyway*."

Quinn laughed. "That about sums it up, Frankie."

"How the hell did we get on this topic, anyway?" The tightness in Aspen's chest released. Quinn made her laugh.

"You started it," Quinn teased. "I was just sitting out here minding my own business, watching the fire."

"Too bad. You let me sit down, so now you're stuck with me."

Quinn pursed her lips, nodded, and pretended to think. "I guess it could have been worse."

"Ringing endorsement. I'll take it." Aspen smiled. "To change the subject from this fascinating conversation. Any concerns about tomorrow?" Aspen began to wonder if Quinn heard the question since she stared into the fire for some time without answering. By the look on her face, she was deep in thought. "Um, did you hear me?"

"Yeah, sorry." Quinn turned to Aspen. "Just trying to figure out how to answer."

"Take your time." Aspen sat back in her chair. Maybe it was the way the fire danced across Quinn's baby face that made her look so vulnerable. Despite her size, there were times Aspen wanted to hug her and tell her it would be okay. It was an odd reaction to such a powerful woman.

"I'd be lying if I said I wasn't apprehensive. Probably why I'm sitting out here when I should be in bed."

Warmth spread across Aspen's chest. Other than Gina, she'd not found many people who were willing to express what they were feeling. Most people in her world hid behind a curtain, only showing a small part of themselves. "What's making you apprehensive?"

"The kayaking," Quinn answered with delay. "I've done relatively well with the rafting."

"Relatively?" Aspen raised her eyebrow. From all she'd seen, Quinn handled everything perfectly.

"I had a moment." Quinn tossed another log on the fire. Aspen suspected it was to delay her answer since the fire didn't seem to need it. "The other day when we capsized. A flashback."

"Oh." *Shit.* Aspen hadn't intended for that to come out of her mouth. "Sorry. Continue."

Quinn shook her head but smiled. "Frankie, you wouldn't make a very good poker player. Your face shows everything."

Aspen laughed and playfully backhanded Quinn's knee. "Would you prefer I turn my chair around, so you can't see me?"

"Nah. It wouldn't stop you from opening that mouth of yours." Quinn winked.

"Keep it up, and I might have to look for another sidekick."

"Too late in the game for that. The trip is almost over."

Aspen's heart plunged, and sadness washed over her. Maybe her poker face would hold.

Before she could answer, Quinn said, "Hey, don't look so sad."

Nope. Obviously, everything she felt inside showed. "This has been an interesting experience for me. I've gone outside my comfort zone." Aspen stopped and met Quinn's gaze. "I've met some really good people."

"Yeah, those locals are pretty nice, aren't they?" Quinn grinned.

"I was talking about my sidekick. I'm going to miss her." *Damn.* She'd really taken to heart being direct. Most of her life, she'd let others pursue her, be it friendship or relationships. The reverse seemed too risky.

Quinn opened her mouth but closed it and cleared her throat. She sat for a couple of beats. "I'll miss you, too. It's not every day someone my size gets to play the sidekick."

"Sheesh, are you still harping on that? Size does not make the sidekick."

"Tell that to every superhero movie ever made."

"Not true. Tell that to Groot." Aspen gave Quinn a haughty smirk.

"That doesn't count. He's a tree, for fuck's sake."

Aspen shrugged. "He's still lots bigger. So you're like my Groot."

"Seriously? You're comparing me to a tree?"

Aspen shrugged and put on her best innocent look.

"Okay." Quinn studied her and nodded. "Now I don't know whether to call you Frankie or Rocket Raccoon."

"Don't think calling me a raccoon is going to get you out of telling me about the flashback." Even though Mick had already told her, she wanted to hear Quinn's version.

"Ah, thwarted." Quinn rubbed her hands together. "I came out of it pretty quick, so none of you even noticed." She stared down at her hands. "I think it was only a few seconds, but it felt like I was back on the river when Stella...when she...when she got hurt."

"Oh, Quinn." Aspen put her hand on Quinn's knee. "That must have been awful."

"Yeah, but like I said, it was over quick."

"What snapped you out of it?"

"Mick." Quinn answered quickly, her voice louder than she'd been talking. Her face reddened, and she looked away.

Aspen stared. That was weird. *Leave it be? Nope.* "What aren't you saying?"

"And you." Quinn's voice came out barely louder than a whisper.

Aspen kept her gaze on the top of Quinn's head, even though she couldn't see her face. She wanted to see Quinn's eyes when she finally looked up. "You? What does that mean?"

"Is it really necessary that I finish this story?"

"Yep. This trip, we are being honest and direct."

"That's what you're supposed to be doing. Not me."

"I changed the rules." Aspen couldn't believe herself. What happened to the woman who didn't want to make any waves or be a bother? "Spill."

Quinn finally looked up. Aspen couldn't read her eyes. They weren't exactly guarded. More like wary. "Mick yelled at me, trying to snap me out of it. She said I stared right through her, and it scared the shit out of her. Then she said, *Aspen needs you.* That's when she said my eyes cleared, and I came back."

"Really?" She put her hand on her chest. It felt full but not in a bad way. "I'm touched. Thank you." Emotion threatened to overwhelm her. Besides Gina, there was nobody in her life she felt would protect her. She knew she should feel that way about her parents but didn't. And Peyton was too self-absorbed. She shook her head as if to clear her thoughts. *Where had that come from?*

"Are you okay, Rocket?" Quinn grinned.

How sweet. Aspen suspected she'd used her new nickname just to lighten the moment. It worked. Aspen felt vulnerable and exposed. Bantering with Quinn would get her on more solid ground. Quinn's crimson cheeks indicated she'd be good with it, too. "I'm good, Groot."

Quinn smiled, and her eyes shined. "Tell me. What's the first thing you're going to do when you get back to San Francisco?"

Much safer ground. She sat up straighter in her chair and bounced a little for good measure. She wanted to reestablish her goofy cluelessness and leave behind the emotional conversation. Tomorrow would be challenging enough without heavy emotions hanging over them. "Doughnuts."

"Doughnuts? Of all the things, you choose doughnuts?" Quinn put her head in her hands and exaggerated a head shake. *Yep,* she was going for an over-the-top reaction, too.

"Don't judge me. I'm obsessed with Krispy Kreme."

"I take back everything I said earlier. Definitely privileged."

"Oh, man." Aspen crossed her arms over her

chest and jutted out her lip. "It's not like I said a pedicure or a massage." She glared at Quinn. "Not even a latte. What is more wholesome and unprivileged than a doughnut?"

Quinn held up her hands. "Whoa, whoa. I stand corrected. Sheesh. You're getting pretty feisty over doughnuts. Who knew they would be such a sensitive topic?"

Aspen bumped Quinn's knee with hers and smiled. "I'll let it pass, this time. Is there anything after Ghostrider? Maybe the Twisting Cyclone of Death? Or Satan's Armpit?"

Quinn laughed and sat back against her chair, the tension in her jaw gone. "Now you're just making shit up again."

"Yup." Aspen relaxed into her chair.

The fire flickered as they continued to talk into the night.

Chapter Twenty-three

*A*hh. *Liquid gold.* Quinn took another sip of her coffee. Damn, this was good. She let the aromatic steam tickle her nostrils before she pulled the cup away from her lips.

She glanced around the circle and grinned to herself. It seemed there were two camps. The morning people and those who weren't. DaKota and Peyton chattered among themselves, clearly ready to take on the day. Tina had eaten a little fruit before heading out for her morning jog. LeAnn and Mick sat next to each other but didn't speak. Their expressions were similar: Don't bother us. They exchanged a few half sentences, but other than that, they drank their coffee and nibbled on their breakfast. With each sip, more life entered their eyes.

Quinn bit her lip when she glanced at Claire. Morning, afternoon, or evening, she looked dazed and confused. This morning was no different.

Aspen was the only one missing. When Quinn emerged from her tent, Peyton and DaKota were already up. She thought of asking after Aspen but decided against it. They wouldn't break camp for at least another hour.

"I take it you two are excited about today," Quinn said to Peyton and DaKota.

"How'd you guess?" Peyton smiled. Quinn hadn't paid much attention before, but this morning, there was no denying how attractive Peyton was. She'd never been attracted to tiny butch women, but she could finally understand Aspen's attraction. Her black hair made her piercing blue eyes stand out.

Quinn squinted into the sun. Had she been that shut down that she noticed nothing before this? She shifted her gaze back to the pair. "Any nerves?"

DaKota held her steady hand out. "Not a one."

"Yeah, right." Peyton elbowed her. "Miss steady. You could barely eat your breakfast."

"I wasn't hungry." DaKota glared at Peyton. She met Quinn's gaze. "Just ignore her. She doesn't have a clue what she's talking about."

Quinn smiled while the two bickered. DaKota wasn't nearly as striking as Peyton, but she had an air about her. A confidence that Peyton only pretended to have.

The more she observed them, the more she realized she had been sleepwalking through the last several days. What did this mean? What would happen when she started noticing things and paying attention to the things around her? She might start feeling again, too. The thought caused her breath to catch in her throat. The past several years, she'd survived by not feeling anything. Could she handle it?

She glanced at Mick, needing a distraction. "Hey, sleepyhead," Quinn said. "If you aren't going to eat that second biscuit, toss it here."

"I'm still working on it." Mick scowled. "Just because you inhale your food doesn't mean we all do."

LeAnn chuckled and stood. "Here. Take mine. I'm not going to eat it."

"No." Quinn waved her off. "You need your nourishment."

LeAnn put the biscuit on Quinn's plate. "Nonsense. I can get more if I get hungry."

"She could shag her ass over to the table and get another one, too," Mick said.

Quinn glanced up at LeAnn. "Ignore her. Nobody should be forced to interact with her until she's had her second cup of coffee."

LeAnn smiled and returned to her seat.

Quinn tore off a piece of biscuit and set it on her tongue. *So good.* She closed her eyes and made happy eating sounds. As she went to swallow, she opened her eyes, and her food caught in her throat.

Aspen pushed out of her tent. The sunlight hit her long blond hair, giving it an almost ethereal quality. If Quinn had seen the vision on television, she'd insist the image was altered. Aspen blinked against the sun and pulled her sunglasses off the top of her head.

Quinn pulled her gaze away. She didn't want to get caught staring, even though she was drawn to Aspen's graceful movement. *Jesus. Enough.* What was up with her this morning? After years of not noticing anything in her surroundings, now she seemed to notice everything.

"Babe." Peyton smiled and jumped up from her seat.

Damn. Peyton must really be a morning person. Her reaction to Aspen's arrival seemed a little over the top, but who was Quinn to judge? Ghostrider apparently had everyone, not just Quinn, acting weird.

"Morning," Aspen muttered.

Put her in the *not a morning person* camp.

"Look, there's a whole spread of food over there." Peyton pointed at the table. "It's got everything. I'll go with you to check it out." Peyton's delivery was rapid fire. "The biscuits are to die for."

"I'm not hungry." Aspen sat on the empty chair next to LeAnn and scowled.

Really not a morning person. Quinn sneaked another glance out of the corner of her eye.

"I'll grab you a plate." Peyton hurried off.

With her sunglasses on, Quinn couldn't tell where Aspen was looking, but she'd turned her head in Quinn's direction. Quinn shifted her gaze fully toward Aspen.

"Good morning," Aspen said. A genuine smile lit her entire face.

"Good morning to you, too." Quinn smiled. *Odd.* "Are you sore this morning?"

Aspen shifted in her seat and grimaced. "A little." She moved some more and groaned. "Maybe slightly more than a little."

"That's typical. I wasn't joking when I said it'll go away once we head out. Adrenaline will take over."

"I can't believe what a beautiful day it is." Aspen breathed in deeply. "I think I might become outdoorsy yet."

Peyton returned with a plate piled with food and a cup of coffee. She set it on the table next to Aspen. "You need to eat something."

Aspen glanced up at her without a smile. "Thank you." The words came out frosty.

Mick pointed at the pile of food. "I highly recommend the biscuits. But watch out for Quinn, she tried to steal mine."

Aspen laughed and picked up a biscuit. "If she tries to steal it again, I'll let you have one of mine."

"Do you want me to get you more?" Peyton

asked and jumped from her seat.

"No."

Quinn caught a glimpse of Mick, who studied the couple. Her lips pursed and eyes narrowed. After seeing Mick's reaction, Quinn felt more solid in her assessment that something was going on.

Aspen snatched a banana from the plate, then tore off the top of a muffin. The rest of the food sat untouched. She sipped on her coffee and looked out at the river.

Quinn thought about initiating another conversation but thought better of it. Whatever was causing Aspen's mood swings seemed to involve Peyton, so she needed to stay out of it. Her nerves were already a little frayed this morning. The thought of kayaking Ghostrider still had her edgy.

"So, Quinn or Mick, are you gonna tell us the real story of how Ghostrider got its name?" LeAnn said, breaking the silence.

Quinn glanced at the still bleary-eyed Mick. "Grumpy over there won't be any use until she's had her second cup of coffee, so I wouldn't ask her anything."

Mick glowered. "To be honest, I'm not sure."

"I still can't believe you pulled that shit," Aspen said, her eyes more friendly than earlier.

"You had us going. Right, Aspen?" Peyton said.

Aspen gazed at Peyton, and her eyes darkened.

LeAnn's gaze shifted between Aspen and Peyton. Her lips parted, but then she squeezed them together. She turned to Quinn. "Ghostrider is the only thing on the agenda today?"

"Yep." Quinn nodded. "The guides will load us up and take us to a spot a little way upriver from

Ghostrider."

"I don't mean to sound dense," LeAnn said, "but couldn't we follow the river to get there?"

"Just like Commercial Suicide, there's some parts that we have to go around anyway. With everyone so excited about Ghostrider, we thought it would be best to get there as soon as possible."

"Yep, we'll be there for a while," Mick added.

"She speaks." Quinn grinned. "Second cup of coffee kick in?"

"Sumpin' like that." Mick scowled and brought the cup to her lips.

"Don't let me stop you from enlightening the group." Quinn gestured that Mick had the floor.

"Like I was saying before I was rudely interrupted." Mick shot Quinn a look before continuing. "It'll probably take us the better part of the day. By the time we get everything loaded up here and get to our put in spot, it'll be mid-morning. Then we'll shoot her in the raft first before we'll be transported back to where the kayaks will be waiting for us."

"Did you confirm with the guides that they'll be there?" Peyton asked DaKota.

"Yep, they've assured me everything will be ready."

"Good," Mick said. "Then you'll go down one at a time. Quinn and I will go down with, as will the local guides."

Quinn's heart began to race. *Breathe.* She needed to be on her game today, so she couldn't afford to be freaking out. Quinn tuned back into the conversation, hoping if she stayed focused, she could keep her nerves at bay.

"And where will Aspen have to go while we're

kayaking?" Peyton said and shot a look at Aspen. Irritation crossed Aspen's face before she turned away. "Come on, babe. I was just asking."

Aspen's head snapped around. "Don't even go there." Her eyes narrowed, and her jaw set. Peyton started to speak, but Aspen pointed. "No. I'm done with this conversation." When she got to her feet, she bumped the table where her nearly untouched plate of food sat. As if in slow motion, the plate toppled onto the ground. She turned and marched off.

Everyone sat in stunned silence before DaKota spoke. "And the Oscar goes to…"

"Knock it off," Peyton said and dropped to her knees.

"What the hell? You're gonna clean up after her?" DaKota said in response.

Peyton continued with her task, ignoring DaKota.

"As you were saying," Quinn said.

Taking her cue, Mick continued. "Safety is paramount, which is why this will take most of the day. It'll depend on how many other groups are also there."

"Why can't we all just go down at the same time?" DaKota asked. "It'd be so epic."

"No," Mick said. "It's all about the safety. Since there's only two of us, we can't keep track of you all at once."

"But we have like eight million local guides," Peyton said, still picking up the spilled food. "That should be enough to keep things in check."

Quinn sighed. She didn't have it in her to argue with Peyton and DaKota. The day had already begun to close in around her. Abruptly, she stood. "You figure this out, Mick. I'm going to pack our gear."

As she was walking away, she heard, "Quinn!"

She thought about ignoring it, but she turned back. "Yes?"

"At least think about letting me and DaKota go down together." Peyton grinned. "Please."

Quinn nodded and turned back to her tent.

Chapter Twenty-four

*G*oddamn *it.* Aspen had not wanted to make a scene in front of the others. Unfortunately, that was exactly what she'd just done. Aspen stared out over the water and inhaled deeply. She couldn't deny how peaceful it was out here, but she doubted she'd have chosen to do this without Peyton's influence.

She wrapped her arms around herself, despite the warmth. Truth be told, she wanted today to be over. Then she could get back to her real life and figure things out. *Interesting.* She'd not allowed herself to think about the future. No, that wasn't true. She already had the answer. She'd had it before this trip but hadn't wanted to admit it.

It would be easy to blame Peyton, pin it on her frat boy behavior, but it wouldn't be fair. Peyton hadn't changed; Aspen had. They'd been drawn to each other's looks but had little in common. Peyton took no interest in the things she liked, but then again, many times, she tuned Peyton out when she talked. *No,* she couldn't solely fault Peyton.

Aspen sighed and sat on a large boulder. Maybe she should see if a guide could take her back to Elephant Camp, so she wouldn't be a burden today. The last couple of days, DaKota made it her mission to remind her that she didn't belong while Peyton sat idly by. Last night and this morning, she'd gone out of her way to rub kayaking Ghostrider in her face, or at least that was what Aspen thought.

She sighed again. Last night, Peyton had told her she was imagining it and being overly sensitive, which resulted in an argument that hadn't resolved itself this morning. She rubbed her temples, hoping to release some of the building tension.

She didn't belong. What's new? She'd never belonged anywhere. Her mood continued to worsen. Maybe she should kayak Ghostrider. That would teach them, show she wasn't some lightweight princess. Then she could hold her head up high and keep DaKota off her back. *Really?* They weren't in grade school anymore. Peer pressure should be a thing of the past. A sardonic laugh escaped her before she could stop it.

Great. Everyone would certainly think she was cracking up if they caught her laughing all by herself. Maybe she was. She glanced down at her trembling hands. Weren't vacations supposed to be for relaxing? She felt anything but relaxed.

She drew her knees up to her chest and rested her chin against them. Meditation might help. At least that was what Molly—or was it Maddie?—taught her. *Ugh.* She'd been through so many she couldn't even remember their names. That was ridiculous; of course she could. She closed her eyes and began ticking off the women she'd dated.

Shit. She'd missed one, so she started over. After three unsuccessful tries, she buried her head against her knees and let the tears flow.

She didn't know how long she'd been there, but the tears had been cathartic. The tightness in her chest was gone, and she could breathe again. Although, she'd come no closer to knowing what to do. *Oh, well.*

She couldn't sit out here all day.

As she got closer to their campsite, she surveyed the area, wanting to get a read on Peyton's whereabouts. She wasn't ready to talk with her.

Neat stacks of gear were piled outside of Quinn and Mick's tent. Quinn was peeking her head inside, probably to make sure she'd not forgotten anything before she took it down.

Aspen made a beeline toward Quinn. Maybe she could give her some words of wisdom. Her pace had been sluggish, but now a bounce returned to her step. *Yep.* Quinn was just what she needed.

"Hey there," Aspen said as she approached.

"Hey." Quinn stood and smiled. "Things better now?"

She considered lying, but that would break the rules she set. Her shoulders slumped. "I don't know."

"Decisive," Quinn said.

Aspen started to bristle but then saw the mischief dancing in Quinn's eyes. "So you think taunting me is going to break me out of this mood?"

"It's worth a try." Quinn grinned. "Plus, it's fun. A win-win for me."

Despite her bad mood, Aspen laughed. Funny, but Quinn had that effect on her. Something about her playfulness coupled with the wound that lay just under the surface put Aspen at ease. "Keep it up, and I just might find another sidekick."

Quinn chuckled as she bent and pulled up one of the tent stakes. "I hear there's a shortage of them, so I wouldn't go firing yours before you found another."

"Hmph, just be forewarned, you're working on borrowed time."

"Good to know." Quinn moved on to the next

stake. "You gonna tell me what's eating at you?"

Aspen took a deep breath. "I feel like a burden to the group. Everyone else will be kayaking, and I'll be sitting on the sideline like a loser. Maybe I should just do it."

"That's ridiculous. You don't have any experience." Quinn moved on to another stake without looking up. "You're not doing it."

Heat rose up Aspen's neck all the way to her cheeks. Aspen's jaw tightened. "Who the hell do you think you are telling me what I'm not doing?"

Quinn chuckled and moved on to another stake. "Remember, I'm the guide, Frankie."

"Don't call me Frankie."

Quinn's head snapped up. Her mouth hung open, and her eyes held a mixture of confusion and hurt. "Whoa. What's going on?" She stood and walked toward Aspen but abruptly stopped.

Aspen clenched her fists at her side and took several cleansing breaths. By the look on Quinn's face, she'd had no idea Aspen was upset.

Months of Peyton dictating everything she did. The countless girlfriends she'd blindly followed. Hell, if she were honest, it started with her parents and never stopped.

Quinn took another step toward her and held out her hand. "Aspen, I'm not sure what's going on, but I'd like it if you'd talk to me."

Fuck. This wasn't fair, but here she was about ready to kick the innocent puppy that happened to be in the way. She needed to get a grip. She hoped her voice wouldn't crack when she finally spoke. "I am so sick and tired of people telling me what to do." She pointed at Quinn. "And you will not be another in a long line that came before."

"Whoa. I'm not into telling people what to do. It's your life. But—"

"No!" Aspen pointed her finger. Rage burned in her. She tried to push it back, but there didn't seem to be any stopping it. "No! There is no but. It is my life to do what I want with it."

"I don't have any idea why you're taking this out on me." Quinn's cheeks turned ruddy. "But you need to relax and talk to me." Quinn's voice quivered.

Relax? The word bore into Aspen's skull and unleashed a new level of anger. She fought against herself. Why was she doing this? It was so unfair to Quinn, but she couldn't stop the anger boiling inside. "Stop. Telling. Me. What. To. Do," Aspen said between gritted teeth. "I will relax when I am damned good and ready."

Quinn took a step back, her face even more flushed than before. She opened her mouth but then closed it. Without a word, she walked back to the tent. With one yank, she pulled another stake out and moved to the next.

Was Quinn dismissing her? Casually going about her business as Aspen came unhinged. Years of hurt and anger bubbled inside of her. Despite knowing she shouldn't unleash it on Quinn, she was the only one here. Aspen bit the inside of her cheek, willing herself to calm down. "So you're going to ignore me now?"

Quinn's shoulders stiffened, and she stopped removing stakes. She remained kneeling but didn't turn around. "I think you should leave now."

Aspen stared at Quinn's back. *Unbelievable.* She thought they were becoming friends, but she'd obviously been wrong. "I get it. The first time I show any sign of unpleasant emotions, you want nothing more to do with me." Irrational thoughts pinged in her head. As much as she wanted to control them, she was losing the battle.

Quinn remained beside the tent where she knelt, not moving or responding. Her shoulders rose and fell with her breath.

Quinn's lack of response only infuriated Aspen. Why was she on this stupid trip anyway? One of the few bright spots of being here was Quinn but no more. Aspen glared at Quinn's back, willing her to do or say something. The longer Quinn remained motionless, the hotter Aspen's face became. A tremor surged through her body. She clawed at her arms to stop the sensation of worms crawling under her skin. "Goddamn it, look at me."

"No. Please go," Quinn said in a measured voice.

Listen to Quinn. Aspen needed to stop and walk away. Get some control back before she made things worse. She wasn't being fair. She walked to where Quinn knelt and stopped inches from her. "I thought you wanted frank and direct. Didn't you mean it?"

Quinn didn't react to her proximity. "If you're looking for an argument, you've come to the wrong place." Quinn duck walked to the next stake and reached for it.

Great. Another person who thought of her as a doormat. *Go away, Aspen. You're bothering me.* Story of her life. Not this time. "Do *not* ignore me. Do you hear me, Quinn?" Aspen tried to control the volume of her voice, so the others didn't hear. She sneaked a glance toward them. *Good.* They seemed to be engrossed in conversation.

Quinn had dropped to her knees next to the last

stake on this side of the tent. "I'm going to go around the backside now. I would appreciate it if you would be gone when I return." Quinn stood and disappeared behind the tent.

Aspen hated herself in the moment. She needed to stop and do as Quinn asked, but she might never see Quinn again if she did. She fought to get her emotions under control, but her chest felt as if a whale were sitting on it. Maybe she should go jump in the water to cool off.

Quinn had walked away from her. She couldn't leave it like this. Aspen strode around the tent and came face to face with Quinn, who was about to bend. A look of shock crossed Quinn's face before she took several steps back.

"Please, go." Quinn's gaze darted around. There was an unfocused look in her eyes. Her bright red face showed signs of strain, and sweat beaded on her brow.

Aspen stopped in her tracks and gaped. The transformation of Quinn startled her, her earlier anger gone. "Are you okay?"

"I need you to leave." Quinn swiped at the sweat that rolled down the side of her cheek. She backed up against the tent and nearly tripped over one of the stakes. She caught one of the poles and steadied herself. The canvas rippled where Quinn's trembling hand grasped it.

Aspen took another step forward. "Quinn, it's okay. Talk to me." She touched Quinn's clammy hand.

Quinn jumped and retreated several steps away.

"I'm sorry." Aspen held out her hands with her palms up. Somewhere she'd read it was a sign of conciliation. "I took out my frustration on you. It wasn't fair."

"You're not going down Ghostrider in a kayak." Quinn crossed her arms over her chest. "And that's final."

Aspen's pulse quickened. *Not again.* She'd calmed down, but she was still sick of people telling her what to do. "It's not your choice to make." Aspen stared defiantly.

Quinn's eyes blazed, the sweetness gone. "My decision is final. You are *not* doing it."

"Really?" Aspen took another step toward Quinn, which forced her to look up into Quinn's eyes. She would not be bullied. *Wow. How irrational.* Quinn was the last thing from a bully.

"I'm telling you. It's not safe." Quinn bent and grabbed a stake.

"Fine. Back to ignoring me again, I see." Aspen spun around to leave.

She made her way to the front of the tent, which had begun to collapse. The stakes clanked as Quinn tossed them into a pile.

The tent deflated. Aspen should leave and let them both cool down, but instead, she stood rooted to the spot. She stared across the expanse at Quinn. By the set of her jaw, Aspen suspected that Quinn knew she hadn't left, but she made no attempt to acknowledge her.

Quinn pulled the last stake and hurled it at the pile. It clanked against the other and ricocheted several feet away. Quinn stomped to where it had landed and snatched it off the ground.

Once she completed her task, Quinn finally looked up. Her eyes still seemed off. Her gaze lacked focus, almost as if she were looking straight through Aspen.

Aspen knew she'd blown it. Who got in a fight with a new friend this soon after meeting? She needed to explain it to Quinn, then everything would be okay.

Aspen cleared her throat. Quinn didn't meet her gaze. Aspen cleared it again. Still no response. "Can we finish this conversation?" Aspen kept her voice low.

"Nothing to talk about," Quinn said. "I'm the guide, and I said no."

"Damn it." Aspen moved closer. "Would you stop and look at me? Talk to me."

Quinn met Aspen's gaze. Her mouth set in a thin line, and her jaw clenched.

"I'm sick of being the pathetic joke." Tears welled in Aspen's eyes. "I thought you were different. That you respected me. Maybe you're right that I shouldn't do it, but I never thought you'd just flat out say *no*. Couldn't you have had a conversation with me, instead of bossing me around?"

"Seriously? You think risking your life in a kayak is going to prove something to anyone? Why would we even need to talk about it?"

"I'm so damned sick of people telling me who I am and what I can do. What gives you that right?" Aspen took a deep breath. How had they gotten into such a ridiculous fight? How stupid. It was like doubling down on a pair of deuces.

"Because I'm the fucking expert, that's why. Who in their right mind decides to take such a stupid risk?" Quinn's voice rose again, and her gaze darted around the area. She moved quickly and grabbed the corner of the tent.

Button. Pushed. Bile rose in Aspen's throat. Now she was too stupid to make her own choices?

That was exactly how everyone treated her. At least Quinn had the guts to say it to her face, but it still stung. "That's right. I'm a fucking idiot. Thirty-three years old and never done a damned thing without someone telling me what to do. But guess what? Not this time. Remember, this is my fucking movie." Aspen marched toward Quinn and pointed. "And I will choose the scenes in my movie. Not you. Do you understand me? I will choose."

Quinn stood still with her arms at her sides and her back straight. A vein throbbed in her neck, and her face turned fire engine red.

"What's the matter? Don't have anything to say to that? Huh?" Aspen blinked and stepped within a foot of Quinn. She needed to get a grip. Taunting Quinn was not only unnecessary, but also unfair. She'd done nothing to deserve this treatment and would probably hate Aspen after this trip. Aspen hated herself, so how could Quinn not? *Breathe.* She needed to make this right before it was too late. She took another step forward.

Quinn's lips quivered, and her eyes were unfocused. She thrust her face within an inch of Aspen's. "Goddamn it, *Stella*, I said you're not going." Spittle flew from Quinn's mouth.

Aspen gasped and stumbled backward. Oh, god, what had she done?

Quinn's face went white. She put her hand over her mouth. Tears streamed down her face. Then she turned and ran.

"Quinn, wait!" Aspen called after her, but Quinn kept running.

"Aspen." She heard her name called and turned. Mick and Peyton ran toward her.

"What the hell is going on?" Mick asked when she arrived.

Tears streamed down Aspen's face. "It's all my fault. I'm so sorry. It's all my fault."

Mick put her hand on Aspen's arm. "Can you tell me what the hell just happened? Did Quinn just scream Stella's name?"

Aspen nodded. "Oh, god. I caused it. What an idiot."

"Babe, calm down." Peyton put her hand on Aspen's shoulder.

She recoiled from Peyton's touch. She couldn't do this right now, not with Peyton.

"God, what's your problem?" Peyton barked.

Mick held up her hand. "Okay. I have no idea what's going on, but right now, I'm worried about Quinn." She waved her hand between Aspen and Peyton. "Whatever you two have going on will have to wait."

Aspen nodded. "She's right." She met Peyton's gaze. "Can you please let me talk to Mick alone? This isn't about you and me."

"To hell it's not. If Quinn did something to upset you, then I should know."

Aspen counted to ten in her mind. She'd already done enough damage, so she needed to stop before she did more. "Please." She smiled and put her hand on Peyton's arm. "Quinn didn't do anything. It was me. I think I triggered a flashback of some kind. I wasn't thinking, and I pushed her. Can you let me talk to Mick, so maybe she can fix things?"

"Is this gonna fuck up our run today?" Peyton said.

Unbelievable. That was the first thing Peyton

thought of. "I'm going to talk to Mick, and you need to leave us alone."

Peyton's jaw tensed. "I think we need to talk."

"No." Aspen raised her voice but kept it controlled. "I am going to tell you one more time. You need to go. We will talk later."

Peyton's face flushed, but when Aspen held her gaze, she lowered her head and turned. As she walked away, Aspen thought Peyton said, "Fuck me. I won the bet but lost my girlfriend."

What the hell did that mean? Aspen didn't have time to deal with that right now. Her only thoughts were of Quinn. Once Peyton was out of earshot, Mick took both of Aspen's hands and looked her in the eye. "I need you to tell me everything that just happened."

"Oh, god. I was such an idiot." Aspen's words poured out. "I was upset and took it out on her when she didn't deserve any of it. I'm such a selfish bitch."

"Whoa." Mick squeezed Aspen's hands. "Slow down and tell me what happened."

"I saw it in her eyes." Tears streamed down Aspen's face. "I knew something wasn't right, but I was so wrapped up in myself. Oh, god. What is my problem? I can't—"

Mick brought a finger to her own lips. "Shh. What say you relax for a minute? I'm not understanding what you're telling me."

Aspen took a deep breath. In a rush of words and tears, Aspen relayed the story.

"Oh, fuck," Mick said after Aspen finished. "Sounds like a flashback to me."

Aspen slammed her palm against her forehead. "Why didn't I realize? It was as if she were somewhere else. But I kept at her until she blew."

"I need to go find her." Mick let go of her hands, and Aspen immediately missed the comforting warmth.

"I am so sorry. Please...please tell Quinn I'm sorry."

"I understand you're upset, but this isn't the first time it's happened, so you can't blame yourself too much."

Aspen's stomach lurched. "Oh, god. Just last night, Quinn told me about the flashback she had when our raft tipped over."

Mick's eyebrows rose. "She did?"

"Yes, we had a really great talk. I couldn't sleep."

"And she told you about it?"

Aspen studied Mick. "Yeah." The word came out more tentatively than she planned.

"Don't you see how huge that is?" Mick took Aspen's hands again. "Quinn let you in and trusted you. She doesn't do that."

Mick's words were like a knife to her heart. Aspen rubbed her chest. "And then I betrayed that trust."

"We'll make it right, but first, I need to find her. She's probably hiding out somewhere. I'm sure she's embarrassed that she lost it in front of you."

"No. I'm the one to blame." Aspen's chest tightened further. "I'm so ashamed."

"Exactly, and that's how Quinn is feeling about now." Mick patted her arm. "Sitting around here chatting isn't gonna help me find her."

"I don't suppose I can go with you."

Mick shook her head. "She doesn't need an audience. Let me assess what's going on. Then maybe you can have a word with her."

"Please, tell her I'm sorry. Tell her I know I acted like a jerk. I want to make it up to her. Tell her I need my sidekick, now more than ever."

Mick's brow furrowed. "Sidekick?"

"Long story, but she'll know what it means."

"Okay. I better go find her."

Tears welled in Aspen's eyes. She grabbed Mick's hand and held it tightly. "Tell me she'll be okay."

"She'll be okay. I've walked through many a flashback with her. It's just been a while, but she always comes out of them. I'll bring her back."

Chapter Twenty-five

Quinn threw another rock into the river. She used to skip stones as a kid, but the raging water didn't allow for a single bounce before the water swallowed it up. The way she felt, she wished the water would take her away, too.

No! She couldn't think that way. The last time she did, it hadn't turned out so well. She ran her thumb over her cheek before she slid farther down on the boulder. The spray from the river spritzed her face. It helped cool her burning cheeks.

Quinn couldn't believe she'd lost it in front of Aspen. It probably scared the shit out of her, having Quinn yell Stella's name in her face. Aspen would never want to talk to her again. She still couldn't figure out why Aspen had been so angry. She'd been sitting here trying to make sense of it, to no avail.

The first friend she'd made in so long, and she'd screwed it up. *Fuck.* She thought she'd been getting better. It had been a while since she'd had a flashback, well, except for when they capsized on Gulliver's Travels. She slung a rock into the water and scowled.

"Hey, buddy. Care if I join you?" Mick's familiar voice said from behind her.

Quinn slid over on the rock, making room for Mick. "Afraid I'm not much of a conversationalist right now."

"I see some things never change." Mick

hopscotched several rocks before landing on the one where Quinn sat. "You've never been a good conversationalist."

Quinn couldn't muster up a laugh or a witty response, so she gave Mick a halfhearted grin.

Mick landed on the boulder where Quinn sat, and her feet slid on the wet surface. She grabbed Quinn's shoulder to steady herself before sitting next to her. "Want to tell me what's going on?"

Quinn remained silent for several minutes. She continued tossing rocks into the water one at a time. Without a word, she held out a handful of stones to Mick. Soon both were hurling the rocks into the waves.

Mick waited her out, not saying anything. She tossed rocks as if they had all day, while in reality, they were scheduled to depart for Ghostrider within the hour.

"I lost my shit again," Quinn said. "I felt it coming on, and I tried everything to stop it."

"Whoa, wait? You knew it was coming?"

"Yeah."

Mick grabbed Quinn's arm and shook it. "Oh, my god, that's wonderful."

Quinn shot her a sideways glance. "Seriously? There's nothing wonderful about flashbacks."

Mick shook her head. "Don't give me that clueless look. This is the first time you knew they were coming. Normally, they just smacked you upside the head without warning."

Quinn sat up straighter, and a surge of warmth spread across her chest. "You're right. Maybe I *can* stop them. I held it at bay for a while, but Aspen just kept at me and at me."

"How did you know? What signs did you get? How did you manage to hold it back?"

Quinn smirked, nearly laughing. "Whoa, partner," Quinn said in an exaggerated drawl. "I don't believe I've heard you talk that fast since Karen Hightower asked you out on a date."

Mick playfully punched her arm and groaned. "God, don't remind me. Seriously, do you see how big this is?"

Quinn nodded. "I'm beginning to after your rapid-fire delivery."

"So answer me."

"I can't remember all the questions now."

Mick groaned. "You're impossible."

Quinn bumped Mick with her shoulder. She felt human again. Still upset by ruining things with Aspen, but at least she could breathe. "Care to give them one at a time?"

"Simpleton." Mick rolled her eyes. "How did you know it was coming on?" Mick said with an exaggerated drawl.

Quinn gazed at the water, contemplating the question. "Hmm." She put her hand next to her head and moved her fingers around in a chaotic pattern. "It was like my brain started going fuzzy. You know when we used to have the old TV my grandma gave us that had that antenna?"

Mick nodded.

"And the picture would come in and out," Quinn continued. "It was like that. Things started to get fuzzy. I could feel it. Then flashes of Stella would come, but then I'd be back there with Aspen."

"Was it all happening on its own or were you doing something?"

"I was talking with Aspen, and for some reason, she was pissed off at me. She wasn't exactly yelling, but she was talking loudly. I still don't know what I did." Quinn ran her hands through her hair and frowned.

"That's not what I meant. I meant how did you hold it at bay when it started happening?" Mick paused. "No, keep telling me what happened. Maybe there's a clue in there somewhere."

"She was worked up about something. She seemed angry or at least upset. I tried joking her out of it while I took the tent down. Then it turned. It gets a little fuzzy from there." Quinn closed her eyes, hoping it would make it easier to remember. "She said she should kayak Ghostrider." Quinn put her hand on her chest. "I felt tight, like I couldn't breathe. Then I pushed through it and told her it was ridiculous. That's when she really lost it on me. Telling me that I had no right to tell her what to do. She was so irrational." Quinn squeezed her eyes tighter, trying to remember.

"Are you okay?" Mick asked after the silence dragged on.

"Yeah, just trying to get it straight in my mind." Quinn opened her eyes and met Mick's gaze. "It was like I kept coming in and out. I tried to ground myself. To calm down. Stella's face kept flashing. Aspen was upset about people telling her what to do, but I thought I was on firm ground. When she said she would kayak Ghostrider if she wanted to," Quinn put her hand against her forehead, "it got really black. And I yelled at her." Quinn pulled her hand from her face and met Mick's gaze. "Oh, god, did I call her Stella?"

Mick nodded. "You did. I heard you yell Stella's name, so I came running."

Quinn shook her head. "Fuck me. I've ruined

everything."

"How so? I think it was a breakthrough."

"Aspen must hate me. I'm such a jerk."

Mick chuckled. "Aspen certainly doesn't hate you. When I left, she was a puddle of goo, saying she'd screwed everything up." Mick winked and elbowed Quinn. "I think she likes you."

"Really? We're not in junior high. And how many times do I have to tell you, she's got a girlfriend?"

"Sheesh, I didn't mean she likes you that way." Mick's eyes shimmered with amusement.

"Do you always give the wink, wink, nod when you're telling me someone wants to be my friend?"

"There was only one wink, no nod, and an elbow. Get your story straight, will ya?"

Quinn put her hand against her chest and feigned contrition. "I stand corrected."

"Honest." Mick slapped her hand on Quinn's knee. "She was going on about how she'd taken her shit out on you and that she didn't want to screw up the friendship you guys were developing. She wanted to come with me to talk to you, but I told her to let me go into the lion's den first." Mick scrunched up her nose. "She said to tell you she needed her sidekick."

"Really?" Hope rose in Quinn. "She's not mad?"

"At herself, but certainly not you." Mick studied Quinn before continuing. "Want to go back and talk to her?"

Quinn looked away. "No, I can't. Everyone saw the whole thing. They'll be staring."

"How 'bout I bring her to you?"

Quinn sucked in her breath. "Do you think she'd come?"

"In a heartbeat. My guess is she'd run here."

Quinn wrapped her arm over Mick's shoulders and squeezed her. Mick's eyes widened, and her mouth dropped open before she smiled.

"Thanks. You're not half bad sometimes," Quinn said.

"Ringing endorsement coming from you." Mick jumped to her feet. "I'm gonna get her now." She put her hand on Quinn's shoulder. "We still have Ghostrider to tackle."

"I'll be ready."

"I knew you would be." Mick hopped up two boulders and turned. "You're getting better. I see it. Just keep going, and you're gonna make it."

"Thanks." Quinn felt the heat in her cheeks. She took another rock and threw it into the river.

⚜⚜⚜⚜

"Are you sure about this?" Aspen turned and met Mick's gaze. "She's not mad?"

"I promise you, all will be fine." Mick motioned to Quinn sitting on a boulder in the distance. "I think you need to do this on your own. It'd change things if I awkwardly lingered."

Aspen chuckled and grabbed Mick's hand. "I can't imagine you awkwardly doing anything."

Mick's cheeks colored. "She feels as bad as you do. You'll work it out."

"What if...umm...what if it happens again?"

"You mean a flashback?"

Aspen nodded. The words caught in her throat.

"Thing is, you know what you're looking for now. I think if you'd known, it would never have happened." Mick's gaze darted around, and she picked at her fingernail. "Would it be all right if I said one more thing?"

"Of course." Aspen braced herself.

"I'm not sure what happened to you back there. I know it wasn't a flashback, but I don't think Quinn did anything to upset you so bad."

"God, no. It wasn't her fault."

"No offense, but I'd say you have some of your own demons to slay." Mick's gaze continued to light everywhere but on Aspen.

"No offense taken. You're right. Quinn got the backlash from years of resentment, which certainly wasn't her fault. But thanks for having the courage to call me out."

Mick smiled. "Now I see why Quinn likes you so much." She tilted her head toward Quinn. "Go set things right. We have some rafting to do."

"Aye, aye, Captain. Oh, wait, that'd be Quinn. What does that make you?"

"First mate."

"Then, aye, aye, First Mate."

Aspen took a tentative step away from Mick, but with each step, her stride became more confident. The sun shone brightly and reflected off the raging water. She just needed to get through the next fifteen minutes or so. It might have been her imagination, but the closer she got to the river, the cooler the air seemed. A slight mist kissed her skin.

Quinn's back was to her, but she must have heard her approach because she sat up straighter and squared her shoulders. Aspen focused her attention on the last couple of boulders since they were covered with water, making them extra slippery.

She didn't want to startle Quinn, even though

she suspected Quinn knew exactly where she was. Aspen cleared her throat.

Quinn turned, her movements slow and deliberate. A shy smile lit her face. "Hey there."

Casual. Good. Quinn had set the tone, now Aspen just needed to keep it going. "Hey there, yourself."

Quinn pointed to the space on the boulder next to her. "Have a seat? If you're not afraid I'll lose it again." Quinn diverted her gaze.

"I'm afraid I could say the same thing." Aspen tiptoed toward the spot next to Quinn, making sure each step was solid before taking another.

Quinn reached up her hand. "Here, we don't want you falling in. Neither of us has a vest on."

Aspen took her hand and moved with more confidence. "Thanks." She didn't say anything more until she'd sat and made herself comfortable. She slid close to Quinn, their shoulders nearly touching. "I'm sorry."

"I'm sorry, too, Fran..." Quinn shifted. "Um... Aspen."

Aspen bumped Quinn's shoulder. "That's Frankie to you."

"But you said...um...you said—"

"I was in a snit. Being an asshole. I never want you to stop calling me Frankie."

Quinn visibly relaxed. "Good. Can I ask what happened? What did I do to upset you so bad?"

"No." Aspen put her hand on Quinn's arm. Quinn's face dropped. "No, I didn't mean you couldn't ask. I meant that you didn't do anything wrong. I'm so sorry. I took my frustrations out on you." Aspen blinked a couple of times. She would *not* cry. She didn't want Quinn to feel like she had to forgive her because of the tears.

"Apology accepted."

"Wow, no. That was too fast. You need to make me feel bad for a while. Hold my feet to the fire. Not let me get away with my shit—"

"Whoa, slow down." Quinn laughed. "I think you're giving yourself enough hell, so I don't need to."

"But I spiraled you into a flashback."

"Actually, you helped me. I felt it coming on. I thought I almost had it under control."

"And then I said something else stupid," Aspen said.

"Maybe." Quinn grinned. "But now I know there's a chance to rein it in."

Aspen's pulse raced. "Yes. If you knew it and told me, maybe we could have stopped it from happening."

"Exactly." Quinn ran her hand through her hair. "Not that I want to test it out anytime soon."

"But this is big." Aspen bounced on the rock. "A breakthrough."

"Damn, you don't need to be quite so excited about my trauma," Quinn said.

Aspen laughed, recognizing the playfulness in Quinn's tone. "Oops, my bad."

Quinn turned and met Aspen's gaze. "Enough about me. I want to know what's up with you."

Aspen squirmed. "I like talking about your issues better."

"Nope, that's not how it works."

"How what works?" Aspen asked to delay the conversation.

"Friendship."

"Oh, so now we're friends. I thought you were my sidekick." The tightness in Aspen's chest had nearly dissipated as they talked. She knew it would likely come back if she allowed the conversation to go in the direction Quinn steered it.

"Friend. Sidekick. The rules are the same."

"Ah, how come I haven't seen these rules?"

Quinn crossed her arms over her chest and scrunched up her mouth. "Nope. I'm not going to let you get away with stalling any longer. Talk to me."

"Okay." Aspen sighed and held up her hands. "I guess you could say I was mad at the world, but in reality, probably more at myself." Aspen paused and glanced at Quinn. "Are you sure you want to hear this?"

"Absolutely."

"I told you I tend to do whatever anyone wants me to. Always following someone, letting them dictate what I do."

Quinn frowned, and sadness filled her lively eyes.

"No," Aspen said. "Don't feel bad for me. I did it to myself. I'm an adult, but I let everyone treat me like a kid. This trip... This trip wasn't anything I wanted to do, but Peyton wanted me to."

"That's wrong of her." Quinn's voice held conviction.

Aspen shook her head. "Don't blame her. I've never told her no. Hell, I haven't even told her what I like. You want to know the truth?"

"Always."

"She doesn't even know me. Just the person I pretend to be. I'm not even sure that I know me." The tightness returned to Aspen's chest. "How pathetic is that?"

"Didn't you just tell me it was a breakthrough

that I recognized what was going on inside me? Why can't this be a breakthrough for you?" Quinn leaned over a couple of inches, so their shoulders touched.

Sweet. Quinn's gesture reassured her. "You have a point. We all must start somewhere. I just can't lose my shit on an innocent bystander when I'm having a growth spurt."

"I'll agree with you on that." Quinn smiled.

"It was like years of being a doormat bubbled to the surface, and I was mad. Furious. Mostly at myself."

"So hell or high water, right at that moment, you decided nobody would tell you what to do."

"Yep. And you were the lucky one to be there." Aspen pinched the top of her nose, hoping to relieve the tension. "I was loaded for bear. And when you told me I couldn't kayak Ghostrider, I lost it."

"Why did you want to do it?"

What? That wasn't the reaction she expected. She thought Quinn would unload a litany of reasons she shouldn't do it. The question took her by surprise. "To prove I can."

"Prove it to who? You or Peyton?"

"Good question." Aspen leaned back and put her arms behind her, her palms resting on the slippery rock. "I suppose to get them all off my back. To show I'm not the princess."

"Any part of you that wants to do it for yourself?" Quinn's gaze bore into her. "If you were sitting in your house in San Francisco, would you say, *Gee, I think I'll go kayak Ghostrider to prove something to myself*?"

Aspen laughed. "Damn you. Stop being so logical."

An audible sigh escaped Quinn. "So would you?"

"No. It would be stupid." Aspen gazed at Quinn.

"And it would be unsafe. And not fair to put that kind of stress on my sidekick."

"Pretty sound logic." Quinn smirked.

"Well then. Let's at least go shoot Ghostrider in a raft before you guys kayak it."

"All right." Quinn rose to her feet and held out her hand to Aspen.

Aspen's small hand was lost in Quinn's. She held on to it, even after she'd risen. "Thank you."

"For?"

"Being the best sidekick a girl could ever have."

Quinn burst out laughing. "Words I never thought I'd hear. Ever. But I like the sound of them."

"Me too." Without giving it any thought, she wrapped her arms around Quinn.

At first Quinn stiffened, but after a beat, she relaxed and returned the hug. Aspen sighed. She felt right for the first time in a long time.

Chapter Twenty-six

It had taken longer to load the equipment and get to the put in spot than Quinn anticipated. The group remained in good spirits with the earlier drama forgotten. Quinn glanced at Peyton, who seemed buoyant, despite what Aspen told her about their earlier argument.

"I can feel it," DaKota said, strapping on her helmet. She adjusted the camera on the top. "I can't wait to see the footage."

Peyton jumped around in front of her, waving at the camera and sticking out her tongue. Quinn smiled in spite of herself. Where did those two get their energy, and how did they run multimillion-dollar companies?

Aspen shook her head and winked at Quinn.

Quinn returned the wink and smiled. "All right, team. We're about to hit the river. Any questions?"

Tina waved her hand. "Did you decide how many of us can kayak at one time?"

Mick stepped up. "Two at a time should be fine."

"Any chance we can all go down together?" Tina asked.

"Nope," Mick answered.

"Hear me out." Tina held up her hands. "Now that LeAnn has decided not to go, there are only four of us and you and Quinn. Every summer during college, I took people down the Colorado River with kayaks. I'm not a rookie. If you'd let me, I could act as an additional guide."

Mick shot a look at Quinn and raised her eyebrows. *Shit.* She didn't want to be drawn into the decision. Although, it wasn't fair to pin it all on Mick. "Quinn and I will have a conversation about it later. Right now, we have some rafting to do."

Tina nodded. "Fair enough. I just wanted to put it out there. That way, we'd probably have enough time to make two runs at it for those of us that crave adventure."

"Or maybe we're just insane," Claire said.

"That too." Tina laughed.

"Let's do this." Mick pulled the raft to the edge of the water and hopped in.

They'd put in farther upriver from Ghostrider, so they could enjoy the spectacular scenery and get loosened up with some light paddling. Quinn dug her paddle into the river. Even this far from Ghostrider, the current had some pull to it.

Was she ready for this? She'd wanted to do this for nearly twenty years, but what if she had a flashback in the middle of it? She hoped that her talk with Mick and then Aspen would keep any negative reaction at bay.

"Is this the longest rapid on the river?" LeAnn called over her shoulder.

"Nope, but close. Gulliver's Travels is longer," Quinn said. "It might not be the longest, but most say it's the best."

"Ugh. Sorry, didn't mean to jinx us." LeAnn put her hand over her face.

"I'm holding you personally responsible if we end up in the water again." Aspen pointed and pretended to give her an angry stare.

"We ain't going in," Quinn said.

"See, our captain is confident. And so am I." LeAnn moved her shoulders with attitude. "We're gonna tame this bitch."

Quinn laughed. "Let's not get too cocky. We don't want to piss off the river gods." But she did feel confident. She'd watched so many videos and read about Ghostrider for years. They needed to run from the center to the right, and they'd do fine.

She allowed the crew to paddle leisurely down the river until they were about a hundred yards from the start of the rapid. Her heart rate accelerated as adrenaline raced through her.

"Okay, kids," Quinn shouted. "It's show time."

A loud cheer went up. Peyton and DaKota raised their paddles into the air in emphasis.

"Forward," Quinn called.

Mick and Tina picked up the pace, obviously eager to meet Ghostrider head on.

Quinn went into autopilot, her instincts taking over. "Forward. Lean in. Forward." A large wave loomed up ahead. "Get down."

The wave hit the raft square and turned them nearly sideways. The waves pummeled the raft, and the spray made it nearly impossible for her to see. She ducked under the frothy water that skimmed over the top of her head. Without anyone paddling but her, it threatened to turn them farther. Without hesitation, she called out, "Forward."

The others jumped into position and paddled hard.

They were moving too far to the left. "Right. Right. Forward." The group dug their paddles in hard, and they shot off to the right. She called out "Right" one final time until they were back on track.

She surveyed the crew. A wave smashed into Claire, and she teetered on the side. Tina grabbed her and pulled hard, nearly sending her sprawling into the center of the raft. She scampered back onto the side, hunkered down, and continued paddling.

"Forward. Forward," Quinn yelled as the next wave bore down on them. They needed to hit it with force, or it had the potential to tip the raft. They needed more power, so she yelled, "Forward." They lurched forward before she yelled, "Get down." As if they'd been doing this together for years, everyone dropped to the floor. It worked. They'd hit it with enough force to crash through. The wave skittered over their heads, without landing a knockout blow. *Holy shit.* They were going to make it. One more wave. How did she want to play it?

Quinn took a deep breath, sucking in as much air as she could before another torrent of river water struck her.

"Forward," she called out. *Once more.* "Forward." The next wave threatened. "Get down." Quinn took a cleansing breath as the last of the large waves harmlessly hit the raft as they edged through it.

Quinn jumped to her feet. "Fuck, yeah." *Oh, god.* Did she just say that out loud?

The others cheered and raised their paddles over their heads. Aspen threw her paddle to the floor and stood. Her gaze met Quinn's, and she launched herself at Quinn. Laughing, Quinn caught her in her arms and lifted her up.

"We made it," Aspen yelled, her mouth near Quinn's ear. Quinn flinched and then laughed.

"Sorry," Aspen said in a quieter voice.

"That was the best two minutes of my life," DaKota shouted and bounced on the side of the raft.

"Minute," Mick said. "I don't think it was much more than a minute."

"Holy shit," LeAnn said. "It felt like twenty."

"I take it you haven't changed your mind about kayaking then," Claire said and shot LeAnn a smile.

"Hell to the no." LeAnn slapped her hand to her chest. "This was enough excitement for one day. I'll take video from the shore."

"You know, I just might join you and Aspen," Claire said.

"Really?" Peyton whipped around and stared at Claire.

"Really." Claire smiled her sleepy smile. "That was a perfect run. Felt good, so why ruin perfection?"

"To a perfect run." Mick held up her paddle and bumped it against Tina's. The thumping echoed loudly above the sound of the water.

"Holy shit, Mick. Careful. You're gonna knock Tina out of the boat with that kind of power."

"I'm good." Tina slammed her paddle back against Mick's.

They continued their celebration as they made their way to the riverbank.

❧ ❧ ❧ ❧

Kayaking was anticlimactic after their run in the raft, at least for Quinn. The way Peyton and DaKota were carrying on, it had been the highlight of the trip for them. While fun, it hadn't been the same. Or maybe it was just Quinn. She'd missed the camaraderie of the larger group. She'd missed Aspen. Being in a solo kayak left her feeling isolated. Alone.

She shook her head in disbelief. The woman who had been hiding out in the Ozarks for the past few years felt lonely in a kayak surrounded by people. This trip had changed her. She didn't know what to make of it nor did she have time to contemplate it with the frenzy of activity around her.

Mick sidled up and wrapped her arm around Quinn's waist. She'd not dried off completely from their second run. "Thanks for agreeing to let everyone go down at once. It was a blast."

"With only three, it seemed silly not to. Especially when Tina could probably teach us a thing or two."

"No doubt. Did you see that move she made when the water flipped her?"

Quinn nodded. "It was a pro move. I'd started digging to get to her, but bam, she popped back up and shot out of it." Quinn laughed. "I almost ran myself into a mess. I had to paddle like hell not to wipe myself out."

Mick chuckled. "I saw that, too. Thought I'd have to come save your ass."

Tina strolled over. She hugged Mick and then Quinn. "Thank you so much. You guys are rock stars. I've shot many rapids, but this trip ranks up there with my favorites. I didn't realize how much I missed this."

Mick grinned. "If you're ever looking for a job, look me up."

Tina's eyes twinkled, but then she slammed them shut. When she opened them, they held a sadness. She nodded. "I'll keep that in mind." She gave Mick another sideways hug. "It was amazing matching strokes with you."

Mick's cheeks blazed, and Quinn held back a laugh. *Hysterical.* Tina embarrassed the hard-to-embarrass Mick.

"Any time," Mick stammered.

After Tina walked away, a chuckle escaped Quinn. Mick shot her a look, so Quinn clamped her lips together, but the laugh still reverberated in her throat.

"Hey, guys," DaKota called. "The locals say the helicopter will be here shortly." DaKota's shoulders dropped. "I suppose we can't do this again tomorrow, huh?"

"Oh, god, no." LeAnn held up her hands and glanced at Aspen. "Me and Aspen are going to hit the closest spa and get pampered. My body hasn't been beat around like this since the four-car pileup I was in several years ago." For emphasis, she rubbed her lower back with her knuckles.

"It's been great, but I'm with LeAnn," Aspen said. She smiled at Quinn. "Much thanks to our incredible guides."

"Hear, hear," DaKota shouted and raised her fist. "To Mick and Quinn."

The others raised their fists and called out, "Mick and Quinn."

Heat rose into Quinn's cheeks, but she smiled.

As they made their way to the helicopter, Quinn's chest tightened. All this anticipation, and now it was over. She'd put so much on Ghostrider. Was that why she felt empty now? Just like a kid at Christmas, the excitement rose, but then the packages were ripped to shreds in a two-minute frenzy. Then it was over. What happened next?

She knew the trip had changed her. A shift had

happened somewhere around Gulliver's Travels, and she doubted she'd ever be the same. But did she even want to be?

When had she turned so poetic? She pushed the thoughts from her head as the helicopter loomed.

Chapter Twenty-seven

Aspen glanced around the helicopter. The boisterous group had quieted. Everyone looked tired, except for DaKota. Even Peyton slumped in her seat.

Without being obvious, Aspen studied Quinn. She didn't look as exhausted as the others, but she seemed far away, her gaze unfocused as she looked down at the river. Aspen wanted to ask her what she was thinking but thought better of it. Maybe they'd have another late-night chance meeting, and she could ask then. Better yet, Aspen would make sure it happened.

She wasn't sure how long they'd been in the air when the pilot dipped the craft. A helicopter pad loomed in the distance. She'd never been a big fan of heights, so she wasn't looking forward to the landing. She took a deep breath and closed her eyes. *Count.* Sheep wouldn't be appropriate. Maybe she would just count numbers. *One. Two. Three. Four.* She got the odd feeling of being watched.

She opened her eyes and met Quinn's gaze. Quinn jerked as if she were going to quickly look away, but she stopped and smiled. Aspen wondered if she were as green as she felt. Her stomach lurched as the helicopter turned for its approach.

"It'll be okay," Quinn mouthed and gave her a thumbs up.

After returning the thumbs up, Aspen leaned back in her seat and let her head fall back. She didn't want to watch, so she stared at the ceiling.

With a slight bump, they landed, and Aspen sighed. That was almost too easy. Maybe things were looking up. Now all that was left was to have the conversation with Peyton; it wouldn't be fair to wait until they got home. There never was a good time, but gauging Peyton's good mood, maybe it wouldn't be as hard as she thought.

༄ ༄ ༄ ༄

"I'm starving," Mick said as soon as they stepped out of the van that took them on the final journey back to Elephant Camp.

"Of course you are." Quinn wasn't sure if she was more hungry or tired. A nap sounded good but so did food.

DaKota waved her hands over her head. "We've got another surprise for y'all."

"If you follow me, I'll lead you to a feast to beat all feasts." Peyton beamed and motioned to the others. "Right this way."

Quinn's decision was made for her. Food it was.

Mick leaned over. "Hey, I'm going to run back to the room and grab my cell. I should check on Kaycee since I left the business in her hands while we've been gone."

"Mind grabbing mine while you're at it?" Quinn said. "Not that I expect anyone to call, but you never know. Maybe someone wants to give me a million bucks or something."

"No problem." Mick peeled off from the others

and jogged down the path leading away from the dining hall.

The two knew how to throw a feast. Champagne chilled in a large tub when they walked in, and hors d'oeuvres filled one entire table. An empty buffet table was off to the left of the appetizers. The warming units were already lit under the large steel pans, so Quinn suspected they wouldn't remain empty for much longer.

Waiters descended, and corks soon popped. Was there any more festive sound than champagne corks? Somehow, they'd managed to pop all four bottles in unison, adding to the spectacle.

Aspen pulled her toward the food. "Come on. I'm starving."

She let herself be led by the tiny woman. What a difference a week made. She remembered their first meal in this room. She'd wanted to get in and out as soon as possible. Today, she didn't mind lingering, even if she could use a nap.

She'd just popped a cocktail shrimp in her mouth when Mick burst into the room. Sweat beaded on her forehead, and she panted, trying to catch her breath. The color had drained from her face. Quinn stared. Something was wrong.

Mick's gaze darted around the room until it landed on Quinn. Her normally mischievous eyes were wide and appeared panicked.

What the hell? A surge of worry pulsed through Quinn.

Mick sprinted across the room and held Quinn's cellphone out. "I think you better sit down."

҈ ҈ ҉ ҉

Aspen gaped at the spread of food. Ostentatious was the first thought that came to mind. *Odd.* A few days ago, she would have thought nothing of eight people having enough food to feed a classroom of twenty, and this was just the opening course. Today, it made her uncomfortable, embarrassed even.

She'd been so lost in her own thoughts she hadn't seen Mick enter the room, but she stood in front of Quinn with a cellphone held out. *Something was up.* Mick's eyes were wide, almost watery. The hand holding out the phone had a slight tremor.

Quinn stared at Mick but didn't reach out. Quinn's eyes were questioning as she studied Mick. "What's got you so stirred up?" Quinn finally said.

"I need you to see this." Mick pushed the cellphone farther toward Quinn.

"Can't I finish filling my plate first?"

"Damn it, you need to see this. Now." Mick snatched the plate out of Quinn's hand and marched to a nearby table.

Quinn shot a look at Aspen and shrugged before following Mick.

What in the world had Mick so agitated? With a half-filled plate, Aspen followed Quinn. If something was up, she wanted to know what it was.

Mick sat and put Quinn's plate and the cellphone on the table. Mick didn't look good. The healthy glow from being outdoors had become pallid. She didn't seem to register that anyone else was in the room. Her gaze stayed focused on Quinn.

"Mind telling me what's got you so riled up?" Quinn asked, taking the chair.

Something told Aspen to hold back, so she

remained standing.

"I think you should take a look at your phone." Mick pushed it closer.

"Is this some kind of prank?" Quinn asked and glanced around the room.

The others gathered around the food, apparently missing Mick's dramatic entrance. Aspen put her hand on Quinn's shoulder. "Why don't you see what Mick's talking about?"

Quinn narrowed her eyes. "Are you in on this?"

"Goddamn it. There's nothing to be in on." Mick pushed the phone again, this time bumping it into Quinn's hand.

"Sheesh. Okay." Quinn picked it up. Her eyebrows shot up. "What the fuck? Eight missed calls and thirteen texts. I don't usually get that many in a month."

"Just listen to them," Mick said.

"Natalie." Quinn glanced up. "All from Natalie."

Mick nodded.

"It looks like she only left three voicemails." Quinn punched the keypad and then set the phone on the table.

A robotic voice announced that the call came in on October 7 at 9:08 p.m. *"Quinn, I need to talk to you. Right away."* The pleasant voice, which must have been Natalie, filled the air. *"I know you're in Africa, but it's important. Please!"* The message ended.

The next call came in at 8:32 a.m. October 8. Yesterday. *"Quinn. It's urgent. Oh, god. I can't believe this is happening. They are pure evil. I can't let them do this to her. I won't. Even if I have to take this into my own hands."* The message paused. Sobs came through the phone. *"I wish you were here. I need you here,*

Quinn. Please call me as soon as you get this. I need you. Stella needs you."

Quinn rubbed her chest with one hand and lightly touched the phone with her other as if she were comforting Natalie. The gesture touched Aspen.

The final message began. This one dated October 8 at 7:26 p.m. *"I can't wait anymore. They've intubated her. She's got tubes everywhere. This is not how she'd want to live. I can't believe they did this. I begged them not to, but the press, the fucking vultures, are everywhere. My parents are monsters. They're eating it up. Performing for their audience. I think I'm going to vomit."* Several seconds passed without a word or sound. A loud inhale came from the phone. *"I can't believe this nightmare never ends. But I'm going to end it. I have to. I can't live off their blood money anymore. I love you, Quinn. Stella loves you."* A sob came from the phone, then the call ended.

Quinn pulled her hand away from the cellphone as if it had scorched her.

Was Natalie planning on killing herself? It certainly sounded like a goodbye to Aspen. Without thinking, Aspen put her hand on Quinn's shoulder and rubbed it.

"What the fuck did that mean?" Quinn gazed at Mick. "What is going on?"

"I'm not sure. Read your messages."

Quinn reached for the phone, but her hand recoiled when she touched it. She stared at it as if it were a rattlesnake. She pushed it toward Mick. "You read them."

Mick took the phone. "These started coming in late this morning." She began reading.

Quinn. This is Natalie's friend, LaTasha. She texted me with your number and told me if anything happened that I needed to contact you right away. She told me to come to Stella's care facility. That's where I am now. Please call me. I need to talk to you ASAP.

I couldn't talk her out of it. I tried!!!

I need you to call right away!!

It's urgent!!

The police are going in. I've begged them not to.

They kicked me out. I can't see what's happening. Her parents are evil. I pleaded with them to let me talk to her, but they wouldn't let me.

Oh, fuck. They just brought her out in handcuffs.

I don't know what she did. Nobody will talk to me.

Oh, god. She's bleeding. I got close enough to yell her name before they grabbed me and pulled me away. She has blood running down her face.

I'm going to sneak inside. They might arrest me if they catch me, so don't be surprised if this is my last text.

Mick cleared her throat. "There was a gap of about forty-five minutes before the next one came in."

Aspen exhaled loudly. She hadn't realized she'd

been holding her breath while Mick read. Quinn gazed up at her with haunted eyes. Aspen wanted to comfort her but didn't know how.

"Go on." Quinn's voice was hoarse when she spoke.

Mick nodded.

That was close. They almost caught me, but the staff got me out before the police could find me. Thank God.

This is what I discovered. Stella is still alive. Natalie had been holed up in her room for the past four hours. She barricaded the door. She told everyone she had a gun. The staff don't think she did. The staff said she was in there talking to Stella. Crying. Singing. Her parents and police tried to talk her into coming out. Well, at least when they weren't hamming it up for the cameras. She refused. She turned off Stella's machine. That's when the police broke down the door and took her. Apparently, not without a fight. She's ok though. Physically. Just a bump on head. Resisted police.

I'm going to police station now. Please, please, please call me as soon as you can.

Mick set the phone on the table. "Last one came in about half an hour ago."

Quinn startled Aspen when she jumped to her feet. Aspen stepped back and studied her. Her gaze darted around the room as if she were trying to figure out what to do next. She bit down hard on her lip, and Aspen feared she'd draw blood if she didn't let up on it.

Mick had made her way around to Quinn's side of the table. She tentatively put her hand on Quinn's arm. "We need to figure out what to do."

"We've got to get back to Boston. Now," Quinn practically shouted.

The others had finally noticed that something was happening and milled around. Aspen motioned for them to stay back. She suspected Quinn wasn't registering much about her surroundings, but having people closing in on her wouldn't help.

"I think you should probably call LaTasha first," Mick said.

Quinn swiped at her cellphone screen. "How the hell do we get a flight out of here?"

Aspen gazed around Quinn's shoulder. Google popped up on the screen, and Quinn's thumbs flew over the keyboard.

"Buddy, stop. Let's call LaTasha first."

Quinn's eyes turned misty. "But I need to be there."

"I know you do." Mick's voice was low and soothing. "But we need to know what's going on first."

Quinn continued typing on her phone. She shook it. "Fucking thing. How do I find a flight out of Africa on a moment's notice?"

Aspen waved her hand. "I'll get you guys a flight." She glanced first at Mick, who nodded and mouthed a *thank you*. "Quinn?" Aspen waited until Quinn met her gaze. "I'm taking care of the flight. I will get one for you as soon as possible. You call LaTasha and gather up your things."

Quinn blinked several times as if trying to process Aspen's words. Eventually, she nodded. "Okay. Thank you." Without another word, she turned and strode across the room.

"I'm following her," Mick said.

"Go. I'll take care of everything else."

Mick smiled and hurried off.

Aspen's heart raced. As if the adrenaline rush of the past few days wasn't enough, this took it up another notch. *Poor Quinn.* She might never forget the haunted look in Quinn's eyes. Aspen stood staring until the two disappeared out the door.

The others all started talking at once. She patiently answered the questions, knowing she'd never get anything done until their curiosity was sated.

"We've got to find a way to get them back to Boston as soon as possible." Her gaze shifted between DaKota and Peyton. "Have any connections?"

DaKota nodded. "I can try."

"You can keep the bet money," Peyton said. "Use it to help pay for the flight."

Aspen put her hand on her hip and met Peyton's gaze. "Are you going to tell me about this damned bet?"

"I won. That's all you really need to know," Peyton said.

"Damn it, would one of you just tell me?" She glanced back and forth between the two. "I'm waiting."

The two exchanged glances.

Aspen turned to LeAnn and Tina. "Do you know what it's about?"

They both shook their heads.

"Just tell us." Tina leveled her gaze at DaKota.

"It was stupid. We never should have made it, but I'm glad Peyton won."

"Just say it," Tina said. "The truth shall set you free."

"Fine." Peyton threw her hand in the air. "We bet whether Quinn would be able to do it. Or whether she'd flip out and not be able to make it the whole way."

Blood pounded in Aspen's ears, and she stared at Peyton in stunned silence. How did she respond to this? Anger rose in her chest.

"Are you fucking kidding me?" Tina said. "What is wrong with you two?"

Aspen finally found her voice. "That's someone's life you're betting on. That's sick."

DaKota held up her hand in a defensive gesture. "I know. We feel like shit about it. Once I got to know them, I wanted to lose."

"Is that supposed to make it okay?" Tina glared at her. She turned on Peyton. "And what about you? What do you have to say about it?"

"I bet for Quinn, not against her." Peyton's voice came out in a whine.

Aspen stepped up to her and pointed. "No, you're not getting away with that. Admit you were wrong."

Peyton's face reddened, and she opened her mouth to speak. Her eyes were full of fire, but Aspen maintained eye contact. Peyton deflated and stared at the ground. "It was wrong." Her voice came out in a whisper.

"What? I didn't hear you," Aspen said, still angry. "Be an adult and say it so we can all hear you."

Peyton looked up. Aspen was shocked to see tears in her eyes.

"I fucked up," Peyton said and looked toward DaKota.

DaKota walked up beside her and draped her

arm over her shoulder. "*We* fucked up. And we take responsibility for it. It was despicable."

"And we're embarrassed by it." Peyton seemed to draw courage from having DaKota next to her. "We can't take it back but hope we can make it up to Quinn by helping her get home."

"We'd prefer they not know. What good can come of it?"

Aspen's knee jerk reaction was to insist that they come clean, but who would it hurt the most? *Quinn.* "If I didn't think it would rip Quinn's heart out, I'd insist you tell her."

LeAnn waved her hand. "It would do more harm than good."

"Agreed," Tina said.

DaKota and Peyton visibly relaxed.

Tina must have noticed because she turned toward the two and pointed. "Don't think that lets you off the hook. What you did was cold and cruel. I hope it will force you to look in the mirror and develop some compassion." Without another word, she stomped out of the room.

DaKota turned to follow.

"No, you don't." Aspen's words stopped her in her tracks. "Get your ass back here and help us get a flight for them."

DaKota longingly looked at the door Tina had exited. Her shoulders slumped, and she said, "Okay. Peyton and I will take care of it."

❧❧❧❧

A knock interrupted Quinn's pacing. She'd packed in record time, but now all she could do was wait. She swung open the door.

"Are you guys ready?" Aspen said without pre-amble.

Quinn stepped back, so Aspen could enter. "Um, Mick just got out of the shower. Should be out soon."

"DaKota's company does a lot of work for a business in South Africa. She was able to convince them to lend her one of their private jets." *Convince, sure.* Likely, a large sum of money changed hands, but she wouldn't tell Quinn that.

"Seriously?" Quinn's eyes lit up. "When can we leave?"

"It should be at the airport shortly. A car and driver are coming to pick you guys up."

Without warning, Quinn bent and wrapped Aspen in a bear hug. Warmth spread over Aspen's chest as she returned the hug. It was like hugging a giant teddy bear.

Quinn released her grip and stepped back, her cheeks a deep red. "Oh, sorry. I didn't...I mean, I—"

"It's okay." Aspen put her hand on Quinn's arm. "You've had quite the shock."

Tears welled in Quinn's eyes, but she blinked them back. She sighed. Suddenly, she looked exhausted. She ran her hand through her short hair. "I can't believe I wasn't there."

"You can't think that way." Aspen guided Quinn toward the table. By the look of Quinn, it wouldn't take much for her to collapse.

Quinn allowed herself to be led and flopped into the seat. Aspen pulled a bottle of water out of the refrigerator, opened it, and set it in front of Quinn. Absentmindedly, Quinn took a large gulp. She put her head in her hands and breathed in deeply.

Aspen sat in the chair across the table from her and waited for Quinn to regain her composure. Once Quinn glanced up, Aspen said, "Did you talk to LaTasha?"

Quinn nodded.

"Do you mind if I ask what she said?"

"Oh, yeah, sorry." Quinn sat back against the chair. She took another drink of water before she spoke. "Not much more than what we got from the messages. Stella coded, and the stupid fuckers brought her back. Then her parents had her intubated." The pained look on Quinn's face was heartbreaking. "Natalie lost it. Who wouldn't? Maybe if I'd been there to talk her down, maybe it wouldn't have ended this way."

"No," Aspen said. "You can't do this to yourself. Is Natalie okay?"

"As far as LaTasha knows." Quinn sighed. "She's still being processed. LaTasha is there waiting to find out how much bail she'll need. Who knows how long it will take?"

"Thank god," Aspen said. "Do you know LaTasha? Are you comfortable she'll take care of things?"

"I've never met her, but Natalie always speaks highly of her. I felt much better after I talked to her on the phone. She's solid. I just want to get back to Boston. I probably can't do anything, but I need to be there."

"Of course you do. We'll get you there as soon as humanly possible."

"Hey, Mick," Quinn shouted. "They've got us a plane. You about done?"

"Finishing up." Mick's voice came from the bathroom. The bathroom door started to open. "I've just got to put some clothes on."

"Stop," Quinn called. "Aspen's here."

A bare leg retreated back into the bathroom. "Shit."

Aspen tried to stifle a giggle. Quinn let out a loud laugh. "She almost saw more of you than she'd ever want to," Quinn said.

"Shut up and bring me my clothes. They're on my bed."

Quinn glanced at the clothes and smirked. "I don't see them. I guess you'll have to come out and find them."

Aspen smiled, happy to see that Quinn could still joke. It would be a long flight back to Boston, so a little comic relief would do her good.

"Knock your shit off and bring them here." Mick's voice held only amusement.

Once Quinn returned from the bathroom, Aspen stood. "I suppose I should go and make sure the car is ready for you guys." She wasn't sure what else to say. Now she would never get the opportunity to have one last late-night conversation with Quinn. Her chest ached. She'd been looking forward to it more than she'd realized.

Quinn shuffled her feet, and her gaze diverted to the floor. "Um...yeah. Thank you again for everything."

"I should be the one thanking you. Maybe whitewater rafting isn't my thing, but you made it bearable."

Quinn surprised Aspen with a genuine laugh. She met Aspen's gaze. "I won't tell Mick you said that. Somehow, I don't think she'd use that for the Pink Triangles slogan, either." Quinn held up her hands and stretched them out as if they were a billboard. "Pink Triangle...we make things bearable."

Heat rose in Aspen's cheeks, and she brought her hand to her mouth. "That came out so wrong."

Quinn laughed again.

"I am so sorry."

"It's okay, Frankie. I knew what you meant."

Frankie. Her chest thumped. She had a nickname. That had to mean they were friends. *Straightforward.* That was what she was supposed to be. Now or never. "Um, would it be okay if I gave you my telephone number....um, I'd kinda like to know how things turn out."

Quinn smiled. She unlocked her phone and handed it to Aspen. "Don't forget to put it under Frankie, or I might not be able to find it."

"Does that mean I should put you under side-kick?"

"If that's how you'll remember me."

How would she remember Quinn? What was wrong with her? Quinn was in the midst of a crisis, and she felt sad seeing her friend leave early. *Get a grip.* She needed to stop being selfish. She quickly entered her number in Quinn's phone and shot off a text to herself, so she'd have Quinn's number.

"All done." Aspen handed the phone back. "I should be going. I'll see you out front. The whole gang will be there. Everyone wanted the chance to say goodbye."

"Good. I want to thank DaKota for arranging the flight." Quinn shifted her weight from foot to foot. She opened her mouth as if to speak and closed it.

"I'm sure she'll appreciate that." *Ugh.* How lame did that come out? "Well, I'll hear from you later?"

Quinn nodded. "Yes. I'm not sure when. But I'll let you know when I know something."

"Thank you." Aspen ran her fingers along the seam of her shirt and pulled at a loose thread. "Be safe. And thanks again." She turned toward the door.

"Wait." Quinn's voice stopped her.

Aspen turned back. Quinn's expression was unreadable. Maybe a cross between sadness and something else. Aspen narrowed her eyes and studied her. "Was there something else you needed?" *Lame.*

"I was wondering, well, since you had an adequate time and all, would it be wrong to ask for a hug goodbye?"

Aspen smirked. "Sidekicks can be so needy." She threw her arms around Quinn and was engulfed in her arms.

Quinn chuckled as they hugged.

Chapter Twenty-eight

A spen flipped her pen onto the table and put her head down. Heaviness descended on her. Ever since Mick and Quinn left, Quinn's eyes burned in her mind. Somehow, it seemed worse to see someone so big and strong looking so defeated. They'd hugged again, and she'd held on longer than she'd intended, hoping to give Quinn some of her strength.

When they'd separated, there was a shimmer of light in Quinn's eyes, but the enormity of the situation weighed on her. There wasn't a dry eye in the bunch as they said their goodbyes. Quinn and Mick had touched them all, and this was a trip none would soon forget. Even DaKota and Peyton had been subdued. Reverent.

She'd feigned a headache, so she could return to the room and collect her thoughts. Writing was the best therapy, so she'd pulled out her notebook and filled ten pages without stopping. Her thoughts tumbled out of her in waves that turned to emotions. Soon tears dropped on the page, causing the paper to crinkle as they dried.

Gina. She needed to talk to her best friend. Besides, what if Quinn tried to reach her? True, it would take them nearly twenty-four hours to get to Boston, but still, Peyton had no right to take her phone in the first place.

She pulled Peyton's bag from the closet and rifled through it. Peyton will be pissed. She shrugged.

Oh, well. She dug to the bottom and finally located it. Apparently, Peyton wanted to make sure it was buried well. She felt around. *Interesting.* Only one phone. Where was Peyton's?

Curiosity got the better of her, so she tipped the bag and let the contents spill onto the ground. One by one, she returned the items to the bag. No second cellphone here. *Unbelievable.* Had Peyton had her phone all along?

Aspen didn't have the energy to be upset. The only thing she wanted was to hear Gina's voice. She went onto the back patio and pulled a chair near the mini swimming pool.

She hit the call icon and let her head fall back against the chair. Aspen closed her eyes, listening to the phone ring and willed Gina to pick up.

"Oh, my god. You've been freed." Gina's loud voice filled the air.

Aspen smiled and let out a loud exhalation. "Gina?"

"Who the hell else would it be?" Gina chuckled at her own joke. "God, I've missed you. I wrote a list of all the important topics I needed to tell you." Rustling came from the other end of the line. "Where the hell did I put it?"

Aspen's chest filled. Just hearing Gina's voice made her feel grounded. She hadn't realized how out of her element she was until now. Tears welled in her eyes, but she brushed them away. She wouldn't cry, or Gina would pick it up immediately.

"Found it," Gina said. "I'm armed with my list, so we're good to talk now."

"Gee, thanks. What would have happened if you didn't find it?" Aspen asked.

"I would have hung up on your ass." Gina cackled. "Damn. It's good to hear your voice. Steph says I've been moping around all week, but what does she know?"

"Um, since you've been with her since pterodactyls flew the skies, I'd say pretty much." Aspen grinned. The familiarity of Gina's antics settled her.

"Details. So how did you escape your captivity? I didn't think I'd hear from you for at least another week."

"I'm a rebel. I said fuck it and dug my phone out of Peyton's bag."

"You go, girl. I see the trip has made you sassy. Did you swallow some of the whitewater or something?" Gina drew in a sharp breath. "Oh, god, that's it. You almost drowned, didn't you? Are you in the hospital?"

"And you wonder why I call you a drama queen. No, I am not in the hospital nor did I drown."

"I didn't say you drowned. Or you wouldn't be calling me. Oh, fuck. Or maybe your ghost is calling me." Gina did a bad impersonation of spooky music.

"Please let me know when you're done, so I can tell you what's going on."

"Okay." Gina continued with her horrible rendition of scary music for several more beats. "Now I'm done. Your turn."

Aspen opened her mouth to speak, but before she got a word out, Gina let out a low whistle. "Wait," Gina said. "I have some pretty important things on my list."

"I doubt if you can top my week," Aspen said.

"Maybe not, but I have some intel on Quinn."

"What?" Aspen tried not to snap. After everything they'd been through, she had a protective streak when it came to Quinn.

"Do you know about Stella?"

"Yep, I know all about her."

"How?"

"Quinn told me."

"So she told you that she tried to kill herself?"

"Stella didn't try to kill herself. It was an accident. Are you reading shit on Facebook again?"

"Not Stella. Quinn."

Aspen sat up in the chair she slumped against. "What?"

"Apparently, about three months after Stella's accident, her parents got a restraining order against Quinn. Holy rollers that wanted to pray the gay out of their daughter, so of course, they couldn't have the lesbian lover hanging around. Let's see...oh, here it is. Let me read this part to you."

Aspen clenched her hands into fists.

"After losing her court battle with the Parsonses, it appears that Ms. Coolidge may have attempted to take her own life late Friday." Gina used her best newscaster voice. "Witnesses claim that the car driven by Quinn Coolidge was traveling south on Willard Street and made no attempt to stop until moments before slamming into a tree. Early reports put her approximate speed at sixty miles per hour. An anonymous police source reports that the accident was likely a failed suicide attempt. Hospital sources say it was a miracle that the only injury she suffered was a large laceration to her face."

Aspen drew in a breath. *Oh, Quinn.* Her heart ached for her new friend. How hopeless things must have seemed for her to do something like that. "It says likely, so how do you know it's true?"

"I don't. So she didn't tell you?"

"Why would she? I've known her for a minute," Aspen snapped. "People don't exactly run around saying, *Hi, my name's Quinn. See my scar. I got it when I tried to kill myself.*"

"Chill. I just asked. No need to get so defensive."

"Sorry," Aspen muttered. Why hadn't Quinn told her on one of their late-night talks? *Stop.* Quinn had shared a lot, but it wasn't exactly something someone brought up.

"Are you even listening to me?" Gina's voice penetrated her thoughts.

"Um...no. I got distracted. What did you say?"

"I asked how big her scar is. The newspaper made it sound like her face was torn up bad. You saw it, didn't you?"

Leave it to Gina. Of all the things she could ask, she wanted to know about the scar. "Yeah, I saw her scar. How could I not since I've been with her the last week?"

"She could have had plastic surgery. Besides, newspapers exaggerate all the time. So how bad is it?"

Bad? No, it wasn't bad. It gave Quinn's face more character, but would she still feel the same way now that she knew where it came from? "It was visible and long. It ran from the corner of her eye almost to her mouth."

"Oh, god. Poor thing. I bet it was hideous."

"No! It isn't."

"Sheesh, what is wrong with you? You don't have to yell."

Aspen put her hand against her forehead. "It's been a rough day. Week. I just want to come home and have this conversation in person." The words slipped out of her mouth.

"Then do it. Hold on."

Aspen could make out the sound of talking, but Gina's words were garbled. She must have put her hand over the phone.

"Steph says come home. You can stay with us when you get back. It sounds like you could use some TLC. She says she'll cook all your favorites."

Tears streamed down Aspen's face. *What the hell?* Why was so much emotion bubbling up inside her? She couldn't even identify it. *Grief? Disappointment?* She wasn't sure, but whatever it was hurt. "Are you sure?"

"Definitely." Gina's strong voice brought her comfort. "Babe, would you find a flight for Aspen?"

"On it," Stephanie called in the background.

"Tell her thank you." All of Aspen's remaining energy left her body.

"Are you going to tell me what's going on?" Gina said, her voice gentler than her normal bluster.

"I'm not sure I know."

"Was it horrible?"

Was it? "No. Not horrible. I conquered some fears and learned a few things about myself. Things I probably knew all along but hadn't let myself think about. I'm raw and emotional. Hell, I can't even explain it."

"How many pages have you written?"

Aspen laughed. Gina knew her so well. "Fifteen."

"Holy hell. A new record? I think your previous one was only eight."

"Yeah, when Nana died."

"Shit. That's seven more pages than Nana. I

need to hear all about it."

"Not now. Not on the phone." Aspen stared out at the mist. The same mist she'd watched with Quinn. It seemed like months ago, but less than a week had passed. "I want to be stretched out on your couch with a big bowl of popcorn and a glass of wine."

"Whew. At least you're still classy. I was starting to worry."

Aspen laughed. "Thanks." The word held so much meaning. She suspected Gina knew.

"Steph has you booked. She's texting you the confirmation as we speak."

Whenever they traveled together, which was often, Gina and Steph always made the arrangements. It paid off now since they already had all her personal information for booking. "Tell Steph she's the best."

"We just want to get you home safe and sound, honey," Steph said.

"I'm gonna let you go. I need to tell Peyton I'm leaving and get myself packed."

"We'll be waiting for you," Gina said. "Chin up. You'll be home soon. We love you."

"I love you guys, too."

"Safe travels," Steph called out.

"See you soon," Aspen said before ending the call. The tightly wound coil inside her loosened, and for the first time since Quinn left, she was able to breathe. She inhaled deeply and slowly let it out.

She needed to let Peyton know of her plans, but she didn't want to be tromping all over Elephant Camp looking for her. Aspen stared at the phone in her hands and grinned. *Hmm.* What would Peyton do? Answer and give away her secret or let it ring?

Aspen hit the call button. After several rings, it

went to Peyton's voicemail. She tried again with the same result. Maybe Peyton didn't have the phone on her after all. A twinge of guilt rose inside of Aspen. She'd probably stashed it in another bag, and Aspen just hadn't found it.

She let her head fall back against the back of the chair. Now she'd have to go looking for Peyton, but maybe she should get packed first. Her limbs felt heavy, but she needed to get moving or she might fall asleep. The last thing she wanted to do was miss her flight.

Reluctantly, she rose to her feet. Her body rebelled. The pounding waves over the past few days had left her stiff and sore. She groaned for emphasis, even though no one was around to witness her plight.

She'd only been packing for a couple of minutes when the door burst open. Aspen tried to hide her smirk.

She might have believed Peyton's arrival was a coincidence until Peyton's gaze frantically darted around the room. No doubt, she wanted to catch Aspen with her cellphone, but she'd nestled it into her carry-on bag, so Peyton couldn't *accidentally* find it.

"What are you doing back?" Aspen casually asked. She normally didn't like game playing, but this one amused her. Watching Peyton try not to give herself away while wanting to catch Aspen in the act, priceless.

"Um..." Peyton's gaze landed on her bag. "I just wanted to change my shirt. I'm grimy."

"After you've finished, I need to talk to you about something."

Peyton's eyebrows rose when her gaze finally landed on Aspen's half-packed suitcase. "Going somewhere?" Peyton tried to keep her voice calm and patient, but Aspen caught the anger in her tone.

Keep it simple. "Home."

"Care to tell me why?" Peyton took another step toward her but remained several feet away.

Aspen sighed. "So many reasons. Most have nothing to do with you."

"Most?"

"I'm homesick. I'm sore. I'm done with the rapids."

"Are you done with me?"

Peyton's question caught Aspen off guard. Made it easier. "I think so."

"Wow. You're breaking up with me with an *I think so?* Who does that?" Peyton's entire neck was red, along with the tips of her ears.

"I don't know what I'm doing. But we've both known this hasn't been working." Aspen's words demonstrated her newfound ability to be direct.

"So that's it?" Peyton slammed her bag onto the bed. "On what grounds?"

"Incompatibility." Aspen shrugged. Peyton's nostrils flared. It went so much deeper, but she didn't plan on sharing the results of her soul searching. At least not until she'd stretched out on Gina and Steph's couch. Peyton would just have to be angry.

"And you're just figuring this out after seven months?"

"Nine, but who's counting?" Apparently, Peyton wasn't. "Doesn't that say everything that needs to be said?"

"What? Just because I don't celebrate our anniversary every month doesn't mean I'm not into this relationship."

"Not the way you're supposed to be."

Peyton let out a half snort. "Care to tell me how it's supposed to be?"

Aspen shrugged again, and the color on Peyton's cheeks reddened further. "I'm not sure. I've never had it."

"Let me get this straight. Because you have a shitty track record, it means that you're an expert on relationships?"

Aspen shook her head. "Not at all." How could she explain it? "This trip has opened my eyes. Changed me. I can't go back to the person I was before. And I don't want to."

Peyton put her hands on her hips. "Care to enlighten me about what happened?" When Aspen didn't speak immediately, Peyton forged on. "I've been on the same fucking trip as you, and I didn't see anything unusual." Peyton's nose turned up as if she'd just taken a whiff of a dirty diaper. "Unless it was all that time you spent with Quinn and Mick."

Was it? Possibly. The conversation had turned exhausting, and it wasn't fair to Peyton. She wanted to sit on the plane with her journal and work it out, but how could she explain that to Peyton? "It's not like that. I've just been lost for so long. I'm not sure who I am."

"Eat. Pray. Love." Peyton threw her hands in the air and flopped onto the bed.

"What the hell are you talking about?" Did Peyton just have an aneurysm?

"The movie. Didn't she go on some outdoor quest and find herself? Or some kind of bullshit like that."

Aspen began to raise her shoulder in another

shrug but stopped herself. Every time she did, Peyton's face grew redder. "Never watched it. Please, let's do this amicably."

"I took you on a once-in-a-lifetime trip. That cost a small fortune, and this is how you repay me?"

"I'll reimburse you." Aspen turned and put more clothes into her bag.

"That's not the point, and you know it." Peyton leapt from the bed. "This is unbelievable."

Aspen turned and met Peyton's gaze. "I need for you to answer one question. The answer will determine what happens next. Fair?"

Peyton sneered. "Nothing has been fair to this point, so why do you care now?"

Choosing to ignore the attitude, Aspen said, "Promise you'll answer honestly."

"I've never been anything but honest with you." Peyton's glare held a challenge.

"Okay. Will you miss me or the thought of me?"

"What the hell does that mean?"

"Will you miss having *me* in your life, or will you miss having a girlfriend?"

Peyton opened her mouth to speak but let it fall shut. Their gazes met.

Aspen nodded and gave Peyton a sad smile. "Thank you for being honest with me. I think that about says it all."

Peyton's gaze fell to the floor. "Are you planning on saying goodbye to the others?"

"I'd like to. If it's okay with you."

"Of course." Peyton nodded. "When's your flight leave?"

"In a couple hours, but I'd like to head to the airport soon. I just have to grab my things out of the bathroom."

"I'll get them."

Aspen watched Peyton leave the room. After any other breakup, she'd cried for days. Her eyes remained dry. It had nothing to do with Peyton and everything to do with her. She doubted that she'd have cried for any of the others had she been the person she was now. They all blurred together because in many ways they were all the same.

None of the women had fallen for her. They'd been attracted to the façade she put on. Each persona different. She'd become the ultimate chameleon. They hadn't loved *her* because they didn't know her. She didn't know herself, so how could they? And each time, when they peeled back the layers of the onion and found nothing, they moved on.

This trip was the first time in so long that she'd just been herself, and it cost her another relationship. Somehow, she didn't think Peyton would like the real version of her anyway. Ironically, she'd found someone who seemed to like her for who she was, but she was on a plane back to Boston and would likely fade from her life.

Aspen shrugged. It was probably for the better. They both had emotional baggage to unpack. Besides, Quinn never showed any interest in anything other than friendship. *Stop.* How sick was it to be thinking this way while Quinn frantically returned to her fiancée's bedside? And she'd soon be saying goodbye to her now ex-girlfriend. This was what Gina harped on her about, jumping from one relationship to another to fill her world. For once, she needed to be enough all on her own.

Peyton returned with her toiletry bag. She placed

it next to Aspen's nearly full suitcase. "I guess this is goodbye then?"

"Yeah." Aspen smiled. "I'd tell you to keep in touch, but somehow, I don't think you'll want to."

"Not right away. But I do care about you, Aspen. I hope you find what you've been searching for."

Aspen tried to hide her surprise. She hadn't realized Peyton had that level of insight. "Fair enough." Aspen took a step forward. "You're a good person, Peyton. And someday, you'll find a woman that will turn your world upside down. I really did enjoy some of the adventures you took me on. Even this one."

For the first time, Peyton gave her a half smile. "It's been nice knowing you."

"Ditto."

Peyton leaned over and gave her a peck on the cheek, and then she left.

Aspen fell back onto the bed and lay staring at the ceiling. Such cordial breakups. Most had been, except for the one who'd been in it for the money, but that didn't count. She had considered it a badge of honor that she could have such mature breakups. The reality hit her. None of the women felt enough for her to have an ugly reaction. Their emotions for her ran as deep as if they were changing phone companies.

She let out a sardonic laugh. *No.* She'd known people to show more passion about their phone carriers. Aspen rose, went to the mirror, and stared. Her normally perfectly coiffed hair showed the effects of being outdoors. She reached up to straighten it but stopped. The windblown look didn't look so bad on her. Even without makeup, she knew she was pretty. Everyone commented on her piercing blue eyes. No, it wasn't her looks that ran people off.

She stared harder. Or maybe it was. Plastic looks for a plastic personality. She leaned in. She'd need to cover the freckles around her nose that were more pronounced from being in the sun.

Aspen laughed. Not this time. She rifled her hand through her hair, making it splay out even more. Her eyes danced with amusement. Freckles. Windblown hair. A twinkle in her eye. She looked good.

She turned from the mirror, ready to get on with her life.

Chapter Twenty-nine

D o you think I'm in shock?" Quinn blurted out. "I can't seem to focus. I feel like I'm in a daze." She continued following Mick, who weaved her way through the airport crowds.

"How's that any different than normal?" Mick shot Quinn her million-watt smile.

Quinn managed a smile. Being morose and brooding wouldn't solve any of her problems. "I'm sorry. This is just such a mess. The first time I allow myself to relax and believe maybe I can start living again, this happens. God is sending me a clear message."

Mick stopped walking and grabbed Quinn's shirt to stop her. "No. You can't think that way. God isn't punishing you. He's testing you."

People streamed around them. Some shot dirty looks. They'd become *those* people, who stopped in the middle of the walkway. Mick pulled Quinn off to the side, away from the bustling throng.

Quinn shook her head. After Stella's accident, she wasn't sure she believed in God anymore. But if there was a God, she must have done something really wrong to be caught in this never-ending nightmare. "God's pissed. He's been pissed at me for a long time."

"Did you ever think he might have saved you?"

"Saved me?" Quinn's eyes widened. "Are you on crack?"

Mick put her hands up. "If you'd have been here, things could have turned out much worse."

"Worse? But I could have stopped Natalie from doing it."

"Or..." Mick leveled her gaze at Quinn. "Both your asses would be locked up for murder."

Quinn's stomach dropped and bile rose in her throat. "But..."

Mick pointed at Quinn's face. "You're white as a sheet because you know I'm right."

Quinn gazed over Mick's head at the rushing travelers. She took several deep breaths before returning her gaze to Mick. Mick's dark brown eyes were comforting. "This is so fucked up, isn't it?"

"We'll figure it out." Mick gestured with her head that they should start walking again. "We need to get to Natalie."

"If she'll let us in." Quinn's heart sank. After traveling all this way, they faced the real possibility that Natalie would turn them away.

Mick dug in her bag and pulled out a wad of keys. "Then we'll let ourselves in."

Quinn shot Mick a sideways glance. *Mick has a key to Natalie's place? Sure.* Natalie needed someone she could count on once Quinn flaked out and ran away. Mick was as solid as they came.

Their Uber had arrived by the time they'd made it through the terminal. The heavy traffic made Quinn impatient, so she closed her eyes and leaned her head against the seat. Maybe if she couldn't see how slow they crept along, she wouldn't be so agitated. *Right.*

"We need to agree on a game plan," Quinn said. "We don't want Natalie flipping out when we show up unannounced."

"Game plan seems simple to me." Mick peered out the front window and scowled at the cars lined up bumper to bumper. "We let Natalie rant for a bit if she needs to get it out of her system. And then we figure out how to get her out of this mess."

"What about Stella?" Quinn asked. When Mick shot her a puzzled look, Quinn continued. "We need to figure out how to help her, too."

"Agreed." Mick nodded. "I'm afraid this doesn't change your status any. You're still the former lesbian lover, and her parents are next of kin."

"Don't remind me." Quinn wanted to scream or rip her own face off, or maybe both.

"I don't mean to sound like a dick, but right now, Natalie comes first."

Blood pounded in Quinn's ears. "I know," Quinn answered in a near whisper.

Mick clapped her hand on Quinn's leg. "It sucks. And I'm sorry, but Natalie's been carrying a lot of the load. It's time for us to carry her for a bit."

Quinn nodded. Tears welled in her eyes. "I feel so fucking guilty. I ran away and left everything in her hands."

"Didn't we already talk about this? God is not punishing you."

"No." Quinn held up her hand. "I'm not talking about going on the trip. I'm talking about running away to the Ozarks."

"I'm afraid I'm going to have to agree with you on that."

Quinn waited for anger to rise, but it didn't. She'd been selfish. "I never should have left Natalie to shoulder all the burden." Quinn clamped her mouth shut. Her stomach lurched. "Oh, god. I'm such a jerk.

I didn't mean it. Stella isn't a burden."

"It's okay to be truthful." Mick's gaze met Quinn's, and she gave her a half smile. "You loved Stella with all your heart, but she's gone. Been gone for a long time. But you haven't been able to move on with your life because you're stuck in this horrible limbo. Purgatory." Mick flicked her wrist at Quinn. "Lighten up on yourself. You're doing the best you know how."

Finally, the cars moved, and their driver gunned it. He expertly weaved in and out of traffic, never slowing. Quinn had to look away. Soon they'd be at Natalie's. Maybe wishing away the cars had been shortsighted. *Too late.* They rapidly approached Boston Harbor. "I'm not sure if I'm ready for this."

"Gotta be. Nat needs us."

Why did Mick always know what she needed to hear? Her focus should be on Natalie, nothing else. She could do this. Quinn sat up straighter and steeled her back. "You're right. It's time to do the right thing."

Once they pulled up outside of Nat's condo, time passed unnaturally fast. It seemed like only seconds ago they'd tumbled out of the Uber, but now they stood in the hallway outside Natalie's door.

The door flew open, and Natalie shot through it. She wrapped her arms around Mick and sobbed into her neck. Quinn gaped, taken off guard by Natalie's actions. She shuffled from foot to foot as she uncomfortably gazed around the hallway.

Mick offered comforting words. The muscles in her forearms bulged as she squeezed Natalie as if she could hug away the pain. Maybe it was working since Natalie's sobs subsided, and her breathing became more rhythmic.

Quinn wasn't sure how long they'd stood in the corridor with Natalie clinging to Mick. Eventually, Natalie stepped back. When her gaze met Quinn's, her eyes were clear, despite the pain that lay just below the surface.

Natalie opened her arms. "Quinn." Without another word, she closed the gap between them and wrapped Quinn in a bear hug.

Quinn hadn't realized how tightly wound she was until the layers of tension melted away as she held Natalie. They'd have to talk soon, but for now, she simply wanted to hang on to this lifeline.

Movement caught Quinn's gaze as a neighbor walked past and eyed them suspiciously. Mick cleared her throat. "Maybe we should take this party inside."

"Oh, sure," Natalie said, shaking her head. "I guess the neighbors don't need to be up in my business. I'm sure they'll hear enough on the ten o'clock news."

When they entered, Quinn surveyed the room. She'd expected LaTasha, but she was nowhere to be seen.

As if reading her mind, Natalie said, "I sent LaTasha home. She has a couple young kids, so she didn't need to be babysitting me. She finally agreed once I assured her nothing would keep you guys away." Natalie motioned toward the couch. "Where are my manners? Would either of you like something to drink?"

"I'll have a water," Mick said.

"Make that two," Quinn added.

When Natalie returned with their drinks, Quinn studied her. If she didn't know Natalie so well, she might have missed the strain that pulled at her eyes and left her forehead taut. Once Natalie sat, it was as if all her remaining energy drained from her body. She slumped against the arm of the chair.

Her beauty, although still evident, was muted by the stress etched on her face. Quinn wished she knew how to comfort her. Mick took the lead and slid to the end of the couch nearest Natalie's chair. Sitting on the edge of her seat, Mick put her hand on Natalie's leg.

"How are you doing?" Mick asked.

Tears welled in Natalie's eyes. "Three guesses and the first two don't count." Natalie smiled at her own joke.

"Would you care to share what happened?" Mick asked.

Natalie rubbed her temples but didn't speak. She stared out the large window overlooking the bay. "It was horrible," she said in a low voice.

Quinn had to strain to hear.

"Stella coded. My fucking parents happened to be in the facility at the time, and they told the medical people to do whatever was necessary to save her. What the fuck is wrong with those people?" Natalie put her hand against her forehead. "Stella could have gone peacefully and finally gotten relief. But no."

"I'm so sorry, Nat." Mick squeezed Natalie's knee.

"I lost it. The more I thought about it, the more upset I became. Something in me snapped. I barricaded myself in her room, and we talked."

Quinn narrowed her eyes. *Talked?* Had Natalie lost it?

Natalie gave Quinn a half smile. "Okay, I mean I talked. To Stella. She didn't answer. I held her hand. I hugged her. I cried. The last call I made to you guys, I was in her room." Tears streamed down her face.

Quinn wanted to offer comfort, but instead, she remained in her seat. Natalie's pain pounded against Quinn's chest, making her ache.

"The cops had gotten there and were trying to talk to me, but I wouldn't let them in. All of a sudden, I knew what I had to do. I had to save her, so I went to the machine that pumped oxygen into the tube they'd shoved down her throat."

"The ventilator?" Mick asked.

Natalie nodded. "I turned it off." She bit her lip, and the pain in her eyes was heartbreaking. "I went to her bed and held her hand. I told her we loved her and that she could finally be free. I told her goodbye. The next thing I know, the police knocked down the door. Somewhere along the line, I got this." She touched the gash on her forehead. "They handcuffed me and hauled me out."

Mick touched Natalie's forehead. "I think you need to clean that out. It doesn't look like they did much for it."

"They didn't."

Mick jumped to her feet and disappeared into the bathroom.

"And now Stella lives forever on a ventilator?" Quinn said.

Natalie let out a loud breath. "I guess. But I'll probably never see her again because I'll be banished just like you." Natalie's voice wavered, and tears began again. "Oh, god, what did I do? What if they won't let me see her again?"

"Surely, your parents won't be that cruel."

Natalie shot Quinn a sideways glance but didn't respond.

Mick rushed back into the room with an armful

of first aid supplies. She dropped her take onto the coffee table and stood looking down at Natalie. "That needs to be treated."

"Seriously?" Natalie touched the wound and winced. "It's not that bad."

"You flinched," Mick said.

"Just a little, but I'm fine." Natalie's gaze settled on Quinn. "She's not going to take no for an answer, is she?"

"Afraid not," Quinn replied.

"Here," Natalie tossed the television control toward Quinn. "If she's going to insist on doctoring me. Look at the bullshit on the news. Find one of the conservative ones, if you want to hear about how evil I am. You two should be careful being here with such a godless creature."

"That bad?" Quinn pointed the controller at the television.

Mick went into motion. She dabbed Natalie's wound with a cloth, wiping off the dried blood. She examined the wound with her brow furrowed.

Quinn flipped through the channels, looking for a news segment.

"Damn. They did a number on you," Mick said.

"It's fine." Natalie waved her hand at Mick.

Quinn flipped the channel, and her heart jumped into her throat. A reporter stood outside Stella's care center. She turned up the volume.

"Earlier, I spoke to Stella Parsons's parents. Many of you will remember her tragic story. A fluke accident while kayaking has left her in a vegetative state. But her dedicated parents have never given up hope..."

"I can't listen to this shit again," Natalie said. "My

parents were in their element during the interview."

Quinn lowered the volume as Stella and Natalie's parents came onto the screen. Mr. Parsons stepped up to the podium with a stern look on his face, while Mrs. Parsons stood off to the side with one hand clasped over her chest.

"Cue the waterworks. Millie Parsons knows how to put on a show." Natalie's voice dripped with sarcasm. Dramatically, Natalie thumped her hand to her chest, and with the other, she waved it in front of her face as if to fan herself.

Mick flinched, and the gauze pad she held against Natalie's forehead fluttered to the floor. "You scared the shit out of me."

"Sorry. I just can't stand them and their bullshit lies." In a high-pitched, exaggerated voice, she said, "My evil daughter, Natalie, nearly killed my precious miracle Stella. Praise be to Jesus for saving her."

"Do you want me to turn this off?" Quinn asked.

"No, go ahead and turn it up," Natalie replied.

Quinn adjusted the volume, just as the segment shifted back to the studio. A familiar host stared into the camera with a pained expression. He placed his hand over his heart and said, "This is so heartbreaking. The Parsonses have spent the last five years sitting vigil at Stella's bedside and hoping the power of prayer would bring her back to them. And now more tragedy has befallen them." A picture of Natalie flashed on the screen.

"Turn it off!" Mick said.

Quinn stabbed at the power button. She'd have to watch this later without Natalie.

Mick finished applying the bandage and stepped back to observe her work. "All patched up."

"Thanks." Natalie smiled. "I'm sorry, Quinn. I thought I could watch it, but I just can't."

"Fair enough. Besides, we need to come up with a plan."

"A plan?" Natalie said.

"Yeah, first, we need to find you a lawyer," Quinn said.

"Public defender, here I come." Natalie put her head into her hands. "Why did I make a deal with the devil?" Her gaze flitted around the room. "I let them buy me out. All my savings went into decorating this place because they told me not to worry about money."

"The two hundred thousand is yours," Quinn said. "I couldn't save one of the Parsons sisters, but I can help the other."

"No." Natalie shook her head. "I can't take your money. You were going to use that for Stella."

Quinn looked down at her hands and blinked away tears. "I had a lot of time to think the last couple of weeks. I even talked to Aspen about it." Mick's eyebrows shot up, but Quinn pretended not to notice. "That money isn't going to do any good, even if I had ten times that much. What court is going to take the power out of Stella's parents' hands and give it to the lesbian lover? Even if we did plan on getting married."

Natalie's eyes filled with tears. "Remember the Terri Schiavo case?"

Did she remember? She'd secretly read everything she could on the case, but just like Natalie, she'd never brought it up. "Yes. It took years for the husband to finally be allowed to remove her feeding tube, and they were married. What chance do I truly have?"

Mick let out a loud exhale. "Hallelujah. Finally."

Quinn stared at Mick and suddenly realized how hard this had been on her, watching Quinn in pain all these years and never being able to get through to her. "This has been hard on you, hasn't it?"

Mick nodded. "I don't want you to run away again. I've missed you."

"Me too," Natalie said.

"Stop. I can't have you two making me blubber." Quinn ran her hand through her hair and stared at the floor. "I know the courts will never go against your parents. They have all the power." Quinn's stomach lurched. Finally, she'd said what she'd known all along. She looked up, and her gaze met Natalie's. "Please, take the money. At least it can do some good."

"But—" Natalie started to protest.

"No!" Mick interrupted in a loud voice.

Quinn and Natalie turned and stared.

"Oops." Mick's face reddened. "I didn't mean for that to come out so loud. Natalie, please take the money. I'll throw some in, too. This whole situation has torn us all apart." She glanced at Quinn. "I lost my best friend. I lost Stella, who was like a sister to me. We can't lose you, too."

"Okay," Natalie said in a voice barely over a whisper.

Mick slapped her hand on her knee. "Let's find you a lawyer then."

Chapter Thirty

The stale air closed in on Quinn, and heat blanketed the room. She pulled at her collar, hoping to cool down. She suspected her face glowed red, which would look terrible on camera. Luckily, Natalie's attorney wanted her and Mick nowhere near the press. They would be behind the scenes to offer Natalie moral support, but they wouldn't be anywhere near a camera. *Optics.*

"He's supposed to be here soon." Natalie glanced at her watch. "It's nearly noon."

"Probably eating his lunch. Nails," Mick said.

Quinn smiled. Mick wasn't wrong. When they'd talked to Broderick Taylor yesterday, Natalie immediately decided he was the one. He came off as tough, no-nonsense, and insanely confident. Also expensive. Quinn was glad to pay if he could get Natalie out of this mess.

Broderick's assistant scurried into the room. "Mr. Taylor will be in shortly. He wants to go over your script." She nodded to Natalie. "The press is already gathering in our media room. We'll have makeup in shortly."

Natalie's eyes rose. "Makeup?" she whispered.

The assistant turned. "Yes, Ms. Parsons. Mr. Taylor wants you to have just the right look on camera." She studied Natalie's perfectly made-up face. "This will need to go. You look too rested. Too good.

He'll want to show some signs of stress and strain. Bags under your eyes. Things like that."

This time, Natalie waited until she left the room before she spoke. "Wow. That's crazy."

"Apparently, he wants to start by winning the court of public opinion," Quinn said.

Natalie scowled. "Do you really think that's necessary?"

Mick put her hand over Natalie's. "He knows better than we do. Let him do his job."

Natalie put her other hand over Mick's and squeezed. "You're right. It's just so…so much."

Before anyone could say anything else, a flamboyant man burst into the room carrying a makeup case. "Which one of you ladies is my subject?"

Natalie raised her hand. "That would be me."

The man looked at her over his glasses, narrowed his eyes, and then smiled. "Perfect. Perfect." He held his hand out as if framing her face and closed one eye. "Such a beautiful canvas to work with."

Quinn bit her lip, stopping herself from chuckling. The whole thing felt surreal. She had to find something to laugh about, or she might never stop crying.

※ ※ ※ ※

Quinn's mouth dropped open. A short balding man strode into the room. Surely, this couldn't be Broderick Taylor.

"Ladies," he said with a nod. Then his focus shifted to Natalie. He scrutinized her for several seconds with pursed lips. Finally, he nodded again. "Very good. Perfect. They'll eat you up."

Natalie fidgeted. "Um, sorry. I didn't catch your name."

"Broderick Taylor." He extended his hand. "I presume that you're Natalie Parsons." Without waiting for an answer, he shifted his gaze. He pointed and said, "Quinn." He shifted his gaze again. "Mick."

They both nodded.

"Great. Great." He turned his attention back to Natalie. "We need to get down to work. I want to make sure you are ready for this news conference. It'll only be you and I out there." He shot a glance at Quinn and Mick. "No offense, but we're keeping you as far away from the press as possible. We're already going to have to do damage control since the press has pictures of you visiting Natalie's condo. My sources tell me you spent the night there." He shook his head. "We can't have that happen again."

Quinn bristled, and the hair on the back of her neck stood up. *What the fuck?* Were they living in the fifties?

Broderick must have caught her reaction. He held up his hands. "Hey, no offense. I'm just telling it to you straight. This isn't me. It's what we need to save Natalie. You want to save her, don't you?"

"Of course," Quinn said. Before she could say more, Broderick turned away.

"Then that's settled."

Mick shot Quinn a look. Quinn shrugged. Before this was over, she might need Xanax.

Chapter Thirty-one

G ina rushed down the stairs of her condo. Obviously, she'd been watching for Aspen to arrive. Fumbling with her purse, she extracted several bills and shoved them toward the driver. "Keep the change."

His eyes widened. "Thank you, ma'am."

Aspen opened the door. It weighed a ton, so she kicked it open the rest of the way with her foot. She felt as if she'd been traveling forever. If she hadn't watched the sun rise at the airport, she wouldn't have a clue what time of day it was.

The scowl on Gina's face told her that Gina had picked up on Aspen's physical and emotional state. Before she could speak, Gina had her in a bear hug.

"What the hell happened to you?" Gina squeezed her tighter. "You look like shit."

Ahh, the eloquence of Gina. She'd missed her friend. All she wanted to do was curl up on Gina and Steph's couch. They would feed her, wrap her in blankets, and hopefully take away the emptiness in her chest.

"Let's get you inside," Gina said and let her go. "Steph made your favorite comfort food. Although, I had to convince her that it was lunchtime somewhere."

"Homemade mac and cheese is perfect for breakfast." A little life returned to Aspen at the thought of the meal that awaited her.

"Yep. It's baking in the oven and should be done any minute. Plus…"

"Fresh banana bread?" Aspen sprang up the stairs.

"Keto's worst nightmare. Carbs for days." Gina laughed.

"Sign me up."

After freshening up, Aspen wandered into the dining room. She breathed in deeply; the entire house smelled of fresh-baked banana bread. Her mouth watered.

Gina had set the table, and Steph brought out a steaming pot of mac and cheese and set it on the potholders.

"You guys are the best." Aspen breathed in deeply. "I already see my future, hours of time in the gym to combat this feast."

Gina glanced at her watch. "We've got about an hour for you to tell us all about your adventures before the news conference."

"News conference?" Aspen narrowed her eyes.

Steph put her hand over her mouth. "Oh, god. You haven't seen any of it, have you?"

Aspen's chest tightened, and she tried to take a deep breath, but it was shallow. "I came straight here from the airport."

"Oh, shit." Gina glanced at Steph. "I was so excited to have you back that I didn't think. Your guides, Quinn and Mick, have been all over the news. Well, more Stella and her sister, Natalie. And their psycho parents. The press is eating the story up."

"How stupid of me. Of course it made the national news." Aspen ran her hand through her hair. "Who's giving the news conference?"

"Natalie and her lawyer," Gina said. "It's supposed to start at eleven o'clock."

Steph pushed the pot toward her. "You need to eat."

Aspen gazed at the steaming dish; she'd lost her appetite, but it wouldn't be right after Steph went to so much trouble. She put a small helping of mac and cheese on her plate and snatched a piece of bread. Gina glanced at her meager meal but didn't say anything.

"What are the reporters saying?" Aspen asked.

"Depends on which station you watch," Gina said. "Natalie and Quinn are being demonized on some of them. Did you expect different?"

"Fuck." Aspen's jaw clenched. "Did Stella survive?"

"Yes, thank God." Steph put her hand against her heart.

Aspen's shoulders slumped. It would have been easier on Quinn if Stella passed. *Dumbass.* Then Natalie would probably be charged with murder.

Gina studied Aspen. "Why do you look as if someone just told you Santa Claus isn't real?"

"Oh, nothing." Aspen tried to keep her voice light-hearted.

"Nice try, but no," Steph said.

"I've spent the week with Quinn. This has been so hard on her." Aspen turned to Gina. "Just imagine if it were Steph in that bed, and you couldn't see her or help her."

"Oh, god, I hadn't even thought about that." Gina looked green.

"Just when she'd started living again, then this. Mick had been so hopeful that the trip would finally pull her out of her self-imposed isolation." Aspen blinked back tears. "This could spiral her back down."

Gina studied her for several beats. "You seem to know quite a bit about Quinn." She narrowed her eyes. "Care to tell us what went on in Africa?"

"Ugh." Aspen put her hands over her face and left them there. She peeked out between her fingers. "There's so much to tell. I don't even know where to start."

"Did you really think you could come here and get wooed with mac and cheese and not be expected to put out? I want to hear it all."

"It's not like that," Aspen said too quickly.

"Not like what?" Gina raised her eyebrows and glanced at Steph. "I think she protests too much."

"Steph, help. She's taking advantage of me because of my jet lag."

"Sorry, sweetheart. But you have me intrigued, too."

Aspen groaned. "Fine. Where do you want me to start?"

"At the beginning," Steph and Gina said in unison.

Aspen launched into her story. As she told it, at times, her fingernails dug into her palms while other times her body relaxed as she remembered the moments.

Gina chuckled. "You're obviously Team Quinn."

"There is no Team Quinn or Team Mick." Aspen glared.

Gina rolled her eyes and turned to Steph. "Are you going to let her get away with her obvious delusion?"

"Hun, she does have a point," Steph said. "While you talked, your fists were clenched so tight I thought you might draw blood, but every time you mentioned

Quinn, your hands relaxed and you got that grin on your face."

"I did not." *Did I? No!*

Steph gave Aspen a knowing smile. "Are you and Peyton over?"

Aspen's eyes widened. She hadn't expected them to figure it out this quickly. She nodded.

"Yes!" Gina raised her hands into the air.

"Could you not be quite so enthusiastic about it?"

Gina raised one fist only a couple of inches above her head and shook it. "Yay."

Aspen rolled her eyes. "Really?"

"You said I shouldn't be quite so enthusiastic, so I wasn't."

"Gee, thanks."

"Tell me more about Quinn." Gina pursed her lips and looked over her glasses. "You like her."

Aspen caught that it was a statement, not a question. "She was a great guide."

Gina laughed. "Seriously? Good try. You like her as more than a guide."

"She'd make a good friend." Aspen crossed her arms over her chest, daring Gina to push the boundary.

"You're single now," Steph said. "Doesn't that open the door for Quinn?"

"Even if I were interested," Aspen said and quickly added, "but I'm not saying I am. But if I were, the obstacles are too big."

"Like?" Gina said.

Aspen held up one finger. "First, her fiancée has been lying in a hospital bed for the past five years, and god knows what's going to happen next."

Gina nodded. "I get that, but she can't stop

living forever."

"And second, *you* told me that I have to stop jumping from one relationship to another. Remember? I'm supposed to be finding myself."

"So have you?"

Aspen shrugged. "I'm trying." With her new-found frankness, she needed to level with Gina. "There's something I haven't told you."

Gina's eyebrows rose.

"I submitted one of my manuscripts to a publisher—"

"Hot damn, it's about time." Gina clapped her hands while Steph cheered.

Aspen waved them off. "Don't get too excited. I've been waiting three months. Not a word."

"One rejection doesn't mean you should give up. There's plenty of publishers out there," Steph said.

"I know. When I was out on the Zambezi, I made a vow to myself. I'm going to keep submitting because writing has been the one constant in my life. My passion."

"If I'd known whitewater rafting would knock some sense into you, I would have sent you a long time ago." Gina grinned. "Next time you get squirrelly, I'll just take you to the wave pool at the water park and let them thrash you around."

"Really nice." Aspen pretended to scowl.

"That's what friends are for." Gina rubbed her chin and looked into Aspen's eyes. "Seriously though, I feel the difference in you." She turned to Steph and clasped her hands to her chest. "Our girl is growing up. Soon she won't need mac and cheese anymore."

Aspen took a big spoonful and shoved it into her mouth. As she chewed, she said, "Don't go taking my food away from me."

Steph laughed. "Honey, my kitchen is always open to you."

Aspen gave Gina a dirty look before turning to Steph. "Thanks."

"Now that you've found yourself, doesn't that put Quinn back on the table?" Gina asked.

Aspen threw up her hands and laughed. "Would you make up your mind? You've only been hounding me for ten years. Now you want me to go against everything you've told me?"

Gina shrugged. "I don't know. There's something different in your eyes this time."

"I can't keep jumping from one woman to the next." Aspen sighed. "Do you realize the longest I've gone without dating someone is two weeks at most. As soon as one relationship ends, I'm on to the next."

"Good thing you're hot." Gina laughed. "Most mere mortal women wouldn't be able to keep the revolving door going."

"This is all they see." Aspen ran her hand in front of her face and down her body. "I doubt any of them choose me because they like who I am. Hell, I didn't even know who I was. How sad is that?"

Gina opened her mouth, closed it, and then looked toward the ceiling. Aspen's dad would have joked that he could see her wheels turning.

"I'm throwing you for a loop, aren't I?" Aspen said.

Gina met her gaze. "I guess you are. Fuck! This might be the first time in my life that I don't know what to say."

"I love it." Aspen laughed. "Something changed in me on that trip."

"I feel it." Gina smirked. "You're not quite such a hot mess."

"Keep the compliments coming." Aspen motioned with her hands as if to say, *bring it on.* Then she smiled. "I don't feel like such a hot mess, either."

"I've been there for every one of your breakups. And I've always known what to say and do."

Aspen nodded. "Yep. We have our shtick. I have an emotional meltdown about how my heart was broken by...."

"Insert name here, or should I say girlfriend X?" Gina said.

"Exactly. Too many to name. I'd cry. You guys would feed me and pat my head. I'd recover after a few days. You'd lecture me about not losing myself in a relationship. And then you'd release me into the wild."

Gina glanced at Steph and nodded. "Sounds about right."

Steph gave Aspen a sad smile as she nodded.

"And then a couple days later, I'd call you all excited because I'd finally found *the one.*"

Gina sighed. "Yep."

"But this time, I'm not doing any of that."

"I know." Gina's eyes widened. She dramatically ran her hands through her hair, leaving it to splay in all directions. "And you're freaking me out."

Aspen wadded up her napkin and threw it. Gina didn't try to move and let it bounce off her head. "Dork."

"Now that you've had this epiphany. Or awakening. Or whatever you're calling it," Gina said. "What's next?"

"Whitewater awakening." Aspen smiled. "I'm

going to get my book published. Even if it isn't a *real* profession." Aspen made air quotes when she said real.

"Product of our parents, huh? My dad still thinks Steph doesn't have a real job since she teaches."

"Yep, finance and business are the only viable career paths." Aspen snorted. "It's crazy. It's okay for me to live off my trust fund and do nothing, but how could a child of theirs stoop to being a *creative*?"

"Eek, that's like the worst thing ever." Gina pretended to shudder.

"Definitely." Aspen grinned.

Gina's eyes filled with mischief. "Who do you think will play me?"

"Play you?"

"In the movie."

"What movie?"

"Duh. The one they make out of your memoir." Gina flipped her hair back and pursed her lips. "I'm sure I'll have a prominent role in your book."

Aspen groaned and wadded up another napkin.

"While I'm enjoying this conversation, it's about fifteen minutes before the hour," Steph said as she stood from the table. "Why don't you guys go turn on CNN, and I'll clean up really quick?"

Aspen started to protest, but Steph stopped her. "Go! I don't want you to miss anything."

As soon as the TV sprang to life, images of Quinn filled the screen. Aspen gasped, and pain shot through her chest.

They'd found some of the most unflattering pictures of Quinn. Most looked to be taken when she was competing in kayak races. Her bright red face full of determination could be mistaken for anger if taken out of context, which was exactly what they'd done. They'd painted Quinn as a dangerous and angry lesbian. It stopped one step shy of accusing her of being an abuser. Every picture of Quinn with Stella was used to accentuate their size difference. Quinn towered over Stella, making her look vulnerable, which wasn't the impression she'd had after listening to Quinn and Mick's stories.

"What the hell channel is this?" Aspen growled.

"Oh, god, sorry." Gina scrambled to pick up the controller. "I was watching earlier to see how the morons were covering the story."

The picture flickered and was replaced by different images. Scenes from yesterday of Mick and Quinn entering Natalie's condo played on the screen while the newscaster droned on about the tragedy.

Suddenly, the picture was replaced by a car with the entire hood crumpled into the front seat. A lump caught in Aspen's throat. Photos of Quinn's accident. She wanted to close her eyes, but she couldn't look away. How had Quinn survived? And had she done it to herself? Aspen pushed the thoughts from her mind.

"This is the same thing they keep playing on a loop," Gina said. "Some of this is tough to watch."

Aspen looked away from the television, but the images of Quinn were burned into her mind.

Gina did her best to distract Aspen with an irreverent story about her trip to the grocery store. Anything to keep her occupied.

Music on the television drew their attention. The newscaster sat up straighter and announced, "We will be going live to the offices of Broderick Taylor, where Ms. Natalie Parsons will be speaking to the press. I'll hand this off to you, Tessa."

Chapter Thirty-two

A young, blond reporter filled the screen. "Thanks, Daniel. Natalie Parsons and her attorney, Broderick Taylor, are expected soon."

As if on cue, the camera cut away from the reporter and focused on the podium. A petite woman with dark hair was led by a short balding man.

"That must be Natalie," Aspen said, and then turned back to the screen.

Damn. The bags under her eyes would make a basset hound jealous. She looked pale and drawn. The media had splashed her picture everywhere. She was an extremely attractive woman, but the stress had obviously taken its toll.

Broderick held on to her arm as if to steady her. He attended to her before he approached the microphone stand.

Aspen narrowed her eyes and tried to take in the rest of the room. Where were Quinn and Mick?

Broderick had already begun speaking, so she caught him midsentence. "...appreciate the support. As you can see..." He glanced at Natalie with a sad smile and paused. "...this ordeal has taken a great deal out of Ms. Parsons. I ask that everyone put themselves in her shoes and show compassion for the plight she's endured the last several years that has led to this moment."

Several reporters yelled out, but the words were

garbled.

Broderick raised his hand for silence. "Ms. Parsons will be answering your questions shortly. I just want to make it clear. I am acting on behalf of Ms. Parsons, and all inquiries should be directed to my office. I want to assure you that this travesty of justice will be righted. Ms. Parsons will be exonerated." He forcefully brought his hand down on the podium as he delivered the line.

Natalie stepped to the microphone. Broderick gave her an encouraging nod. He looked more like a concerned father than an aggressive attorney. *Likely by design.*

Natalie cleared her throat. Her eyes widened as she looked out toward the reporters and into the camera.

Poor thing. Aspen's heart went out to her. How hard must this be, and why the hell weren't Quinn and Mick there offering support? It wasn't fair that she had to do this alone. She looked so vulnerable. *Duh!* Of course, that was what Broderick wanted.

It made her more sympathetic. The poor woman alone in the world, with only her fatherly attorney by her side. Broderick certainly wouldn't want the big, strong Quinn standing with her. The lesbian aspect would probably be frowned upon, too. *Poor Quinn.* She was probably pacing a hole in the floor not being allowed to be there.

Aspen pushed the thoughts out of her mind. She wanted to hear what Natalie had to say.

Natalie cleared her throat again, and Broderick gave her an encouraging smile. "I want to thank everyone for the support they've given me over the last forty-eight hours." She put her hand on her chest.

"It has been the second-worst time of my life. The first being my sister's accident."

Aspen stared at the screen, riveted. The camera loved Natalie, despite the bags and worn-out look. How could anyone not feel bad for her?

Natalie had stopped talking and looked toward Broderick. He approached the microphone. "Natalie, why don't you tell these fine people what was going through your head when you barricaded yourself in your sister's room?"

Natalie visibly flinched. *Perfect.* She must be scoring major points with the audience.

Natalie took a deep breath. "I walked in and saw my sister…Stella…" Natalie stared into the camera with her lip trembling.

"Go on," Broderick said.

"She looked terrible. She's been through so much, but now there was this tube shoved down her throat." Natalie stood up straighter. "If you'd seen how full of life she was before her accident. So vibrant. More energy than anyone I've ever met. To see her like that…it was too much. I don't even remember barricading the doors. The only thing I could think of was saving my sister. I couldn't let them do this to her." Natalie blinked back tears, and her hand resting on the podium appeared to be trembling.

Broderick stepped up and put his hand on her back. "It's okay, Natalie." He looked into the camera. "Are you up to taking a few questions from these fine people?"

Natalie looked up and nodded. Her brown eyes glistened in the lighting, making her look more vulnerable.

Broderick pointed to a reporter in the front row.

"I'd like to ask Ms. Parsons what she thought she'd accomplish by doing this."

Natalie opened her mouth, but Broderick spoke. "I believe she already answered that question. The only thing she was thinking about was saving her sister." Broderick pointed. "Next question."

"There's been speculation that the district attorney will charge Ms. Parsons with attempted murder."

Broderick shook his head and flipped his hand toward the reporter. "I don't think anyone believes that our fine DA would be so callous. So heartless. This is a family issue, not a legal one. Ms. Parsons needs our compassion and help, not jail."

Natalie stood beside him with a rigid posture. Her gaze darted around as several reporters shouted questions.

"We have time for a few more," Broderick said. "Stanley, how about you?"

"It has been reported that Quinn Coolidge visited you yesterday," the reporter said. "Is this true?"

Broderick nodded at Natalie.

"Yes," Natalie said. "She heard what happened and came by to check on me."

What? Heard what happened? Heat rose up Aspen's neck. Natalie had frantically been trying to get in touch with Quinn. Now she'd dropped by. Aspen took a calming breath. The lawyers knew what they were doing.

"She was your sister's long-term girlfriend but hasn't been seen around for some time. Why would she show up now?" the reporter asked.

"You know Ms. Parsons can't possibly speak to the motives of someone else," Broderick said, his tone scolding.

"But Ms. Parsons spent quite a bit of time with Ms. Coolidge, so I thought she'd have insight."

Broderick looked away from the reporter and scowled into the camera. "The reporters need to stick to questions related to Ms. Parsons. If you have questions for Ms. Coolidge, you will have to ask her." He glanced around the room. "Are there any more questions for *my* client?"

The room grew loud as questions were shouted out. Broderick pointed at another reporter.

"Will your parents support you? Or do they want you incarcerated?"

Aspen leaned in toward the screen. At the mention of her parents, Natalie's face became paler.

"I remind you again. Ms. Parsons will not be able to answer any questions concerning people that are not here."

"Your parents are so pious and caring," a voice called out. "How did they raise such a godless daughter?"

Natalie cringed, but her eyes narrowed, and her jaw clenched. Before Broderick could stop her, Natalie spoke. "I believe my definition of God and yours are two different things."

Broderick put his arm around Natalie. His hand clenched Natalie's shoulder. Aspen suspected that his grip sent a message to her. "Ms. Parsons is rightfully upset. Daily, she prays for her sister, so it's painful for her to hear people who've not walked in her shoes say such hurtful things."

Natalie's gaze dropped to the podium. "Sorry," she mumbled.

Broderick nodded. "It seems we aren't going to

get any legitimate questions, so I think—"

"Do you think the DA will throw the book at you?" a reporter called out.

"No," Natalie said, her voice stronger than it had been seconds before. "I believe he is a fair man who will look at the circumstances of this case and then do the right thing."

"But he's in a tough battle for reelection," the reporter said. "Don't you think he'll use this case as a springboard for his campaign?"

Natalie shook her head. "No. He has shown himself to be an honorable man, so I don't believe he would use my family's pain for political gain."

Good answer. Natalie seemed to be hitting the mark, but then again, Aspen wasn't an attorney. If it went to trial, the jury would love Natalie. She had just the right mixture of vulnerability and grit.

"Ms. Parsons will take one more question." Broderick raised his voice above the reporters who'd begun to shout out questions again. He scanned the room and then pointed. "Cynthia, you have the last question."

"Thank you, Broderick. I would like to know what Ms. Parsons wants for her sister."

"Peace," Natalie said without missing a beat. "I don't want her to suffer any longer."

"So you want her dead?" another reporter yelled.

Broderick scowled and shook his head. "That question is beneath you, Thomas. Ms. Parsons clearly stated that she wants peace for her sister. You're the one who extrapolated an erroneous assumption." Broderick stood up taller and looked directly into the camera. "On behalf of Ms. Parsons, I would like to thank all of you for coming today. In the days ahead,

I am sure the DA will do the right thing and drop all charges. This is a tragic situation that doesn't need to be made more tragic. Please pray for Ms. Parsons and her sister, Stella."

Broderick abruptly turned from the podium as he was peppered with questions. He put his hand on Natalie's elbow and led her out of the room.

Aspen exhaled and sat back against the couch. "That was intense. I've always watched things like that on TV, but it's different when you know the people."

༄ ༄ ༄ ༄

Thank god it was over. Quinn didn't know how much longer she could sit and watch before she crawled out of her skin.

Mick turned off the television. "I can't watch these commentators any longer." She continued to pace around the room as she'd done during the entire press conference. "Broderick will bring her right back here, won't he?"

"I hope so," Quinn answered.

Quinn's phone vibrated. She snatched it from the table. Maybe it was Nat. Her heart pounded in her chest when she saw it was from Aspen.

She opened the message.

Aspen: *Thinking about you. Just watched the press conference. How are you doing?*

Quinn: *Thank you for thinking of me. Hanging in there. Natalie was a pro.*

Aspen: *Definitely. Why weren't you out there?*

Quinn: *Lawyer said it would be better for us to hang out behind the scenes. Waiting for Natalie to come back.*

Aspen: *So you guys are there?*

Quinn: *Yep. Waiting in Broderick's office.*

Aspen: *I'm so sorry you're going through this.*

Natalie burst through the door. Before she'd gotten more than two steps in, Mick rushed to her. Natalie threw her arms over Mick's shoulders and buried her face against Mick's chest.

Quinn: *Nat just arrived. Can I call you later?*

Aspen: *Yes. Please. I would love to hear from you.*

Quinn: *Talk soon, Frankie. :)*

Quinn leaned back in her seat and watched her friends. Her eyes narrowed. *Nah.* It was a reaction to the crisis. Natalie just needed someone...although she and Mick looked awfully comfortable in each other's arms.

As if reading Quinn's thoughts, Natalie broke from Mick's embrace. She motioned for Quinn, who skyrocketed to her feet and hugged Natalie with all her might.

"How you doing?" Quinn asked.

Natalie held out her trembling hand. "I doubt if I'll be doing any fine embroidery any time soon."

"And you were so looking forward to it." Quinn smiled. She hoped to lighten the heaviness in the room.

"What now? Do we just go back to your apartment?" Mick asked.

Natalie's gaze fell to the floor. "Apparently, I'm supposed to stay as far away from you guys as I can." She made eye contact with Quinn. "Especially you."

The words stung. No, they downright hurt. Quinn's breath caught in her throat.

"I'm so sorry." Natalie snaked her arm through Quinn's. "That came out so wrong."

Quinn held up her hand. "No. I understand. We need to do whatever it takes to get you out of this mess."

"One I created."

"No," Mick said loudly. "Your parents created this mess. Not you."

Natalie's genuine smile lit up the room as she smiled at Mick. "Thanks."

Quinn's gaze shifted between Natalie and Mick. *Chemistry? Nah.* People needed each other during a time like this. Natalie was no exception.

"Will you have to go to court?" Quinn asked.

"Nothing moves fast with our legal system. It could take months or longer before I go to trial. In the meantime, Broderick wants me to lay as low as possible."

"That's fucked up." Mick's dark eyes flashed. "So you sit in limbo?"

"Sumpin' like that," Natalie said and flashed a cheesy grin at Mick.

The tension in the room broke, and they all laughed harder than the joke warranted.

Chapter Thirty-three

Aspen lay staring at the ceiling. The bed was so comfortable. She suspected that Gina and Steph had bought the memory foam one especially for her since she used the room so often.

Jet lag finally caught up with her. She glanced at the clock. It had been over two hours since she'd texted Quinn. Aspen checked her phone again, which must have been the fifth time in the last fifteen minutes. She pushed the volume button several times to ensure it would be loud enough.

Maybe she should try to contact Quinn. *No.* Quinn would call when she could. Her plate was overflowing, so she didn't need Aspen pestering her. Some of the things the people said on the news programs made Aspen's blood boil, so she could only imagine how it affected Quinn.

Despite wanting to stay awake, her eyelids fluttered. She hadn't realized how tense she'd been until she'd finally relaxed while talking to Gina. She pulled the covers up under her chin and allowed herself to close her eyes.

Loud music woke her. Instinctually, she snatched her phone. *Quinn.*

"Hello," Aspen said into the phone.

"Hi. Sorry it took me so long to call you back. It's been a crazy day. And lawyers sure can talk."

"No worries. You sound tired," Aspen said.

"Exhausted." Quinn sighed. "Jet lag on top of being unable to sleep isn't a good combination."

"I hear you. I wish I could reach across the phone and give you a hug."

"I'd like that."

Aspen's chest filled with warmth. "I saw the press conference. Natalie did great, but she must be a wreck."

"She's a rock star. It's so hard...so hard to see her falling apart. I think she might be the strongest person I know. When I flaked out, she just kept going and going. She never let Stella down."

Aspen wanted to say something comforting. Something to reassure Quinn that she'd not let Stella down, but something told her Quinn wouldn't accept soothing words right now. *Questions were safe.* "What is the lawyer telling you?"

"The man never shuts up, so it might be better to ask what he's not saying."

"Surely, he can't be that bad."

"Don't call me Shirley."

What? Was Quinn losing it? Who was Shirley? Aspen wrestled with how to respond.

Quinn chuckled. "I think that pregnant pause was the best thing I've heard, or should I say not heard, all day."

Aspen pulled the phone from her ear and stared at it. She'd heard of people losing it under extreme duress, and there was no doubt that Quinn would qualify. "Um, I...um...I'm not sure I'm following this conversation."

Quinn laughed. "Oh, Frankie. Thank you. I needed to laugh. Obviously, you've never seen that old cheesy movie. Shit. I can't even remember the name now. Where anytime someone says surely, the other character says don't call me Shirley."

Aspen smiled. "What the hell kind of movies do you watch?"

"Good ones." Quinn paused and hummed under her breath. "Well, at least I found them funny. Once I figure out what movie it was from, we'll have to watch it sometime."

"I'm game." Aspen's chest expanded. Quinn wanted to stay friends. "Then I can make fun of you for your poor taste."

"That's an elitist comment if I've ever heard one." Quinn's voice had more energy than it had at the beginning of the conversation.

They spent another twenty minutes talking about old movies and everything but the situation at hand.

"Hold on," Quinn said. A muffled sound came through the phone. She must have covered the microphone. "It's just Mick, trying to get on my nerves."

"Hi, Aspen," Mick yelled in the background. "And I'm not annoying, don't listen to her."

"Tell Mick hi," Aspen said. "Does she need you for something?"

"She can wait." There was a grin in Quinn's voice. "She wants to drag me to the gym. Says it will do me good."

"Earlier, it sounded like sleep might do you better."

"That's exactly what I said, but she wasn't having it. Besides, Alex, a good friend of ours, owns it, so it will be nice to see her."

"I should let you go."

"Nah. I'm not done talking to you. Unless you need to go."

"No." *God.* Could she sound any more eager? "I mean, I would like to hear the rest of the story of what's going on."

"Good. And it's an added bonus that I can annoy Mick," Quinn said.

"I heard that," Mick shouted.

"Where are you guys?"

Quinn let out an exhale. "Still at Broderick Taylor's law office."

"What are you still doing there?"

"Hiding."

"Hiding?"

"Yeah, Natalie left about an hour and a half ago. The press is everywhere. Broderick doesn't want us seen anywhere near her, so we have to be whisked out of here in secret."

"Are you serious?"

"I wish I wasn't."

"Oh, Quinn. That sucks. I'm so sorry."

"Thanks." Quinn paused for a few beats, but Aspen remained silent. "Um, I'm sure you've been watching the news."

Aspen didn't like the sudden change in Quinn's tone. "Yes," she answered tentatively.

"I'd like to talk to you about...well, not really like, but I think I should..." Quinn sighed.

Aspen tensed. "What is it?"

Quinn's exhale was loud in Aspen's ear. "I'm sure you've seen the pictures of the accident."

Oh, god. Now she understood. "Yes."

"And you've heard the stories?"

"Uh-huh." Could she be any less supportive?

She wanted to tell Quinn it was okay and that she understood, but instead, she remained silent.

"They're not true."

Aspen hadn't realized she was holding her breath until it rushed out of her. She hoped Quinn hadn't heard. "Tell me what happened then."

Quinn sighed. "I'm not sure. I'd just left the hospital. They wouldn't let me in to see Stella. I was so upset. I took off out of there like a bat out of hell, but I wasn't thinking of hurting myself. The next thing I knew, I was in the hospital."

"Flashback?"

"I think so." Quinn's voice held a note of relief. "Thank you for not thinking the worst. The media plastered it all over the place. How do you prove you had a flashback? It wasn't worth it. Besides, people will believe what they want to believe."

"Oh, Quinn. I am so sorry."

"It's okay. I've learned to ignore it." Quinn chuckled. "I guess I can't with this ugly scar as a constant reminder."

"Chicks dig scars," Aspen said before she could censor herself. "I have got to stop being so forthright with you."

Quinn laughed. "I like it, Frankie. Never change."

Warmth spread across Aspen's chest. In all her years, everyone wanted her to change to be the chameleon they wanted, so she'd hid herself. But now, she'd let someone see the real her, and Quinn didn't want her to change.

"Are you okay?" Quinn asked.

"Yeah, sorry...it's just...." Aspen struggled to find her words. "Damn it, it's just great talking to you.

Hearing your voice. I'd been looking forward to one last late-night conversation in Africa, and I was afraid I'd never get to talk to you again." Aspen put her hand on her head. Was she ever going to shut up? "I don't know what's gotten into me. Jet lag. Just ignore me and my rambles."

Quinn chuckled. "I missed you, too, Frankie."

With that short response, Aspen's heart filled. Quinn missed her already. She wasn't the only one.

Another twenty minutes flew by as they talked about nothing, just enjoying each other's company.

"Are you going to stay in Boston?" Aspen asked.

"I'm not sure what the point is. The press will just chase me around. I can't see Nat or Stella. And I have my Jet Skis and boats to winterize. But Mick wants me to stay."

"What do you want to do?"

"Hell, I don't even know anymore." The tiredness returned to Quinn's voice. "But I suppose I better get my butt moving, or Mick is going to throw a hissy fit."

Aspen's shoulders sagged. "Can I call you or text you again soon?"

"I'd like that," Quinn answered immediately. "Can I do the same?"

"Absolutely." Aspen's answer was just as quick.

"I'll catch you later then, Frankie."

"Catch you later."

The line went dead. Aspen held the phone to her chest and lay back onto the pillow. The conversation rolled around in her mind, but sleep soon overtook her.

Chapter Thirty-four

Quinn slammed the screwdriver onto the dock and buried her head in her hands. *Fucking Jet Ski.* It was the same one she and Mick had fixed when Mick showed up unannounced on her doorstep. *Damn.* Nearly three months had passed since that Labor Day weekend. It seemed like another lifetime.

She'd been back from Boston for three weeks. Since returning, she'd had no energy, and everything felt like a chore. So much needed to be done to get the place in tip-top shape. The Realtor wanted her to put lipstick on this pig. Apparently, it would sell better.

It would be so much easier and faster if she had help, but something held her back. Mick would turn cartwheels when she discovered Quinn planned on selling her business. No doubt, Mick would be here in a heartbeat to lend a hand. So why hadn't she told her?

Probably, in case she changed her mind. Until she signed a contract, nothing was final. She and Mick had a heated exchange when Quinn left Boston. It still played in the back of her mind, even though they'd made up before she left. Things went back to normal, at least Quinn thought they had, but the last couple of days Mick had been acting strangely.

Maybe Mick had given up hope that Quinn would come to her senses. Regardless, something wasn't right. Quinn took a deep breath and let it out slowly. Thoughts of tension with Mick only slowed her down more. She needed to focus and get things done.

Abruptly, she rose from her seat and grabbed the screwdriver. She smiled at the tool in her hand. If she pulled out all the drain plugs, maybe she could sink the stupid Jet Ski. *No.* It would be just her luck she'd damage it and the damned thing would still float.

She glanced at the fading sun. It would be dark soon. She'd work on it until she couldn't see any longer.

One more try. She picked up the wrench to remove the rotors when a noise caught her attention. *Fuck no.* Who the hell would show up here this late in the season? One of these days, she'd learn to lock the damned door.

She glanced around her and found the rag sticking out of her toolbox. Why had she put it there? Without thinking, she snatched it and sent several bolts skittering across the dock. *Shit.* Now she remembered. She'd put the screws on the cloth for safe keeping. Her head certainly wasn't in the game.

A voice called from inside, but she couldn't make out the words. Maybe if she ignored them, they would go away. She dropped to her knees, searching for the errant bolts.

"Anybody here?" The voice grew louder.

Persistent asshole. Quinn gathered up the last bolt and shoved them all into her pocket. Maybe it was someone who wanted to buy the place. If so, she needed to put on a smile. She took a deep breath before she walked across the dock.

As she reached for the door handle, the outside light turned on, practically blinding her. "What the hell did you do that for?" *So much for being pleasant with a potential buyer.*

"I came fourteen hundred miles, and that's how you greet me?" the familiar drawl said from inside.

Quinn's heart soared, but she couldn't let Mick know. "What the hell are you doing here? Just passing by?"

"Sumpin' like that." Mick chuckled. "Actually, I came to meet a friend."

"Really? I didn't think you knew anyone out in the middle of nowhere. Don't you hate Missouri?"

"She doesn't live here. Thought we'd meet halfway."

"But she cheated," a familiar voice said. "I had to come two thousand miles."

Quinn's heart raced. It couldn't be. *Aspen?* Her palms immediately began to sweat. Quinn couldn't speak, so she stood on the dock peering through the screen door into the dark room.

The screen door flew open and almost hit Quinn. Before she could react, Aspen was in her arms. "God, it's so good to see you," Aspen said. "I've missed my sidekick."

"Hey, you two," Mick said, wrapping her arms around both.

Quinn blinked back tears and removed one arm from Aspen, so she could draw Mick in. The three stood in a circle laughing and hugging for several beats.

After they released one another and stepped back, Mick smirked. "Were you planning on telling me about the for sale sign out front?"

"You saw that?" Quinn drew her shoulders in and tried to go for a sheepish look. "My bad."

"Does that mean you're coming home?" An unmistakable tone of hope was in Mick's voice.

"Maybe."

"Yes!" Mick pumped her fist. "I knew it."

Quinn rolled her eyes and gazed at Aspen. "I can't believe you came all this way to see her."

Aspen smirked. "I might have come to see someone else, too."

"Hmm, who might that be?"

Aspen playfully punched Quinn on the upper arm. "Very funny."

They'd been excitedly talking for several minutes when Mick hit herself in the head with her palm. "Shit. We forgot the others in the car."

"Others?" Quinn glanced around the dock. "You brought someone else to this dump? Oh, shit. You found out I was selling, and you brought a buyer?"

Mick waved her hand. "Whoa, slow down. We didn't bring a buyer."

Quinn's eyes narrowed. "Then who did you bring?"

Aspen put her hand on Quinn's arm. "You need to hear us out."

"Never a good way to start a sentence," Quinn said. "Are you about to drop a bombshell on me?"

"I've been talking to Peyton and DaKota," Mick said.

"For?" Quinn shifted her gaze between Aspen and Mick. "Wait. Are you going to sell Pink Triangle to them?"

Mick shook her head. "Nothing like that." Mick shot a desperate glance at Aspen, as if to say help.

"Would one of you tell me what's going on?" The nerve endings in Quinn's arms tingled, but she resisted the urge to scratch them.

"But you're not going to like it at first."

"I didn't like it when I first heard it, either." Aspen gazed into Quinn's eyes. The deep blue pools always mesmerized her. "But the more I thought about it, the more I realized it might be the only way out."

"How long have you guys been talking about this?" Quinn asked.

"Since shortly after you left," Mick said. "I couldn't let you disappear again. Hide out, away from us, so I called Aspen. We decided that Peyton and DaKota might be able to help."

"How?" Quinn asked.

"At first, we were just talking money," Aspen said. "Create a legal fund for you and Stella. But then they came up with a different plan."

Quinn turned to Mick. "Have you heard the plan?"

Mick nodded.

"What do you think of it?"

"To be honest, at first, I was against it, but the only way to fight fire is with fire."

"Can we bring them in to tell you about their idea?" Aspen asked.

"Okay," Quinn said and wondered if she'd just made the biggest mistake in her life.

❧❧❧❧

Aspen's heart raced. Now that the greetings were done, it was time to get down to business. How would Quinn react?

She suspected Quinn was stalling as she meticulously gathered the papers off the tiny table shoved into the corner of her office. She'd brought two stools from outside on the dock to have enough seating. The table wasn't necessary and looked ridiculous plopped down between them. All the chairs were different heights, which made it look as if they were at the kids table at Thanksgiving dinner.

"*So*," Mick said and waited for the others to quiet. "Quinn, we've been worried about you…. I've been worried." She looked around the room and shook her head. "I didn't know that you put the place up for sale."

"I wanted to surprise you," Quinn said.

Mick smiled. "Now that you're coming home, I'm tempted to call this off and scrap the plan." Mick sighed and looked down. "But I couldn't do that to Stella."

Aspen's gaze shifted between Quinn and Mick as if she were watching a tennis match.

"You're freaking me out," Quinn said. Her expressive eyes, which Aspen loved, were guarded.

"Not trying to do that." Mick gazed around the table. "I just want you to understand that what we are about to share wasn't an easy decision." Mick nodded toward Aspen. "We struggled with what to do, but we love and respect you too much not to tell you the entire truth."

"Do you think you can start with it *now*?"

"After you left," Mick began, "Natalie and I had a long talk, trying to figure something out. That's when we contacted Aspen, who suggested that DaKota and Peyton might be able to help."

Mick smiled at DaKota and Peyton. "They graciously offered to send an investigator out to Boston."

Quinn's eyebrows shot up. "I suppose in your line of business, you need that."

"Definitely," DaKota said. "You can't believe how many false claims are leveled at us from people hoping to hit a payday." DaKota snorted. "We learned the hard way. Once you give into someone like that, they keep coming back to the well. That's when we hired a corporate investigation firm."

"It's saved us a boatload of money, and more importantly, it's saved our reputation," Peyton said. "We sent one of our best to see what she could find."

DaKota put her cellphone on the table. She gave Quinn a sympathetic look. "This might be a little hard for you to listen to."

Quinn nodded but didn't speak. She focused on the phone sitting in the middle of the table.

The only sound in the room was water lapping at the dock outside. Then a voice came through the phone.

"Hi, are you here to see your daughter?" a perky voice asked.

"Is Natalie here?" a man's voice said.

Quinn stiffened, and her jaw clenched. She'd obviously recognized Mr. Parsons's voice.

"No, I meant Stella," the woman replied. "She had a rough night last night."

"I'm afraid we won't have time today, but thanks for letting us know, Donna," Mr. Parsons said.

"Oh, okay. Did you want me to get Betty for you?"

"Please, be a dear," Mrs. Parsons said. Her voice dripped in sweetness.

"Okay, I'll be right back," Nurse Donna said.

After a couple of beats, a loud sigh came from the phone. "God, I hate that woman. She's always so perky," Mrs. Parsons said. "She works in the most depressing place in the world, and she acts like she's at *a carnival."*

Aspen glanced at Quinn out of the corner of her eye. Quinn's face was flushed, and her gaze remained glued to the phone.

"It's as if the woman actually believes Stella will wake up someday. I can't believe there are so many stupid people in the world." Mr. Parsons's voice was low, but his words were unmistakable.

Even though Aspen had heard the recording several times, she was still riveted each time she listened.

"Pathetic. I'm sure she prays for a miracle every night." Mrs. Parsons chuckled. *"She's an idiot, but she makes good brownies. Do you want one?"*

"Sure," Mr. Parsons said before DaKota picked up her cellphone, and the audio stopped.

"Let me play this one," DaKota said. "It was recorded shortly after Natalie's arrest." She swiped her phone a couple of times before setting it back on the table.

"You must be so relieved," Donna said. *"I can't imagine how upset you are. I've reserved this room for you, so nobody bothers you. If you'd like to see Stella, please let one of the girls know, and they'll find me."*

"That's so kind of you," Mrs. Parsons said. *"I'm just so distraught that I'm not sure I can right now."*

"Yes, it's been a rather trying day for both of us," Mr. Parsons said. *"Please, let Betty know we're here."*

"Of course," Donna said. *"Are you sure this room is adequate? The reporters are all over, so I thought this would be the best."*

"It's lovely," Mrs. Parsons said. *"We appreciate everything you do for us and our Stella. Please pray for her."*

"She's in my prayers every day. I better get back to the floor. Betty should be in soon."

"Thank you," the Parsonses said in unison.

What sounded like a door clanking shut was the only sound for nearly twenty seconds.

"Shoot me now," Mrs. Parsons said. *"If she gives me that cow-eyed look of sympathy one more time, I'm going to vomit."*

"Now, Millie," Mr. Parsons said. *"She's exactly what we need to sing to the press."*

Rustling came from the phone and what sounded like a couple of mumbled curse words. *Mrs. Parsons sighed. "Damn it. I forgot to pull my tissues out, but I've got them handy for when we leave this broom closet."*

"It's not a broom closet. You need to channel some of that drama for later."

A creaking door could be heard faintly in the background. *A loud voice rang out. "Jonathon. Millie. So glad you could make it."*

"You could have saved us from that simpleton if you'd met us at the door," Mrs. Parsons said in a sharp voice. *"Where were you?"*

"Doing damage control for you, so I'd cut the attitude," Betty said.

"Ladies, please, we don't have time for bickering. We need to work out a strategy."

Quinn placed her palm against the edge of the table. Her hand trembled, and her knuckles turned white the harder she gripped it. Aspen debated reaching out to Quinn, but she thought better of it. No. Quinn needed a little space.

"What's the word on the floor?" Mr. Parsons asked.

"There's a lot of sympathy for Natalie and Stella,"

Betty said.

"*What about us? Surely, there's sympathy for the steadfast parents,*" Mrs. Parsons said.

"*Unofficially, at least on the floor, Natalie and Stella are getting much higher ratings for likability,*" Betty answered.

"*What the hell do they know?*" Mrs. Parsons said.

Aspen glanced at the others. The hypocrisy was laughable. The Parsonses were unbelievable, but Aspen knew the worst was yet to come. She kept one eye on Quinn as the conversation continued.

"*It's probably time I work the crowd,*" Mrs. Parsons said. "*There's nothing more sympathetic than a heartbroken mother.*"

"*Um...I have an...another idea.*" Betty said. "*I think it's time we get some pictures of you in Stella's room. People are noticing you never go in. I keep running interference, telling them how hard it is on you. I think it's worn thin. You're in danger of losing the court of public opinion.*"

"*Oh, for Pete's sake, maybe it's time we stop this whole sick charade,*" Mr. Parsons said in a loud voice. "*We have one daughter in jail, and the other one is dead.*"

"*Jonathon,*" Mrs. Parsons said. "*Lower your voice before someone hears you.*"

"*Face it, Millie. She's been dead for years. Now she has a tube shoved down her throat. And you're considering going in and doing a photo shoot.*"

"*I think I should leave you two alone for a bit,*" Betty said.

"*No!*" Mrs. Parsons's voice was strong. "*Jonathon needs to get it together. If we must go in and take pictures that somehow get leaked to the press, then that's what we do."*

"*Isn't there another way around it?*" Mr. Parsons said. "*I don't want to go into that stench-filled room. It smells like death. Can't we just go on Tucker Carlson's program or something?*"

"*Both,*" Mrs. Parsons said. "*We can make sure Tucker gets the leaked photos, and then I'm sure we'll be able to get on the show. It'll be worth it.*"

"*You mean it'll be lucrative,*" Mr. Parsons said. "*While we lose both of our daughters.*"

"*I bet the donations are already rolling in,*" Betty said. "*Just imagine how much more we... you'll get after the pictures get out.*"

"*Don't worry. You'll get your cut.*" Mr. Parsons's voice dripped with disgust.

DaKota swiped the phone, and the sound went dead.

Nobody said anything for several beats, all attention on Quinn. Without warning, she abruptly stood; the stool she sat on crashed to the floor. Her bulky frame seemed too big for the room, and when she rushed out, her leg cracked against the table, knocking it crooked.

Aspen's heart ached for Quinn. The pain that lay just under the surface inside Quinn had erupted. There were several more recordings, but Aspen suspected Quinn couldn't listen to more.

Mick sighed. "Well, that went about like I'd expected."

"Should you go talk to her?" Aspen asked.

"We should," Mick said.

"I don't think it's a good idea to have all of us descend on her," Aspen said.

"No. Just you and I."

"Us? But—"

"She'll want you there, and I could use the reinforcements."

Peyton and DaKota nodded but remained silent.

Aspen's heartbeat throbbed in her ears, and she struggled to breathe. "Are you sure?"

"Only one way to find out," Mick said. "Let's go before she does something stupid."

❧❧❧❧

Quinn leaned over the side of the dock and vomited again. What little dinner she'd eaten today came up, so now all she had left was bile. Her throat burned. She could use some water, but she wasn't going back inside after she'd made such a scene.

The shack's old door squeaked open. Footsteps trod on the deck. The reverberation sounded like two people walking toward her. *Aspen?* She knew Mick would come, but would Aspen join her?

"How ya doing?" Mick asked.

Quinn didn't turn. Instead, she continued to lean forward over the side. Her stomach still churned. "I've been better."

"Understandable." Mick paused. The water lapped against the side of the dock. Mick waited for several seconds before speaking again. "I brought Aspen with me. I hope that's okay."

"It is," Quinn responded. "Sorry, I just needed to get out of there."

The sound of shuffling feet came closer, but Quinn kept her back to Mick, even though her nausea had passed.

"Quinn?" Aspen said. "I'm so sorry."

The sound of Aspen's voice caused Quinn's

knees to buckle. No, it was more than that. It was the concern and caring that overwhelmed her. Quinn swayed, afraid she might go down. She lowered herself to her knees.

"Are you okay?" Mick grabbed her by the shoulders.

Quinn nodded, and then put her hands over her face. "What is wrong with those people? She's their daughter."

"I know." Mick kept her hand on Quinn's back.

Pain started in her stomach and spread up her chest. She struggled to breathe. Every time she tried to inhale deeply, she coughed. Her body still trembled.

"What can we do for you?" Aspen asked.

Good question. What was the proper protocol in a situation like this? She sat back on her buttocks and wrapped her arms around her knees.

Aspen sank to her knees beside Quinn. Their shoulders brushed together. A sense of comfort ran through Quinn when Aspen increased the contact between them.

That was all it took. Her emotions boiled over. The next sob was louder and caught in her throat. She pulled her legs tighter against her body. Tears streamed down her cheeks, and her nose ran. She wanted to wipe it off but only had her sleeve. That made her laugh, but it came out like a hyena as it mixed with her sobs. Her emotions were unleashed.

Aspen wrapped her arms around Quinn. Soon she felt Mick's vise grip encircle her from the other side. She couldn't fight it. This must be what grief felt like. Her shoulders relaxed, and her jaw unclenched.

All her pain bubbled out. She sobbed as her friends held her.

Chapter Thirty-five

Aspen squeezed Quinn's hand, not sure if it was Quinn or herself who needed it more. Despite the room being crowded, the mood was subdued. Even the normally boisterous Peyton and DaKota were quiet.

It had turned out to be a whitewater reunion. Tina, LeAnn, and Claire had insisted on being there to support Quinn. Life was strange. Aspen suspected the group would have a bond that would last a lifetime. It had been a life-changing experience. Gauging by the concerned faces around the room, she wasn't the only one who felt that way.

Natalie and Mick sat on the loveseat shoulder to shoulder. The last couple of days, as they prepared for this moment, Aspen had wondered at the cozy nature of the two, but it was probably her imagination. Natalie, of all people, needed comfort.

Peyton sauntered over and put her arm around Aspen. "Are you sure you want to do this?"

Aspen gave Peyton a sideways hug. "Nope. But I'm the logical choice." When they'd discovered that Aspen's parents ran in the same circles as the Parsonses, it was a foregone conclusion that she'd have the best chance at success. Many times, she'd wished it wasn't the case, but she wouldn't let Quinn down.

"I could do it," Peyton offered.

"Thank you." Aspen smiled. Peyton truly could be sweet. They just had nothing in common. "I know you would, but I make a much better good cop than you."

Peyton pretended to bristle but smiled. "Are you saying I'm too aggressive?"

Aspen laughed. "Afraid so. You sit in board rooms. You direct people. I've never had a backbone in my life."

"Until now," DaKota said from across the room.

The group laughed, happy for the diversion.

"No way will they want the Kennedys' daughter to see them in a negative light," Aspen said. "Besides, I can still channel that sweet, innocent doormat. Make them love me."

"And hate me." DaKota had a gleam in her eye as she said it.

"I think you might be enjoying this too much." Peyton chuckled.

"For the record," Quinn began, "I want to say one last time, you guys are walking dangerously close to doing something illegal."

"Another reason I'm the best one for the job." Aspen shot a cheesy grin at Peyton and then DaKota. "Put these two together, and that line might get crossed. I won't do it."

"Win at any cost," Peyton said.

Aspen shook her head. "Nope. That's why there has to be an adult in the room."

DaKota glanced at her watch. "Well, Miss Adult. We're on in five minutes, so let's wrap this conversation up."

Butterflies danced in Aspen's stomach. Quinn squeezed her hand tighter. She'd been exceptionally quiet, saying little the last half hour.

Quinn stood. Her eyes were strained, but a slight smile played on her lips. "I want to thank all of you for what you're doing for Stella. For us." She glanced at Natalie. "I think I can speak for both of us. We will forever be in your debt."

A round of hugs and well-wishes ensued, which helped keep Aspen's jitters at bay. She approached Quinn and gazed into Quinn's brown eyes. Her breath caught. All of Quinn's emotions were written there. Pain. Sadness. Hope. Relief.

Aspen took Quinn's hands and held her gaze. "This is going to work. I promise I'll do my best."

Quinn smiled, and the corner of her eyes crinkled. "I have faith in you. Just don't do anything you don't believe in. Regardless of the outcome, I appreciate everything you're doing."

Aspen's heart raced. She hadn't wanted to admit that she feared Quinn's reaction if they failed. "Promise?"

"I'll forever be your sidekick, Frankie. Nothing will change that."

The words set Aspen free. Ironically, it made her feel more confident that she would succeed. Words escaped her, so she moved forward and wrapped her arms around Quinn.

Quinn's strong arms enveloped her. Aspen didn't care if anyone else watched. She needed Quinn's strength to propel her forward.

"Show time," DaKota called out.

Aspen reluctantly stepped out of Quinn's embrace. "I'm ready."

❧❧❧❧

Aspen straightened her jacket and ran her hands down the front of her dress, pressing out imaginary wrinkles. She knew she looked good in business attire. Confident, yet still feminine.

The elevator doors slid open, and they stepped into the corridor. DaKota took a step down the hallway, but Aspen stopped her. "Wait."

When DaKota turned, Aspen reached out and straightened her suit coat and tucked her shirt collar in. She looked formidable and confident.

"Presentable?" DaKota said with a smile.

Aspen nodded. "You'll do." And then she winked.

DaKota started to turn but stopped. "I just want to tell you. I think it's pretty cool that you're doing this." DaKota's gaze darted around before it settled back on Aspen. "I know we haven't always seen eye to eye, but you've shown that you've got more courage than I realized."

"Does that mean you like me?" Aspen teased. Despite the conversation being awkward, it also kept her from thinking about what would soon come.

"I think it might." DaKota smirked. She held out her elbow. "Are we ready to do this?"

"No." Aspen took DaKota's offered arm. "But let's go."

The door opened almost immediately after DaKota knocked. A stately man of average height opened the door. His tailored navy blue suit fit impeccably. Although his thinning white hair was combed over, there wasn't a strand out of place. He had a military aura.

After swinging open the door, he offered his

hand. "You must be Ms. Kennedy and Ms. Lee."

In turn, they shook his hand. "Please, call me Aspen, Mr. Parsons."

"Very well, Aspen." She noticed he didn't return the gesture.

"Please, come in. My wife is inside."

"I hope you like the room we selected for you," DaKota said.

Subtle. A reminder of who paid for the luxury suite and how much money might be involved.

"Yes, it is very nice."

A matronly woman in a long dress that nearly reached the floor stood up from the table. The first thing Aspen noticed was how short she was, but she wouldn't let the small stature fool her. Aspen had listened to the recordings several times to get a sense of her adversary.

"Mrs. Parsons, it is so good to meet you," Aspen said, approaching her.

"You must be Aspen Kennedy." Mrs. Parsons smiled. "You resemble your mother."

"Thank you." Aspen faked her best smile.

"Lovely people," Mrs. Parsons said. "Shall we sit down? Jonathon, bring the ladies a bottle of water."

Good sign. She might not be offering one later.

Once seated, DaKota laid her hands on the table and cleared her throat. "I'm sure you're wondering why we asked you to meet with us today."

"On the phone, Aspen had mentioned that the Kennedy Foundation might be interested in donating to our cause," Mr. Parsons said.

"We know you're busy people," Aspen said, continuing with her script. "With all of your charity work, we appreciate how valuable your time is." Aspen couldn't look at DaKota. When they'd rehearsed earlier, DaKota always stuck her finger in her mouth as if pretending to force a vomit.

"Thank you for saying that, dear." Mrs. Parsons put her hand against her chest. "So few people realize how trying philanthropic work can be, but I'm sure you've grown up with the burden. Shall we get down to the details of your donation?"

"There is one thing before we do that." Aspen nodded at DaKota. "If you would."

DaKota placed her phone on the table and pointed. "I recently received some rather disturbing recordings that I thought you'd want to be made aware of."

Mrs. Parsons's eyes narrowed, but her expression didn't change.

"Why don't I just play a couple?" DaKota swiped the phone, and Mrs. Parsons's voice filled the room.

DaKota played three before she stopped. "There are more, but I do believe you get the gist."

Aspen had been studying the Parsonses as the audio played. Mr. Parsons's face reddened to the point of crimson, but Mrs. Parsons's face remained impassive. *Impressive.* Other than a slight tic in her right eye, there was no reaction.

Mr. Parsons leapt to his feet. "What is the meaning of this? Where did you get this trash?" He stomped across the room and flung open the mini bar.

"Jonathon, return to the table." Mrs. Parsons's intense look was enough to shatter glass.

He mumbled under his breath but returned.

Mrs. Parsons's gaze landed on Aspen. "Young lady, I'm surprised you'd stoop to blackmail. I'd have thought your parents had set you up nicely."

Perfect. Mrs. Parsons was playing right into their hands. Now if she could only pull it off. Aspen put her hand against her chest. "Oh, no. Did you think we were here to blackmail you?" As practiced, she gazed at DaKota. "Did you hear that?"

DaKota nodded. "I assure you, we aren't after your money."

"How did these recordings come into your possession?" Mrs. Parsons asked, still not giving away anything.

"I don't think that's important," DaKota said. "What is, is that they exist."

"Somebody at that place is going to pay for this." Mr. Parsons slammed his fist onto the table. "We will hunt down whoever's responsible."

"I don't recommend that." DaKota picked up her phone and stashed it in her pocket. "I think you have much more to lose if this gets out."

"That sounds like a threat to me." Mr. Parsons's jaw clenched.

Aspen turned to the Parsonses, trying to channel her most angelic look. "I'm sorry that DaKota is coming off so crude. She's just trying to help you see what the consequences may be if this was leaked to the press."

"The press?" Mrs. Parsons said. "Are you suggesting that *you* plan on turning these over to them?"

"Oh, my, no." Aspen put her hand over her mouth. "Of course not. We would never do that. I am so sorry for the misunderstanding."

Mrs. Parsons narrowed her steel blue eyes, and her gaze locked on Aspen. "On whose behalf are you here?"

Aspen smiled and nodded. "Very astute, Mrs.

Parsons. You are correct in assuming we have mutual acquaintances. Although, in this case, I wouldn't call her an acquaintance."

"Her?" Mrs. Parsons's eyebrows raised.

"Natalie," Aspen responded. "It must be horrible having lost one daughter and now possibly the other."

Mrs. Parsons patted her chest. "Oh, dear. You don't know how hard it is on a mother."

Paydirt. Things were going well. Even though Aspen saw through Mrs. Parsons's act, it was a good sign she was playing it.

"I can only imagine." Aspen gave Mrs. Parsons a sympathetic look. "I don't have children *yet*. But when I do, I would hate to think of such a tragedy befalling my family."

"Don't you want the world to see this version of you, not the one on the recordings?" DaKota said, pushing the knife in a bit.

Good. That would remind Mrs. Parsons there was still a bad cop in the room.

Mrs. Parsons leveled her gaze at Aspen, ignoring DaKota. "Darling, it's been a nightmare. And our attorneys won't let us speak to our dear Natalie. We've been ripped apart. Haven't we, Jonathon?"

Mr. Parsons pulled his trembling hands off the table when Aspen gazed at them. He thrust his chest out, trying to exude confidence, but Aspen suspected there was little of that left. "Yes. We would like for this nightmare to be over." Aspen almost felt sorry for him until she remembered his words on the recording.

"Of course, we do have others to think about," Mrs. Parsons said. "I'm sure you'll understand." She locked gazes with Aspen as she spoke.

"Others?" Aspen said. Even though Mr. Parsons

crumbled before their eyes, she wasn't sure Mrs. Parsons could be broken. It didn't matter if she saw the wisdom of their plan.

"Our...how should I say it? Our...um... followers," Mrs. Parsons said, feigning humility. "There are many people who have been inspired by our story. By God's message. We wouldn't want to let them down."

Aspen swallowed the bile that rose in her throat. She'd joked they'd be making a deal with the devil, now she knew it was true. "Goodness no. We would never ask you to let down your followers. In fact, we believe you might even become more popular with them."

Mrs. Parsons's eyebrows rose slightly. It was the biggest reaction they'd gotten from her since they'd sat down. "Go on. We're listening."

Aspen turned to DaKota and nodded.

DaKota rose to her feet. "I knew you were intelligent people. Imagine this," she said and spread her arms out like she were presenting a picture. "The heroic parents who have faced so much tragedy make the final sacrifice for one of their children, but this time, it's Natalie."

Mrs. Parsons nodded as DaKota spoke, while Mr. Parsons looked as if he wanted to punch DaKota.

Dramatically, DaKota clapped her hand against her chest. "You take a stand for your daughter. No longer listening to the attorneys that have kept you apart."

"You want us to go to bat for Natalie?" Mrs. Parsons narrowed her eyes and cocked her head.

Savvy. Mrs. Parsons knew there was more, but she would make DaKota declare it. Aspen bit her lip, knowing this was a crucial juncture in their plan.

"Hear me out." DaKota put her hands out for calm. "Things have changed. Stella is no longer just on a feeding tube but a ventilator." DaKota paused for effect. "God tried to call her home, but the overly ambitious doctors thwarted his plans. But *you...*" DaKota raised her hands and looked to the ceiling. "You have prayed on it, and God's will shall be done. The ventilator will be shut off. If God wants Stella to live, she will breathe on her own."

Damn. DaKota had channeled her inner preacher. Aspen almost believed what she said.

Mr. Parsons buried his head in his hands, but Mrs. Parsons sat silently with her lips pursed.

"Or you can take your chances." DaKota pulled the phone from her pocket. "And hope nobody ever leaks these."

Game. Set. Match. Aspen kept her face impassive, even though she wanted to smile.

"And how will we be guaranteed that it wouldn't leak after...after this is over?" Mrs. Parsons said.

"Of course, since we don't control it, we can't make any promises," DaKota said. "But we believe the people behind the recordings would be satisfied with this outcome."

"I see." Mrs. Parsons turned her gaze to Aspen. "What about you? What do you think?"

"I assure you that my family would not take kindly to someone of your ilk being taken advantage of by such unscrupulous people," Aspen said. "But I doubt that will happen."

"Jonathon?"

Mr. Parsons shrugged. "Do it. I've wanted this nightmare over for a long time."

"Jonathon!" Mrs. Parsons's eyes blazed. She turned to Aspen. "He's under a tremendous amount of stress."

"Of course." Aspen smiled. *Unbelievable.* She was worried about what he said now. "Would you like to discuss this in private?"

"I don't think that will be necessary," Mrs. Parsons said. "We'll arrange an interview with a reporter of our choice. I'm sure Natalie will be okay with that."

"Definitely," Aspen said. They'd expected this, and despite Natalie's distaste, she'd agreed not to make this a sticking point.

"I believe we could have that arranged by tomorrow," Mr. Parsons said, finally rejoining the conversation.

"Excellent. Natalie will be pleased," Aspen said. "You are doing the right thing."

"We will contact Natalie after this meeting." Mr. Parsons sighed. "We can assume she will take our call?"

"She will," Aspen said. Now that the deal was almost finalized, they'd agreed that DaKota would take a backseat. "I'm so glad that we could help you solve this unfortunate problem."

"Very unfortunate." Mrs. Parsons's intense gaze bore into Aspen. "Do tell your parents hello for us."

"Of course, they'll be so pleased that I saw you."

"If there is nothing else." Mrs. Parsons stood.

They were being dismissed. Aspen rose and walked to where DaKota stood. Her heart raced, and her palms were clammy. They'd practiced this, but could they pull it off?

The Parsonses ushered them to the door.

When they reached it, DaKota cleared her throat. "There is one other request."

"And then the other shoe drops," Mr. Parsons said. "How much money do you want?"

"No, no." DaKota gestured with her hands. "We don't want your money."

"Then what is it?" he asked.

"Natalie has requested that she and Quinn Coolidge get the opportunity to say goodbye to Stella. Together."

"Absolutely not," Mr. Parsons said. "That woman will never be allowed near my daughter."

"Oh, that's a shame," DaKota said. "Did I forget to mention that it's non-negotiable?"

"This is absurd." Mr. Parsons raised his voice. "Millie, are you going to stand for this?"

Mrs. Parsons's neck reddened, but she said nothing. She leveled her gaze at Aspen. "I presume you have something to say."

Smart. If there were any doubt that Mrs. Parsons had their number, it was eliminated. "In fact, I do. This visit can happen late at night when there are few staff around. Of course, it would never be sanctioned by you. This would be something that the rogue staff and Natalie cooked up should anyone discover it, but I doubt anyone would. No mention need be made in your interview with the press. You will be none the wiser that it happens."

Mrs. Parsons shrugged. "Well, since I'm not aware of it, why are we having this conversation?"

Victory. Aspen wanted to do a happy dance, but she maintained her poise. "Indeed. It's been a pleasure meeting you." Aspen held out her hand.

Mrs. Parsons looked at it for a beat before she

took it. "My best to your parents."

Mr. Parsons opened the door. Aspen's gaze met his. Something in his eyes gave her pause. *Relief?* He reached out his hand. "Ms. Kennedy, thank you for coming."

As she shook his hand, she suspected he meant it.

Chapter Thirty-six

Things moved fast after Aspen and DaKota met with the Parsonses. Quinn wasn't sure if she'd truly processed everything. Tonight, she and Natalie would be brought in under the cover of darkness to say goodbye to Stella.

Poor Natalie. She'd have to do it all over again tomorrow, but she'd be standing with her parents and a select group of invited guests when Stella's ventilator was removed. Who invited guests to something like that? *The Parsons.*

Quinn ran the towel over her hair, getting the last of the moisture out. Being so short, it would be dry before she finished dressing. She'd agonized over what to wear. Was it stupid she wanted to look good for Stella?

She pulled on a pair of black jeans, the ones Stella always said made her butt look yummy. Quinn smiled through her tears. Two shirts hung on the back of the bathroom door since she'd been unable to make a decision. *Gray or purple?* Did she want the occasion to be solemn or festive? Her hand lingered between the two shirts before she made her decision.

⚜⚜⚜⚜⚜

What did you say to someone who was going to say goodbye to her sister for the last time? Aspen couldn't think of anything appropriate, so she remained silent.

The others had already returned to San Francisco, but she stayed for Quinn and Natalie. It had been an emotional day, full of laughter and tears. Natalie had gotten out her childhood photo albums, and later, Quinn pulled up her electronic pictures from the cloud.

Aspen's sides hurt from laughing. They'd told so many stories of Stella's escapades. At one point, she'd felt she was intruding on their private moment, but Quinn assured her she was welcome. She only wished she'd had the opportunity to meet Stella. In every picture, she seemed so full of life.

Natalie had been sitting quietly with her head resting against Mick's shoulder, but she'd suddenly hopped to her feet. She paced her condo and stopped at the window. She stared out into the darkness.

The door to the bathroom creaked open. Aspen stiffened. Quinn had been in there a long time, and Aspen wondered how she would be when she emerged.

The fresh scent of Quinn's shower gel arrived before she did. Spruce. Aspen scooted to the edge of her seat and prepared to stand.

"Nice shirt," Natalie said with a smile when she turned from the window.

Quinn's cheeks reddened. "Stella loved purple. She'd be pissed if I showed up in funeral clothes."

"Truer words have never been spoken," Mick said. "The car should be here in about five minutes. Are you ready?"

Quinn nodded. "I think I am."

Natalie's gaze shifted between Mick and Aspen. "You two will be here when we get back?"

"We're not going anywhere," Mick said.

"Thank you." Natalie let out a loud breath. "Does your chest hurt as bad as mine?"

"Afraid so." Quinn put her large hand just above her breasts.

Aspen's heart broke. Somehow, Quinn looked small, standing there in her nice outfit.

Mick rose from the couch, so Aspen followed suit.

Natalie picked up her purse, while Quinn adjusted her belt. Their actions were so normal as if they were getting ready to go out on the town. Aspen pushed the thought from her mind.

Quinn's cellphone dinged. "The car's here."

Natalie clutched her purse tighter against her chest.

"It's cold out." Mick picked up Natalie's jacket. "Let me help you."

No words were spoken as Natalie allowed Mick to help her on with her coat.

"Hey, you big lug," Mick said. "I expect you to take care of Nat."

Quinn put a protective arm over Natalie's shoulder. "We'll take care of each other."

Natalie smiled. "Quick hugs. I can't stand here any longer."

"Understood," Mick said.

Aspen bit the inside of her cheek as she hugged Quinn. She would not cry. Quinn didn't need Aspen making things more difficult. Their embrace, something Aspen treasured, ended quickly. Aspen suspected Quinn couldn't handle anything longer.

When the door closed behind Natalie and Quinn, Mick dropped to the couch. "Oh, fuck, that was brutal."

Aspen went and sat next to Mick on the couch, needing her proximity. "It's going to be a long evening, isn't it?"

"For all of us," Mick said. "Do you want to watch some Netflix or would you rather talk?"

"If you don't mind, can we talk for a bit?" Aspen shifted uncomfortably.

"I'd like that." Mick took her hand.

"I'm sorry you couldn't go with," Aspen blurted out. *Oh, god.* She hadn't intended on saying it like that.

"It's okay," Mick said but looked anything but okay.

"Still hurts."

"Sumpin' like that." Mick attempted a smile.

They'd debated taking Mick with them despite the agreement, but Mick adamantly refused. She wouldn't be responsible for tonight going wrong. "Maybe we should have got the Parsonses to agree to all of you."

Mick shook her head. "I wouldn't have let you do it. It wasn't worth the risk of them saying no. This is how it needed to be. The two of them need to be alone with Stella. Besides, I said my goodbye to Stella every time I visited in case she died before I returned."

A sharp pain twisted in Aspen's chest. "You're a good friend."

"I try to be. I just hope it goes well. I think I'll be clinging to the ceiling until they return."

"It sucks. I can't believe they have to sneak in like thieves in the night." Aspen's tone held more venom than she'd intended. "It's so unfair."

"It is. But maybe it's a blessing. Quinn isn't much

for crowds and commotion, and you know tomorrow will be a shit show of press and well-wishers."

"Poor Natalie," Aspen said. "She's got it the worst."

Tears welled in Mick's eyes, and she looked to the ceiling. "She truly has."

"She's going to need lots of TLC."

"I aim to give it to her."

The last couple of days, Mick and Natalie had stopped hiding their budding relationship. Mick's words solidified it. "Good. I think you two are perfect for each other."

"What about you and Quinn?"

Aspen breath caught. "Quinn?"

"You heard me." Mick smiled. "When are you going to admit what all of the rest of us see?"

"The rest of who? Quinn hasn't said anything, has she?" Aspen hoped her voice didn't come out as excited as she felt.

"No, you and Quinn seem to be the only ones not in on it."

"That's because there isn't anything to be in on." Aspen wanted to look Mick straight in the eye and deny everything, but she knew she couldn't. "Besides, her fiancée dies tomorrow." *God.* That sounded crude to her ears.

"Her fiancée died years ago. Stella's body will finally follow."

Aspen sighed. "Still she's going to need to grieve again."

"She's going to need some TLC, too." Mick gazed at Aspen.

"I'm sure you and Nat will do a good job of that."

"So you're not sticking around?"

"I can't," Aspen said in a voice not much louder

than a whisper.

"Can't or won't?"

"Is there that much of a difference?" Aspen wanted out of this conversation, so maybe answering a question with another would work.

"What are you running from?"

Aspen paused. "You might not believe this, but I'm not running from anything. I'm finding myself."

"But still away from Quinn."

"I've bounced from one relationship to another, and with each one, I've lost more and more of myself. I can't do that again. I have to fill myself, instead of relying on someone else to do it. Can I let you in on a secret? With everything going on, I haven't even told Quinn yet."

Mick's eyes narrowed. "Sounds mysterious."

"I heard back from the publisher. They've sent me a contract for my memoir."

"Holy hell. Congratulations." Mick smiled. "Why didn't you tell anyone?"

Aspen frowned and gazed around the room. "Not the best timing."

"You've got a point." Mick's eyes shined. "But this is great. Now that you've found your purpose, who's to say you can't find the woman of your dreams, too?"

Aspen's heart clenched. Was she making the biggest mistake of her life? "It's too soon."

"But you like Quinn?"

Aspen put her hand over her heart. "Very much. Unfortunately, it is the absolute worst time for the both of us." Aspen shook her head and sighed. "Just my luck."

Mick studied her for several beats before she

nodded. "Should we watch a movie?"

"Yes, please."

⁂

Quinn and Natalie traveled in silence, neither wanting to talk in front of the Uber driver. It wasn't a topic that the poor driver needed to overhear. Besides, Quinn was lost in her own thoughts.

"Quinn." Natalie finally broke the silence. "Can I ask you a question?"

"Certainly." Quinn's stomach roiled. She didn't want to discuss Stella in front of a stranger, but if Natalie needed to talk, then she'd have to suck it up.

"What do you think of Aspen?"

The question caught her off guard. "Um, she's great. Why do you ask?"

"Don't let her get away."

Quinn's cheeks reddened. "For fuck's sake, I can't talk about this."

"Why not?" Natalie met her gaze.

"Are you serious? They're pulling the plug on Stella tomorrow, and this is what you want to talk about?" Quinn said louder than she intended.

The driver glanced at her in the rearview mirror but quickly looked away. *Great.* He'd have stories to tell his family when he got home.

"Stop the outrage. I see how the two of you look at each other."

"And how is that?" Quinn tamped down her agitation.

"The way you used to look at Stella."

Fuck. Not helpful. Quinn shook her head. "Now is not the time, even if I were interested."

"You know what?" Natalie said. "If this experience with Stella has taught me anything, it's to hold on to the people you love as tight as you can because you never know when it will be over." A tear ran down Natalie's cheek.

Quinn's chest ached. Gently, she wiped the tear away with her thumb. "Let me get through Stella's funeral before you start hooking me up with other people."

Natalie winced. "Low blow, Quinn."

"Oh, shit, that came out so wrong. I'm sorry." Quinn glanced down at her hands. "My emotions have been so churned up lately that I don't know which way is up."

Natalie slid over in her seat and wrapped her arm around Quinn's neck. "I'm sorry, too. I shouldn't be pushing you right now. I just want you to be happy."

"I will be...someday."

"Aspen makes you happy...now."

"Please, I can't." Tears welled in Quinn's eyes.

"Okay." Natalie hugged her tighter.

Chapter Thirty-seven

As promised, there was a skeleton crew working at the convalescent center. Most of the staff would be working tomorrow in light of the circus that would take place.

Donna, Natalie's favorite worker, met them at the back door and spirited them inside. She greeted them both with a hug and a sympathetic smile. They made small talk as they walked through the corridors.

This late at night, the unit was eerily quiet. The lights had been turned down, and no other staff bustled in the hallway. Each step reverberated off the walls, seeming to get louder as they approached Stella's room. Quinn knew it must just be in her mind, but she couldn't shake the feeling.

They paused outside Stella's door, and Donna gave them a sad smile. "You take as long as you want."

"Thank you," Natalie said and took her hand. "Thank you for everything."

"I'm just glad I could help bring this day to pass," Donna said before she walked away.

Natalie pushed open the door and entered first.

Quinn took a tentative step into the room. A dim light bathed the room. A machine purred inside, as well.

Natalie took Quinn's hand. "Come on. It'll be all right."

When Stella came into view, Quinn froze, and

her knees buckled. Natalie grabbed her around the waist.

"Are you okay?"

Quinn righted herself and stood up taller, her heart still beating out of her chest. How could she have forgotten about the ventilator? It was why they were here in the first place. "Sorry."

"You weren't prepared for the ventilator, were you?"

Quinn shook her head. "What have they done to her?"

"Come on." Natalie gently pulled her forward.

There were already two chairs pulled up to the bed, sitting side by side. "Donna thought of everything."

"She's a gem."

They walked the last few steps with Quinn never looking away from the tube shoved down Stella's throat. Natalie motioned for Quinn to sit on the chair closest to Stella's head, and she took the seat next to her.

A whoosh of air pushed through the tube, followed by the hiss of the air escaping. The rhythmic sound continued. Whoosh. Hiss. Whoosh. Hiss. Quinn struggled to inhale with the sound.

Natalie grabbed Quinn's arm. "Sweetheart, you need to breathe normally."

A rush of air escaped her lungs. "I'm so sorry. How are you so strong?"

"I'm not. I've just had more practice at this than you. Trust me, when we leave here, you're going to have to be the strong one."

"It's a deal." Quinn took Natalie's hand in one of hers and Stella's in the other. Natalie's hand was warm and clammy, while Stella's was cold.

They sat like this, not speaking, for some time. Quinn found that her breathing had synced with the rhythm of the machine. What did loved ones normally do in a situation like this? After nearly hyperventilating earlier, she found herself numb. The emotions that swirled in her earlier were gone. Had she cried too many tears the past week?

It didn't seem normal to be sitting by Stella's bedside with dry eyes. Maybe she'd become heartless. All feeling might have been sucked out of her. Panic started to rise in her, and she didn't realize she'd tightened her grip on Natalie's hand until she flinched.

"Ouch," Natalie said. "Don't crush my hand."

Quinn met Natalie's gaze. Her eyes so much like Stella's. The way Stella's eyes used to look. *What the hell?* A surge of emotions, of pain, rose from her stomach and clobbered her in the chest. Her breath caught again, almost doubling her over. Her gaze darted around the room, looking for an escape. Without any warning, she began to cry.

Her sobs came from the depths of her soul and drowned out the whoosh, hiss. She drew her shoulders in and rocked in her chair. Natalie stood and wrapped her arms around Quinn's neck from behind.

Natalie held her while she cried. Years of pain poured out of her, and she let herself go.

When her rocking subsided, Natalie let go of her and returned to her chair. Now that she'd quieted down, all she heard was whoosh, hiss. Whoosh. Hiss.

"We've been here nearly an hour," Natalie said. "I think we need to say our goodbyes."

Natalie's eyes were slightly red, but she'd not shed the tears Quinn had. She'd been mourning each time she'd visited Stella, so she'd had a head start on Quinn.

Quinn stood and leaned over the bed railing. Gently, she brushed the hair off Stella's forehead. "Baby, I'm sorry you've had to go through so much hell, but it will be over soon. You'll be free."

Natalie stood next to her and pressed against Quinn's side. Quinn put her arm around Natalie and pulled her closer. Natalie grabbed Stella's hand and brought it to her lips. "Goodbye, sister. You'll always be in my heart." She drew Stella's hand to her chest and held it there.

"We love you, Stella. More than anything." Quinn bent and kissed Stella's forehead. She left her lips there for several seconds before standing upright.

Natalie did the same. She glanced at Quinn. "How do we leave? Do we just walk out?"

Quinn's chest ached. Tomorrow, Stella would be dead, but tonight, they would have to leave her while she was still alive. "No, Nat. We have to think different." Quinn grabbed a handful of her shirt. "I wore the festive shirt for a reason. This is what Stella would want. She never wanted to live this way. We have to celebrate with her. She needs to leave this world feeling happy vibes, not this."

Natalie took a deep breath. "You're right. Just in case she knows we're here, we can't do this to her. She'd haunt our asses."

Quinn laughed. "No doubt. WWSD?"

"Huh?"

Quinn grinned. "What would Stella do?"

"Easy." Natalie's eyes lit up. "She'd dance."

"To?"

"You don't know the answer?" Natalie asked.

At the same time, they said, "Eighties music."

"*Livin' on a Prayer?*"

"Bum, bum, bum," Quinn said, imitating the beat.

"Dun, dun, dun, dah, duh," Natalie joined in.

Quinn picked up one of the water bottles Donna must have left for them and began to sing the chorus. She flipped the top of the bottle toward Natalie, who sang into their makeshift microphone.

"Oh, oh," Quinn sang backup.

"We're halfway there." Natalie pumped her fist into the air.

They danced to the music they made; their hands raised over their heads as they sang. Their singing more robust with each word.

Quinn cupped her hands and pretended to be the crowd roaring in excitement, while Natalie jumped up and down, hands outstretched.

They forgot all the words, but it didn't matter. They made them up as they went.

When they reached the end of the song, Natalie let loose with a belly laugh. Quinn joined in. They sang and danced to two more songs, and sweat poured down their faces. The release better than any tears.

When they wore themselves out, Quinn smiled down at Stella. "That's the way you wanted to go out, isn't it?" She pulled Natalie up beside her. "We're gonna go now. I love you, and I will love you until the day I die."

Natalie kissed her forehead. "I love you, Sissy. Forever and always. Godspeed."

Quinn and Natalie left the room, holding hands.

Chapter Thirty-eight

Quinn brought the phone to her ear. "Hello."
"It's over," Natalie said. "She's gone."
The phone fell to the floor.

Chapter Thirty-nine

Quinn pulled her coat around herself. Early December in Boston was colder than she'd remembered. Mick's three-season room wasn't equipped for the winter, but Quinn still loved it out here. It looked out over a small pond that was surrounded by pine trees. She was tempted to open a window so she could smell the damp earth and the pine needles, but she was chilled enough.

She hadn't gotten warm since the graveside service, but she suspected it was more than just the weather. Surprisingly, Stella's parents hadn't tried to keep her from the funeral. Maybe they'd learned something. *Right!* Likely, they were afraid that one of the recordings would get out if they behaved badly. Whatever the reason, she was thankful she'd been able to attend. The Parsonses had pretended she wasn't there, but it didn't matter since she was surrounded by her friends.

A tear trickled down her face, and she swept it away. It shocked her that she had any more tears left to shed.

The door creaked. Everyone had gone to bed an hour ago. She turned, expecting to see Mick.

"Aspen," Quinn said with a smile. Her smile got bigger when she noticed the wool coat, mittens, stocking cap, and boots. "Going skiing?"

"I might freeze out here." Aspen exaggerated

a shiver before sitting next to Quinn on the hanging swing. "I'm a California girl."

"I suppose I better not tell you that I was contemplating opening a window to let in some of the smells from outside."

"Are you crazy?" Aspen pushed against Quinn's knee with her own. "I'm afraid it's me or the smell of pines. I'm already an ice cube."

Quinn rose and walked toward the window, trying to hide her smirk.

"Seriously?" Aspen said. "Are you trying to get rid of me?"

Quinn opened the cedar chest under the window and pulled out a large fleece blanket. "Just getting this." She held it up and shook it open.

"You did that on purpose." Aspen managed her best glower.

God, she's cute. Quinn tried to push the thought from her mind, but the stocking cap was adorable. She handed the blanket to Aspen and sat.

"Oh, I thought you were giving me this so you could open the window."

"Did you want me to open it?"

Aspen held up the blanket. "With this and your body heat, I should stay warm enough. I know how much you love the outdoors."

"You sure?"

"Yep, we can always close it if we get too cold."

Quinn jumped to her feet before Aspen could change her mind. She threw open the window. A blast of crisp clean air rushed in. With a deep inhalation, she took in the mixture of earthy smells. "God, isn't that like a slice of heaven?"

Aspen made a show of sucking in a lungful of

"No, I meant it in a good way." Quinn puffed out her chest. "Your bad self," she said with attitude and finished it with a head thrust.

"Ah, now I get it. But don't do that again." Aspen crinkled up her nose. "You're not hip enough to pull it off."

"Gee, thanks. Why did I invite you out here?"

"You didn't. Remember, I keep showing up."

"Or you throw yourself in the pool to lure me in?"

Aspen laughed. "Oh, my god, that seems like a million years ago. We were destined to be friends after that."

Quinn frowned. "We had some fun, didn't we?"

"Hey, why so sad?" Aspen asked and leaned against Quinn.

"What happens next? My entire existence has been in limbo. Revolving around how I failed Stella. Now what?"

"You start over." Aspen smiled. "You finally start living again."

"I think I've already started. I'm staying here with Mick until I can get my own place, and I'll be back at Pink Triangle Adventures once I sell my property in the Ozarks."

"The trip changed things, didn't it?"

Quinn nodded. "Yeah, regardless of how things ended with Stella, I think I'd be heading in the same direction, but now I can do it without this heavy weight on my chest. But..."

"But?"

Quinn felt Aspen's gaze on her, but she continued staring out at the pond. "I'll always love her."

"Of course you will." When Quinn remained

silent, Aspen said, "What aren't you saying?"

Honesty. Could she say this to Aspen? "Can I eventually love someone else, too?" Quinn finally met Aspen's gaze.

Tears welled in Aspen's eyes. "Aw, Quinn. You absolutely can."

"But wouldn't it make the new woman feel...I dunno...weird? Uncertain?"

"Only if she's an idiot," Aspen said with conviction. "It's not a competition. Your new relationship will be different than the one you had with Stella. Do you plan on keeping a tally sheet to determine whether the new woman or Stella is better?"

"Oh, god, no!"

"Then why do you think the new woman would?"

"Damn, Frankie. Apparently, the trip changed you, too." Quinn smiled. "Or maybe, it's just you've gotten smarter now that you're going to be a published author."

Aspen chuckled. "Yep, my IQ went up by at least ten points. I keep waiting for the publisher to send me an email and tell me it's all been a mistake."

"Now who's being insecure?"

"I know, right? Gina says I behaved like a train wreck for the past decade, so I'd have material for my books."

Quinn laughed. "Sneaky." Aspen's hand still rested on Quinn's leg, so she put her hand on top of it and squeezed. "I'm proud of you."

"Did you just say you're proud of me?" Aspen's voice cracked.

"I did. And I meant it. You should be proud of you, too."

Aspen sat up straighter. "I guess I should." She

glanced at Quinn. "It's kind of a big deal, isn't it?"

"A real big deal. Lots of people want to do it, but not that many succeed."

"But is it a real career?"

Quinn turned her head and narrowed her eyes. "Yes. A thousand times, yes. Don't let anyone tell you it isn't."

Tears streamed down Aspen's cheek.

"Oh, god, I broke you." Quinn shuffled in her seat. "What did I say wrong?"

Aspen elbowed her. "Nothing, you big lug. Don't you know happy tears when you see them?"

"Whew, you had me worried." Quinn sighed. "Do authors need sidekicks?"

"Duh, obviously." Aspen bumped Quinn's knee. "And since I've already got one, the publishing house won't have to assign me one."

"Oh, don't you think they might want to replace your old one with a better model?"

"I'll find a new publisher before I let them do that."

"Good." Quinn's chest filled with warmth. "Do you think we should go inside? Get some sleep?"

"Nope." Aspen lay her head against Quinn's shoulder and yawned. "I'm comfortable and warm right here."

"So Mick's going to find us here in the morning?"

"Maybe. We've never watched a sunrise together." Aspen yawned again.

"I'm not sure you're going to stay awake until then. At least let me close the window."

Aspen held up the blanket. "Hurry up before it gets cold."

Quinn scurried to the window and closed it.

"Quick. The warmth is escaping," Aspen said with a furrowed brow.

Quinn returned to the swing and made like she was going to dive back into her seat. "Incoming."

Aspen laughed and opened the blanket farther.

Once Quinn was back in position, she said, "Do you seriously plan on staying out here?"

"Yep. My flight is booked for next week."

"What does that have to do with it?" Quinn asked, puzzled.

"I've only got three more days to hang out with my sidekick."

"Oh." A stabbing pain punched Quinn in the chest.

"Then we both have to get on with putting our new life together," Aspen said.

The pain in her chest increased. Aspen had been such a big part of her journey back. It would feel empty without her here. "But you've found your dream, so what do you have left to do?"

Aspen sighed. "This seems different. Finally, I'm doing what I love, not just following behind someone else, but I'm kinda like one of those colts trying to walk for the first time. My legs feel like they're splayed out, and each step feels shaky. I need to prove to myself that I can make it in the world on my own. Without my mom and dad or someone else doing it for me."

"I have faith in you. You're going to be one hell of an independent woman." Sadness washed over Quinn. Maybe if they'd met at a different time, but they both had too much work to do on themselves. *What the hell?* She quickly pushed the thought away. She'd found an incredible friend, so what did she have to feel sad about?

"Thanks," Aspen said and closed her eyes.

☙ ☙ ☙ ☙

Aspen stared out at the pond. Quinn had fallen asleep nearly an hour ago, but sleep escaped her. She was warm, almost too warm, with Quinn's inferno-like body heat radiating under the blanket, so she couldn't blame the cold for her inability to fall asleep.

She gazed at Quinn. The peaceful look on her face made her look younger. Her scar the only evidence of the strain she'd endured.

Aspen's heart hurt. Even though she wouldn't admit it to anyone, it would be easy for her to fall in love with Quinn. Why did the timing have to be so wrong? Quinn needed to finish grieving before she'd be ready for a relationship, and Aspen had to find her independence before she would be good for anyone.

She let out a heavy sigh. Quinn was like none of her other girlfriends. It wasn't a big rush of hormones but something softer and sweeter. They talked to each other. Shared their innermost feelings, well, except for these thoughts. Quinn was solid and trustworthy, all the traits Aspen craved in a companion. She shrugged to herself; it wasn't like they'd stop being friends.

Maybe that was all her feelings were. Friendship. *No.* She loved Gina with all her heart, but this felt different.

But it didn't feel like any of the other women she'd lusted after through the years, either. So it couldn't be an attraction. *Right?* She'd just been friends with Gina so long that she'd forgotten what it felt like to have the new friendship rush.

That must be it. It wasn't sexual, even though

Quinn was one of the sexiest women she'd ever known. Those expressive brown eyes melted her, and that little mischievous smile caused her heart to do flips.

Oh, crap. Aspen burrowed into Quinn's side. Quinn mumbled in her sleep and pulled Aspen closer. And those muscles. She loved Quinn's broad shoulders and solid build. She'd seen enough of her in her swim clothes to imagine the rest of her.

Stop! Good god, what was the matter with her? She couldn't do this to Quinn or herself, so she forced her eyes closed. She fell asleep to the sound of Quinn's heartbeat.

Chapter Forty

Quinn stepped out of the way of the surging crowd. She'd been bumped by several passengers who apparently were on a mission. Travelers could be ugly.

Aspen followed her to the tiny space devoid of people. "Damn, you'd think it was Thanksgiving weekend with these crowds."

"No doubt. It's almost like a zombie apocalypse. I think they might eat their young if they got in the way."

Aspen laughed. "Yep, they must hurry up and wait. I bet most of these people will be sitting at their gates for at least half an hour. Speaking of, I should probably make my way through TSA. I'm cutting it a little close."

Quinn's shoulders dropped. She wasn't ready for Aspen to leave and probably never would be no matter how long she stayed. "I'll miss you." Had she really just said that?

"I'll miss you, too." Aspen blinked several times. *Tears?*

"I need to thank you for everything you've done for me. For us."

"Nonsense." Aspen flicked her wrist. "That's what friends are for. I'm happy I was able to be here."

"Will you keep in touch?"

"Of course. I have to make sure my sidekick

doesn't try and sneak back to Missouri."

Quinn smiled. "Mick won't let me. I've given my Realtor and attorney all the power they need to sell the place. Plus, Mick's insisting on going with me when I collect my things."

"Pink Triangle Adventures will be back in business. With all three sides."

"I still can't believe it." Quinn's heart soared. Natalie had agreed to take the other side of the triangle. They'd be together again. "Funny how much life can change in a heartbeat."

"Will you be okay seeing Natalie every day? I mean, will she be a reminder of...?"

"Stella." Quinn smiled. "She will be, but each day, it will get easier. My heart's full being back here in the city I love. With the people I love. What about you? Are you looking forward to getting back to San Francisco?"

Aspen shrugged. "I don't know. I guess. I miss Gina, but it's been nice being here, too."

Quinn's heart raced. Was Aspen giving her a hint? *No.* She wanted to get home. "It's been nice having you." When had they become so stiff with each other? This seemed like an awkward romance movie. *Romance.* She needed to stop thinking.

"I guess I better go then."

"You'll let me know when you get a release date for your book?"

"You'll be at the top of the list, right behind Gina. She'd kill me if she weren't the first to find out." Aspen smiled. "I hope you get to meet her one day."

"Me too." Quinn shuffled from foot to foot.

Aspen glanced at her watch. "We'll talk soon." She stepped into Quinn's arms.

So many times, Aspen's hugs helped heal her, but today, it just hurt. She squeezed Aspen tightly. When they separated, Aspen quickly looked away.

"Later, Frankie."

Aspen smiled, then disappeared in a sea of people.

Epilogue

FOUR MONTHS LATER

Quinn looked at her reflection in the library window and straightened her tie. Butterflies danced in her stomach. She'd only seen Aspen once in the past four months, but she'd promised to support her at her first publishing event.

They talked on the phone frequently. Their last conversation played in Quinn's mind. Aspen had been giddy as she told Quinn about the event. Quinn's palms went cold just thinking about standing up in front of people doing a reading.

Quinn found a seat near the front and scanned the crowd. Likely, Aspen would be backstage until it was her turn to read. Would she be allowed to come out to the crowd afterward, or would they keep her the entire time? *Dumbass.* Questions she should have asked earlier.

She glanced at the program on the seat next to hers. Why hadn't she gotten one? *Shit.* Maybe she had. Subtly, she lifted her butt cheek. Yep, she'd sat on it. She yanked it out from under her and casually smoothed out the wrinkles. While she flipped through the pages, her gaze landed on Aspen's picture. *Beautiful.* The professional photographer captured her in just the right light, making her blue eyes practically glow.

After staring at Aspen's picture and reading her

bio, Quinn thumbed through the pages looking for an itinerary. Second to last. Quinn sighed. She might as well sit back and relax. It would be a while before she saw Aspen.

⊱⊰⊱⊰

Aspen paced around backstage and peeked out from the curtain for what must have been the tenth time. Her breath caught. Quinn sat three rows back. *Damn, she looked good.* She'd always had a thing for a woman in a tie, and Quinn looked better than most. Her square shoulders somehow made the tie look better.

"Aspen," someone called.

She reluctantly let the curtain fall back into place. "Yes?"

"Since this is your first time, the publisher's representative would like to talk to you," her agent said.

"Of course."

"Are you nervous?" her agent asked and put a supportive hand on her arm.

Was she? Her sweaty palms told her she was, but did it have to do with the reading or a particular audience member? *Focus.* Now wasn't the time to think about Quinn, even if she was someone Aspen thought about often. "I'm okay. I just hope my voice doesn't crack when I read."

"Even if it does, your writing is so compelling I doubt anyone will notice."

Heat rose up Aspen's neck to her cheeks. "Thank you." She took one last look at the curtain before she said, "Let's go meet with the publisher."

≈≈≈≈

Aspen had nailed it. In Quinn's estimation, hers was the best reading of the day, but then again, she was biased. Aspen had texted her that she had to do a few publicity photos with her publisher before she'd be done.

Quinn wandered into the lobby and scoped out a secluded nook. *Perfect.* There shouldn't be much foot traffic here. She'd been to the bathroom twice and circled the lobby several times. She'd even purchased water and snacks in case Aspen was hungry.

She needed to just sit and relax. Once seated, she pulled out the program. She could kill time by rereading it. The program shook in her unsteady hands, so she threw it down in disgust.

"What, you didn't like my reading?" a familiar voice said.

"Aspen." Quinn jumped to her feet and knocked over the bottles of water sitting on the table in front of her.

Aspen laughed. "Wow. Do they let you out much?"

Quinn busied herself retrieving the bottles that rolled around on the floor. When she set them back on the table and looked up, she met Aspen's amused eyes. "It's so good to see you. I—"

Aspen flew into her arms, cutting off any further words. "God, it's good to see you."

Quinn laughed and hugged her tight. Her heart thumped out of her chest. "You did an amazing job with your reading."

"You're just saying that because you're biased,"

Aspen said as she stepped back.

"Not true. You were great."

Aspen leaned toward Quinn. "Are you all right? You look pale."

Quinn held up her hand and opened her mouth to speak.

"Oh, my god," Aspen said. "You're trembling. Did you eat?" Aspen rummaged through the snacks Quinn had purchased and picked out a candy bar. She ripped open the package. "Your blood sugar is probably low."

"Whoa, slow down. It's not my blood sugar."

Aspen's eyes widened. "Something else is wrong. That's why you came here. You wanted to tell me in person."

"Would you slow down?" Quinn chuckled. "Yes, there was a reason I wanted to see you in person, but it's not because anything is wrong. Well, at least not yet."

Aspen paused and cocked her head. "So there *is* a reason you're here other than the reading?"

"Yes." Quinn wiped her sweaty palms on her pants legs. "Do you think you could let me get all my words out before you interrupt?"

"It'll be hard." Aspen lifted one shoulder. "But hey, I can give it a try."

"Thank you. There's something I've been wanting to ask you for a long time."

Aspen opened her mouth, but Quinn put her finger to her own lips. Aspen closed her mouth and smirked. She motioned for Quinn to continue.

"I've probably wanted to do this since we wiped out on Gulliver's Travels. But I knew you needed to find yourself and forge your own path first. I vowed to Mick that I wouldn't do this until your book was published."

Aspen nodded.

"Aspen Kennedy, I would like to take you on a date. A real one. That is if you'll have me."

"But I'm not published yet. My book doesn't come out for another six months," Aspen said.

Quinn's face dropped. It was a no. She'd waited all this time only to be rejected.

Aspen laughed. "I was teasing."

"Seriously? Are you trying to kill me here?" Quinn gave her best glare.

"You should have seen the look on your face. Scary. I thought you were going to pass out."

Quinn threw her hands into the air. "Tell me why I've been pining for you?"

Aspen put her hand against her chest. "You've been pining for me?"

"Shit. I need to shut up now before I say anything else embarrassing."

"I think you're cute when you're embarrassed." Aspen winked.

"You do, huh?"

"Yep."

"Do you plan on answering my question?"

"What question?" The twinkle in Aspen's eyes gave her away.

"You are determined to make this as awkward as possible, aren't you?"

"Awkward is cute, too."

"So are puppies and kittens, but you wouldn't date them."

"Oh." Aspen opened her mouth wide in mock surprise. "Are you asking me out on a date?"

"I was, but I might just change my mind."

Aspen shook her head and linked her arm through Quinn's. "Sorry no takebacks. I would love to go on a date with you, Quinn Coolidge."

Quinn exhaled loudly. "Finally."

"Will it count as our first date, or since we've known each other for a while, does it qualify as a higher number?"

Quinn narrowed her eyes and shrugged. "I don't know. I hadn't thought about it. Why?"

"I need to know what undies to wear." Aspen raised her eyebrows.

Quinn's face burned. "Oh."

Aspen gave Quinn a sideways hug. "This dating stuff is going to be fun. If that's all it takes to embarrass you, wait until I start talking about my bra."

"Stop. Frankie, you're killing me." Quinn held up her hands in surrender. "Can we get to our first kiss first?"

"I suppose if we must." Aspen turned and met Quinn's gaze.

Quinn leaned in, and their lips met.

About The Author

Rita Potter has spent most of her life trying to figure out what makes people tick. To that end, she holds a Bachelor's degree in Social Work and an MA in Sociology. Being an eternal optimist, she maintains that the human spirit is remarkably resilient. Her writing reflects this belief.

Rita's stories are electic but typically put her characters in challenging circumstances. She feels that when they reach their happily ever after, they will have earned it. Despite the heavier subject matter, Rita's humorous banter and authentic dialogue reflect her hopeful nature.

In her spare time, she enjoys the outdoors. She is especially drawn to the water, which is ironic since she lives in the middle of a cornfield. Her first love has always been reading. It is this passion that spurred her writing career. She rides a Harley Davidson and has an unnatural obsession with fantasy football. More than anything, she detests small talk but can ramble on for hours given a topic that interests her.

She lives in a small town in Illinois with her wife, Terra, and their cat, Chumley, who actually runs the household.

Rita is a member of American Mensa and the Golden

Crown Literary Society. She is currently a graduate of the GCLS Writing Academy 2021. Sign up for Rita's free newsletter at:

www.ritapotter.com

IF YOU LIKED THIS BOOK...

Reviews help an author get discovered and if you have enjoyed this book, please do the author the honor of posting a review on Goodreads, Amazon, Barnes & Noble or anywhere you purchased the book. Or perhaps share a posting on your social media sites and help us spread the word.

Check out Rita's other books

Broken not Shattered - ISBN - 978-1-952270-22-2

Even when it seems hopeless, there can always be a better tomorrow.

Jill Bishop has one goal in life – to survive. Jill is trapped in an abusive marriage, while raising two young girls. Her husband has isolated her from the world and filled her days with fear. The last thing on her mind is love, but she sure could use a friend.

Alex McCoy is enjoying a comfortable life, with great friends and a prosperous business. She has given up on love, after picking the wrong woman one too many times. Little does she know, a simple act of kindness might change her life forever.

When Alex lends a helping hand to Jill at the local grocery store, they are surprised by their immediate connection and an unlikely friendship develops. As their friendship deepens, so too do their fears.

In order to protect herself and the girls, Jill can't let her husband know about her friendship with Alex, and Alex can't discover what goes on behind closed doors. What would Alex do if she finds out the truth? At the same time, Alex must fight her attraction and be the friend she suspects Jill needs. Besides, Alex knows what every lesbian knows – don't fall for a straight woman, especially one that's married…but will her heart listen?

Upheaval: Book One - As We Know It - ISBN - 978-1-

952270-38-3

It is time for Dillon Mitchell to start living again.

Since the death of her wife three years ago, Dillon had buried herself in her work. When an invitation arrives for Tiffany Daniels' exclusive birthday party, her best friend persuades her to join them for the weekend.

It's not the celebration that draws her but the location. The party is being held at the Whitaker Estate, one of the hottest tickets on the West Coast. The Estate once belonged to an eccentric survivalist, whose family converted it into a trendy destination while preserving some of its original history.

Surrounded by a roomful of successful lesbians, Dillon finds herself drawn to Skylar Lange, the mysterious and elusive bartender. Before the two can finish their first dance, a scream shatters the evening. When the party goers emerge from the underground bunker, they discover something terrible has happened at the Estate.

The group races to try to discover the cause of this upheaval, and whether it's isolated to the Estate. Has the world, as we know it, changed forever?

Survival: Book Two - As We Know It - ISBN - 978-1-952270-47-5

Forty-eight hours after the Upheaval, reality is beginning to set in at the Whitaker Estate. The world, As We Know It, has ended.

Dillon Mitchell and her friends are left to survive, after discovering most of the population, at least in the United States, has mysteriously died.

While they struggle to come to terms with their devastating losses, they are faced with the challenge of creating a new society, which is threatened by the divergent factions that may tear the community apart from the inside.

Even if the group can unite, external forces are gathering that could destroy their fragile existence.

Meanwhile, Dillon's budding relationship with the elusive Skylar Lange faces obstacles, when Skylar's hidden past is revealed.

Thundering Pines – ISBN – 978-1-952270-58-1

Returning to her hometown was the last thing Brianna Goodwin wanted to do. She and her mom had left Flower Hills under a cloud of secrecy and shame when she was ten years old. Her life is different now. She has a high-powered career, a beautiful girlfriend, and a trendy life in Chicago.

Upon her estranged father's death, she reluctantly agrees to attend the reading of his will. It should be simple—settle his estate and return to her life in the city—but nothing has ever been simple when it comes to Donald Goodwin.

Dani Thorton, the down-to-earth manager of

Thundering Pines, is confused when she's asked to attend the reading of the will of her longtime employer. She fears that her simple, although secluded life will be interrupted by the stylish daughter who breezes into town.

When a bombshell is revealed at the meeting, two women seemingly so different are thrust together. Maybe they'll discover they have more in common than they think.

Betrayal: Book Three - As We Know It - ISBN - 978-1-952270-69-7

Betrayal is the exciting conclusion to the As We Know It series.

The survivors at Whitaker Estate are still reeling from the vicious attack on their community, which left three of their friends dead.

When the mysterious newcomer Alaina Renato reveals there is a traitor in their midst, it threatens to tear the community apart. Is there truly a traitor, or is Alaina playing them all?

Dillon Mitchell and the other Commission members realize their group might not survive another attack, especially if there is someone working against them from the inside. Despite the potential risk, they vote to attend a summit that will bring together other survivors from around the country.

When the groups converge on Las Vegas, the festive

atmosphere soon turns somber upon the discovery of an ominous threat. But is the danger coming from within, or is there someone else lurking in the city?

Before it's too late, they must race against time to determine where the betrayal is coming from.

Other Sapphire books from Sapphire Authors

Thundering Pines – ISBN – 978-1-952270-58-1

Returning to her hometown was the last thing Brianna Goodwin wanted to do. She and her mom had left Flower Hills under a cloud of secrecy and shame when she was ten years old. Her life is different now. She has a high-powered career, a beautiful girlfriend, and a trendy life in Chicago.

Upon her estranged father's death, she reluctantly agrees to attend the reading of his will. It should be simple—settle his estate and return to her life in the city—but nothing has ever been simple when it comes to Donald Goodwin.

Dani Thorton, the down-to-earth manager of Thundering Pines, is confused when she's asked to attend the reading of the will of her longtime employer. She fears that her simple, although secluded life will be interrupted by the stylish daughter who breezes into town.

When a bombshell is revealed at the meeting, two women seemingly so different are thrust together. Maybe they'll discover they have more in common than they think.

Diva – ISBN – 978-1-952270-10-9

What if...you were offered a part-time job as the personal assistant to someone you have idolized for years? Meg Ellis has just completed the school year as a nurse in the Santa Fe school system. It isn't her first choice of profession, but a medical problem derailed her musical career years ago. The breakup of a bad relationship is still painful. The loving support from her close-knit family and good friends has buoyed her spirits, but longing still lurks below the surface. She can't forget the intoxicating allure of the beautiful diva who haunts her dreams.

Nicole Bernard is a rising star in the world of opera, adored by fans around the globe. When Meg learns that Nicole is headlining a new production at the renowned New Mexico outdoor pavilion—and then is asked to accept a job offer to be her personal assistant—she is beside herself. After a short time learning the routine and reining in her hormones, Meg discovers that Nicole's family will be visiting for the opening. Her responsibility to the charismatic singer immediately becomes more difficult when Nicole's young husband Mario shows up and threatens the comfortable rapport between Meg and the prima donna.

The two women brace for a roller-coaster interlude composed by fate. Will the warm days and cool nights, the breathtaking scenery, and the romance of the music create summer love? A heartbreaking game? Or something very special?

Keeping Secrets – ISBN – 978-1-952270-04-8

What would you do if, after finally finding the woman of your dreams, she suddenly leaves to fight in the Civil War?

It's 1863, and Elizabeth Hepscott has resigned herself to a life of monotonous boredom far from the battlefields as the wife of a Missouri rancher. Her fate changes when she travels with her brother to Kentucky to help him join the Union Army. On a whim, she poses as his little brother and is bullied into enlisting, as well. Reluctantly pulled into a new destiny, a lark decision quickly cascades into mortal danger.

While Elizabeth's life has made a drastic U-turn, Charlie Schweicher, heiress to a glass-making fortune, is still searching for the only thing money can't buy.

A chance encounter drastically changes everything for both of them. Will Charlie find the love she's longed for, or will the war take it all away?

Swann Song - ISBN - 978-1-952270-63-5

Christine Swann is a world-famous singer/songwriter and lesbian icon, known for her edgy style and heart-pounding songs. Gorgeous, rich and miserable. Her music has always been her life, her escape from an unimaginable childhood, and choices no thirteen-year-old should have to make.

Now, pushing thirty, she wants out. From all of it.

Willow Bowman lives in the farmhouse her beloved grandmother left her, with her husband. A pediatric nurse and small-town girl, she relishes in the safety of her marriage that keeps difficult questions at bay and keeps her life quiet and peaceful, because that makes sense to her.

Until one night when Willow is driving home and is about to cross the old, rickety Dittman Bridge not far from the farmhouse, and she sees a figure jump off into the cold waters below.

The moment she jumps in and pulls the woman dressed in leather pants out, both their lives change forever.

Encore Performance - ISBN - 978-1-952270-52-9

Grey Rickman, a journalist for The New York Times, is offered the opportunity of a lifetime and a huge boost to her career—ghostwriting a memoir for one of the world's most beloved actors. She is deeply in love with her girlfriend, dancer Christian Scott, and her world couldn't be better.

Christian, though proud of Grey and all that she's accomplished, is facing her own career dilemma. All she's ever wanted to do is perform and create, her body her kinetic canvas. But, in one of the few industries where youth matters above all else, her time is coming to make decisions that no woman in her mid-thirties should have to make: is it time to retire?

As the career of one begins to explode into the stratosphere and the other's implodes after a career-ending injury that makes any retirement discussion irrelevant, Grey and Christian begin to drift apart. Changing priorities and newly built walls lead to fears and accusations, further tearing at the fabric of the love they've worked years to create.

Will cooler heads prevail to warm up the hearts of the deeply passionate couple in time to create a new dream for their second act?

Survival – ISBN – 978-1-952270-18-5

After surviving a school shooting, Mona Ouellet moves from Montreal to Peterborough, switches her PhD discipline from English Literature to Psychology, and tries to move on with her life. Unfortunately, her nightmares follow her—and so do a host of "bad men" who seem to appear around every corner to make her life difficult. Her only escape is to fall into her research completely, where she soon becomes obsessed with retelling true crime case studies and enamoured by a waitress at a local diner.

Kerri Reznik is a waitress by day and horror writer by night, where she turns elements of her two-month long captivity in the wilderness with her survivalist father into stories to scare others. Though over a decade has passed, Kerri is still haunted by her brother Lee's absence in her life and her inability to reconcile with it. She seeks camaraderie with Absalom Lincoln, a detective on Peterborough police's force, where the two bond over mysteries, both true and imagined.

As Kerri and Mona's connection becomes stronger, their past traumas begin to intertwine and both of their worst nightmares begin to evolve and intensify. Each character must struggle to negotiate how to live in a world where survival is never guaranteed, and even when it is possible, there is always a cost.

Made in the USA
Middletown, DE
22 November 2023

43239090R00265